THANH DINH

Kill My Darling

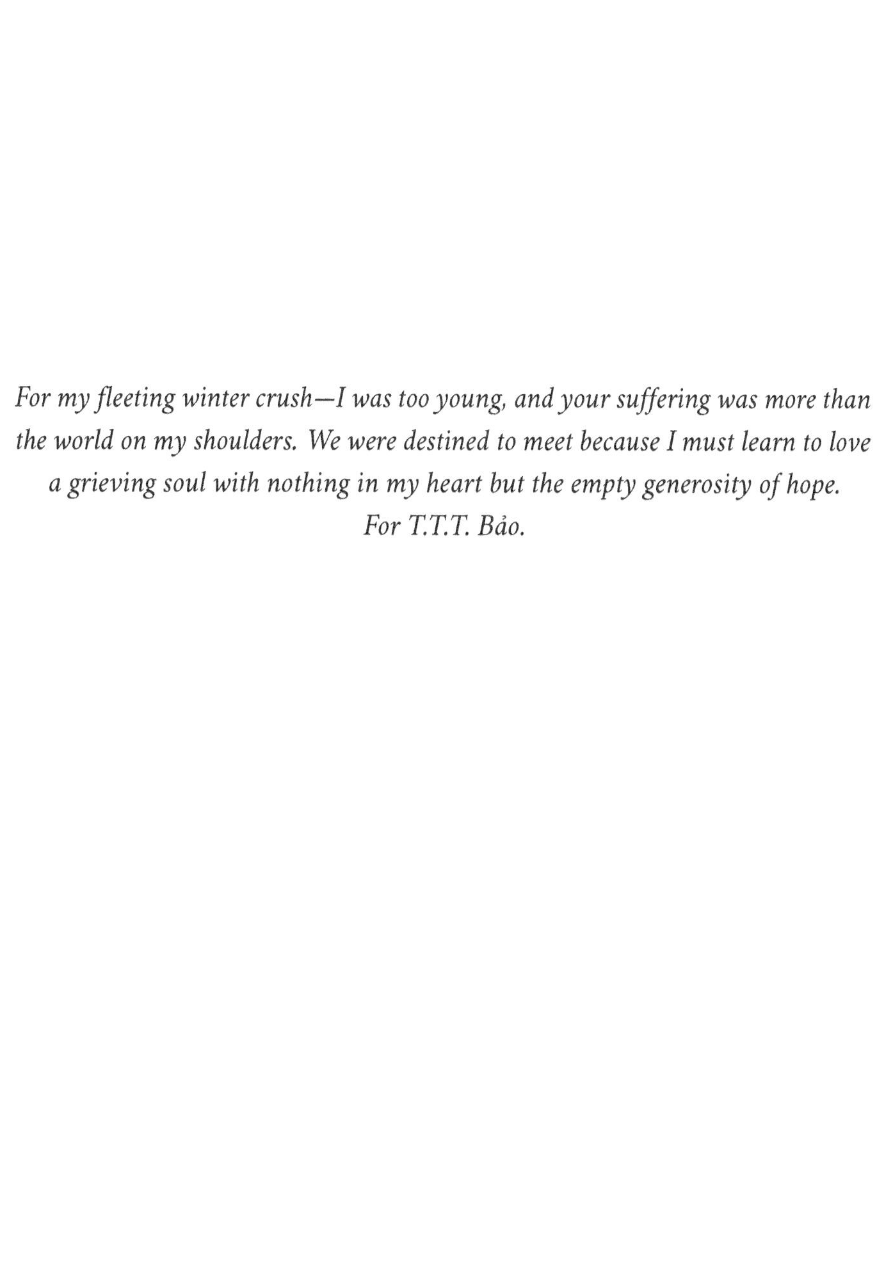

For my fleeting winter crush—I was too young, and your suffering was more than the world on my shoulders. We were destined to meet because I must learn to love a grieving soul with nothing in my heart but the empty generosity of hope.
For T.T.T. Bảo.

Contents

Foreword

This book isn't about softness or poetic prose. Neither is it about a happy ending and a good old love story. If you expect to find inside these pages and between these lines an ounce of gentleness, please put it down.

Kill My Darling is about the test of faith, the failure of reason, the unanswered questions, the endless search for meanings in the madness of living—in short, it is a story about Bertrand Russell's narrow hopes and faithless religions.

From the first chapter, where the female protagonist, Angela, confesses to a crime she indirectly participates in, to the last chapter, where the ending is a new beginning, Kill My Darling sings a mourning song. The sadness lies in the fact that it is a song we know far too well: life goes on, and what doesn't kill us, doesn't kill us. Period. Who pushes Jean-Paul "Bambi" Raymond into that desperate fate? Who forces Angela into the narrow hopes that she keeps holding onto like the bitter salvation of Judgment Day? And who takes away Pierre Raymond's chance to escape the prison he trapped himself in so willingly?

It is not I, the author, who decides their destiny as such. Look at them, read their lines out loud, then look at you in the mirror.

Angela's will to freedom, Jean-Paul's existential nausea, Pierre's struggle to be human, all too human—aren't they so familiar now?

Because my dear readers, it's you who decide their fate.

That's why, if you still think this book serves high-stakes thriller and suspense to chase after the mass market, and everyone will have their own happy moment, please, put it down.

Preface

This section is to protect my dear readers as well as myself. Please read the bullet points and consider them carefully, as they are the book's trigger warnings:

This book discusses severe and potentially dangerous issues and topics such as:

- Mental health, up to and including: depression, anxiety, panic attacks, potential self-harms, hallucinations, and addictions.
- Drugs uses.
- Mentions of suicide and suicidal attempts.
- Murder.
- Dispose of corpses.
- Discussion of philosophical topics and religious matters.
- Other adult and mature content.

Please proceed with the highest caution.

Acknowledgments

Kill My Darling is the fever dream that is actualized thanks to the hard work of my sweetest, most talented editor, Cynthia Constantino. She is, by far, a blessing that I keep thanking Heaven every day, and perhaps will do so forever. The cover is designed by Tiago Araujo, a talented individual with superb taste, who understood my novels and collection so well, and I couldn't ask for a more perfect artist.

During the period of writing this novel, I was diagnosed with chronic fatigue syndrome and two other chronic mental disorders, which, for the comfort of readers, I shall not name. It was the best of times, it was the worst of times, as Charles Dickens would have said. My mom, sister, and my dear father were there, bearing the heaviest burden (namely, me) and pulling me through the darkest phase of my life. Thanks to them, I survived the storm once more.

My friends, Tam Nguyen and Hoang-Anh Nguyen, who send me memes and funny videos every day, keep me updated with the latest trends on the internet, and are another blessing in my somewhat dull life. It is a joy to see the cats dance, and I am yet to understand what she (Tam) meant when she sent me the video of the snake yawning, but well, I'm getting old.

My dear doctor, Dr. Le Minh, who has been helping me through the recent diagnosis and keeping my medication in check—thanks Heaven for his existence. It is a joy to have him by my side when I was in my delirious state, babbling and screaming into the imaginary void of nothingness.

Friends and family, I can't thank you enough for always standing by my side, raising me on your invincible shoulders, and putting your faith in me, time and again. This is me at my best yet, and my success always bears your name.

Chapter 1: The Murder

February 14, 2025 – Downtown Toronto, red light district

I inhale the cold, arid winter air of the city made from broken dreams. The putrid smell from the gutters and the rotting trash filling the waste bins placed along the moldy walls add a perfect touch to the day of Saint Valentine's sacrifices. The couples pass me by in a hurry, no doubt running to their late reservations in some gaudy restaurants which are branded "niche" for this special event. I want to vomit my dinner for reasons more than disgust.

All the lovers in the night and I have a corpse in my trunk.

I stride toward the club and plunge myself into the deafening noise. The disco ball is making my brain doubt its own existence. My ears ring with the booming noise from the dance floor. *Hi, my name is. Hi, my name is. Chicka-chicka-chicka.* I pull out a cigarette, light it up, and hungrily breathe in the delicious nicotine like my life depends on it. Fuck, I need air.

"Angela. Sweet Angela. Hey, darling." A voice deafens what is left of my hearing ability. I turn to walk away but a strong hand bars my escape route. "Where's Bambi?" the oily, leering man in the flashy, colorful suit asks, smiling. Markus never stops being trash. That's why he belongs here, in this city that reeks of decay.

"Fuck you, Markus. Leave me alone." I scowl.

"If I could, I would.. Do you know men have an erogenous zone inside their asses? Just kidding. Anyways." Markus, the lecherous voice in the figure of a Greek God's appearance, leers. His hair is combed back, polished and reeking with the smell of filthy money. The deep shade of brown makes me sick to my stomach. He sneaks one lanky arm around me, breathes in my ear, "Bambi owes me a few grand. For the last drug delivery, you know."

"I don't." I push him away, trying to repress the urge to vomit.

"Yes, you do, baby girl. He said if he's gone, I can talk to you." The sweet voice is now tinged with a hint of annoyance. He blabbers on and my stomach churns at the thought of pouncing on him and tearing him to shreds. Someone should make all the noise stop.

"I seriously don't. And you've had your talk. Let me go," I hiss.

"Come on, angel. He's not—"

"Listen here, Markus." I turn on my heels, yank my arm away, grasp his collar, shove my face close enough so that he can feel my raging breath and the little bit of wine I downed before coming here for courage. I piss these words into his ears: "I'm done with him. With you. And with anyone who's involved. Fuck Bambi. There's no him anymore. There's only me. You either get away from me or I swear there will be blood."

"Whoa, sorry to ruffle your feathers."

Markus watches in bewilderment as I stomp out of the crowded bar. The fucking coward shouts after me, "What's wrong with that fucking bitch?"

Sure, let him bark all he wants. He doesn't know how to bite, after all.

The most important thing is that Markus has seen me here, in the club. He now knows that I'm not in contact with Bambi. As far as he is concerned, I have enough alibi to be innocent.

Pulling my coat's collars up, I trod down the block to get to my car. Outside, the sky is lit in a tacky, red, neon color. The air is filled with the sickeningly sweet smell of garbage and rotting waste. The red light district. On the evening news, the mayor slams his fists like a petulant kid, claiming he will wipe out all things immoral. Well, who knows. Maybe I will see his face among the frequent clientele. Bambi once said he loved this city because the life inside killed all the dreams everyone ever had. What's the harm in buying a little bit of fun, deceiving ourselves once in a while in the embrace of a whore, then? "Angela, people love playing just and righteous," he replied.

But never mind. From dust thou hadst cometh; to dust thou shall return.

I chew the last bit of my cigarette butt, feeling the tears swelling up. Since when have I sunk so low? I look at my reflection in a dirty store window. The long, thick brunette hair is now thinning fast, the face I once was so proud of is sagging in both cheeks, the lips that whisper vows of forever to my one true love now die on the lies--I'm gradually blending into the neon lights and the garish billboards, fraying at the seams like a cheap doll thrown out after Christmas. The stars peek out briefly behind the dark, gathering clouds. I can hear them laughing; the person who keeps rejecting this city's hypocrisy has become a testament to its success at mass-producing mannequins. In a trance, I trace the blurring lines of my existence on the glass window. How do I find myself when the road back has long been erased in the whirlpool of shitty things I lived through? And how do I climb out of this trap when I'm already six feet deep? The people around me echo in their daydream, begging me to stay, because at least I'm happy here.

I argue with the girl in the window glass just for fun's sake, telling her there's only one of me and she's the ghost of the past. But who am I kidding? Roaring with laughter, I trudge down the pavement, leaving her in that grieving state, her jealous eyes glowering after my back like a haunting shadow. Isn't it sweeter to believe in the words of a human because God has abandoned us? I never walk the path of the righteous and my faith in His benevolence is as thin as the next day's luck. So I choose to follow a man I can see and embrace with both hands. What's there to lose? When he fails, and he did, from time to time, I just need to off him before following the next best stranger.

The cold makes my whole outlook on life miserable. I wipe my nose. It's sticky, with a thin trickle of blood. I feel the panic settle in. Guessing what will come next has always been a mad pastime of ours--Bambi's and mine. Will it be a seizure next? Or will I just straight out faint, lying there on the muddied, oil-stained road, becoming a ridiculous spectacle for every passerby? The odds are always in my favor. But not now. My sanity is the last thing I want to lose. The craving for sleep is creeping onto my skin. My hair stands on end. I shiver with the knowledge that somewhere in the glove compartment, Bambi hides his usual stash. The cocaine, the amphetamine, the fairies that would make him a greater man than the sorrow on his bare shoulders.

Markus asked, "Where's Bambi?" In a strange, fucked-up way, I don't know. All of us lost Bambi in one way or another. Some of us believe in his farce––the comedy where he played the puppeteer, masquerading as the fool. Markus would laugh if he heard those things. Melancholic sentimentality from a madwoman, lovelorn and dying with yearning, he'd ridicule in the same sleazy tone. People like Markus fall in love with themselves more than anything or anyone else. It's a blessing; it's a punishment. One day, Bambi tossed a coin, saying, "Markus's a lucky guy. He's ignorant enough to not know any other suffering besides his own." He tossed the coin again, laughing, "Now he's a very unfortunate guy, because to him, there's no other suffering larger than his own."

Getting to my car, I yank the door open, throw myself into the driver's seat. The nauseating feeling inside my stomach scorches my blood and flesh. The pain is suffocating me. Drowning in my madness and agony, I want to scream at the world: He's gone. I killed Bambi. Instead, all I can do is hit my head against the steering wheel, crying in silence. The scent of him is still here, lingering in the cheap Toyota car like a grieving ghost. I suck the air as if it is life's golden, narcotic elixir. His name stays on the tip of my tongue like a prayer. If ghosts were real, would he come back to haunt me as his last mercy for a lost cause?

I watch the cars speed by, racing nowhere fast. Leaning back on the driver's seat, I put a playlist on. Bambi's raspy voice raps to the beat, "Just turn back and I will be here, waiting for you with cigarette smoke and coffee." His lyrics are so agonizingly sweet and tender, so filled with promises and ever-after that I have to laugh at my pathetic stupidity. But my tears have long dried and my heart burns with the little love I never knew I still possessed.

Yes, everybody wants to fuck Bambi. The silver-streaked hair, slicked back, hard to the touch, the arrogant smirk bordering on a contemptuous snicker, the wide grin when he's high on ecstasy, the beat ringing through the night in those drug parties as he spits out flow after flow, living on the edge of hell and heaven. What I would give to have it all back. What I wouldn't trade to never have known the sweet taste of his poison. I say, "There's no him anymore." What I mean is, "There's only ever been him."

I check the rearview mirror. The blue neon light flickers in the dark, giving off an eerie feeling. The billboard hanging above a crumbling house with a "For Sale" poster stuck on the door says, *We can show you Heaven.* It's almost a cheap act of divine comedy, how the people going there are looking for hell instead. I inhale the sharp nicotine taste. Sweet Bambi. Cruel Bambi. Smart Bambi. Everything Bambi.

My youth has been wasted away in a chaotic whirlpool of madness and longing, reduced to the shape and sound of the two-syllable name, Bambi.

I turn on the ignition and take a final glance at the bar, Rendezvous. So long, misery. I'm so glad I have other options besides dying with you in this whole mess. There are better things out there.

The glass gets foggy after a while with the heater on. The February night is piercingly cold. But I can't spend another moment breathing in the stinking smell of rotting flesh. I roll down the windows, stick my head out, and breathe in the dearly needed fresh air. The cozy restaurants along the upper side of Lakeshore Boulevard are filled to the brim with couples enjoying their romantic dinners. How I wish to barge in each luxurious diner, throw a tantrum, kick up a fuss big enough for everyone to remember me. The world is moving on; life is happy. I told you, Bambi, your death won't change a thing.

Bambi once said in his high after a gig in a dimly lit room, behind an old diner in Chinatown, "You must possess an inhuman bravery and determination to believe that humans are fundamentally good at heart." The damn bastard has some wisdom to spare when the amphetamine occasionally releases his brain from its fatal claws. Ironically, in his version of divine comedy, the amphetamine never let me go. I swallow his words, thinking they are universal truth. He was once my faith, an idol only my hands could reach. The sweet delusion of an addict's drug ballad. No one ever teaches me how the faithless will act when they betray their God. I hear someone say Judas wasn't a traitor by choice; he acted on holy guidance.

And Caesar's murder had to happen for history's wheel to move forward. What about my religion?

I blow rings of smoke to the wind. On nights like this, I can always taste the saccharine flavor of his name on my tongue. He says it is the right thing to do. What he means is it's alright to sin. He says people can kill for worse. What he means is he holds no responsibility over the life he left behind. A field of corpses covered in white powder and the liquid dream.

No one was enough for Bambi. Perhaps I will be in this finale. When the curtain draws, the grandiose scheme ends, and I will be the last one standing, waiting for his ovation. I bite my nails; my teeth start chattering. I'm speeding toward my limit, and my mind is screaming defeat. Just a little more and this will be all behind me. The nightmare barely begins drawing the velveteen curtains. Don't tell me the show is ending. Not yet. I hit the brakes. The tires screech on the unmarked road.

The lake is calm and peaceful, holding inside its bosom a thousand secrets deep. Slamming the door, I jog to the back of the car and open the trunk. My whole body becomes giddy. Every movement causes me to choke on air. In the total, silent darkness of the winter night, I kick at the jammed car trunk, cursing my fate, nearly doubling myself over from the exhaustion of the whole ordeal. The thought of someone seeing me here drives my paranoic nightmare skyrocketing. The glittering darkness and the moon's reflection, like liquid silver cascading over unfathomable depths, make the idea of a double suicide so endearing and alluring. I rub my stomach, feeling the warmth seeping through. The tears I try so hard to hold back now stream down my face in a torrent. I can't. It is no longer my own decision to make.

From the trunk, the pungent smell of decaying flesh pervades my nose. I look at the blind heaven above, helpless and cold in the newfound solitude. The help won't come. Salvation is not needed. I sink to the abyss, take a deep breath, and with another kick, push the trunk open with my sheer willpower, fervently praying that God is real. The black plastic bag lays neatly inside the closed space.

I heave it out, drag it to the edge of the freezing water, and sit down beside it. In the slight crack of the black plastic, his face is drowning in the gentleness of eternal sleep. I stroke the handsome features, the long eyelashes, the still-soft lips, grown cold with death, the pair of azure eyes, even more ethereal than the whole sky, that cut me into tiny pieces, now lying hidden behind the thin lids. He is nothing but a child, and I can save him. I really can. Where did I fail? I open the crack wider, revealing the pale skin and the hollow cheeks. Peace has found him, but the world has abandoned me.

I snuggle into the crook of his long neck, bruised with the thick line of rope, and inhale the sharp scent of sandalwood. The smell of decay is overpowering his warm, comforting cologne, but it doesn't matter. Memory is stronger than reality. Placing a soft kiss on his forehead, his nose, then his frozen lips, I wonder about forgiveness. He said he wouldn't consider it a good thing. "Angela, baby, you must kill yourself along with your enemy when you decide to forgive them," Bambi smiled, his eyes glazed over.

I never knew what he saw in those off-the-floor moments. He was somewhere else—the past, the future, the could-be and the never, the whatever—as long as it wasn't real. He forgot the fact that no matter how much he loved those illusions, the fever dreams wouldn't love him back. "Angela, why are you named Angela?" Bambi toyed with my hair as he laughed at nothing at all. "There's no angel on Earth. You weren't meant to be here, my sweet Angela." And he was right. He was so goddamn right. Sometimes, it takes a whole lifetime of mistakes and regrets to know that things are simply never meant to be. My lips remain on his, sealing the fate I choose. The tears keep flowing for the life I gave away. Holding his stone-cold face in my heating palms, I whisper the final goodbye, knowing it is too late because I'm too far down the road and the way back has long vanished.

"Raymond, this is the first time and the last time I will call you by your last name. You spent your life rejecting that last name, and I don't want to disappoint you, so I dare not mutter it in your presence. It's funny what fear will do to you, because I love it. Bambi or Raymond or Jean-Paul, they are all you. The magnetic rapper and the discreet lover in the night—I love them all. I loved you when you were on stage, performing your songs with the band. Standing in the spotlight, your sweat glistened and I never saw anything shine so bright. You were born to be a star. No one can convince me otherwise. My brain is addled with the singular thought: I adore you. But to you, I was probably just another speck of dust among the heaps of bodies piling in front of you. You had the right to choose, after all. Fame. Power. Money. Why, Jean-Paul "Bambi" Raymond, you have it all. So it keeps bugging me, Bambi, why did you choose me? Why must you bestow the sweet gift of your torturous love on me? Is it fun, watching me dance as I burn myself in the flame of your creation?"

I choke. My nose is bleeding again as the panic and the paranoia claw through my brain on a high-speed rollercoaster. The red spatter of blood smears his otherwise paling, perfect face. For a moment of quiet revelation, I am mesmerized by the beauty of his death. Out of reach. Even in the moment when all is considered equal, he finds a way to be more equal than the rest. He makes his followers chase after his shadow, hunting him down like the last shred of relief in a nation with eternal starvation. He brings his faithful devotee, his lover, the mother of his child––me––the masterpiece of his show, the testament of his miracle, and the atonement for his sins. As the legacy is rolling like the credits of a horrendous, horrible movie made in bad faith, Jean-Paul "Bambi" lays in his grave, smiling, knowing all along that his scheme is the best laid plan. How does it feel to be a human playing the role of the Creator?

"Hey, Jean-Paul, tell me. Do you still feel that threatening, suffocating solitude after death?" I snicker, remembering the first time I laid my eyes on his haunting beauty, only to be forever trapped in that honey-poisoned embrace I'd thought was freedom

It was four years ago, in that crowded bar, Rendezvous. The noise almost gave me a seizure. The pungent smell of sweat and cheap perfume filled my nostrils and reminded me how ugly and grotesque human existence was. I held onto Cecilia's shoulders, barely able to keep myself from throwing up the crappy orange juice I swallowed to stay afloat. Cecilia, still alive then, was a good student at an art college uptown. She had this special talent for turning the swamp of this mess into something beautiful enough to make strangers cry. But being that good at drawing wasn't enough to save her from the comfort dreams in the embrace of the White Fairy—one night, she decided that a cocaine and amphetamine overdose was worth more than her meagre life on Earth.

I didn't see her bleak future then. I was too busy hanging onto her thin arm for dear life, wondering for the thousandth time that night why I had decided to come to that place. I was in my gap year, busy preparing for my university application. The future was so bright I had no other option but to be blinded by everything. Raymond entered the scene when I finally let go of the hold on my stomach and vomited all over his leather jacket and expensive designer baggy pants.

"Oh hey, look who's coming to meet me tonight?"

His voice was sweet like the most potent honey I could buy in the flashy, upscale supermarkets, or the glistening places I never thought to enter. Not mine to hold. All mine to lose. He smiled at me, catching my drooping body in his strong arms. As his minty breath fanned over my overheated face, I kept thinking, *This is it*. The platinum silver hair, slicked back to perfection. The cigarette hung loosely at his lips. The lopsided grin when he squinted his sparkling eyes, unfathomably dark, as he asked me in that same hoarse voice and low baritone: "What's your name, cutie pie?"

"Angela." I spoke without realizing my own voice in the trembling noise of the bar. There was no Cecilia. No crowd. No cigarette smoke and cheap perfume smell. The world came back to life with just the two of us.

"So, Angel?" He smirked. I thought he found the name funny. It wasn't that.

"Yes."

"You look a bit uncomfortable here, Angel." He drew another smoke and flicked off the ash, gestured to the door. "Mind coming outside a bit with me? For some air, you know."

"I don't. I mean, that's what I was thinking of doing, you know, before." I pointed vaguely toward the dance floor. "Before you came."

"Really?" He cocked his eyebrow, seemingly saw through the lie I told, and many lies afterward. "Good. Big ideas often find a way to each other.

Let's go, then?" He jerked his head toward the exit.

And I ignored Cecilia's protest, Bambi's friends' groans, the guards in dark clothes surrounding him as he walked casually out of the bar with me in tow. Someone shouted out, "Bambi, you fucker, don't steal my girl." And he put up his middle finger with a mocking tease. "Too bad. Go fuck yourself, Markus."

The bar door closed behind us, shutting the door to what my professor would call the next best alternatives, and I simply called the prison I never wanted to live inside. Turning my head away from Cecilia's tortured expression, I had a dark premonition that it was my first step on the ladder descending into madness. But madness wasn't the only thing Bambi Raymond would bring. Madness was his middle name.

To think that I loved him that much, and I love him still. What has become of the woman in me? She was destroyed. Not because she had no options. She chose her ending, didn't she? So many escape routes, and I settled for the simplest way to be free. Special K OD. An obvious ending for all drug junkies, especially someone like Bambi who has plenty of dough to spend on the deathly, delicious stuff. I stay out long enough, hang around places, show my face. My alibi should be strong. Biting my lips, I think about the last goodbye, hoping no one smells the decaying flesh in the back of my trunk.

"It's okay, Jean-Paul. You won't feel the pain of living anymore."

Tying the heavy bags of rocks to his cold feet, I push the corpse down the bank and watch it sink down into the dark, winter lake, dragging with it the human in me. The weeping willows shift their branches in the night air. An ending so befitting to the Emperor of Madness. Hamlet. Too bad I wasn't good enough to be his Ophelia.

The surface of the water ripples for a while, calculating the weight it must take into its bosom. After a long, arduous moment, the lake goes back to its indifferent calmness. An unsettled peace on a stormy night. I light a cigarette, draw in a smoke, throw it down into the lake, and walk away. Farewell, my only reason for living.

For now, I have another reason: Revenge.

The corpse smirks in the dark, watching me drive away on the dimly lit road, saying, "Angela, if you want revenge, you must prepare two graves: one for me, one for you."

Chapter 2: The Meeting

February 14, 2020 – 5 years before the so-called 'murder.'

Every saint has a past, and every sinner has a future; I remember one ill-fated writer once said so. Was it a lamentation for his destiny or simply a cry of haughty vanity before he ended up in the same grave as all of us? I will never figure it out.

My saintly past started quite boring, an anticlimactic arc after a thunderous opening act. My family was well off. My studies couldn't have been going better. My life stayed true to the faith: be good, pray, and obey. I thought the road would be smooth sailing until I grew old. Perhaps I would die like Oscar Wilde, minus the prison sentence. Or I'd be a nondescript slave in the machines of those phantasmagoric worldwide corporations, helping to further others' lives along. Then Bambi came.

The first thing he said when we were out of Rendezvous was, "Angela, it takes a pure obedience to form the foundation of man, and it will take an act of disobedience to rebuild humanity." Right then and there, I knew that no matter where or when or how, as long as it was him, I would fall a thousand times and more.

Following his lead, I trudged down the dim alley segregating the two sides of the city: the side of bustling happiness, and the side of hustling dirty. The stink from the gutter made me feel so alive, like I belonged, like my life was built for this, no matter what it was. We were trash, but trash looked like art when put together. Leaning against the whitewashed wall, looking at the hideous graffiti someone had drawn, I prayed for the paint's agony. Why, God? The graffiti must not have wished to be born that ugly. So bad was the color scheme that I thought Cecilia would cry from anger if she saw it. Her desperate voice when I left her behind in the bar still rang in my head, "Angela," but I didn't listen. Couldn't pay attention to the pleading in her tone when Bambi took my cold, sweaty hand in his long, nimble fingers, carved with grace and beauty, and dragged me away from the crowded place as if that was his right all along. What use would it do me to think about Cecilia now? But somehow, I couldn't shake off her face, a badly burned afterimage in my retinas. The night was long. Who among us would wake up tomorrow?

I kicked the pebbles, trying to make myself busy. To not think. To not focus on the eerie silence around me. The smell of decay and rotten food attacked my nose in waves, telling me how we were living on waste, day after day. My breath came up short. I wasn't used to these filthy dumpsters, where danger was everyone's second skin, and the chance of ending up in prison was nothing more than a daily occurrence. The crippling anxiety wasn't helping.

Bambi hadn't said anything apart from the statement about disobedience since we arrived at this godforsaken alley with the putrid smell of a serial murderer's backyard, only lit one cigarette after another. The smoke added yet another layer to the myriad, suffocating smells that pushed me toward the edge of my precipice, but I doubted he cared. His profile was stark against the dim moonlight. I stole a glance now and then. His platinum hair befitted his ghastly white skin. It seemed almost like he was glowing. Like he was transparent. The soul of a person before a person acquired a physical body. Ethereal beauty.

His eyes were a soft brown. A mystical twinkle sometimes sparked up in them, challenging my stare, asking me what I was looking for, what I was trying to accomplish. The tenderness born from too much sorrow. The burden of living a life borrowed from time, stacked with high interest. I didn't know then how much sadness was buried underneath the layer of darkness in them. I wished I had never noticed. But that was a story for later, when things no longer needed saving.

Lighting up another cigarette, Bambi curled his lips, cracking a smug smile.

I was forever caught in that moment, when the pale pink peony bloomed amidst the white moonlight and the petals brushed my heart with their feathery touch. I caught them, and they turned to sharp blades, tearing my flesh to leave behind fiery scars, lest I ever forget an existence that glorious.

"Had your fill yet?" Bambi said, squinting with one eye. A habit whenever he was high, or happy, or excited by new prey, or all of them combined.

"My fill of what?" I replied, coughing awkwardly, trying to compose myself. He was not from my world, and I was the farthest thing from what he usually knew or saw or touched in that sphere of red-light districts, drugs, and discreet rendezvous.

"All of this." He gestured vaguely at his whole body. "Jesus, I thought I would be eaten alive with the way you were staring, you—?"

"Angela."

"Right, angel."

"No, it's Angela." My voice hitched. A part of me was screaming at myself for opposing him, while another part of me was raising all the flags. It was a danger worth dying for, I had naively thought at the time.

"Whatever. Angela comes from the word 'angel,' does it not?" He took another drag from his cigarette. The smoke swirled around his face like an enchantress with her own will. His long, nimble fingers squeezed the cigarette slightly before crushing its remains in a swift motion as he threw the whole thing to the ground. "Nice name. Makes people want to do stuff."

"It does come from the word 'angel,' or to be more precise, the Greek word 'angelos,' yes. But I'm no angel. And excuse me, but what stuff?" My mind swirled in the hazy, billowing smoke. My heart already yielded, pleading, *I don't mind what you do. I never will mind it.*

He moved closer; his face jerked and twitched, like it was deciding on which expression was best suited to the situation. His jaws went slack; he shook his shoulders, snapped back to reality, put the cheeky smile back on. He was high. I didn't know it at the time, but I would get used to it later on. The warmth of his body slowly reached my skin. I breathed in the intoxicating scent of his sandalwood cologne. Mixed in was the scent of the desert, a campfire in a pine forest, the indigo-blue night sky cascading over a head full of dreams. A firefly landed on the tip of my nose briefly and flew away. *Freedom*, I thought, *and the disaster that so often came with it.*

"You know, when I saw you standing over there with your friend—Cecilia, wasn't it? She was a regular, but you were a new face—I thought, wow, someone dropped a newborn babe into the filth. Now, don't be so quick to anger," he chuckled, stroking my face, then with a force I've never known before, he pulled me to his side, caught me between his arms, and framed me there forever. "I was interested. I didn't know what caused an angel to have enough love in her heart to descend there and bear the suffering with us mortals. Can you enlighten me, Angela?"

"Cecilia said—"

"Hm? So it was Cecilia the antichrist?" His face inched closer. His arms caged me in, cornered me on the wall, drowned under the pungent smell of rot. His breath was ticklish on my skin. My mind wanted to run but my heart was fighting with every beat to stay there, to long for more, to immerse in his gleaming eyes' dark ocean. I was drowning.

"Cecilia said she needed someone to take her home. She said she wanted to drink. Said she was heartbroken over some rejection." I swallowed thickly. Danger. But it was so sweet, so damn delicious, so fucking alluring.

"And you would do that for her? Even though you clearly were killing yourself to stay on your feet then? Even when you would murder someone for fresh air? I saw you crouching over and I thought..." Bambi lowered his voice to a sultry baritone, his breath tracing my neck. I was doing everything I could to stay sane. "I thought, *Oh, she wants to escape. A way out. To be free.*"

"You know, being free is an illusion." I kicked the empty can at my foot, watching it roll noisily down the road. "We're all trapped here."

"Is that your thinking? Or is it someone's thought you assume to be your own? Skinner? Or another lonely guy who had nothing else to do but watch the boring specimens of our days?" He scoffed, leaning into my ears, penetrating my peace. The war was on; I tried to stall my losing battle.

"You talk much for someone who looks like he learns very little."

"And you think much for a person who has many blessings but is nothing without a mask." He grins. "See? We pair perfectly with each other."

"Do you talk like that with everyone else? Do girls find that interesting?" I screwed up my eyes, huffing at him.

The truth was, my heart was louder than the sound of cars passing by. My hands clutched my purse, desperately holding the last ground. Did I want to lose? I wasn't sure. All I ever knew was in that moment, when his eyes stared at mine, fiery and tempestuous in their promise of the dance to a disquieting symphony, I begged on my knees for him to emerge victorious and spirit me away like a spoil of the war I waged. It was funny to see how we fight against the beast within to be the human we think will make us happy.

"Tell me, then, Angie." The use of a nickname surprised me. I froze in place as his graciously long fingers caressed my cheeks, stopped at my lips, and pressed them open: "To be or to have, which will you choose?"

"I…" I swallowed, the words coiled inside my throat like a tangled web. "Cecilia is calling me back there." I fumbled for an excuse, lame and cowardly.

"Be my guest." Bambi waved his hand with a comically exaggerated motion. But I couldn't move.

There was something in those magnetic eyes, soft with sorrow. The smile lingered on my heart and memory like a Rembrandt painting. He was haunting. The strong arm hooked around my waist, not holding me back nor letting me go, just barely leaving me stranded, and the moonlight shone on his silver hair, a starry night with dreams and nightmares above his head. I wasn't in love then, but I was mesmerized by his beauty and sadness. The one-of-a-kind feeling, rarely seen in a human, that when you touch the other person's skin, they will turn to sea foam. I didn't know how long I had stood there in my mess of indecision and half-reverence of a man who was lost beyond redemption, until he spoke again: "So you choose to be?"

"I don't know. I have much, but I'm nothing. I can get a reputable degree, I guess. Live a normal life. Is that what you mean by 'to have'?" I took one step back. His arms were wide open. The road to Cecilia was still there.

"Then strip it off. Throw away the things you have. Find the things you want to be. See, it's easy. You said freedom is an illusion, Angie. Freedom is more than that: it's a punishment, an eternal condemnation of consequences, an unsolved question of what would happen if things were different. Skinner meant exactly that when he said it was an illusion. Angie, don't live a life borrowed from dead men and their pedagogy. Be, Angie; between to have and to be, always choose to be."

Bambi's eyes were aglow. Who wouldn't be fascinated by the mirage of the dying stars when they shone their last light before death? I was enraptured, and before I knew it, my back hit the corner of the wall. The road leading to where Cecilia had been was gone, replaced by Bambi's entire existence. I should've known, but knowing never guaranteed understanding. "Yes," I told him, breathless and fervent, "I want to be."

Bambi laughed. I thought it was because of my straightforwardness. But no. When I sank deeper, knew better, and lost myself in the whirlpool of his cheap-man philosophy just to be, I realized that he was laughing at my stupidity and his easy victory. The prey had fallen into his lap without him moving a finger. Only a few sweet words, a charming smile here and there, striking the right chord at the right moment. I was the easiest hunt in his life. Devastating. Yet, laughable, right? Sometimes, it came as a marvelous wonder to me how easy it was to ruin a girl.

He cradled me in his arms, whispered into my ears, telling me how I was the gift God bestowed on him, an angel with hair a gentle shade of blue, the color of heaven on the brightest day, of hope, of freedom in a locked cage. What he meant was I belonged to the collection of girls he got, right between his unfortunate ex, who had offed herself, and the next whore he made love with briefly because she had enough curves but not a lot of brains. So no, he never had faith in any man other than himself. As he led me out of that dank, narrow-to-the-point-of-suffocating alley and boarded a taxi to his apartment, I couldn't shake the feeling that if I opened the car door, I could still escape.

But escape what? Wasn't this what I had always wanted? A person. A reason to keep moving forward. More than that, freedom. Untainted. Untouched. He was everything I ever wished for, manifested in the body of a man and a predator. The danger palpitated in the air and I drowned, intoxicated on the addicting flavor of his nicotine breath as his lips traced out the shape of my neck. On the ride along the busy Burnhamthorpe Road leading toward the quiet Lakeshore Boulevard, I was giddy, thinking that this was what I had lived for; this was what I had dreamt of, forgetting everything else. The world in my eyes was reborn and reduced to this one name: Bambi.

I wondered if he found the spectacle ridiculous. I wondered if he told this story to his friends, his bodyguards, to Markus, his close partner, and jeered about it. "You had to be there," I could imagine him saying with roaring laughter, "and see the look on that girl's face." I wondered if he had ever looked back on that day and spared a merciful thought for me. A shred of dignity. A sliver of pity, ragged though it may have been, bequeathed on me in his most benevolent moment, too high on ecstasy to be cruel. Far too many times, in those nights when I woke up in my own vomit, I still dreamt of our first night. Of his eyes. Of his smile. Of the gleaming light in the unfathomable darkness as he said, "Be, Angie. Between to have and to be, always choose to be."

"Here we are." He opened the car door, inviting me out.

In a trance, I stepped out of the taxi, walked blindly behind him along the path to the mid-rise building. We climbed the rusty staircases. Bambi tickled me just to hear my laughter, and I responded to his touch fervently, satisfied with the shadow of a smile on his face. We reached the shabby apartment. The dark yard was doomed with empty bottles and beer cans like our future would be one day. All the lights were out. The stars were fading. The only living thing in that immeasurably lonely and desolate void was Bambi.

"I thought we were—" I said, still high from being his chosen one.

"Well, sorry it isn't a castle. I'm moving soon anyway. To some better place," he said nonchalantly, pulling the keys out of his jeans' pocket and fumbling with the lock, never missing a beat.

We danced the tango of passion, our legs swirled into the apartment, not even bothering to close the door. I followed his footsteps, beguiled by the melody he whistled and the gentle caress of his fingers wrapping lithely around my wrist, tugging my heartstrings with every move. Falling never needed much: he commanded, and I abandoned the whole world. Nothing was ever that simple. No one could imagine a scheme that elaborate.

Bambi opened the door to his bedroom. It was old with paint the color of wooden casket and a weathered bedframe. But the decorations were immaculate. The furniture was simple and cheap, I could tell at first glance, and yet, the way he sprinkled his magic on them made each piece looked like it came straight out of Crate and Barrel's latest catalogue. The caramel-colored rug laid snugly under the coffee table with an accompanying cream sofa; it screamed nouveau riche. Nobility. New aesthetic. The hardwood floor and the terse flower decorations reminded me of a Japanese inn. I asked him later if he ever visited Kyoto for his decor's inspiration. He said Kawabata came by his abode one day and left the footprint. We were fucking high then; everything was as real as the billowing smoke and the fleeting illusion of happiness on loan with double interest.

That was a future I had no access to viewing. A premier to a movie where I had no invitation, even though I was the lead actress. Too bad, from what I heard on the street; it was a blockbuster. That night, as I took my shoes off and tip-toed into his living room, all I could glimpse was something more fragile. A palpitation of the heart. A lost innocence. A hope that somehow, tomorrow would come, and I could still go on hoping.

"You look like you've seen a ghost's grave." Bambi threw himself on the mattress and spread out his long limbs. He seemed at ease. A lion in his lair.

"No. Maybe. I mean, I expected, well, something different." I tried to find the right words, but the feelings kept going astray.

"You mean, you expected to find a dumpster." He winked, resting his cheek on his hand; a bashful smile beamed on his face.

"No, well, technically speaking—"

"Technically speaking, I'm right."

"You're not wrong. But I never said you were right. I mean, I don't want to be rude." My voice grew smaller as I cowered in his larger-than-life presence. It was all too late, and I never felt an ounce of remorse.

"Well, be rude, then." He lit up a cigarette and started pulling a few drags.

"Life is too short for niceties. And I didn't drag you here to listen to praises and compliments. How's it? Satisfied?"

"It's a nice apartment." I fidgeted on my feet, not sure whether to sit down or keep standing there until sunrise. Bambi cocked his eyebrows at the spectacle, clearly enjoying it, and didn't seem like he would release my anxiety anytime soon.

"It is. Ex-girlfriend's an interior designer. Can't complain. Well, too bad she's not here anymore, and I'm moving next month. This place is up for rent now."

"Is that so? Excuse me, your what?" I caught myself in a whirlpool of information.

"Heh, what's tripping you? Moving next month or the ex-girlfriend thing?"

"I don't, I mean, you don't need to share that with me."

"Is this going to be how the whole night goes?"

Bambi crushed the cigarette, stood, and walked toward me. The lion was done playing. He stopped close enough for his breath to trace my face and his body warmth crept through every pore on my skin. It was eerie. It was strange. His heat instilled fear and the shadow of his fingers dancing on my skin made me tremble. His hand hovered over my cheek, never quite touching it, but close enough to make me aware of his presence. Haunting. Obsessing. Never letting go. My throat closed. My mouth dried up. Words refused to come out. I felt like a child who had committed a serious crime, who needed a fatal punishment, and only Bambi could deliver me from the sins I had committed.

"Didn't you say you want to be? Show me, then, Angela, how do you want to be?"

At that command, my world spun. My legs gave out. The earth beneath me vanished and I drowned in the lava ocean. Darkness closed in. I choked, trying to breathe, but the harder I did, the more fire burned in my lungs. I slid down to the floor, convulsing; my heart was struggling to beat. My whole existence became so painful I wished something would stop it. And Bambi was there, laughing. "No kidding," he said through my hazy moments of a full-blown panic attack, "You're a gem, Angela. Like no other." In a split second, I was out of my body, looking at my grotesque self, kneeling at his feet, clawing at his pants, trying to formulate a word, a prayer for mercy. Tears were flowing automatically without my control. I was drooling, gagging with every breath I fought to catch. He just watched it happen. *Help,* my mind screamed, *Help me.*

After ten minutes of agonizing pain, my limbs lost their final strength. Bambi, with the same bored expression on his face, crouched down to the mess that used to be me, picked me up, cradled me in his arms, and held me there, completely still. I drank in his warmth like the sweetest elixir God had ever created. The scent of sandalwood calmed me. Unconsciously, or rather, the survival instinct of the animal in me, urged me to burrow my nose into his neck, greedily inhale whatever was there. The source of my living. The essence of my existence. I grasped his jeans jacket with ragged breathing, knowing he was a beast, hoping I had shown him what I wanted to be, and that was to be loved. All along, I was the lost cause, swimming in the Great Flood, currying favors with the devil. Because I was a human God abandoned when Noah built his ark.

"Angela, sweet girl, listen to me," Bambi said, or I thought he said in my half-crazed state, "I don't need a saint. I don't need another person walking in here, telling me I need saving, saying they can get me out. Sweet Angela, do you ever feel like you need a way out?"

I nodded my head, more to appease him than to agree.

"I thought so. When I saw you at the club, I knew what you were. Those eyes have seen far too much sorrow. That smile has tolerated far too many burdens. I looked at you and I thought, 'Oh, she is me.' Sweet Angela, if God were real, maybe He bestowed you in my arms as the last mercy. Don't you think so?"

Again, I nodded without understanding the weight of his meaning.

"I never once believed in the mercy of gods. They're far too cruel; they have too much free time for that. But hey, if you're their grace, wouldn't that be beautiful? Who wouldn't believe in something like that? A love that could cure everything. Angela, don't you believe that love has such an immense power?"

I didn't believe it. Never. But I was too weak to protest.

"So stay here, Angela. Fall. Be. Let yourself go. Join the free and the damned. And I'll be there, building a special kind of hell that befits both of us."

He looked at me; his hand finally touched my face. It was cold. The fingers were tremulous and tender. The soft caress trailed down my cheek, my jaw, and reached my neck, feeling for my pulse. It unearthed something primal within me. Something I never knew was there, dormant, waiting for a call to war. He placed a kiss on where my vitals were beating, stealing my life and my reason for living. His lips were rough with dried skin, but the tingle sparked a wild forest fire in my whole body. I froze, trying to ground myself in the fact that it was all wrong, that I shouldn't believe his words, that temptation was the first threshold to Lucifer.

But there were days when a person would be desperate enough to think that Lucifer belonged to the good side. And who could resist Bambi when his eyes were glistening with childlike joy and suffering happiness?

Falling was easy. He said it first. I just needed to let myself go. As the night raged on outside the beautifully decorated windows of the old apartment, I forgot that the world existed, that human nature was prone to cruelty, that we both were children, entertaining ourselves in the grandiose scheme that love and only love could win in the final battle against the theory of everything. I lost myself in Bambi, trusting in his Hell and denouncing others' Heaven. In the wild embrace of the strange man and the chase of human warmth, we consoled each other with the wounds we undressed.

If he had known then I would be the one to end his theatrical act on the stage of his Divine Comedy, where he was the sole director, I wonder if he would still have let me into the theater and allowed me to live through the next day. But what was the use in asking? All the what-if questions were just that: black ink on white paper. They couldn't solve anything, and they wouldn't leave behind even a trace of regret. Humanity is still a fucking child in a cradle, crying for mother's milk. I wonder if our mothers ever wanted us to be free. If they did, why would they raise us to be so selfishly, cruelly narcissistic?

Bambi, did you ever love me? Or did you just pretend?

Chapter 3: The Morning After

March 27, 2025 – A month after the death of Jean-Paul "Bambi" Raymond

I wake up from the nightmare of the past. Strange bed. Cold room. The lingering smell of forgotten passengers whose lives I will never know—and never care to—pervades my nostrils. The dust whirls in the stale, early morning air. It's weird. I thought I had left the ghosts behind when I watched his corpse sink beneath the darkness of the lake. The Psyche-style mirror reflects me, smiling. You, my love—you are the shadow of that ghost you are trying to outrun.

Asphyxiation is a strange condition. For a creature who survives solely on air, there is such a thing where the body just stands up and goes, "That's it, I'm not going to breathe for you anymore."

I flick the cigarette and watch the embers glow in the twilight of the new day. Perhaps this is why Bambi always wanted to cover all the mirrors in his home. He feared something would come out and strangle him. It was the superstition of an addict. Delirious paranoia. Or worse, the fear was himself, buried under layers of aluminum foil and reflections. Who knows. Now it's my turn to find out.

The tank top is not enough to make me warm. I reach for the old cardigan I threw on the floor last night before I drank myself to oblivion, knowing full well I will discard it again in a few moments. The instantaneous satisfaction—that's what I'm after, and the liquor does a good job. Who cares what will happen when the light comes through the windows later? I curl into a ball on the twin bed, scrolling through my phone. No news about his disappearance. No messages from Markus. Is it good? Is it bad? I wonder. The life inside my stomach kicks me out of my apathy. This is no time for questions: I need to act. The crossroad is far behind me now, and I must keep walking on. Angela, how many lives do you want to lose?

A tiny ring echoes in the quiet dawn, waking me up from a temporary nap. Sleep has come as second nature since the day I cradled the sweet blessing in my bosom, hoping it would flower. In a trance, I look at the brightly lit phone screen. The reminder says, in its piercing kindness and bliss: "Happy Birthday, my sweet Angela. XOXO. B." I stare at the message— a timed reminder on an untimely day. Did Bambi think he would be dead by the time I reach the next stage of my life? Or he simply never bothered to care for such trivial stuff? I scroll through the calendar in my phone. The reminder is on at the same time, on the same day, only the year is different. The sadness in Bambi's final little act is enough to break the Earth apart in gentle oceans.

My thoughts evaporate, the room vanishes, reality merges with delusion, and the dream gnaws at my feet with its savage fangs, biting my bones, swallowing my flesh as I try to breathe, to survive, to exist, to hold on to whatever could keep me going. Futility reduced to the small frame of a haunting memory. Pathetic.

A teardrop falls on his smile. Then it becomes two. Three. Until the floodgate opens and the ocean rises forth. I let the salty stream flow, stunned at the fact that my body still knows how to cry. After all, it was Bambi who said, "Angela, do you know how beautiful a teardrop is?"

It was an evening in the last days of summer. The breeze passed by us, never to return, but it etched on our skin the soft caress of the brightly lit happiness as the sunlight slanted through the windows. Bambi sat there on the chaise-longue, fucking higher than the Empire State building. His head was lolling off the edge of the chair. A glass frame of some crystalized object in his hand. His fingers toyed with the piece in different angles. A childlike glee shone in his deep blue eyes.

I was kneeling by his side. At that time, I wasn't keen on drugs. The effect of twenty years of proper education and the tradition of moral high ground were keeping me sane. Or rather, it was sorting me into a different category. A social caste Bambi couldn't reach with his grimy hands and his smoke-hoarse voice. He needed me to fall of my own free will. And it would be sooner than I cared to admit. Sooner than I thought it would be.

"Teardrop? Isn't it similar to crystallized salt?" I asked, twirling my fingers in his soft, silver curls.

"Kind of. But what makes it special is the sadness from which it was born. A thousand nights of longing. A thousand stabbing pains without screaming. A thousand unnamed sufferings. Then one day, this single teardrop falls. It crystalizes under the microscope for the human eyes' entertainment. No one knows the tragedy behind the birth of such beauty. That is the holiness of its divine comedy, Angela. That is the heavenly allure of a teardrop. Dangerously gorgeous in all its purity and innocence."

"Bambi," I said, mesmerized by his dictation and the gospel of my newfound religion, "Bambi, your mind is acting on you again."

"And is it a friend? Is it a foe?" He smiled languidly. His eyes were searching for something nonexistent. Something that hadn't been there since the birth of the universe and probably would never be as long as the Earth still turned on its axis. He was looking for an abyss. For destruction. Annihilation of normalcy.

"Why don't you take a rest? Markus said he would come by to pick you up at eight. Don't you have a show at eight-thirty?"

"Yeah. Fuck Markus." He laughed. Bambi was crazy. It was contagious. I giggled, falling over his spread-out body. "Fuck Markus," I echoed, reveling in the shared feeling. Granted, I didn't know Markus that well then, but from Bambi's voice, I decided with firm conviction that I would hate him, curse him, and cut him up if need be. He was a villain to me before he had a chance to prove himself to be anything else. The role was assigned. I doubted he had a choice in it, or even a show of hands to protest in silence.

Bambi stroked my hair, still holding onto the glass frame of the crystalized object. I looked at it, my skin prickling with curiosity. His eyes grew vacant for one moment, then they became glazed over the next. He was in a trance. In these instances, I could get almost anything out of him. At least, the unimportant stuff. After many failed attempts, I learned that the key to success with him was patience. Bambi might be out of it, but the moment danger got close, he pounced back like a leopard on the hunt. So I bit my tongue, swallowed my words, chewed over my thoughts, and waited until he settled down in his cozy place of calm before dropping a sneak attack:

"Is that a crystallized teardrop in your hand?"

"What?" His voice was groggy, which was perfect. I clutched my chest, trying to temper my heartbeat.

"The crystallized teardrop. In your hand."

"Oh? This? Yeah. It was mine."

"Your teardrop?"

"Yeah. When I was a med student, I cut myself once. The pain was intolerable enough for me to shed some tears. So I thought I might as well collect them. I was curious. What would a teardrop look like under a microscope, you know? And here we are, a crystallized teardrop framed in glass. Pretty narcissistic, if you ask me." He chuckled, still unwilling to let the frame go.

"But why?"

"Why what?"

"Cut yourself. Collect teardrops. Frame it. Isn't it, I don't know, painful?"

"Perhaps it was. But that is all there is: It was. Now it's not. Funny how time changes the worst things in history, eh?" He giggled, and I knew he truly found it hilarious. The spark in his eyes proved that. "Look at us. We almost forgot how bad World War II was. Perhaps we'll get ourselves into another World War. Angela, time doesn't mean shit to a race that is so fragile it could end itself on sadness."

Bambi laughed, resting his head on the armrest, eyes closed, fingers tapping a silent, unknown melody. He was no longer on the balcony of our shared condo--no, he wasn't even inside the world I was living in. His mind was traveling to a faraway land, where there was no sadness and sorrow. He longed to reach home; that was what he always professed to anyone who would listen, but he never knew where that home was, except when he was in his euphoric state, when things no longer had a price, but just were. And

Bambi sang, sweetly, in his low, rumbling voice that could shake the earth underneath anyone's feet:

"Strangers in this town

They raise you up just to cut you down

Oh, Angela, it's a long time coming

Oh, Angela, spent your whole life running away--"

It was The Lumineers. The song didn't have a direct relation to me, but I cried like a newborn child in his arms, knowing in my heart that even if I could bend God's will my way, He would never bestow my lover back to me.

I didn't know if he meant anything then. He had a habit of saying whatever when he was high on drugs. He never remembered his words later. The promises, the ever-after, the fever dreams—it was better to forget, he said; remembering them only made reality more like a hell he never chose. And he wished to love it more than he did. For a person who vowed to believe in goodness, he did a terrible job at being a disciple of God. He often said Judas Iscariot betrayed God on a holy order, and people didn't want to listen to that version of the fairy tale because it was less convenient for them as a cause to wage a war.

"Antichrist?" Markus once asked him in a heated debate. Despite the shady drug dealing business and the lecherous personality, Markus was a devout Catholic.

"No, more like a hypocrite. But as long as it fits your narrative." Bambi shrugged and wrapped his arm around my shoulders, continued drowning himself in scotch and whisky. By then, I caught his madness from the kisses we had and the love we made, so the smallest gesture from him, a caress or a touch, was enough to made me feel special. A world was living out there, moving, chasing, racing ahead, trampling on each other to be the last ones standing. But we were there, side by side, quietly watching, letting life slip through us, satisfied with being abandoned, settling for the bottom of the ladder.

I knew then that I had fallen. The drugs weren't necessary. His name on my tongue was enough to make me take the jump.

A soft melody brings me back to the shabby motel room. "Cigarette Smoke and Coffee," the song he wrote when his ex-girlfriend went crazy on X and offed herself in the pool of bloody mess. Come to think of it, which ex was it? The third? The fourth? Or the one who designed his old apartment's interior decoration? Who keeps count of the dead when they no longer love you back? The moment they stop breathing is the instant their existence becomes meaningless. The void. A drop of water merges into the ocean. Whoever came up with the phrase, "They live on in your memory" must be some desperate wino, drunk on false hope and illusion.

The ring keeps blaring incessantly like the devil's hound from the deepest level of hell. With the sluggish reluctance of a sloth, I pick up the phone. It's Markus. A prickling premonition and nauseating hatred creeps up on me like claws scratching at my throat.

"Hey." I cough. The phone stays silent for a suspiciously long while, then Markus's subdued voice replies in a whisper:

"Angela, is Bambi there?"

"No."

"Weird. I can't reach him. No phone call. No text messages. He isn't at home or the club. His car is there but it hasn't been used for quite some time. Where the fuck is that guy?" Markus sounds more and more frustrated as he lists his causes. Then he softens the volume just as immediately. My brain catches the clue and shouts the alert to my whole body. Somebody's listening.

"I don't know. He didn't tell me anything. Never tells me anything." I swallow, replying with measured words. It was a half-truth. The rest of the truth stares at me from the Psyche mirror: grotesque and ugly in all its blood and decaying flesh. Tears are swelling in my eyes. Don't blame me, Bambi; it was you who said humans can die of sadness.

"You're his girl, Angela. If you don't know, no one does. Come on. I'm at the end of my tether here. He has Saul's contact. He's the only one who can reach that fucker now, and I need that new stash. Angela, help me," Markus pleads. It is so fake in his plastic tone and his thinly veiled contemptuous treachery that I almost vomit. He doesn't mean to beg. He means to command.

A silent beat falls through. Saul. How could I forget? This whole charade is a special performance for him. Smiling through the fury, I can hear my voice sounding back in my ears like it belongs to a stranger's:

"I'm one of his girls. And no, I can't help you. Maybe you can try your luck with another girl, Markus. Some Sophie or Marie or whatever the latest fallen angel's name is." It used to work on me, that tone in Markus's voice. But the girl who feared the fall of the Babel Tower is here no more. She's dead, gone with the cold body beneath the calm and peaceful water. Markus's fate isn't a wise man's role.

"Come on, don't tell me you're still jealous of his habitual one-night stands?" Markus groans, then quickly cuts to the chase. "You must at least have his contact, right?"

"I'm not. And I don't. What use is it anyway?"

"Angela, baby girl…"

"I'm not your baby girl. Or anyone's baby girl. Leave me alone."

"Angela, I—"

I hang up, leaving the pleading Markus to his own devices. It seems no one has filed a missing person report for Bambi Raymond yet. Leaning against the padded bedrest, I feel a hollow cave open wide inside me, devouring me whole. I don't know if it is sadness or pity that is making my heart weep with such biting sorrow. For the first time in a month, it hits me.

Bambi is gone and no one even cares. No one except me. I lie there, looking at the white-washed ceiling, thinking how much misery he had borne when he was living his life that way, all alone, knowing that there would be no soul missing him. No love lost. No love found. He was standing there, watching everyone walking by, leaving. There's never been any greetings in his short life. Only farewells. And he tolerated it all, like a child waiting for the last act of a magic show, the kind where the parents would come by to pick him up and tell him they were going home.

Living a life like that, so utterly lonely at night and crying his soul with every step he takes underneath the bright blue sky in the day, Bambi chose bitter acceptance and grudgingly let go of hope. It made sense enough for him to tell me on our first meeting, "Angela, I don't need saving."

I open the calendar app and check the events of the day. Anything would do, as long as I can escape his ghost. While fumbling with the phone, my hand knocks on the nightstand and the old, scratched glass frame falls over. A crystalized teardrop. I pick it up, place it under the nightlight, and twirl the glass piece in different angles. The crystal shines with beauty in a reverie, almost as if this world was never meant for something as mesmerizing as a human's tear. The little branches reach out their tiny hands, so fragile, so delicate and graceful in all their transparent structure I can almost feel their heartbeat, though they are inanimate objects. I touch the glass surface, tracing each line and contour of the crystalized piece, lost in the world of the poignant, untold tales from the land of the broken and the maimed. In the faint light of the hushed dawn, I think I hear the cry of the unborn babe, palpitating in my eardrums, dancing to the rhythm of the life he dreams God would give him as the gospel promises.

The blessings upon us are the suffering that makes us the humans we are. But how can a babe who is sheltered in a cradle know that?

"Angela, time doesn't mean shit to a race that is so fragile it could end itself on sadness," Bambi once said.

It didn't hurt then. It shouldn't hurt this much now. But the sun has come out of the dark cloud of a stormy night, and as the light shines through the slanting curtains, I realize how lonely a human can be sometimes. The fucking desolation of a person washed up on a deserted island. Stranded. Out of breath. Out of escape routes. Hanging onto hope because there is nothing else to do but hope. And like all things Bambi predicted, I cry, letting the tears flow like the beautiful sadness that they are. I don't know what I am mourning for: Bambi's death or mine. A literal loss or a metaphorical one. Either way, the trap is closing in. Bambi has paid his dues. Now it's my turn to bargain with the interest.

Chapter 4: The First Man

February 15, 2020 – Early hours of the morning after the first meeting

The thunder shattered through the quiet bedroom. Even the thick velveteen curtain and the double glass windows couldn't temper the tempestuous howls of the beast outside. The rain beat on the windowpane of the apartment, peeling off the already stripping layer of moldy paint on the outer wall and whatever was left of the once-pristine, colorful bricks.

I lay there in the dark, wide awake, waiting for the storm to pass. Something changed in the brief turn of the clock's hands, though I knew not what. Beside me, Bambi curled into a ball, so small I could gather him up and wrap his entire being in my bosom, shielding him from the world. His arm clung to my waist, desperate in its coldness and tremor. He wasn't sleeping, but for more than three hours now, I couldn't get him to say anything, much less move. Monsters and men, they were all scared of a thunderstorm.

"Bambi, hey, it's okay, it's only a storm. It'll pass," I whispered, stroking his temple, drenched in ice-cold sweat. Hell, I didn't even know if he was afraid of the bellowing gust shaking his windows, or something worse. Something like the place where that suffering began.

He refused to budge. His eyes squeezed shut. The frigid arm only clung tighter to my waist as a response, pinching my flesh hard enough to bruise. I bit back the yelp, telling myself he needed help and I was his last salvation. In that fleeting moment, I forgot his first warning when I crossed the threshold: he never wanted to be saved. The revelation of being the one and only saint in someone's life, revered and sanctified in all the holiness of the living—it was the sweetest elixir I had ever tasted, and the addiction came as naturally as breathing.

With as much tenderness as a kitten's paws, I ran my fingers through his silver curls, now relaxed from hair gel and dampened with sweat. He shivered slightly, then remained still. "Bambi, come on. Where are you, Bambi?" I coaxed him like a child, placing soft kisses on his forehead, trailing them down his cheeks and the sharp, masculine jaw. It was almost soul-wrenching to see a human breaking apart in such desolation and—what was it again?—a vulnerability so tangible I could hear the sound of its fall in the dark. "Bambi," I called, my voice barely reaching through his thick wall of solitude, "I thought you were going to wreck me."

He remained still. Listless and cold. A body without soul. His breathing grew faint, but the pulse was screaming into the vanity of the raging night how much he wanted to live. How he was trying with every fiber in his being to exist, to hold onto life, to simply be. I wondered what had happened in that short period—that span of over three hours—to turn him from a savage and menacing leopard to a defeated soldier on his own battlefield. He took me to his bedroom just to make me witness his downfall. One must laugh at the stupidity of the whole fiasco. I thought my panic attack was the end of me. I was wrong, as I would be far too often later in our macabre relationship, where the only thing good was the deadly ending of one of us and the madness of the other. He lost his grip on reality the moment the thunder struck. As the rain started to fall, Bambi shattered in the gentle night like a vase made of the cheapest clay.

"Bambi," I called again. No answer. He trembled slightly as a form of quiet acknowledgement, then went back to his stubborn silence.

Thinking back on it now, there were so many red flags raising on that night when I still had him in my embrace. When I pick them up now in those sleepless, strange bedrooms in motels that smell like vomit and last night's leftovers, I can build a tower of desperation and hopelessness out of them. Warning signs. Exit boards. I should have taken the first flight when the metaphorical neon lights went on like a fucking Christmas tree. And Bambi was lying there in my arms, waiting for the storm to pass by his nightmarish life like anything else in the tepid days he had been through. Bambi said he kept waking up one morning and waiting until one day, he wouldn't need to wake up anymore, and mused that much like Sisyphus, he must believe that somehow, he was happy. Time slipped through the cracks of his fingers, and he let it be. Maybe since the day he learned that he belonged to the world of the grown-ups, he knew there was a kind of hopeless beauty in tolerating the grinding wheel heading toward the same ending. Moving or not, he would reach that goal, so why bother trying?

Lightning pierced the darkness of the disquieted room. I looked on with boredom. My mind was drifting away from the present; my thoughts were reaching home. Maybe Cecilia would understand him better. Maybe Markus would know how to deal with this severely wounded beast. Meanwhile, I was left alone, stranded on a barren shore of hurt, trying to resuscitate a soul who had already refused to go on, and I was barely keeping my balancing act together, walking on the thin rope of now and never, trying to see before me what I would have and watching my back to understand what I had lost. Breathing in hope. Holding on to nothing. Blessed was the curse of suffering and pain, for without it, we could never be human.

A soft noise stirred me awake. Bambi held himself up with the strength of a newborn deer.

"Hey," he said. His voice was weak and hoarse.

"Hello, thy name is Darkness," I teased, hoping it would somehow release the tension in his eyes. But what stared back at me was worse than death.

"Darkness wishes it were me. Anyway." Bambi quickly changed the subject, avoiding my inquisitive gaze, rubbing his nose viciously, as if he couldn't feel the pain. "Where were we?"

"You almost stripped me naked, then it rained, and you collapsed. Next thing I knew, I had to piggyback you to your bedroom without any knowledge of your floorplan. You were no easy baggage, either. I tried to go home for the last, let's see, it's past 3 a.m. now so, four hours. But you gripped me like a lifeline, and I couldn't leave you there, dying in your own house. So there. We were about there."

Bambi looked at me. A strange glint of something like amusement mixed with anger and a dose of curiosity shone in his bewitching blue eyes. "Has anyone ever told you that you lack communication skills?"

"And no seduction skills either. Yep, heard that plenty." I swung my feet down the bed, ready to go home. I never planned to stay inside the cage of another dying beast, considering myself as one.

Bambi halted his hand mid-air. Then he burst out laughing.

"Seriously? You're not the least bit curious about how I got to that stage? Do men collapse on you that often?"

I pondered his question for a moment, then shrugged it off. "Not really my problem. I mean, the one who collapsed was you, right? Then the one who should be worried is you. I was simply there. Also, men don't collapse on me. Usually, I'm the one collapsing. On other men. Women. Walls. Tables. I don't have a choice in the subject matter."

"Panic attack?"

"Focal aware seizures. You?"

"Post-traumatic stress disorder. Sometimes, drug overdose."

"Ouch. Must sting."

"That's it? 'Ouch. Must sting'? You take it way better than—well—all the people I've ever met."

"Try meeting more people then."

"You do drugs?"

I blinked, twisting my neck at him so fast it almost snapped. Bambi, still calm and composed, reached over me to get the pack of cigarettes on the nightstand and lit one up. The white smoke billowed up to the pale ceiling. In the fleeting moment when his body warmth blanketed my thighs, I could breathe in the cologne that would haunt me for dear life. The drugs. The addiction that one day I would breathe with hunger and thirst, like air, like water, like the barest food when there was nothing left on Earth to eat. I crave that scent still; passing through the mall in my ragged clothes, and with just the sheerest hint of that smoky sandalwood, I would chase it down, hunt the scent with fervor, until the realization hit me, each time more brutal than the last: There's no meal to satiate a beggar by the door of love.

The more generosity I receive, the greedier I become, until it burns into a dying match in a silent prayer by a closed church gate: Lord, please take me with him, because I've already dug out my grave.

But at that time, drugs and addiction were a foreign concept to me. Living a life forever depending on something that could disappear any moment, I thought I wouldn't succumb to that mediocrity. So I said, half in jest, half in provocation:

"I do enough to keep me sane." A flame was burning hot in my stomach. The pain turned more and more excruciating. The tiny voice in the back of my head whispered, If you had done some kind of drug, maybe he would consider you the same kind of addicts. Bambi ignored my awkward answer.

"What kind?" He cocked one eyebrow, blowing a cloud of smoke toward me.

"Xanax. Clonazepam. Something else but I forgot the name. I have them at home."

"Oh baby girl, we don't talk about medication. That shit never helps." He cackled like a madman.

Under the glimmering night light of the bedroom, his pearly white teeth reflected the beauty of shadows and stars, and that eerie scene would make anyone with a normal sense cry out in fear, but I was strangely attracted to that monster's alluring hideousness. My eyes followed the curve of his lips as he spoke my name with so much tenderness, I could learn to love myself again. "Angela, I'm talking about the real shit. Cocaine. X. Amphetamine. Ever heard of those?"

With deft movements, he pulled the drawer of the nightstand out and picked up a film of tablets. Bambi popped two of them into his mouth like they were nothing, and I stared on in fear and trembling. A sort of mesmerizing worship creeped up my spine and I lurched toward him unconsciously. Instinct. Primal urge. The basic need of a human to protect and shelter what she thought was rightfully hers. Fifteen minutes later, I caught him in my arms right when he went completely lax and pliant. My mind screamed for the phone, but my hands refused to let go of his cold body, dripping with sweat. His face muscles grew taut. His jaws clenched tight. The titillating azure eyes dilated until all I could see was a bottomless abyss. I thought I was staring Death in the face, but that wasn't the end of me. Not yet. As the tears stung my eyes, ready to stream down my cheeks to celebrate the uselessness of a damsel who was grudgingly trying to save herself from this mess of disquiet, Bambi jerked up.

The stark profile lit up in the dark room by the lightning from the windows was so eerie and uncanny, it nearly shattered my heart. I whispered the name of the monster I had just woken from the deep slumber of the deathly hollow: "Bambi." He didn't answer. His teeth were grinding so loud I could hear the sound gritting on my ear canals, and it hurt. "Bambi," I repeated his name like a fervent prayer, ready to escape the dungeon I was unwillingly trapped inside. One of my legs was touching the floor. My hand grasped the blanket, trying to fend for the attack of the newborn beast.

But Bambi wasn't having any of that nonsensical premonition shit. Before I could launch down the bed, he caught both my wrists in one swift motion, caging me inside the frame that was his existence. The smile on his face was weirdly gentle and yet so sinisterly euphoric that my thoughts and my soul left the scene. I heard him speak, but the words seemed to lose all their meaning. Fear and trembling. So this was what Søren Kierkegaard was talking about.

"Ah, that hits the spot. See? It's easy. You pop them in your mouth and the next thing you know, you're deep in paradise. I don't call it heaven, Angela. I don't believe in a place no one ever sees. Hell, who has ever returned from that place? At least we have seen hell, have we not? We created it—still living inside it—and we called it Earth. Angela, you need a special kind of bravery to wake up every morning without wanting—actually trying—to slit your throat. There comes a time, my angel, you realize that everyone is leaving. Such is the natural course. Remember the rivers? They flow to the ocean. What makes you think, or even believe, that humans will be different?"

Bambi stopped his monologue, seemingly out of breath. He was heaving. The pain, I thought, was such a sudden rush of ecstasy that his mortal body could barely keep up. Within a few minutes, he started again. The words tumbled on top of each other. The thoughts were almost incoherent. His body toppled over mine; pale, bare skin gliding onto my fishnet top, his hands grasping whatever body parts within reach could give him a sense that there was a life here with him. I tried to remember how to breathe, then I tried to remember that Bambi also had a heartbeat. His chest pressed onto mine, and I counted to the rhythm of the weirdly shaped clock on the wall. One, two, three--

"Angela, people hope because there's nothing else to do. And they hold onto hope for the sake of keeping the hope alive. Do you see the desperation in that? Truth be told, Angela, I abandoned my hope a long time ago. Since the day God decided to take my sweet girl away, what use would there be for me to keep fueling something that was barely existing? The flame was gone before I had the chance to see it burn. Angela—"

Fourteen, fifteen, sixteen. I didn't pay attention to his rambling anymore. My eyes focused on the tattoo hidden beneath the layer of his shirt. Twenty, twenty-one, twenty-two. A thorn vine wrapped neatly around his left arm, climbing upward toward his bicep, with the inscription of a foreign phrase. I tried to make out the words amidst Bambi's fast speech:

Jos liedelle käy käteni
Sen heti vedän pois
Jos kadulla on lompakko
Sen varastaakkin vois

"—but perhaps God has always wanted it darker. Perhaps God wants the suffering children. The misery and the pain. What kind of heaven is God building, I wonder. Angela, do you understand?"

"Bambi, what are those words?"

He stopped rambling. With the same dilated, deep azure eyes, brewing storms and reflecting the thunder outside, he stared at the tattoo on his left arm with a childlike innocence. I wondered if he fully registered the meaning of my question. A long silence passed between us, then his eyes grew tender, almost too tender for a person who was so high he could see the Halley comet fly by him. A soft voice flew out of him like a breeze:

"Love this?" he asked, his fingers tracing the words.

"I don't know what it is--"

"What's the difference? When I sing it to you, whisper it into your ears, so the world is locked outside, and there are only the two of us living here, tell me, Angie, would you love it then?"

His eyes stared at me, and from that moment on, I learned to fear silence. My limbs became paralyzed. My brain shouted, No, no, no. Yet, like a puppet on a string, whose end was in Bambi's hands, as he traced his tattoos like that, I kept leaning forward, moving to his beat. "Yes," I said, "I would love it anyway."

"It's a Finnish song. I got it when my ex committed suicide. The general meaning is, nothing we ever do will leave a trace in history so."

"So?"

"So, fill in the blank. There are many options, right?" He held me by the waist and locked me in his embrace. The thorny tattoo wrapped around me, the other tattoo, a glorious, beautiful snake, crawled up my back, holding my head in place. "So, love doesn't mean a thing. So, keep on suffering. So, scream I love you to me forever and see if I want to love you back, how about that?"

"I--" Speechless, I felt the surge of another hyperventilation episode rushing in. "I never--"

"Angie." Bambi reached for the unfinished cigarette, took a long drag from it with relish, then, with as much hunger and passion, he devoured my lips.

The bitter taste of cigarette smoke made me tear up, but he was the first one to cry. "Angie, I also want to go back, you know?"

"Where?" I asked, feeling the need to appease the lost child within him, never understanding the assignment I was given.

"I need to go back to the time when I was happy. And safe. When there was no sadness."

He smiled again, but this time, there was no strangeness to it. It was just a normal, tranquil smile. But his eyes betrayed that normalcy. The hazy, clouded look let me know that he wasn't there with me. It was as he said: he was going back. And where was that place? Only Bambi knew. We were stranded in the same room, but the sky we were looking at wore different colors. Mine was thunder, filled with the wails and howls of the gust as if something sacred had been stolen, and Pandora was sitting helpless in their bosom. His was darkness with a tinge of something like remorse. Like building a spaceship to reach the moon. Two hundred fifty thousand miles on a clear night in June, and Bambi never reached it.

Like Jesus to a child, Bambi became subdued. A rare tranquility on a blank canvas that used to be his sharp face filled with sarcastic remarks and mockery. I barely recognized the transparent look in his eyes. My hands involuntarily reached out for the beauty of the innocence that was gleaming in the moonlight—a reflection of a picture-perfect sadness on a still, autumn lake. But just before I could catch its shadow, the beauty slipped through my fingers and the cracked Bambi returned, fueled with a renewed vigor. "Angela," he said, grinning like the Cheshire cat in Lewis Carroll's *Alice in Wonderland*, "let me tell you a secret."

"Bambi, I think you should…" I swallowed, quite speechless, not knowing how to react. The stories about every addict's violent tendency in their highs kept revolving in my brain. Fear, I thought, was the definition of all things human, but I'd rather not have it. "I think you should rest."

Bambi's pupils dilated with keen interest. My words fell on deaf ears. Of course, how could mere mortals' sound reach the realm of his drug ballad's *paradiso*? He crawled toward me as I retreated farther back, almost falling off the edge of the bed. With one swift motion, Bambi caught me in his strong arms, caged me down on the feather-soft mattress, and let the craziness unfold. The first chapter of our descent into madness.

"Angela, I killed all my lovers."

The lightning struck across the sky as Bambi slammed the last punctuation to the night. Sometimes, I had to laugh at the irony of it all: how my life fell apart not because of prince charming's kiss, but a thundering confession of a broken human trying to turn himself into God.

"Angela, they're all dead. What about you?" He smiled, beaming at my wide-eyed expression. In his dark irises, I saw the first sight of the apocalypse: the fall of the first man.

Chapter 5: The Chase

March 31, 2025 – On the outskirts of Montreal

I sit at the bar of an empty lounge in a town called Laval. It was never my intention to come here. I hate the French; their crude contempt hidden underneath the gaudy beauty of all things holy disgusts me. The Eiffel Tower. The Louvre. Palace of Versailles. I wonder how so many people can walk those streets of lights, underneath the burden of the old legacy, and still live. If it were me, I would suffocate. Choke on the inability to escape the prisons I was forced to accept as something sacred. The Catacombs of Paris. Are we not all inside it in one way or another?

The bartender pours me another shot of whisky. The lounge puts on soft, sultry music. It is a weekday night. Not many customers will frequent this place, and it's fine that way. I don't need the crowd to remind me how the world outside is moving on. The yellow liquid burns on my tongue and slides down my throat with fire. I feel like half of my life has turned to ashes. My phone pops up a message. Markus. I switch it off and throw it in my tote bag. The name makes me sick. The sound in the lounge makes me sick. The warm and tender bartender makes me sick. All living things make me nauseated. My stomach churns; bile rises in my throat. I cover my mouth, trying to subdue the feeling, quickly getting to my feet to run to the lounge's restroom. Out of nowhere, like a haunting echo of a ghost from the bygone past, a foreign song plays from the speaker like a toll for my soul:

Jos liedelle käy käteni

Sen heti vedän pois

Jos kadulla on lompakko

Sen varastaakkin vois
Ei teoistamme suuretkaan
Tod näk. Historiaan jää
Jos perin varmaa pelaisin

"Bambi, what are those words?" I said.

"I need to go back to the time when I was happy. And safe. When there was no sadness," he said.

My mind swirls. The earth beneath my feet slips. I am thrown into the eye of the universe's chaos. Someone is chasing me. Is it Bambi's ghost? Or is it my ghost, resurrected from the land of the forgotten? I turn around. The lounge is gone. The chairs and tables are empty and broken. In the corner, Bambi's pale body is standing. Closed eyes, tight lips, tranquil expression; he is sleeping. I run toward him, trying to reach the things I had lost. "Need to go back," he said. "Need to go back, I beg you." To fully understand the verses, the words, the despair in every punctuation and mourning keen of the singer's voice. Oh, how much have I sacrificed to come to this end?

"Excuse me, miss? Are you alright?"

The bartender's gentle voice with a heavy accent brings me back to life as it always does. I am still in the lounge. Another whisky shot is on the bar top. I look around. The melancholic French pop songs are reverberating through the walls. I ask him, half dazed, half in an unawakened state of dementia, "What was that song called, Mr. Bartender?"

"Oh, this one? It's a recent favorite. 'La Bohème' by Charles Aznavour. You might not know it though. It's not popular with the Anglo-Saxons." The bartender laughs in his friendly, disdainful way. But I am in no mood for arguments.

"No, not this one. The one before it. The one that sounds like gibberish. I'm sorry, it's not gibberish, of course, but it's not French. It's another language, something like…Latin, maybe? Or Swedish? It sounds like a European language, but I don't know which one." In my mind, I pray, please let it be Finnish, please don't let it be a mistake.

"You don't know which one, eh?" He scoffs but quickly regains his calm composure. "I'm sure we only have French pop songs here, miss. Perhaps you're referring to La Poupée Qui Fait Non? It was played right before this."

"No. That's not it," I shout in frustration, but as the words escape my mouth, the realization dawns on me.

Yes, that's not it. But is anything ever "it"? Nothing we ever do will leave a trace in history so––fill in the blank, Bambi said. I was left bereft and mourning on the floor, trying to find the correct answer to a test no one has the right to mark anymore. Every reply I come up with is returned with a failing grade––the reason is never fully explained. Isn't the task simple? Just fill in whatever is the most treasured in my life, feeding gold to the monster, begging it to grant me a wish, until there's nothing left but the will to live, beating inside me wildly like a hope sparkling in the dark.

Nothing we ever do will leave a trace in history, so why do I still keep on loving him grudgingly, miserably, agonizingly, bearing the cross as if one day, the dead will love me back?

Now he is gone. And I am all alone in a strange town, struggling to find the remnants of the life he led. I don't speak their language; their history is a blank page in my memory. We keep each other at arm's length—polite enough to share a bit of gossip, estranged enough to forget the faces quickly once we pass through. "Angela, don't trust other people," he once said. "They build you up just to break you." The tears I've been trying so hard to hold back begin to flood through the gate. In front of a sea of strangers, I fall apart. Such is the fate of the betrayer, isn't it, Bambi Raymond?

After all, I did build you up just to break you.

The lounge dims the light. It is nearing midnight. This town never stays awake past the zero mark. The music slows to a drag and finishes when the singer is still mourning mid-sentence, "*Que tu es belle, paroles, paroles, paroles, Que tu es…*" I don't understand a thing she is crying for, but if a man were whispering into my ears with a voice like that, I would destroy myself and beg on the street just for the chance at a second glance. A voice like—

Jos liedelle käy käteni
Sen heti vedän pois
Jos kadulla on lompakko
Sen varastaakkin vois

Ei teoistamme suuretkaan

Tod näk.

I shudder. There goes the same song, resurrected like a mummified version of the sanctified past and the glorified name I dare not call again in my fervent prayers. Looking around, I only see the lone bartender, wiping the champagne glasses and stowing the empty Scotch bottles away. Whose voice is rising from the grave? Whose voice is hunting for me? In darkness and fear, I vomit onto the bar top, but nothing comes out. It is air that I'm getting sick of. The bartender quickly rushes to my side; his large hand pats my heaving shoulders. "Ma'am," he says, "Should I call your friends? Perhaps you shouldn't drink alone this often."

"Friends? I have no friends. Not here. Not anywhere. Not anymore," I reply, dry heaving, convulsing on the stool. It is humiliating, yes, and Bambi would have laughed it off as a joke. He would have distracted the bartender while whipping out a handkerchief—soaked in his cologne and a few ice cubes he put in when no one noticed—placing it on my pathetic face, trying to calm the heating beast inside my brain as it gnawed at my sanity, telling me to die while I fight with tooth and nail to survive. Sensory overload. It's been a long time since I've had an episode.

"But ma'am, your friend's been calling you for a while now."

"What?"

"Your friend. Your phone keeps ringing. A few customers were annoyed by the song, so they moved to the lounge area. I'm sorry, I've been meaning to tell you—"

"What song? Also, what phone? Didn't I shut it down and put it in my bag?" I ask, perturbed and confused. What is real? What is he saying? Which scene is unfolding in front of me?

"No, ma'am, your phone has been on the bar top since you sat down. You've had quite a few drinks tonight. Listen, why don't I call you a cab, get you back to your hotel, and your friend can—"

"I don't have a friend," I scream, louder than necessary. The bartender quickly backs away, well-trained in how to handle a disturbing client.

Just then, the fucking song rings again. I look back, ready to break the bar top in half, using my body as a destructive weapon if I need to, and lo and behold, my goddamn phone is right there, lying diagonally next to my whisky.

The screen is lit up. The caller ID shows the usual name, Markus. And the song I've been hearing since the start of this shit show of a night is my damn ring tone.

"When did…?" I stutter, trying to think of the question, forgetting what I want to ask, remembering the pieces of meaning behind my being here, but the words won't come out. The heaving begins again. The convulsion starts not long after it. I clutch the phone, shutting it down, unable to find the power button, and in my panic, redial the forbidden number.

The number of a person whose existence had been erased. Jean-Paul Bambi fucking Raymond.

In silence, I let the phone slip through my hand and fall to the marble floor. I don't need the leading role in this 80s melodrama television show. I don't need the tears, rivulets in slow motion as the bartender inches closer, trying to appear more human than a working person whose only concern is when the last customer will leave and he can finally head home in peace. I certainly don't need the ring tone echoing against my ear canals. The strange sound of a foreign language that has become a haunting. Daydream and rose-tinted glasses trampled underneath the strong feet of sorrow and melancholic rhythm. Mourning. Suppressed cries in hushed tones. Voice breathing sadness and desperation instead of hope. Why do the Finnish words have such intense and heavy pronunciation? Is that the language of pain? I dare not understand. The fear is gripping my existence: what if the understanding will only push me down the abyss faster than the current darkness that I choose to drown in?

"Ma'am?" The bartender asks. I glance up, noticing for the first time the tattoo on his neck. A spider's web. The trap.

"I think I'm lost." My voice trembles far too much for my liking. I prefer a more confident tone.

Like how, on that august winter night, I took Bambi on a stroll through the thick Lemoine Point Shore trail, screaming to the starlit sky and the snow-laden thicket, "Fuck the free world!" Or when I told Markus on the first occasion I witnessed Bambi's overdosed state, "Either you save him or one of us will walk out of here with both corpses. And I promise it won't be me."

The night closes in. My memory fades. Yes. There's no use lingering on the things that never could be. I pick up the phone, grab my purse, pay my tab at the bar, and walk out the door. It is no place for insanity. Then again, this world has never been a place to belong for me.

Bambi said, "The Lord knows and the Lord dictates that Judas will serve his fate in a prison. But Judas locks himself inside it willingly because he imagines—believes, even—that it is the Lord's promised paradise. The world never belongs to Judas. I wonder if the Lord realizes how tragic that reward disguised as punishment was. Saints and Holy Spirit—their little faith escapes my grasp sometimes. Walking on water needs a second coming's miracle, don't you think?"

And I agreed. Not because I understood what he meant. Bambi and his musings; they were the water I tried with blood and tears to hold onto, but they kept slipping through. He wanted to be free. Judas wanted—what? A star. A name known by all lips. Transcendence. Eternity. A human yearning to no longer be human. I wonder if Bambi found a comrade in Judas. Or did he sympathize more with the Lord, who suffered, sacrificed, and exonerated all sins, only to see the world filled with them to the end of time? On his immortal throne, I imagine the Lord finds a sort of ironic, bitter happiness in knowing all his good work had gone to waste.

Bambi said, "Our good deeds are not the things that define us. It has always been our sins."

My phone rings. The wind turns into a strong gale. I wave to the Uber driver from the shady corner of the plaza. The neon lights at the store fronts turn off one by one. Closing time. Willful ignorance is a kind of bliss, I chant in my mind, dismissing the call from Markus for the nth time that night. Like a sick twist of fate, my finger slips. The call goes through, opening the curtain to show the hideous demon inside.

"Angela?"

Lucifer, thy name is Markus.

"Hey, Markus," I reply with gritted teeth, getting into the Honda sedan. The sickeningly sweet scent of the driver's car perfumes poison my nostrils and every pore on my skin.

"Jesus, it's harder to reach you than the fucking prime minister, I dare say." Markus whistles.

"Been busy. Traveling, getting to know myself, touching grass, those sorts of make-believe things."

"Good, good, it's always nice to touch grass now and then. Anyways, Bambi ever call you these days?" He goes straight to the vital point. The urgency and the fast speech signal how frustrated he is. A dire situation. A grave he digs to bury himself in. A disaster only Bambi can save him from. Too bad for him.

"I don't know. Never heard from him. We parted ways. Told you that much last time, didn't I?"

"But it's weird. I mean, I don't see him anymore. Not a shadow. Not even a sound. It's like—I'm scared to think of this case but—it's like he's already dead."

Cold sweat drips down my spine, prickling my back. I can feel the skin on my face being stripped off like a theatrical mask, leaving behind the bare flesh of a thief. The car disappears into the dark road ahead. I no longer see any form of the future. The present shuts itself down around me. "He's already dead," Markus's voice reverberates against the closed space, like a coffin lid slowly being hammered nail by nail over my frozen corpse. My heart is racing for the last stretch to the finish line, but my breath refuses to catch up. I open my mouth, but the words vanish like air.

"Hello?" Markus asks, and a thousand "hellos" ring in my ears. I claw at my throat, leaving behind burgundy marks and a searing physical pain, grounding me fleetingly in the unsteady reality. Before consciousness leaves me completely, I hear the brakes screech. The car pulls to a stop. The driver rushes to open the door, gets to my side, and decides to call an ambulance. In a haze, his conversation with Markus floats to my brain like the tiny stained-glass fragments of a broken church relic.

"Yes, she—Right now, we're at—I'm taking her to—No—" the driver's heavily accented voice babbles.

"She is—Her boyfriend—Dead—I don't know why. Disappeared for— Laval?" Markus screams from the loudspeaker.

"I'm an Uber driver—Drunk—Sick—Emergency—I—"

"Tell her—He's coming—That guy from the—I will be—Address—"

The rest blurs into the starry sky as I am lifted out of the taxi and loaded onto the ambulance, spit and vomit foaming out from my mouth involuntarily. Panic attack—I make it look easy, don't I? Like a farce for comic relief in bad taste. A mess of what people call high-functioning bipolar depression, what I call surviving, what Bambi called—the most beautiful name of them all—a testament that God is real and He is malevolence. I hold onto the agony, watching the illusions of the past merge with the delusions of the present. Sweet like the apple Eve has bitten to bring down destruction and God's wrath. Such a delicacy, so intoxicating one might mistake it for the elixir of eternal life. Perhaps that is what God meant when He said, "suffer the children."

The sound of the siren is getting louder and louder, and my thoughts retreat to the quiet corner of monsters and men, where the beasts can shelter me from the upcoming wave of human's cruelty, where power doesn't guarantee victory and weakness is not reduced to a single diagnosis: focal aware seizure. I close my eyes, breathing in the oxygen. A sudden urge to cry blooms inside my chest like a nighttime flower waiting forever for its chance to shine. No one ever tells me how luscious a gulp of air can be. Nobody cares to urge how good it is to simply exist. Alive. Between grief and nothingness, the only person who taught me that had chosen nothingness.

A teardrop trickles down my cheek. Bambi, I finally understand. Not all of you, but I finally understand. Despair, thy name is Jean-Paul Raymond.

Chapter 6: The Power

February 15, 2020 – Late in the evening

I woke up with a start, gasping for breath. My right arm reached for something to hold, to anchor me in the dimly lit bedroom. My left arm was numb. How long had I been sleeping? The sky was overcast with the most beautiful gradation of violet and cobalt blue. Amidst the loud beating of my heart, I could hear Bambi's husky voice drift through the crack of the door like a poisoned lullaby.

Historiaan jää

Jos perin varmaa pelaisin –

In the hollow of despair, I tried to call his name. The only living person whose existence my mind could recall. But what came out was just burst after burst of loud coughing. Where was I? The past? The present? The future? Or some ever-after I never signed up for but forgot to unsubscribe to?

Bambi patted my sweat-drenched forehead and I jumped. My whole body levitated for a single minute in thin air, hanging there by a thread of fear. I didn't hear his soft footfalls on the hardwood floor. I didn't catch his shadow creeping onto mine as he approached me in the dark. The devastation from the aftertaste of a nightmare distorted my world, and suddenly, I was nothing but a subject to the reign of my paranoic brain.

"Hey, angel," Bambi smiled, sweet and gentle. His eyes squinted like two subdued crescent moons; their light waned over my ashen face. "Suffering angel, come unto me."

"Where am I?" I grabbed his arms, my fingers wrapped around his wrist, tremulous in their newfound reverence, feeling the beat of his heart through the veins underneath the rough, pale white skin.

"My place. Why?"

"What date is it?"

"February 15. Still the same day as this morning when I went mad with my drug ballad and you fainted due to—what's the clinical term?—overwhelming emotions?" he joked, stroking my head. Something in my eyes must have triggered his worry, because after a brief look at them, he asked, "Why, what's wrong?"

"Bambi, I had a nightmare," I said, trembling.

"Well, I guessed as much. Happens to the best of us." He shrugged, half standing up, brushing the matter aside. I grasped his wrist with the sheer force of a mule. *Never let go*, I told myself, *Whatever happens, do not let it go.*

"Bambi, in my dream, you were dead."

"I guess that's not that bad of an ending—"

"And I will be the one to kill you," I said in a quick breath, the meaning of the words catching up to me only after a pause. A pin dropped in the maddening crowd of a ballroom. Everyone was dancing, and I was there, witnessing the decay, alone in my sanity.

Bambi hummed in silence. He chewed his bottom lip then popped it out with a soft, sensuous noise. I never knew if he did it intentionally, or if luring his prey into the trap of the flesh was simply a part of his being. A sheen gloss shone on the pale pink flesh, and the sight was so captivating I thought he was no longer human. I reached out my hand, tracing the curve of his lips. *A primal instinct*, I thought. *Humans are born slaves to their desires.* Between wanting and being, no one would be crazy enough to choose the latter. Bambi lifted his downcast eyes, watching me with the twinkling curiosity of a mischievous calico cat. His eyelashes quivered slightly as he shook with laughter. "You don't look like you want to kill me now. Or do you?"

"I don't. Kill. Not you. Not anyone."

"But yourself. It's a different matter, isn't it? We're selfish that way." He caught my wandering hand in his, stroking the back tenderly. "Suppose, then, there will be a day you gather enough courage to kill someone. Why would that be me?"

"Because you ask for it." My other hand ran through his soft, silvery hair. "No, not asking, you order it. And I have no choice—"

"Oh sweet Angela, let's not talk about the illusion of freedom and the prison of the will." He stood up, but I was gripping him too hard, so he settled for a crouching position instead. "You always have a choice. If you follow the order, it's because you have faith in the system that produces the order, isn't it?"

"But why would I have faith in a system that would order me to kill?"

"Why wouldn't you? You already are, right now. Do not ask what your country has done for you and whatnot, am I right?" He tried to untangle my spidery fingers, but I clawed his shoulders, unwilling to let go of my lifeline.

"Bambi, do not let me kill you, please," I begged. Somehow, in that singular moment, I thought he had planned his ending. A sick, twisted intuition in me had foreshadowed the day I would become the perfect slave to his little game of being the Messiah of filth and dirty truth. "Do not let me kill you," I repeated, in vain. Words wouldn't help me win, but what else would?

"I don't know what the point is, Angela," Bambi said nonchalantly. "I go my way, you go yours. I don't let anyone do anything, that's my principle. And if you choose to follow the order, that's your problem more than mine. Oh, sweetheart, don't cry..."

He shuffled onto the bed and gathered the whole mess that was my torn being into his embrace. I didn't know who I was looking at, who I was talking to—the mad Bambi, going crazy with a drug-filled mind from that morning, the confident Bambi who saved me from the awkward incident at the bar, the apathetic Bambi who looked at the world as if he was The Creator and this was but another tribulation under his feet. I never understood the real him. The many masks he wore, the soul he tried to hide, the heart he concealed, wounded and mended with no intention of going on.

I stared at the truth with staggering anguish. Beside the name Bambi Raymond, what else did I know about him?

Yet I clung to him, sobbing my lungs out, seeking his warmth, snuggling my face into his neck, inhaling the spicy scent of pepper and sandalwood. It was haunting. It was good. Like the melancholy melody he put on the living room's speaker,

Jos liedelle käy käteni –
Sen heti vedän pois
Jos kadulla on lompakko
Sen varastaakkin vois
Ei teoistamme suuretkaan
Tod näk –

He soothed me like Jesus to a child. I hung onto his neck like Judas listening to the last teaching of the Lord. He saw me as the newborn babe with the sins of the humans before me, and the humans after. I watched him through the foggy curtain of my tears, knowing the fate that awaited me, knowing I wouldn't escape it. And yet, the apple was so sweet, so delicious, so devastatingly appetizing, I wouldn't blame Eve for biting it, nor Adam for going against the Lord to have it. After all, we were born to rebel. Perhaps the line of my life's limit had been reduced to that one figure of a person named Bambi Raymond.

Living for myself or living for another person, I was hesitating on the tightrope. But it helped when Bambi brushed my hair with his nimble fingers, and I remembered that living for myself so far had brought me nothing. Who was I before Bambi came into the picture? There was no evidence of such an existence called Sweet Angela. Wasn't the choice easy?

"You know, I had a nightmare once. Many years ago. Pretty messy and bloody," Bambi said, his tone muted. A sadness as silky as velvet and cashmere wound itself around me. I leaned in, intoxicated from the saccharine sorrow in his voice. "In that dream, I killed someone, too."

"You killed someone? Is that person important?" I mumbled; my consciousness struggled to stay alert.

"Doesn't matter now. Didn't matter then." He tapped my shoulders rhythmically to the song outside. "She was a good friend. We had something between us, but it ended as quickly as it began. She never tried to be understood, and I kept prying. It happens more often than you think, sweet

Angela. People never leave well enough alone."

"So you killed her in your dream."

"Not necessarily. In my dream, she came to me, disheveled and desperate for a place to call home. I was simply a rental room on her road to where she belonged. And in the middle of the night, as we both were high on cocaine, she climbed over the balcony…" His voice thinned out. The chilling azure eyes glazed over. It wasn't the bedroom, me, or the present that Bambi was seeing: All along, it was the dream.

"But it wasn't your fault." I tugged at his shirt collar, trying to bring him back. A dark premonition dawned on me: Will I suffer the same fate? The nightmare would merge into my reality, and one day, I, too, like Bambi, would just—

"Watch it happen. I was there, looking at her corpse blossoming in the most beautiful blood carnage on the cemented pavement, thinking to myself, she was never as pretty as she was then. In that dream, I had a superpower. A weird one, now that I think about it."

"Superpower? To save her?" I asked. My fingers were tremulous from the sheer apprehension of the strange, cruel, almost inhumanly malevolent expression on Bambi's face.

"I could turn back time. But only five seconds. Five seconds to see her step onto the railing. Five seconds to watch her jump. Five seconds to remember the red shade of the blood dripping onto the pavement. Fucking five seconds to relive the hurt, all over again. Weird, isn't it?" He chuckled. His fingers twisted a lock of my hair. Something in me told me that it wasn't a dream. He was telling his story. The suicide. The pain. The agony. They had happened.

Or did they not? Many years after that night, I never found out who the girl was. Her name, her death, her relationship with Bambi—they vanished the moment I opened my eyes. Dreams or reality—which plane was I living in?

"So you were stuck in that five seconds forever?" I asked, detaching myself from his hold, but it was his turn to cage me inside the prison of his soul. His arm wrapped around my waist. His face burrowed in my bosom. I was

Jesus to his wounded, suffering child.

"Sweet Angela, what would you do if you had the power to go back in time, but only for five seconds?" Bambi asked, his eyes squeezed shut, as if there was an excruciating pain eating him inside out.

"I wouldn't use it."

"Why?"

"I don't know, Bambi. I guess… I always think that people live. They move on. No matter what happens, no one is going to stop for another person. Suppose you're hurt. Then who else would understand the pain you suffered except yourself, right? So even if I were to go back in time, to relive those five seconds eternally, what would it help? Not me, not anyone else. I think, as you said, I'm a bit selfish for thinking that way." I tried to laugh but the sound came out awkward and nervous, like a teacher's pet yearning for validation.

"It's not selfish, no." He breathed into my breasts. The warmth flushed down my cheeks. I buried my fingers in his thick hair, feeling the weight of his head fall more and more onto my chest until both of us toppled on the mattress. Without moving, his lips brushing against my palpitating skin, Bambi said, "Sweet Angela, what you call selfish is just the innocence of age."

With all my heart and the dark heaven above me as my witness, I wanted to be angry at his words. To push him off me and prove to him I was more than just an endearment, "Sweet Angela." To be more than a brief nightmare, something he could simply wake up to and walk out on, leaving no traces behind, like a stranger stopping by a train station… But I couldn't. The warmth from his skin was spreading between my flesh and my existence. His breathing seeped through my shirt, hovering over my chest, so painfully fragile I almost thought it was a death rattle. *Primal instinct*, I thought. *Women were born to be the caretakers.*

It wasn't important. He wept in the quietude of a raging requiem. I was, coincidentally, the observer of his fall. One of the many he would have later when we began the spiral dance toward our madness, the malady everyone called love. Holding his face closer to my breast, hoping to comfort him, wanting to make him feel safe—all those thoughts were the proof that

Bambi was right. I wasn't selfish; he met me when I was fully ripe with the innocence of age.

Patting his head to the rhythm of his breathing, I whispered the same question: "So would you use it? The power to turn back time, I mean."

"Mm-hm. I would. Nothing kills a person quicker than the remembrance of things past. And to live in that window of five seconds—reliving the pain, simmering in the ocean of hurt—it's a sweet price to pay for eternal life, isn't it?" He mumbled, half of the sound muffled in my chest. The reverberation made me feel more alive than a flaming torch.

"Wasn't there a man who said—" I ventured.

"Between grief and nothingness and whatever."

Bambi left the matter at that and drifted away to his deep slumber. It was fascinating how fast he fell asleep whenever he came into contact with a human's bodily warmth. I held him in my embrace. The tranquility on his face was too precious; I dared not move an inch in fear I would destroy it. The fallen emperor on a glass throne. The puppeteer sleeping beside his treasured doll. Which one was the truth, and which was fiction? Lies and reality—it was beautiful to see lines blurred together and piled onto each other until they built a sacrilegious tower of sins, thinking there would be forgiveness after death.

Amidst my philosophical musing on his unreal beauty, Bambi's phone rang. The eerie sound of a villain's laughter echoed in the closed space of the apartment. He jerked up, grasped the phone, read the name on the screen with such detestation that his gentle demeanor turned grotesque, then with two clicks, he hung up.

"Was it important? Maybe you should—"

"It was nothing. A reminder of a debt I forgot to pay on time is all." He went back to my side, snuggled in the duvet, and curled into an awkwardly large ball. I giggled at his childishness.

"Wait, you have a debt?"

"Don't we all?"

"But—"

"Sweet Angela." Bambi called my name, not with the same gentle voice, but more like a hatred masked in honey and sugar and all things that were nice. "Let's not talk about things that will make us both uncomfortable."

"I don't…" I retreated, sensing the danger. After knowing him better, I understood where the danger came from. The Bambi I saw would always be sweet like a soft kitten, but if I stroked his fur the wrong way, the Raymond inside him came out like a leopard ready for attack. As for Jean-Paul, he was lost a long time ago when he tried to find the way home on his own.

"And remember, my little angel…" That Raymond enunciated each word, his eyes going a tenth of a degree below zero, his hands grasping my wrists so tightly they left a dark, red mark long after. "No matter what happens to me, do not engage with the man called Saul."

"Who?" I asked, confused, my brain trying to compute how my life had turned one hundred and eighty degrees after just one night out at the bar. "Saul who?"

"Saul. No last name. There will be a day you'll come across him if you're with me."

"What should I do then?"

Bambi smirked. His lips curved up. The smile was so sinister and insidious I thought he was possessed by some sort of darkness outside as the storm was raging on. Leaning closer to my face, with his whole body weight pressing against my bag of skin and bones, he said, more threatening than joking, "Run."

Five years after that night of fury, I met the man called Saul many times. Never once did I run. Never once did I remember the words Bambi said. Shit, remembrance of things past. Between grief and nothingness, he chose the latter. I was left hanging, not knowing which way would lead me to the place of the past. To relive that fucking five seconds, eternally, like a damn broken record gone mad.

Chapter 7: Saul

April 1, 2025 – Hôpital de la Cité-de-la-Santé, Laval, QC

"Can you hear me, ma'am?"

Through the foggy curtain of my tears, I want to scream at the non-descriptive figure in white that yes, I can hear him just fine without the loud yelling. I can hear the thick accent, the hard, rolling 'r' sound on his tongue, the deafening noise of the medical carts scrolling on the ER floor. What I can't hear, what I can't comprehend, is how I ended up in this godforsaken place of the chase against the dead and the living.

"Ma'am, relax. We're getting you the help you need."

I don't know why I need to relax. Can a person simply relax in an ER, like she's in a fucking resort by the seaside, watching people come and pass by her, not knowing who they are, where they will go, or what in God's sweet name she has become this time? Perhaps I yell this at him while the thought runs through my mind. Perhaps the words that were so well-articulated in my brain come out as nothing more than just gurgles and gibberish. Either way, it must be something disgusting, because he can't hide the nauseated look on his face. The scent of decay is everywhere. My safest bet is someone's going to see God after tonight. Or many someones. I hope it won't be me. I wish it would be me.

While trying to lie on my side to lessen the pain in my chest, I realize that I can't move. My eyes refuse to focus. My voice resigns from its position. Every function in my body is quitting. I lie there on the hard hospital bed, thinking, *So this is what people mean when they say when life can't break you, it kills you.* Even coughing causes my whole body to convulse. In madness and dark dreams, I conjure up a situation: everyone here is pretending to fix me, but in truth, they are trying to tear me down. Maybe that white-smocked figure injected me with some toxins when I was out. Maybe the liquid going into my veins now is the cause of my haziness and, eventually, my fading into oblivion. Maybe this is all a scheme. Someone discovered what I did to Bambi—someone close, someone like Markus—and they planned this as the vengeful act they thought Bambi needed. I choke. It is getting hard to breathe again. I need to get out. Either my mind or this starkly, oppressively white ER… I need to get out. The last thing I need now is—

"Angela."

I snap my head to the side at the familiar voice. I don't need my eyesight to know who he is or what he looks like. That raspy, sickly tone with a dry cough in between. Who else could it be but…

"Saul," I say. My voice returns to me miraculously, not in gratitude at having found a family, but in fear. Absolute fear.

"Long time no see, girl." He pats his pockets, takes out a cigarette, looks at the non-smoking sign and feels the hatred in the glances of the nurses, then settles to put it in his mouth without lighting it up. "Anyways, got yourself in a pretty bad situation, eh?"

"No."

"What d'ya mean no? You in a fucking ER. And where's that madafaka flower boy of yourns? What's his name? Bam? Bambi? Eh?" He coughs, making the patient next to my bed jump in her sleep. "Sorry, old habits die hard."

"I don't know where he is. We separated." I try to make it sound convincing. It isn't. Saul's hawkish eyes pierce through my lies, picking apart the flesh of the make-believe world I built. We built.

"That so, eh? You younguns. Getting together one day then saying goodbye the next." He tuts. "Or should I say, this time is farewell?" Saul laughs. There is no menace in his laughter, but the sheer weight of the meaning behind his words makes me tremble with trepidation of what could happen after. "Listen, missum, Bam—"

"His full name is Bambi Raymond."

"Whatever. Bambi or Raymond. He owes us big time, eh? That last delivery of ketamine—"

"Saul, please, this is a hospital."

"What about it? Not my fucking fault you ended up in one. That last delivery—"

"Saul, let me get out of here first before we talk, okay? I'm not going anywhere, I swear."

"Of course," Saul says, standing up slowly, groaning in the process as if he is in extreme pain just by doing that simple action. "Funny you fancy you could—what's the word?—escape."

He walks out of the ER. The coughing trails behind him, haunting like the worst nightmare dressed in sickness and death. It is so real I could almost touch it and feel the fangs gnaw at my bones. He wants destruction, just for the fun of it. Never settle for any resolution less than mere violence. That's Saul. That's bloody, motherfucking Saul Goodwill's motto. I grit my teeth. "Angela, you always have a choice," Bambi said. But Saul never believed in freedom of choice. "Fucking illusions of fucking bourgeoisies. You and your sweet lady friend, Bam, it ain't gonna end well for either of y'all."

Did Bambi ever think of upending Saul's career? Of laughing in his face, sneering at his materialistic thinking, resurrecting himself from the death just to prove to Saul that being free is a choice, and it is real?

I never know. Never will, now. But there's one thing I possess, the one thing that will end Saul's existence.

That last delivery of ketamine. It is inside Bambi's corpse.

"Ma'am, are you okay?"

The heavy accent and the sweeping white smock with the navy scrubs reappears, almost out of thin air, and the worn-out face of the exhausted doctor shows itself in the blinding light of the ER for the first time to me. Without the blurring effect, and if I can ignore the thin layer of suffering ladening his voice, he would be the epitome of the word "kindness." The gentle, piercing blue eyes are visibly red from lack of sleep. The white smock is decorated with a name tag clipped on in willful negligence—he doesn't want his name to be remembered. The dark brunette hair with wavy locks tucked neatly on his head, a few white streaks and some wrinkles by his eyes spice up his appearance to show he has battled with enough demons to know which one he could take on and which to avoid. He wipes his face, heaving a sigh, like before him—me, the crippled soul and battered mind—is the worst burden a higher deity has given him tonight. If he has a belief that the Lord would give him less trouble tonight in his shift, it didn't turn out too well for him. The name 'Bambi' curls on my tongue and dies on my lips as I hold back a choking scream that bursts inside my lungs.

Because that name tag stares at me, screaming, howling from the abyss: Pierre Raymond.

My whole body shakes with a sudden rush of exhilaration. The shiver runs down my spine until my skeleton trembles with a premonition of what will happen. Will it happen again? The same ending that Bambi had gone through keeps haunting me, and the twin who he had entrusted to me, together with the child in my stomach—the stakes has grown monumental, and I am impossibly small under its weight. The darkness of a past conversation creeps up my shoulders, and the monster whispers in my ears: *Find Pierre Raymond, Angela. He's my twin. Yes, find him, ruin him, then bring him back to life, much like what I had done to you, because what goes around comes around, and the flowers of that karma tree are about to bloom.* A tangy, metallic taste immediately fills my tongue; a tearing pain pulls my brain back to the bed, the fluid, the beeping of the machine measuring my vitals; all this time, after Saul left, I have been biting my lips and chewing myself alive. I look at the doctor; his eyes say he has it no better than I. Maybe outside the curtain separating my bed from the rest of this ER, someone is bleeding to death, crying to death, laughing to death—anything to end the suffering. Anything to return to nothingness.

"My lips are bleeding," I manage in a hoarse voice. It isn't an attempt at being funny, but the sentence makes me laugh. He doesn't, though. The same sad eyes, haunting in their silent power, cruel and piercing, watch me as I writhe in agony and in the high of a psychotic episode.

"Ma'am, how about we talk first?" He pulls a metal chair out of nowhere, puts it near the edge of my bed, and sits down. His eyes remain calm, but they possess the same piercing power as Bambi's when he wants to get to the bottom of things. "May I know your name?"

"Didn't they already take that when I—?"

"Your real name, ma'am. Just in case."

"My real name." I scoff. "I only have one name. What makes you think—?"

"Ma'am, that guy you were talking with a moment ago—"

"Hear me out. I didn't know anything about whatever he was talking about. He's batshit crazy. He's sick in the head." I rush out my words; the sheer primal instinct to escape and survive outlive the fear.

"Ma'am, please, calm down. I'm not accusing you of anything." He enunciates each word slowly, ensuring that his intention comes across. The Montreal accent only accentuates his elegance; all that remains is the strong hand trying to pacify my fraying nerves.

"Then, what do you want, Doctor…?" I try to pronounce his name without letting my excitement show. "Doctor Pierre?"

"First of all, thank you for the good pronunciation. Second, let's get back to the man. His name is Saul, isn't it? I know him. Not personally, but well, it makes me understand more about your relationship with him. He is famous—or rather, infamous—around here. Human trafficking. Are you involved in that?" he asks in a quiet and tender tone, but his voice is dripping with concern and grave distress. The strong hand presses on mine, inhumanly cold yet reassuring all the same.

"No, I'm not. I don't have anything to do with him. I don't even know about the human trafficking thing." I shake my head; the pain is splitting my brain in two. The first reply is a half-truth, but the second one is true. Saul and human trafficking? Sounds impossible, but not improbable.

"Okay, as long as we get that sorted out, Ms…?" He stops for a second, waiting for me to say my name. Nothing comes back. "Ms. Angela, then?"

"Yes."

"I would warn you to be extremely cautious with him. The investigators are on his tracks like hunting hounds these days. Not a good picture for this region. Are you a tourist?"

"Visitor. I plan to visit Old Quebec City." Again. One truth, one half-truth.

He can choose whichever he wants to believe.

"And you end up here? Not a good trip, then?" He laughs, but it comes out more like tired gasps and yawns.

"Nothing is ever good. I mean. If you believe a thing is good, then it is, right?" That is Bambi's motto. *Believe in things, Angela,* he said, *because in this modern hell we built for ourselves, without that belief, we are nothing.*

"Ms. Angela, have you been suffering from panic attacks often?" Doctor Pierre switches his attitude on the spot. The mask is on, figuratively. The laughter is off. The eyes go cold. The hands become distant and detached.

"I've been living with it since forever." I crawl away. The last thing I need is *that type of doctor*'s help. "Dr. Pierre, are you a psychiatrist?"

"Yes, I am. Now, it shows here that you had withdrawal symptoms when you were admitted. Are you using recreational drugs?"

"I'm not."

"Have you, then?"

"I don't have to answer your questions."

"Ms. Angela, I'm not the psychiatrist in charge of you, and I can't find their information on your person but as a doctor, no, as a caring person, I must warn you, your mental state is in a dangerous situation."

"I'm perfectly fine, thank you." I retort. Never trust a stranger's kindness, that's what Bambi always told me. How foolish I am to be tricked into his gentle amber eyes with their golden hue and weary demeanor. Who needs saving when abandoning everything feels so good? "When can I be discharged?"

"Ms. Angela, if you must insist on that, then answer me one more question."

"Fine."

Doctor Pierre leans in, shining his flashlight into each of my eyelids and checking my vitals. The fathomless azure eyes never shy away from my scarred soul, like a hawk after its prey. The gentleness is gone. The sudden, dark premonition settles in my gut, and I can feel my body descend lower still, until it reaches the bed of fiery hell. Amidst the beeping of the machine, I hear him say: "Why did you watch me die, my angel?"

With all my strength, I push him away, yanking at the cords and lines and everything that is restraining me to the hard bed. It is Doctor Pierre one second, then, with a blink, it turns to Bambi's face. The bloodshot, fathomless void in his eyes grows darker in the ER's blinding light. The gleaming white teeth—never affected by the consequences of tobacco, drug abuse, or alcohol—beam at me with the same arrogance and indifference Bambi had when we first met. His breath comes in waves of vaporizing whisky, hard liquor, and the heavy scent of nicotine. The ether-filled air gradually slips away, flushing with the faint aroma of burned sandalwood and peppers. "I ask again, why did you watch me die, baby girl?" he says. "Didn't you say you wouldn't kill?"

Four pairs of strong hands push themselves out from the dark, like the weird monsters from my worst nightmares resurrected in the white light of salvation. They grab my upper and lower body and hold me tightly in place. I wonder if they would hear my screams, seeing as they have no head, no ears, no other human characteristics but arms, hands, and fingers. I wonder if Doctor Pierre is a real person. Desperate and cold, I feel my throat going taut with tension, but there is no sound. A hollow is swallowing my existence. My body refuses to move. The commands from my brain are met with a failure notice. The system only thinks with your worst interests at heart, my brain says with every command I enter. Someone calls, "Angela." I think it is Bambi, but my head won't move. "Angela," the voice repeats. Reality is slipping through my fingers. I feel a tiny prick on my skin. An injection. The institution wins. "Ms. Angela." I stare wildly ahead. The same vision of the ER returns, a blurry white smock accentuated by navy blue scrubs. An indistinct face merging between the past and the present, the dead and the living, Jean-Paul and Pierre Raymond. The only difference is the accented voice.

"Ms. Angela, where do you live?"

"I don't." Breathless, I whisper, "Live."

Chapter 8: Helen at the Chelsea Hotel

February 17, 2020 – A cozy cafe in Chinatown

"So, who is Saul?"

Bambi shrugged the question off his shoulders. His slender fingers stirred the silver spoon obnoxiously loudly in the otherwise empty and quiet old cafe downtown. He wanted to be seen. To be noticed. To remain here after all else perished, and humans returned to oblivion. I shuffled my feet. The sneakers were killing me. I switched my comfy shoes with Cecilia, a futile attempt to be cute. She hand-painted her sneakers with artsy decor I never understood, but in certain scenarios, like this one, it would make me appear almost sophisticated enough to draw eyes. The only problem was always the size. Hers were half a size too small for me. Never mind; maybe a second date with Bambi would prove the sacrifice worthy.

"Saul. The man you talked about last time. When you were high." I lowered my voice, not wanting to attract unwanted attention to the word "high." But it was too late. Bambi caught onto it like a hunter chasing after prey.

"Oh, you mean when I was on drugs?" he asked, intentionally and insufferably deafening with his booming laughter.

"Would it kill you to quiet down a little?" I hissed, covering my face with one hand.

"Why? Because it would kill you if I don't?"

He grinned, gleaming white teeth shining in the slanting sunlight as he chewed bread with a showman's confidence. His eyes sparkled with mischief and dark mockery. He hummed to the cafe's melody, waiting for my next reaction, and I could see in those half-moon beams he already had a myriad of counter attacks to any weaponized question I prepared for him. Banter that would make me furious, jokes with double entendres to drown me in silent fever dreams, pillow talk, and warm skin, and a knowing wink here and there to quiet my rambles. He knew me all too well for the short duration of forty-eight hours of our acquaintance, while I was barely crossing the first step over the threshold of his thorny, minefield territory.

"I mean," I said, drawing in a big breath to stifle the rising laughter. I feigned seriousness, fake-touching my nonexistent glasses. "Don't discuss your recreational entertainment here, Mr. Bambi."

"With a voice like that and a face so beautiful Helen of Troy would envy it, the only thing you lack to make that statement into my command is a lacy black silk negligee from Vic," Bambi said, calm and composed despite the dirty intention behind the phrasing. He never looked at me. Not once.

"So, you won't talk about Saul?" I pushed my luck. Like many girls who have fallen before me, and many who would later, I forgot the age-old lesson of Eve and fancied myself to be—what was the right word?—important? No, *irreplaceable.*

"Wrong. It's not that I won't talk about Saul. More like—" he lifted his head, breadcrumbs stuck to his chin, and mimicked my fake glasses touch, "—we don't discuss your intrusive and perverse curiosity here, Miss Angela."

"You—"

"Hush."

Bambi caught my slap just in time before it landed a perfect score on his left cheek. I forced his hand away, but his grip grew stronger. His knowing wink had been directed at me once, twice, too many times for me to remember. Then it happened. His slender fingers wrapped perfectly around my wrist, like it was born to be held by them. They stroked the scarred skin, sliding up, never lessening their strength, until each finger was laced with my own, and with a simple tug, Bambi drew my hand to his lips, placing on it a soft kiss.

It was a searing flame on my skin, the feel of his pale pink lips on my living tissue. He was waking the dead with each second going by as the kiss stayed in place. The hand he touched was burning. My fingers were burning. I was aflame with the sheer will to keep on living. Hamlet's question rang in my head and the answer kept echoing, *To be, to be, to be.* Bambi flicked his eyelashes; those piercing aquamarine eyes stared right through me, stabbed my core, gorged out my heart, and watched it beat to death with the rhythm of his quiet breathing.

Looking back at it now, it is cold, hard proof that Bambi Raymond knew how to kill a person. Man, woman, anything in between—he held the power to dictate how their lives would end. He knew how to make it painful just as much as how to make it sweet. The fucker was God. But before he was God, he was chaos reincarnated.

Blinded by the desire instilled in me through his touch, I followed Bambi out of the cozy cafe. The weather was cold with wet snow, and he drew me to his side, covering me with his large winter coat. We laughed the whole way down the streets of Chinatown, bickering like two giant children. Nobody's son or daughter, we were the freest when we knew nothing about each other. Waiting for the streetcar to go back to his place, Bambi snuggled his face close to my neck like a spoiled child. The warm breath turned foggy, and it tickled me. Being that giddy and high on the newfound addictive emotion, I never quite figured out what he said then, or if he said anything at all. It sounded something like, "I wish it were all different."

When the nights got too dark and lonely, I often thought about that scene in the blistering cold winter. My memory is no longer clear. Perhaps what Bambi was trying to say was, "I'm sorry. For all that will happen. And for all that never will."

Standing there at the crossroad, watching the light turn red, green, then red again, we let so many streetcars run by us. We never boarded any. Did we ever plan to from the beginning? It was hard to say. Bambi kept telling me to wait for the next one, so I did. Like a fucking puppet on strings, I only walked when he pulled the cords. Leaning against his tall body and a million layers of warmth, I mumbled, "It's a bit like the Chelsea Hotel."

"Chelsea what?"

"Chelsea Hotel. You know, that hotel where—"

"Most famous and infamous things happened. Yeah, I know that. Happened to be there once or twice. Caught Leonard Cohen there on a few rare occasions." He smirked. When he talked with so much confidence it oozed from his breath and every living cell, I couldn't figure if it were a lie or a truth he was telling. So I asked, bewildered, half-believing, "You met the real Cohen?"

"No, silly. How could I meet him? When he was staying there, I might have still been swimming around inside my dad's balls." He burst out laughing, leaving me a flushing mess, burning red with shame and untainted naivete.

"You're a real piece of work, you know that?" I clenched each word through my teeth. It didn't affect him. It never did. But it was so tempting to try, to see if I could break through the invincible facade. "When will we board the streetcar? I'm bored."

"I thought we were talking about how this is like the Chelsea Hotel?" He cocked one eyebrow. The same knowing wink. The same palpitation and suffocating feeling of being trapped.

"Because you won't stop being an ass. That's all." I tried to push him away. No one could force me to stay there, so why did I never leave? Because each time I moved away, he pulled the same stunt: "Wait."

Bambi squeezed me in his strong arms and swayed me back and forth. He was twice my size—all seventy-eight kilograms of living and existence wrapped around me, engulfing me in their world. The feeling of being swallowed alive by a marshmallow monster—except with the burnt sandalwood scent and a hint of peppermint—made me breathless. I mouthed, "What?" and the rest of my words were dancing on his tongue, as my will to leave dangled on his tender lips.

"Sweet Angela, this is Chelsea Hotel." He smiled, lips still glossy after the kiss. "Mm-hm. Yeah, I remember eating a strawberry shortcake that tasted like this."

"Fucker." I was breathless, but the anger was dissipating faster than vapors.

"That I am, milady."

Another streetcar stopped. I no longer asked him if he wanted to board it; we simply stood there, a smaller existence inside a larger, more scarred existence, watching people moving on. Two broken dolls stuck in a corner of a time capsule, never thinking about being picked up or choosing another fate. I inhaled the snowflakes, saying, "Maybe we were born for this."

"For what? Waiting for a streetcar?"

"No. Well, maybe. If you think about it, in a way, it's all about getting on the right streetcar. People can get on, but we choose not to. Because we know it will all end up the same. And we keep asking ourselves, Is the destination worth going to after all? Or will we fare better to just stay here? You know, kind of like Schrodinger and his cat. You never know until the right streetcar comes along, and even then, you don't know if it's the right one unless you board it, so we're stuck in limbo. I think. At least." I rambled on. A sane person would call that crazy talk. Cecilia called it this once. Yet, the word was true from the start and the word kept echoing: *irreplaceable.*

Bambi stared at my neck because I refused to face him. The only indication of his movement was the breathing getting nearer and nearer to my nape, and as he peppered kisses on my bare skin, his hoarse voice tickled my heart until it ached. "God, you are so beautiful sometimes I forget you're smart. And you're so smart, sweet angel, people don't see your beauty."

"I'm not beautiful." I froze, my hands holding onto his forearms, my head spinning. To be. To never let go.

"Baby, because God gave humans eyes but required them to see with their hearts, the lesson hasn't been learned yet."

"Bambi, your breath tickles—"

"Wanna head somewhere else? Less cold? Less tickling?" He rubbed his chin against my shoulders, and I yelped in surprise. But "no" was never the answer. "Let me take you to our own Chelsea Hotel then." The grin. The sparkle in his eyes. The universe I was chasing after. The meaning of my existence. And my head kept screaming, *Yes, yes, yes.*

"Will I meet Cohen there?" I said, the strength slowly leaving my body as he took my hands in his and dragged me through the busy street, cutting corners and alleys.

"My sweet Angela, Cohen wishes he met you there."

We ran through Janis Joplin's guitar, Bob Dylan's soulful voice, and the dripping sorrow of Leonard Cohen's lyrics condensed in a mixtape playlist that were shrouding the Toronto sky with fog and a mist of tears. Our feet carried us to a place called "there." Neither of us cared where it was, if it was destined for us as a blessing or a punishment. We thought in that moment, we outran fate, and somehow, lost as we were amidst the crossroads and red lights, we were home. It was freedom. It was youth. It was something we would regret later, but history wouldn't incriminate us for the wrong choices on the road to the loft just outside the busy landscape of the city lights.

Climbing the rusty staircase of the run-down apartment complex, we giggled like two beggars high on borrowed time and the luxury of living. The writing on the wall said, "Everything is possible," and another bit of graffiti beside it said, "worst advice ever." Bambi unlocked the door. The room was infinitely dark. He said the studio was his futile attempt at recreating Olympus and turned the light on. The world cracked open. The carving of Greek on the walls, the bust of Venus still in its cocoon, the withered flowers hanging on the rope, waiting to be inducted into the hall of eternity, reaching legendary status, unforgettable in their decay and beauty, and the dried fruits laying around. What normal people called trash was what he treated like treasure, and I learned to appreciate the beauty in the wasteland of his world.

He picked up the carving tools and began to work on Venus's eyes. Just as I was immersing myself in his deft fingers working on the locks of her hair, Bambi roared in laughter and struck Venus down to smithereens. Another beloved figure had been returned to oblivion through the force of his hands.

"What was that for?" I said, covering my ears as he continued to strike Venus's bust with fatal blows.

"It's so useless. Why am I trying to resurrect the dead?" he replied. His eyes grew hazy with the same trance he had two nights ago, and I knew the monster was rearing its ugly head inside his soul.

"Bambi. Bambi Raymond, you quit that right now."

I lurched forward and took the sharp carving tools from his hands. He was madness. He was destruction disguised as creation. Something snapped inside his brain and the hell hounds started gnawing his flesh until he was reduced to a mess of hurt, reliving the same five seconds, all over again. But what was in that short frame of five seconds? I dared not ask. Pulling his head to my chest, holding him close enough so he could hear the living as it beat inside my ribcage, I whispered to him incessantly, "It's alright. Everything is alright. I'm here." He heaved with hard breaths, as if the simple act of breathing was torture to him. As if living itself was a punishment. The sheer weight of his body overpowered my own, and we fell back onto the soft mattress laid on the floor of the devastating loft. Like a dream, Olympus shattered in fragments of light and stained glass, and we were left with nothing but belligerently harsh reality.

"Bambi," I said, feeling my heart break open, so hopeless, like a bird without wings. "I will never be enough, will I?"

He was sobbing into my breast. I should have taken that as an answer. I should have learned to surrender when the monsters inside him were larger and so much stronger than what my mortal frame could afford to win. But I never did. Stroking his trembling shoulders, I kissed his hair, his forehead, his cheeks, every inch of skin that was visible and within reach. The desire to be—no, the desire to become—irreplaceable.

"It wasn't about you, Angela," he said through the tears. "It was all about me."

"And the five-second time-skipping power?"

"Mm-hm."

"And the girl who danced on the balcony?"

"Mm-hm."

"The weird lyrics you tattooed on your arms."

"Yeah."

"And Saul."

Bambi jerked his head up like a spring released after a long-suppressed hold. A menacing smile graced his otherwise melancholic face, with tears still staining his sharp cheeks. The sparkle was gone from his eyes, the darkness restored. A storm was brewing. I had caught myself in the whirlwind of his malady, and I didn't know it yet.

"Angela, you really are too smart for your own good."

He leaned forward, but it wasn't Bambi. I pushed him away, but he kept pressing against me with his weight. The seventy-eight kilograms of warmth turned into the oppressive power of a sinister hunter. My panic attack started at full force, and the words echoed, *Not to be, not to be, not to be.* He caught my hands in his and pinned them against the mattress. "Saul," the hoarse voice was dripping with hatred and vengeance, "took everything away. Angela, he would take you away from me, too. But worry not, my little caged bird." Bambi smiled, a weird, eerie smile that haunts me still. "I will make him pay. For each thing he's taken thus far, the interest will only accumulate."

"Bambi. Please. Bambi," I pleaded. "This is not you."

"Then who am I?"

He stilled, just a few millimeters from my face. A sudden quietude descended on the previous carnage. The fury was gone, or rather, it was distilled into something in purer form, a whisper of malady for what would come next. His eyes grew vacant and hollow. What used to be a stormy ocean in the darkest night was turned inside out, and I found myself in the embrace of a lost sailor who had fallen out of grace with Poseidon. "Who am I?" Bambi repeated the question.

"I don't know. Someone who needed saving? Is there someone I can call? Perhaps you shouldn't be here alone." I caught him as he fell, deflated like some faithless hope.

"No one comes here," he said, muffled, into my neck. "Talk to me, then. Tell me who I am. Tell me about the salvation I need. Perhaps in your story, Jesus Christ wouldn't have to walk on water to recruit the first disciple."

"Bambi." I paused. The words kept coming and flowing through my brain in waves. Nothing seemed to be the right phrase. Nothing could become the streetcar he had been waiting for. I settled for the less gaudy of them all. "Some of us need a little bit of love to keep going, yeah?"

"Is that the saving you preach?"

"No. Personally, I don't believe love can save anything. Or have enough power to save itself. But…" I kept his face burrowed in the crook of my shoulders, so close I thought I could feel the tears and weeping, but there was no trace of sadness on the skin after. "Sometimes, it's the only thing that keeps us going, no? Holding onto hope because there's nothing else to do but hope. Keep believing in love because there's no larger faith to lean on. Bambi, humans are incredibly fragile. Broken at the core. What makes you think they can outlive the rest of the earthly creatures?"

"Power?"

"Faith."

Bambi stayed silent. Then he chuckled into my neck, making me shiver with the foreign feeling of being touched and breathed in and lived by someone who was not me. "What's the faith I should believe in, then?" he mumbled. I patted his platinum blond hair with silver streaks at the tip, wondering how he had managed to live thus far amongst adults. The world hated beings like him—a child trying to mimic a wise man of old.

"I could love you." I spoke without thinking. It was to appease a crying infant. The primal instinct within every female creature.

"Then try."

"Try what?" Bewildered, I pushed him back to look at his smug face again. But it was such a desolate, defeated, and ghastly painting facing me, and I have never turned my eyes away since.

"Love me. Make me believe in its existence."

With awkward hands and clumsy lips, I tried. Kissing him, whispering sweet nothings to him, convincing him that I was the faith he should lean on. I was so good at it I turned myself into a believer far sooner than he ever did. Because Bambi had an antidote, whereas I had none.

"Angela, Saul was the guy who killed my ex-girlfriend," he announced with a stone-cold voice amidst the rainbow of kisses as he took his shirt off. The glimmer of light reflected the black ink tattooed on his toned, pale body like a prayer for a quick death and final peace. "Or rather, he made me kill her."

Yes. To be or not to be. In the flurry of kisses and promise of an ever-after, Bambi had always grounded himself in the reality of this life, where power ruled, where money always came first, where his only mission was to live until he couldn't. All the while, I was a madwoman chasing after a fever dream, believing because there was no other choice Innocence of age. What kind of flimsy faith was that?

To be or not to be. Isn't it easy to choose if the only way out is through?

Chapter 9: The Word

February 17, 2020 – A loft turned into a studio, downtown Toronto

"He what?" I asked, pausing Bambi as he tried for another kiss.

"Can we leave that for later?"

"Oh, what the hell. For fuck's sake, Bambi fucking Raymond, you listen to me." I pushed him away, gathering my blouse and tucking it in my skirt. "You never planned to sleep with me from the start, anyways. What? Panicking in the middle and making me pacify you like a baby? I'm not here to babysit your traumatized ass."

"Angela." Bambi reached for my arm, his voice vacant like the landscape of a ruined nation.

"I'm not here for this. Sure, I was there for the glitter and the glamor, and you—you're something I've always been searching for. You made me stop. No, rather, I stopped myself. In foolishness and fucking pathetic fervent desire for something out of my reach, I stopped myself. For someone whose hands were never mine to hold. What the fuck, Bambi Raymond? I said, let me go."

"Angela."

Bambi yelled my name and with a brutal strength unimaginable for his gentle demeanor, he pulled me back to the mattress. I struggled to break free. We tangled ourselves in a maze of duvet and blankets, choking in the shattered air of the broken Venus bust and the illusion of what could have been. Each of us was chasing after different things. I wasn't the one he wished for, but I persisted. He would never stop being the person I longed to have, but he resisted. And in all that fight—the scratches on faces and fingers clawing on skin—neither of us thought of letting go. Such was the tragedy of being human.

He turned me on my back and caged me between his arms. The veins were showing through the pale white skin as if they, too, wanted to strangle me, to bind me there, to tie me up inside their suffering and sorrow. I caught onto them like a drowning person holding out for a lifeline. Despite the hatred and my sheer will of strength, the tears kept flowing, mourning for the things I had lost. It was weird; I hadn't owned anything from the beginning, but the loss was insurmountable. Like a wounded soldier, I howled for the country I had failed to defend.

"Angela," he said, hissing, for the first time showing me the ugly anger he suppressed, "Don't fuck with me. You were the one who never wanted this. You were the one who never wanted to sleep with me. You were the one who bailed out every goddamn time. I'm a traumatized pain in the ass, right?" he chuckled. The rage was visible in his popping temple. "Then what does that make you? What makes you scared of the dark?"

"You don't love me."

"Love doesn't mean shit to me."

"Then fucking leave me alone."

"Don't be a stupid fuck. You think you can live without a person who wants your company?" He laughs, mad with fury. "Sweet Angela, when will you realize we fucking need each other?"

"I can't. I fucking can't."

"Then I will make you. Until you can."

Bambi leaned in closer. His face wasn't the tender and gentle person I loved; it was a monster. I kicked his abdomen, but he was resistant to physical pain. "Tell me," he said, more a command than a plea, "who makes you into this mess?"

Heaving for air, I could no longer discern between the real and the fake. The studio turned into the streetcar, the station, the library parking lot, the unwanted hands touching the unwanted places, the sneers in the dark, the forgettable faces in the crowd, a thousand complaints and the voices of many policewomen saying, "I'm sorry, there's not enough evidence to prove..." I was breaking apart in his hands like a piece of cake being crumbled, just for the fun of a naughty child on a summer day. Who did I have to trust then? Cecilia? She was a mess herself. The crowd? It was staring at me, vicious eyes and blurry faces. No one would come. In the darkness, I had always been craving a hand to hold. And all I could utter at that point was, "Bambi, I can't make love to you. I'm scared of men."

The words were spoken. And the fountainhead burst. I laid there like a puppet with all the strings broken. And to my astonishment, Bambi wept.

Quiet and in reverence of a thing sacred that only he knew, Bambi took in the fear on my face, the fear in my eyes, and the hate I had suppressed all these years; he breathed them in and exhaled a tremulous sob. His whole body collapsed onto mine, letting the warmth of his beating heart seep through his bare skin, still trembling intermittently as he struggled against the urge to burst from the reins holding him back. Somehow, I wondered if that was his way of apologizing for the things he had done, or rather, for the things the world had done, which he had no power to stop. Yet, one still hoped, for the sole sake of hope.

I had told my stories multiple times to many people: the sexual assaults by the roadside of the central library, the female investigator coming to my home to apologize because there was "not enough evidence," the robbery and the warning that girls shouldn't stay home alone, the constant reminder that because of my gender, I should learned to act sweet and dress myself in ten layers of wool because showing skin meant I agreed. Recounted them like a broken record—not because I wanted to, but because they thought I needed it. The sympathy. The pity. The blessed be thy suffering because it will bring you nearer to thy Lord. I entertained their little faith until I got bored of the whole fiasco. I had trusted them all, thinking there was no way a person would hurt another person out of nowhere, thinking there was pain behind their actions, thinking perhaps they were the ones who needed saving—the perpetrators, the accomplices, the indifferent passersby, the crowd. Dancing to the music orchestrated for the masses—social goodness, people were good at heart—just like the fairy tale about the dancing girl in the red shoes? Didn't she get tired of being the eternal entertainment for the people in the end? And when the time came, the red shoes got cut off, and the little girl was left bleeding to death. I wonder if there was salvation in that tale, and if the little girl in it still thought that the villagers were good at heart.

After all, no one noticed the scars they left from their half-assed attempts to help or not help. Calling out for the masses was always a risky bet: what was in it for them to save me? The benefits are glaringly obvious in the option of looking the other way and going about their business. Life was about moving on. All they needed was a participation trophy for their good deeds. "Are you alright, sweetheart?" was easier than punching the man who's running away, whose guilty evidence would never be enough, who would stay on the safe side of society because he learned how to take advantage of its dark side.

So, who would blame me for falling into the embrace of the first man to weep at the altar of my wounds without asking why I had gotten them? Who would ostracize me for taking the side of the devil when he was the only one taking my hands without inquiring about my defeats and the failed battles where I bled? The Lord said, "Let he without sin throw the first stone." When I touched the glistening teardrops on Bambi's suffering and desolation-stricken face, I knew the punishment was for me: between the two of us, I was the more loving one, and I bet the life given me by the higher power to save the life of someone who had abandoned his faithlessly.

"Hey," I said, my voice cracking. I tried my best at a smile, but my face settled for a scowl instead. "Shouldn't I be the one crying?"

Bambi didn't answer. He just shook his head. The one trying to comfort turned into the one being comforted. It would always be this way between us: the flip of the switch, as natural as the twitch of a finger, and he was there, wrapped inside my arms. Two broken pieces didn't mean it would make us whole, but damn, the feeling that we somehow fit, for a moment, to a place where suffering wasn't a requisite for living, where pain never equaled the proof of our existence, where we could learn there was as much beauty in a shattered hope as in the illusion of despair. His eyes were soft with sorrow, and I couldn't let go of the face I was cradling in my palms like some sacred treasure of a bygone time, when the gods were gentler and the humans were less intelligent. "Raymond," I whispered his name, my lips crashing against his as the syllables danced a tango between the thin space connecting our breath, "I wouldn't mind, you know, if you had forced yourself in, that first night or just now. But you never did."

"No one deserves to be hurt."

"See? That makes two of us." I scoffed, feeling the hurt swell in my throat like a balloon almost bursting with air. "To hurt or to be hurt. That is the question."

"Hamlet would make an easy choice if that were the question." Bambi chuckled.

The tears fell on my cheeks like tiny dewdrops on rose petals, so frail and beautiful in their fragility I could see my destruction reflected in them. And I couldn't help but adore the sadness that evaporated as quickly as it touched my heated skin. I wanted to kiss him. I never wanted to kiss him. The repulsion and the desire tore me apart; I ran from the fight, thinking I should save my life before the last shred of it was devoured by that monster called love. But it was sweet; it was divine. Like saccharine syrup pouring onto a thirsting tongue and dying lips, it fed the hunger I never knew I had. And against my will, against all that could be, I crawled back, begging on my knees for more, as I pulled him closer, chasing after his soft lips. The scent of burnt sandalwood invaded my nostrils and my living. Never had I known a person could go on surviving based off something so intangible and infeasible as perfume.

"Angela," he said, but I didn't want to listen. All I wanted in this moment was to forget. "Angela, do you think life is a heartless bitch?"

"No."

"Why? It never treats you with tenderness. Nor does it ever treat anyone else as such." Bambi refused to drown in my fever dream. He stared at me, so cruelly real and piercing, searching for something only he knew, something he was so sure that I would know the answer to.

"Bambi—"

"Jean-Paul." He lit a cigarette, took a long drag, and spoke with a wearied defeat. "My real name. Jean-Paul Raymond. As in, my mother had wanted the second coming of Jean-Paul Sartre but there was no man with that last name in her vicinity so she settled for mediocrity instead."

"Jean-Paul is a good name," I muttered, playing with his hair. "It makes me want to question, like, 'Oh, Jean-Paul, why are you named Jean-Paul?' or something like that. I guess." The laugh was awkward. The silence stabbed like sharpened knives on us both. He leaned into the touch, humming as my fingers ran across his scalp, dampened with sweat and gel.

"Say what you want, she named me that because it sounded nice amidst a thousand other names in the rhyming book. My brother's worse. Pierre. Who can bear a saintly name like that?"

"You have a brother?"

"Had. He must have forgotten me. It's better that way." Jean-Paul flicked the ember off the dying cigarette, pondering a memory in his mind for so long I thought I could see the reflection of the past in his eyes. "He's my identical twin. Neither of us wanted that. Just so happened that…we were born." The cigarette dropped to the floor, and he crushed it with his bare hand, then lit up another. "My mother died when we were about ten or so. I tried as best I could to get us both to survive––Pierre and me––until one day, I thought, *Hey, there's life after leaving this city*. And guess what? I imprisoned myself in another fucking city. Gosh, the mistakes we keep on making. Pathetic."

I sat there, letting his words simmer and soak into every pore on my body. He said he made a mistake, and all I could hear was his bellow mournfully in the dim studio, of how much he wanted a life he could never have. Pierre Raymond, the one left behind, and Jean-Paul Raymond, the escaped person, chasing after freedom and the illusion of happiness. I wondered if they ever found what they were looking for, and if the price they paid was worth it. When the nicotine aroma lingering around me thickened into the fervent embrace of a drunken lover, I said, "Remember when they preach, 'Suffer the children to come unto me'?"

"What about it?"

"Jean-Paul, look at it this way. If God allowed the children to come unto

Him, He would have to take them at a very young age, right? But He didn't. He allowed the children to grow up, and growing up means living because there is no other choice until you realize the kingdom of heaven you were promised is proven nonexistent time and again by other humans. Only when you were burning would you know how bright the flame is, and how cruel, too, right?"

"What if I don't want to know?"

"But Jean-Paul, that's the beauty of life. We all burn. In one way or another, we all suffer. It's ironic how languages change and the meanings will play with your mind at times. But my point is, in the end, we are nothing but children. We will come unto Him, who will deliver us from this sorrow. And—"

"And you believe that's all true? The false promises He gave all those thousands of years ago?" Bambi said, or Jean-Paul said, cold and detached, like a soul torn from a body.

"Jean-Paul. Besides believing in salvation, what else do we have left?"

"Forgive and forget. Is that what you're after? Until you can't. Until the world grows far too large for your bosom to hold. Until—"

"Jean-Paul." I yelled his name. Something in his eyes told me he was succumbing to the higher indifference he never wished to turn to. My hands gripped his face in place, anchored him to the studio, the mattress, and the two half-naked bodies colliding into each other. "Jean-Paul. Tell me, would you still wake up tomorrow morning?"

"Of course," he said without hesitation.

"Then that's the beauty of it. Life, Jean-Paul, is all about putting one step in front of another. You think you can't. But won't you still wake up tomorrow morning?" I said, more to myself now than to the wounded beast in front of me.

"What happens to the ones who won't wake up? Not tomorrow. Not ever."

"Then that means they've suffered enough. They turned back to children and they'd come unto Him."

He looked at me, a sheen of tenderness and mockery showing through his glazed eyes. "Isn't it easy, Angela, lying to yourself like that?"

"You laugh, but Jean-Paul—" I was half-mad myself. The adrenaline coursing through my veins let me know I was finally living for once in all these years of tolerating the weight of Atlas. "Isn't it fun to entertain the faith?"

"What are you proposing, sweet Angela?" He drew back, pulling me toward him, my breasts against his chest, my thighs straddling his hips.

"I'll give you all my faith."

"Then I'll give you all the hope I ever have."

"Let's live this life, Raymond."

"It's Bambi."

"Yes." I felt my throat tighten. "Bambi, live, and when we grow enough, we can go back to being children together."

"I don't trust Him, who builds humans up like children who could never grow, only to tear them down in His anger when they couldn't learn their lessons."

"Yes, Bambi, yes."

"But I have faith in a madwoman who faced the cruelty of the world and still had enough heart in her to say, 'Life is not a heartless bitch.' Angela, the next time the world comes at you, don't run. Fight back. If a thing doesn't kill you, you murder it, yeah?"

"Same goes for you. If a thing stops giving you enough reason to go on," I spoke, never knowing that it would be a prophecy, "You don't have to wake up tomorrow morning."

Bambi or Jean-Paul or Jean-Paul "Bambi" Raymond—whoever he preferred to be in that crammed studio in the middle of the February winter—held me like that for hours. Skin on skin. Breath on breath. I stopped asking him about Saul, about the girl who died, about the trauma, the pain, the hurt, the reason he chose me to be a disciple amongst the crippled and the sick. He stroked my hair, humming the same mournful melody, threading in his fingers and his touch the golden thread of dreams about a life so far removed from the snowstorm and the dark winter nights of a country where every life was mortgaged out on a good credit score. Slipping his large, rough hand down my back, Bambi asked if he could unhook my bra. I nodded, wondering why he needed to ask for permission. But he wasn't just any man. He was the one I would sacrifice everything for. Holding me in my gasps, I let him trace the curve of my back until his slender fingers reached the zipper of my skirt and my brain screamed, *Yes, yes, yes.*

He toyed with the zipper, kissing my ears until I flushed a deep red. I asked him if he was waiting for me to refuse again, and he said no. He was waiting for me to accept all of him—the good, the bad, the worse than the rest of the lowest scum on Earth. As he said it, his hand undid the zipper so slowly I thought my mind was tricking me. Wrapping my arms around his neck, I traced the tattoos on his shoulders with my lips. The spiderweb laced with thorns, the weird language of the lyrics from some song I never listened to, the symbols of a faith he used to believe in until it shattered him—all of them tasted like holy water from the purest fountainhead. He hummed a sigh, and I asked if it was painful to hold it all in. He asked what I meant, and I bit his lower lip, sucking on the sweetness from the dripping nicotine and the something from the drugs he survived on, saying I meant *this.*

With a swift movement, he grasped my waist, stripped down my skirt, and heaved me up until my body entwined around his torso. I yelped, laughing. He said I never knew what danger was, all while his hand reached for every inch of my naked skin like a drowning man holding onto the last light. I said I knew danger when I saw it, breathing hard into his ears, feeling the restraint in his arms as he tried to resist the will to destruction. Without a word, he turned me around. The cage looked so much like freedom when the locked-up person looked at it, lying on the ground, thinking the darkness above was just a night sky without stars. He placed a kiss on my left breast, where my heart was, and lifted his eyes, looking at me while the kiss lingered in place. The reverence in those dark irises, the burning desire in his longing gaze set my skin ablaze. There was darkness one wanted to run away from, and there was darkness one was willing to catch. Between the easy choice of existing and the harder choice of living, I did not hesitate to decide which road to traverse. I was blinded, maybe, but it wasn't an excuse.

Wasn't I the one who said I would give him all my faith?

Bambi asked if I wanted out, because he wouldn't let me go once we went through with this act. And I cried again and again, begging him to continue. "Keep me insane. Keep me in the madness of your suffering. But don't ever let me be on this Earth alone for one second," I pleaded as he smothered me with his soft lips and wet tongue. "Bambi, we fucking need each other."

The snowstorm grew into a haze of illusory happiness. The kind that could be quickly traded over the counter of some run-down pharmacy at the price of a lottery ticket. I loved him. I never loved him. He needed me. He never needed anyone else. We grasped onto the mess of skin and hair, not knowing whether it was ours or the other's, deluding ourselves all the same that we were here before the first human on Earth. I cried his name and he prayed mine into the air.

The Venus bust, cracked and fissured, laid there on the floor, like a fuck-you for all the things we ignored. Ah, bliss, thou art a heartless bitch.

Chapter 10: The Same Sad Song

April 3, 2025 – Laval, QC

After much struggle and paperwork, I am released from the vines and grip of the hospital staff. The doctor—or rather, the psychiatrist, whose pallid face and hollow, dark-ringed eyes reminds me of a hungry ghost on the hunt for its next meal—keeps pestering me to register for a session. "Therapy," he exclaims, calm with a weird and obsessed determination, "Is the great product of the twentieth century. You don't want to end up like a certain Virginia Woolf, do you?" And he chokes on his own little phrase, thinking it is funny to recite the tragedy of a literary figure as a hilarious factoid no one needs.

I wonder if that is all life ever was to him, listening to other people's sorrow and suffering, turning it into inside jokes, trying to convince himself, edging him on that that he is still living and standing here, while others are not.

Shutting the pessimism's croaking inside my head, I quietly remove his dry hand from my shoulder. The scene keeps swirling back to that day in the emergency room when he and Bambi appeared as the same person and it's driving me mad. "Thank you, doctor," I mumble, shuffling my feet, "I'll reach out if I need to."

"Oh, you will?" he says. His eyes bore holes into me. The sense of being strangled by his insomniac gaze makes my skin prickle. "Everyone says that, you know. Until there's no need to. Until it's too late for the need." With a languid manner, he waves me away and drifts into the dark hall of the hospital.

There is something almost comically pitiful about the psychiatrist—his weary, staggering feet and the way he shoulders the burdens that are not his to bear. Watching his back disappearing into the long, pristine corridor, which reeks of ether and boric acid, the urge to stay here rises in me fleetingly until I vomit it out and walk away.

The last thing I need right now is sympathy toward a human, psychiatrist or not.

Hauling the light backpack onto my left shoulder, I walk toward the gate, looking for the Uber that is supposed to be there. The high noon sun is gentle enough to make me love living again and remind me how easy it is to breathe. Scrolling through the phone's changing interface, I press the call button and wait with patience. The Uber is not here. A rude click. The call is cut off. The drive is canceled quickly after. And like the storm no one wants but knows for sure will come on the dark, filthy horizon, the black Honda sedan appears from hell. Model 2017. Dusty plate. Almost invisible numbers. A greasy white hand with a long pinky nail waves from the driver's door.

Saul is here.

"Angie. Congrats on getting out," he says as the car inches toward me. "Thought you would be there for good. Damn. When your life was at stake, they sure did every test on the table, eh?"

The roaring laughter makes me sick. His coughing makes me sick. The fact that he is still there, breathing, living, existing despite it all makes me sick unto death. But I grit my teeth and get on with the act. He won't let go of the gold coins so easily. The sleazy slimebag.

"Saul. I said I'd call you later."

"Well, you can never be too sure. Not with you younguns and your temperament."

The car is filled with a cigarette stench and oily smells from the many finished and unfinished meals he's had. Saul reaches for the bag of fries next to him, munches on a bunch of them at once, and throws the bag at me. "Eat some'ing. It'll do you good. Too thin."

"Thanks, but no, thanks."

I refuse to touch the bag of fries with the same aversion and hatred people have for a deadly, contagious disease. My disgust doesn't escape his hawkeyed leer and his sniffling nostrils. He cackles, "Too cheap for your fancy taste?" Heaving a sigh and a train of dry coughs like a broken machine, he stops for breath, or for dramatic effect, whichever will heighten his prey's fear and raise the bar of terror. His eyes grow sharp, the irises dark and constricted in the sunlight, focusing on me, what I am at that moment, what wear, the things I carry, and most importantly, the price tag on my neck. "Get in," he says. The piercing note of threat spikes around each word, trapping me in place.

"Why the fuck do I have to?"

"Watch your words, lady. You don't have to, of course." He gags and spits on the pavement. "You must."

"That's it, I'm calling the police."

"Fuck the police two ways to Sunday. Bambi died, didn't he?" Saul roars his filthy laughter, attracting the attention of the passersby. The mass of his body, the folds of his fat and skin and all that construe his being show him to be more of a monster than a human. But I need to play along. Bambi, he betted all he had for this gamble, and I was his last pawn before the checkmate.

"What makes you think so? It's his habit to not answer anyone when he feels like it." I shift my feet, feeling like shit with every movement. My stomach churns. The smell of oily fries chokes me.

"Yeah. But it's not his habit to leave his condo and his studio empty. Where's the kid? He's been missing for about--let's see--two months? And you don't even throw a tantrum. The Special K disappeared with him. A human doesn't suddenly disappear like that unless he's actually six feet deep, aight? Or do you want more? Angela, baby girl, when I said 'get in,' it wasn't an offer to take you home, yeah?" He grabs the burger and takes a big bite, chewing obnoxiously loudly, with the sauce dripping out of the corner of his lips. "It was an order. So get the fuck in."

Curling my toes, I glance around. The pavement leading to the hospital is getting restless with the growing attention on us. Someone says something on their phone, and I hope it's a call to the police. Bunching my shirt into fists, I pray that Pierre won't pop out of nowhere. I must find a way to divert Saul's attention from the hospital before he finds out about the twins, the true identity of Bambi, the legacy he left behind, the plans, the orchestration he draws out from the other side of life like a master puppeteer high on vengeance, having the last laugh. I look back at the car, weighing the options. The tiny life inside my stomach aches weakly, crying for help. Bambi said run, and I don't. Saul orders me to get in, and I hesitate. *Just another push*, I pray to the corpse underneath the peaceful water of the lake. *If it be your will, give me another push.* Like an answer, a female voice rings like a blessing behind me: "That Doctor Raymond, he--" Without missing a second, I step into the car.

"Saul, what do you want?" I curl up inside the seat. The seatbelt feels like an army of ants crawling on my skin.

"Well, let's find some places. We need to do some talking. Knock some sense into that pretty little head of yourn."

"You do that, and I'll jump out of this car right now. I fucking swear." My knuckles turn white. A million accusatory questions scream inside my head. Why did I ever leave the hospital and the insomniac psychiatrist?

"Don't be hysterical, you mental little thing. Listen, if you don't wanna do that, how 'bout you give me Bambi's current address? That is, if the fucker hasn't died."

"I said I don't know."

"And I said cats can fucking fly, Angie."

Saul slams on the brakes. The car screeches to a sudden stop, and I lunge forward, hitting my head on the dashboard. "You either tell me where he is, or I will see you to your death." He grinds each word through yellow, rotten teeth. "Now, Angie, where's your fucking thank you?"

"I don't know. I don't fucking know where he is. Damn, why do you ask me? Ask Markus. That guy's been with Bambi way longer than I have, you stupid fuck. The whole lot of you. Leave me be."

Screaming, crying, flailing around in the crammed space of the Honda sedan, I try everything I can to escape the last period at the end of my story. Saul catches my wrists with one hand and pins me to the passenger seat. The fear grows like a balloon and my body is too small to contain its existence. I look at him, trying to think of a way out. What runs around my brain instead is Bambi's last conversations, "Angela, kill or be killed. The decision is all yours. Think of Schrodinger's cat."

"What about Schrodinger's cat?" I asked, incredulous and laden with worries as I lay on his stomach, my breasts touching his bare navel.

"People think too much about it, that's all. When talking about Schrodinger's cat, Angela, the only thing you need to know, in Schrodinger's setting, the cat would've been dead. Every cat would've been dead. That's your answer."

As if awakened from a long nightmare, my sluggish body rears into motion. I open my mouth as wide as I can, almost tearing my lips, and bite hard into Saul's oily shoulder. He yells, slapping my face. The sound of the slap reverberates in my ears, and it fuels my next action. The cat would've been dead. I punch open the glove box, grab whatever touches my hand first, and slam it at him. Once, twice, multiple times. The warm blood seeps through my fingers until all I see is red. But the thought that Saul is dead never enters my mind. Kicking open the car door, I jump out and run away as fast as I can, leaving behind a howling Saul.

Kill or be killed. I made my decision because I trust Schrodinger's cat.

Gasping for breath, I don't know for how long I've been running. The many intersections turn into one long, winding road. The red lights blur into the same mess of burgundy wines. I keep on running until the sun dies and the moon shows its first sign of living once more in the starlit sky. The places. The names. The people I bump into. I forget them all, trying to outlive the haunting ghost beside me. It says, *Every cat would've been dead, Angela. That's your answer.*

A hand grasps me and pulls me into a dark, empty alleyway. Under the sickly streetlight and the flickering panels of the restaurants nearby, I look up and see the insomniac eyes of the psychiatrist.

"Ma'am," he says without an ounce of feeling. Sheer boredom glints in his dark irises. A familiar tremor rises from within my heart as his hoarse voice rains on my ears like feathers and the sweetest nectar after a blazing journey across the desert. "Do you feel the need for a psychiatrist now?"

"Help. Me." I grasp onto his long-sleeved sweater with the funny ducks and the French phrase 'Je suis mermaid.' "Save me, Bambi."

"Who?"

"Who?" I echo his question, slowly spiraling in the unending nightmare.

"It's the psychiatrist, ma'am. My name is—oh right, the name tag is not here. Anyways," he flashes a tired smile to no human and no ghost in particular, "the name is Pierre. Pierre Raymond."

A police siren blares on the street a few feet away, harsh and loud, like a hunting hound in the night. I cover my ears; my brain short-circuited the moment he said his name is Raymond. Some things are meant to be buried. Some people never mean to rest in peace. He calls me again with the same disinterested voice, "Ma'am, do you need help?" But I am so far removed from the scene of the streetlamp and the lanky arm wrapping around my shoulders to even utter a proper answer.

"My house is near here, if you want to rest." He pats my back. Maybe that is all in his medical books. Trying to gain trust. The disaster will come after that.

"I don't want another Raymond." Abandoning myself to his lead, I drift behind him out of the alley onto a smaller street where his car is parked. "I'm sorry I couldn't be what you wanted. Forgive me, Raymond. Forgive me, forgive me, forgive me."

"Huh? Who's Raymond?" He tucks me into the passenger seat. My mind is half gone and whatever is left of it is stuck in the whirlpool of the past I long to forget.

"Jean-Paul." I stroke his prominent cheekbones, cupping his shallow face in my palm, smiling at the sweet eyes in my memory. "It's alright, I'm here."

He flinches. A scowl finally appears on his permanently bored face. Detaching himself from my clawing fingers, he mumbles, almost inaudibly, "So you're that Raymond's consequence."

I can't figure out his words. The words slur together and I think I am hearing Bambi's voice again as the car drives through the black curtain of the winding road. The lights are on, but the eyes can't see. What is ahead of me, and what is behind, I no longer have the power to distinguish.

"Jean-Paul, I did a good job, didn't I?"

"How should I know?" His voice drones in a repressed monotone.

"Jean-Paul, is it cold out there?"

"What do you think?"

"Jean-Paul, I can't live on like this anymore."

"Why should I care?"

"Jean-Paul, why are you so cruel?"

"Because I—"

Breaking down under the weight of so many days moving between cities and hotels, I cry like a baby who's just realized with all its senses and being that its mother is lost forever. Every cat would've been dead. I cry for Schrodinger's cat, for every other cat in Schrodinger's experiment, for Saul, for the psychiatrist, for the world that is at war with itself. For Bambi.

And yet, I can't find a reason to cry for me.

Pierre parks the car in front of a nice, cozy townhouse. He removes me from the seat like a bag of potatoes. Another burden no one asks him if he wants to carry. I mumble a soft "Sorry," but he ignores it. Everything happens like a routine. Unlocking the door, throwing the bag of potatoes on the couch, turning on the light, drawing the curtain, and lying face down on the sofa seat. He does them all with the natural talent and smoothness of a professional.

I glance around the scantly furnished living room. Besides the large and comfy sofa set, there is not much to it. No TV, decorations, photographs of his past, or the proud wall of achievements. The greyscale color scheme makes it look like a prison. Even the bunch of flowers in the corner of the room is fake; it is covered in dust and cobwebs. I wonder if he actually lives here, or if this is the grave he plans to remain in for his death.

"Doctor," I venture. My throat is scorching with a dull pain.

"Pierre. I'm off work." He groans, diving his head deeper into the soft cushions.

"Pierre. And Raymond?"

"Yes. Pierre. And Raymond. Anything else to satisfy your curiosity?"

"Do you happen to know another Raymond?" I bite my lips, curling into a ball on the off-white velvet sofa. He is different from what I had heard, but it's alright, I can always dig deeper, go further, because Jean-Paul left his last wish with me. Pierre, he said, who would bear a saintly name like that? Because the man lying like a corpse before me is no saint, but more like a drowning mess waiting for the last judgment.

"Yes, I do."

"Then—" I spring toward his tired, stretched-out body. Before I can finish my sentence, he goes on:

"I have a Richard Raymond in the files. Samson Raymond. Simon Raymond. Martin D. Raymond. When you think about it, the world has a lot of mentally sick people with the last name Raymond."

I heave a disappointed "Oh" and go back to my corner on the sofa. We simmer in silence for an eternity of an hour, then Pierre grudgingly gets up and rolls on his side, punctuating each movement with a guttural grunt. I watch him tormenting himself to stand up, wondering if this is what normally happens when he gets home from work.

"You seem tired," I say, trying to start another conversation.

"If it only 'seems' that way to you, then I fail in my performance," he replies, his hands pushing at the sofa seat to boost himself up, but he drops down again, sighing contentedly.

"If that job is so tiring to you, why do you keep at it?" I feel my guard lowering fast; the grip on my resolve slowly releases without my will. The Raymonds of my life, the agony that keeps on living in the dim light of the dark, stormy night.

"Ma'am, jobs, or rather, employers, have the right to hire whoever they want but," he groans as he stretches his back, "people like me, I choose money."

"Is that alright for a doctor to speak that way?"

"I said I'm off work. I'm free to say what's on my mind. Anyways, hungry?"

"A little bit, yes."

"Then order whatever you like. I'm going to sleep." He drags his feet toward the back of the house. Each step seems more painful than the last one.

"You don't eat?"

"If I can sleep, I'd rather not eat. Good night."

Pierre waves away the living room, the awkward situation with me sitting there like a useless decoration, and the aftermath of something he never signed up for but has to handle out of his doctor's oath. He slams the door of his bedroom, and the world outside ceases to exist. I am left alone again, with a growling stomach and a bewildering question: Among the many Raymonds in his list, has there ever been a Bambi Raymond? And if there was, what was the real registered name of the patient?

A Richard? A Samson? A Simon?

Or a Judas Raymond?

Chapter 11: All About Pierre

April 4, 2025 – A nondescript townhouse, Saint-Laurent, QC

I wake to the sound of multiple alarms ringing. The noise is loud and obnoxious enough to bring down a forest. A normal person would have gone crazy from the sheer amount of panic the mess of different tones triggers in the air. But there is no alarm clock in the bare living room. Behind the closed bedroom door, an animalistic bellow echoes out like a dog from hell who's been jerked awake at the most importune time. A few bangs against the wall. The noise stops as suddenly as it begins.

I observe the bedroom, my ears keen for the first hint of movement. A long silence follows, and with reluctance, the door opens gingerly, ejecting the gloomy and grumpy ghost of a being like a half-finished meal. Pierre. And Raymond.

His hair is curling into a bird's nest. His dark circles are not any lighter. The pallid face is only paler. A sheen of stubble shows on his chin. He still wears the same clothes as the night before. The faded shirt is wrinkled. The pants have already lost their pristine lines. Pierre-and-Raymond doesn't seem to mind. He tugs at the collar, mumbles, "Meh," then walks toward where I suppose the bathroom is located.

All this time, he never acknowledges my existence.

I listen to the shuffling noise coming from the toilet, a few curses thrown in for good measure, and the tap water finally runs its course. Unsure of what to do and why this stupid script was handed to me like the sick turn of a badly written comedy, I tip-toe to where the water sings. Pierre-and-Raymond is chanting something inside the bathroom. I thought it was his morning prayer, but upon closer inspection, it turns out to be a mantra he repeats to urge himself to go to work. A monotone repetition of, "Do not cry, you chose this, you fucking chose this for yourself, you have no right to cry, wake up and go to work—" Hesitating between going back to my peaceful corner and barging in to disrupt his will to make money, I knock on the door, and after a long silence, decide to turn the doorknob.

"Hey, so, about last night…"

"You chose this. You fucking chose this. Get up and get on with it. You— oh, you still here?" He turns back. His eyes half recognize me, but his mind is struggling to remember.

I freeze. It is not important. Because there, on the pale skin of the lanky psychiatrist, Pierre-and-Raymond, just underneath his collarbones, is the tattoo of the foreign phrase, wrapping around his chest and shoulders, like a fucking curse staring right back at me.

Jos liedelle käy käteni

Sen heti vedän pois

Jos kadulla on lompakko

Sen varastaakkin vois

Ei teoistamme suuretkaan

Tod näk. Historiaan jää

Jos perin varmaa pelaisin

A normal person would have shattered; a great person would have gone mad from the sheer illusions of shattering dreams, of nightmarish haunting from the past, of the eternal rerun on the screen when the movie keeps playing the death scene and the hero dies a thousand times his tortuous dead. But I am neither. And in the quick span of ten seconds, I choose to fall slowly to the floor, on my knees, begging to change the cruel fate I was handed without being asked. Weeping is an understatement. Grieving can't describe the sorrow I have.

It is an utter, absolute sense of desolation. As if I am the only person left living on this Earth.

"It's rude, you know, staring at my body and crying like I'm a shame to the whole world." Pierre walks toward me and holds my limp body up; the same detachment shows on his face and in his actions. "People always tell me to not bring my work home. I never listen."

"It's… The phrase… I don't know… I don't—" Language starts to fail me.

"Hush. Let's get you calmed down first."

He sits me down on the same velvet sofa, but the world has changed. It isn't Montreal. I'm no longer in the pristine living room with so little living it is reduced to a hollow void instead. Before me isn't Pierre. Suddenly, a mirage blooms. The face turns loving and ardent. His eyes shine in the morning light filtered through the muted grey curtain. His flushed lips curl up as he chuckles. The present withdraws, and the past takes on the stage as the master of ceremonies. Bambi reappears in front of me, warm and smiling. I always knew the world wasn't prepared for my angel, my one and only Bambi. The stars fall from heaven and the earth was destroyed as I sat there in our condo, miles away, the bustling city streets buried our sorrow as I was crying, begging him to stay, and he said, "But baby girl, do you really believe that love has such a power to cure the darkness within me?"

"Ma'am, I know you must be upset from all the things you've been through, and I'm here to—oh fuck, I'm too tired for this shit. I need my coffee first." He groans. "Alright, let's start again. Ma'am, I know you must be upset—"

"Bambi. Had the same tattoo." I choke, scratching his arms in my onyx haze of lack of oxygen and too much delusion.

Pierre stops his monologue midway; in surprise and with reluctance, he points to the phrase inked on his pale skin like a hex foretelling that his life won't be easy, or happy, or blissful and filled with beauty: "This?"

"Yes. But his has thorns and spider webs added in." I snort, feeling my nose running. My fingers turn cold. I don't know what I'm still holding onto, or if I possess the strength to keep going.

"I see. And does it mean anything special to you? The tattoo and—" he winces with hatred and distaste, "Bambi?"

"I don't know. I asked him about it once. When we first met. He said, 'Nothing we ever do will make a difference in history so, fill in the blanks.' We never talked about it again, and I don't know what I should write in that blank space after the phrase. He's just—so Bambi, you know? So—"

"No, I don't," Pierre replies curtly, then, as if afraid of being caught in an indecent act, he averts his gaze. "Alright, he's just so Bambi, you know. Then?" He repeats what I said in a shrill, comical voice. A derisive act of mimicry. I watch, bewildered.

"You seem like you really hate him. I mean, for someone who says he doesn't know who Bambi was, you hold a strong aversion to his name." I clutch his forearm, poking further. The situation is wretched as can be, but I have no reason to abandon hope, and if he were the twin of that devil, who would say he doesn't share the same malady? Madness runs in the blood, doesn't it?

"So what? I can't hate a name, then? Because I'm a psychiatrist, I can't be the crazy one once in while, or what?"

"No, I mean…" I swallow the lump in my throat, calculating my next word. The chessboard is getting dangerously close to the final showdown, and I need to measure each step against the larger collapse. My gaze lingers on the tattoo. Instinct is an untamed beast, and the beast draws me to trace his inked skin.

He catches my wandering hand before I can touch the sickly white skin. Hissing like a snake spitting out venom to protect itself, he spews anger and fury like nothing I've ever seen before: "You keep that sad soap drama to yourself. I don't get paid enough for this."

"Pierre Raymond. Are you related to a Bambi Raymond? Maybe by a different name, let's say, Jean-Paul? But he has the same tattoo. And the same temperament, too." I grow cold. Something in me dies a little, and I let it go with no regrets.

"Jean-Paul Raymond. That's what he said? Tall guy, eh? Charismatic, silvery hair. Muscular enough to trick you that he's healthy. Smiles like a sunbeam. Talks with poisoned words. Yes, I know a Raymond like that. There's only one of him in the whole wide world. Jean-Paul Raymond. That's who you're talking about."

"So you know Jean-Paul?"

He confirms to no one in particular, stretching himself out on the white sofa, giving up the day even though the morning has just started. "He's my brother."

The world stops moving for a second. Then, it resumes its pace with a torturous drag. I watch the man before me, Pierre Raymond, with a newborn, half-hearted hatred and longing for hope. Hope for what? I dare not dig deeper, lest the grave I dig this time will be the one I lie in forever. The voice in my head roars in deafening laughter like a travesty, the act of a drunken fool on a circus's empty stage. *Great, isn't this what you want? He admitted his identity, lure him in, get him where Jean-Paul wanted him to be, teach him what it means to live with darkness like yours.*

Pierre takes no notice of the blow he just dealt. Clinging to sleep for dear life, he shuts his eyes and runs away from the living sound of the life that is bustling outside, chanting his mantra to go to work again. I wonder why they are so different. Jean-Paul, who was bursting at the seams to live but yearning to be dead. And this ghost of a human, Pierre, a sicklier version of him, who has no life left inside, yet keeps on going. Without much thought, I blurt out, biting my tongue immediately at the stupidity: "Blood related?"

"Unfortunately, and regrettably, yes."

"But—"

"But he's just so Bambi," Pierre mocks. "Yes, I know. He's built that way. Sick in the head. Our parents tried to cure him. Judging from the state of you, he's not that well yet, huh? So, how's he doing, in whatever hell he chooses to be in now?"

"I…" At a loss for words, I hesitate between confessing the truth and telling another lie to cover this sudden plot hole in the divine tragedy dressed as a mortal comedy. "He told me you must have forgotten all about him. He said he had a brother. I guess he didn't want to involve you in the life he chose."

"He wouldn't dare to. It would mean he's still care for brotherly love." Pierre churns the words out, then heaves himself from his prone position with force. The tattoo catches the sunlight, and I am bewitched by its beauty. Noticing this, he says, "It's not anything fancy. This tattoo. It's a lyric from a weird Finnish song."

"I know." Something in me breaks and falls apart on the hardwood floor of the quiet living room. Smiling at the shadow of Jean-Paul walking naked around his condo in the last months of his life, scratching the lyrics on his chest, letting the water trail down each word, sparkling with beauty and sadness. I say, "You both like the same song?"

"No. He's obsessed with that song."

"And you?"

Pierre grimaces. Finally gathering enough strength to stand, he hovers over the coffee table with his tall figure, like a giant, lost child, not knowing what to do or where to go next. "Things are destined to be in your life. Sometimes it's a blessing. Most of the time, it's a punishment."

Without allowing me a chance to ask what that means, he drags his feet to the kitchen and turns on the coffee maker. The process is filled with bangs and curses, much like his morning toilet routine, until the scent of coffee fills the apartment. It smells like peace and order before chaos. My stomach growls. I finally remember the need to eat. But after that fiasco with Bambi-slash-Jean-Paul Raymond, I can't ask for a meal like a shameless beggar at the temple of hurt. Trying to appease the revolt of my hunger, I take my phone out, checking the balance in my account, hoping despite it all that I still have enough money for a decent breakfast. The fact never disappoints: my bank account is nothing but a hollow emptiness to fall through. When I think it's high time, I will take my unwelcome existence out of this pristine apartment, think of another way to weave Pierre into the trap, and go back on the road as the last escape route. A piece of buttered toast is shoved in front of my nose. "Take it or leave it," Pierre says, notably calmer than his previous, non-caffeinated self.

"Why?"

"Why what?"

"The toast. Everything."

I take a bite of the toast. Unsalted butter. Flavorless and tasteless, like the rest of the apartment. "Saving me. Is that a part of your job description?"

"You happened to me. That's all." Pierre sits on the other side of the sofa, munching on his toast, doubtless as flavorless and tasteless as mine. His coffee mug is filled to the brim. He lets the dark and steamy liquid simmer there, until his eyes rest on it and his mind registers that he needs to drink it while it's hot.

Pierre Raymond is a curious man. He hardly has any muscles, just a toned body, enough to show that he is healthy and mentally well, despite the exhaustion. Permanent insomniac. Provides consultations to other people. Listens to their troubles and traumas. Prescribes medication to suffuse their pain, temporarily. Goes to work when the clock strikes 8:30 in the morning. Back home as soon as his shift is over. Never attends parties or socializes as long as he can help it. He lives because he doesn't want to choose the other option. And he makes it clear to everyone watching that it's worth going on instead of giving up and surrendering to the nothingness that he will return to sooner or later.

Life has never been a happy place for Pierre.

"That's your opinion." His hoarse voice, much too similar to Bambi's, draws me back to the sunlit living room.

"I'm sorry?"

"You just said it out loud, you know. Your thoughts. That life is never a happy place for me."

"And is it?"

"Happiness is a curious cat, ma'am. She comes and she goes. You won't just die because one day is sadder than another, right?" He stirs the black coffee, drinks a few sips, and sighs contentedly.

"I don't know. Talking about cats. He—your brother—likes Schrodinger's cat. He says every cat would've been dead. Would your happiness-cat be the same?" I draw my knees up to my chin, giving up on eating the boring piece of toast.

"Well, he's that kind of broken soul. As my mom used to say, 'Blessed be the curse upon us.'" Pierre rolls his eyes so far back I can see his whites standing out like a haunting. "But the purpose of Schrodinger is to posit that you won't know whether the cat is alive or not unless the box is opened. Thus, the cat remains alive and dead at the same time. To say every cat would've been dead—that is purely nihilism."

"So you think he's wrong?"

"He's entitled to his opinion. I'm entitled to mine. We're very different people, ma'am. I can't accuse him of being wrong. I've never been through his life."

"What was he like when you guys were still…" I gesture vaguely. "You know, brothers?"

Pierre stops everything he's doing. The toast remains half-eaten. The mug almost reaches his lips. His eyes grow dark and cold, like the attic on the longest night of the year. After a long pause, he settles for the same mimicry: "He was just so Bambi, you know."

My anger rises at the shrill voice. I raise my hand, but the slap never lands. Not when the person is hurt by what he said more than I am. Not when he suffers so quietly it almost looks like the pain has become his identity. Not when he has been going for so long with the burden, never once letting if off, never once sharing it. Alone in his agony, Pierre keeps simmering the same way his dark coffee ripples in the nondescript mug with the phrase "#1 Doctor."

A thousand words form inside my mind. The primal instinct to soothe a crying child, except this is not a child, and he's not crying. Not outwardly. Holding a tissue to him tentatively, I don't know if I should apologize or just laugh it off so he can go back to his role on the stage. "Hey, I—" Before I can finish, his phone rings. He picks it up. The hurt is gone. The face disappears. The mask is on. Only the dark circles are there—irremovable, against his will.

"*Oui, docteur Raymond de garde. Oui. Oui. Elle est sortie. Oui. Non. Je vois. Non, je n'ai pas de visite aujourd'hui. Je vois. Quand? Je vois. Oui. Oui. Vous aussi. Ouais. C'est ça. À bientôt, hein?*"

After a series of faked cheeriness and pretentious hilarity, he hangs up. The piercing eyes turn to me. I can feel a grave open next to me.

"Angela Carter. A man called Saul Hammerhead was rushed to the ICU yesterday. He reported that you tried to kill him because you wanted to use his car to traffic drugs. You're wanted by the police."

My heart drops. The suffocation kicks in again. It is light, then it is darkness once more. Keep breathing, I remind myself, but I no longer have control over my lungs. The beating inside my ears is so loud I can't hear the life outside. Who's here? Who's saving me? Who's leaving me behind? In my haziness and the mess of horrifying laughter in my brain, I can feel Jean-Paul's calm voice like a soft caress in the form of Pierre's frowning face, painted black with sleepless nights and dreamless days: "I told you. Things are destined to be in your life. Sometimes, it's a blessing. Most of the time, it's a punishment. Breathe, Angela, breathe." His lanky arms hold my shaking and trembling frame with a force I never knew he possessed. "Remember, Schrodinger's cat is not dead yet."

"Why?" I heave. The world is whirling around me. There is no past. The gate to the future is closing on me.

"Why what?" Pierre scowls, and I think I hear Jean-Paul laugh somewhere so far away that it echoes back like a flicker of a cigarette in the dark.

"Why are you being so nice to me?"

"You should reconsider your definition of 'nice.' Also," Pierre wipes his face, pinching the bridge of his nose as if his head is suffering an intense pain. "Jean-Paul left you all alone, didn't he?"

"I--well, he--technically, I don't know." Yes, it is the truth. I don't know who abandoned who. But when I point at the elephant in the room like that, seeing its large frame looming over me, I am protected by its shadow, casted on everything I own. Anything I leave behind, all that I gave away turned invisible, so I don't have to see that I was losing him--lost him, irretrievably so. My hands clutch onto Pierre's shirt, twisting it up into a bunch, and the realization hits me like Haley's comet raining down its debris on Earth. It is devastating, and it hurts, like an impossible promise, like a replaceable love. When he was Bambi, he said, "Angela, don't ever think that nothing is irreplaceable." "I don't know." And it is enough to drive Ophelia mad. "I don't fucking know." Yes, it is enough to kill Juliet.

"Right." Pierre pauses, then removes my hands from his shirt, trying to calm my tense muscles and fingers, which are clawing at air now. "That makes two of us. Because I also don't know whether I left him, or he abandoned me to this mad world. I'm also a victim of his lofty philosophies and grandiose ideas." Pierre smiles bitterly, and it looks exactly like when Jean-Paul talked about his past. "I'm looking for answer. Until then, how about we go on being accomplices in this suffering together, Ms. Angela Carter?"

I should have refused. Because the answer he is searching for died a few months back, and it never bothered to provide so much as a shallow thank you to his waiting all this time. Because that answer, that self-indulgent answer, thought that it loved him enough, that it sacrificed itself so he could go on living, that it had paid its due. Because, like Pierre said, the answer will be nothing but lofty philosophies and grandiose ideas. Yet, the man before me has the eyes of a saint, so forgiving in their sorrow, so lonely in their forgiveness, that I, a starving wanderer in the desert, can't do anything but kneel at his feet, begging, "Yes. Let me be your accomplice."

Things happen to us. Sometimes they are a blessing. Sometimes, they are more like a punishment. Most of the time, they are a reminder from above that living is a constant suffering until we learn to let go.

Chapter 12: The Beginning

February 19, 2023 – A loft-studio in downtown Toronto, early morning

"Schrodinger's cat?"

I repeated Bambi's question. My head propped on my hand, half of my body was entwined with his. It was hard to let go from the start when the warmth was still lingering on my skin. The cold, cruel night was closing in outside the window.

"Yeah. I sat through a lecture about it. Well, not the whole lecture. Part of it, anyways." Bambi flicked the lighter and lit the cigarette hanging from his lips. The tobacco smell pervaded the room in the form of swirling, vanishing smoke.

"What about it?" I cozied up to his neck, breathing in the faint sandalwood scent.

"Well, there's a guy named Schrodinger. And he has a cat. One day, he decided to put the cat into a box. There's a device with a fifty percent chance of killing the cat. Long story short, until the box is opened, the cat is both alive and dead."

"That's silly," I scoffed. "There's no definite outcome in the experiment at all."

"It's called superposition. And it's a thought experiment. Schrodinger never expected it to have an outcome." He played with my hair and kissed the lock twirling on his fingers.

"So, why do you bring it up now?"

"I don't know. Maybe because after a few ups and downs, dying and living, I think that the cat in that experiment will die. Under Schrodinger's experimental setting, every cat would've been dead."

He went silent for a long while. I could hear a soft hitch in his breath, the quivering sadness that shrilled in the air like a string instrument someone decided to play out of tune. I placed my hand on his heart and felt his blood pulsing through the flesh. There was as much beauty in the living as there was in the death. But cocooned in that makeshift mattress and deflated duvet, I thought perhaps Bambi would find more beauty in the latter.

"What would it take for you to love the living?" I mumbled. He froze.

A light in his eyes shattered, and I caught the fray as it dimmed in the dark. We were both falling apart in our own ways. In a way, we were all Schrodinger's cats in someone's thought experiment. A superposition, as Bambi said. We were both moving on and breaking inside our skeletons, bleeding our guts out as our stomachs churned up the defeat and the willing surrender at the same time. Only time would tell whether we were dead or still alive in the end.

"You know, Bambi, if you think less, and start living more, maybe—"

He caught my wandering hand on his chest. The twinkling eyes and the mischievous smile stayed the same; only the strong grip bordering on breaking my bones let me know how furious he was.

"Angela, aren't we all breathing?"

"I'm sorry." Flinching, I apologized like an innate instinct. "I just mean—"

"Mean well. Everyone does that, now, don't they? I only mean the best for you and that bullshit. The world could do with less of that hypocrisy."

"But I do mean well," I protested, flushing a deep red. It wasn't anger; it was sadder than that. A defeatism at seeing how a human failed to convince another human that there was goodness in the world.

Bambi didn't retort. He simply shrugged, kissed my forehead, and went back to sleep, his back facing me. A wall so tall and impenetrable, built with brick and unbreakable suffering, dressed in the scarred skin of ink and tattooed foreign words. I traced the phrase on his back, *Jos liedelle käy käteni*. The meaning was hidden behind a layer of pain I had no right to pierce, lest the shame of facing such monumental torment would render me even more pathetic and foolish. With palpitating breath, I peppered kisses on each word, each punctuation, each spidery web and thorn, across his back to his shoulder and along his forceps. Bambi trembled slightly, but he refused to bow down before my whimsically awkward seduction.

My hand wrapped around his firm torso, reaching his navel and drawing circles there. My chest touched his broad back. Our skin merged with no space in between, and in that one moment, my breath was his. The long, nimble fingers laced into mine, tugging them, pulling them to his chapped lips. Dried skin caressed my fingertips, and the ticklish feeling made me bubble inside with happiness. "It's alright, Bambi." My lips moved against his skin. "We're not the only ones who are suffering."

In the disquietude of the night, I fancied hearing a child's sob. So small and tender, ever so faint; if I breathed too loud, I would miss its echo from a past I hadn't known yet. Bambi let his cigarette burn in the dawning studio, until the ashes faded out on the tray and what was left of our conversation was reduced to ashes. It was hard to love something as ethereally cruel as love itself when the more human deified that sacred feeling, the more it laughed at us from above, on its throne of poison and thorns, watching us writhe in agony for a little bit of warmth, praying that somewhere, someone was waiting for us to come home. My phone beeped twice. Messages from Cecilia. She had been worried sick since the day I disappeared with Bambi in the club. I relaxed my hold around him briefly, thinking it was high time that I meet Cecilia and explain everything because Lord knew that girl was one worry away from a heart attack. The moment my hand left, Bambi pounced back, lunging at the phone, tossing it across the room like the last thing we ever need to live. He rolled me inside himself, as if he was trying to make a pearl out of me. Not letting go, but the moment I sparkled, he would quit.

"What the fuck was that?" I asked for the sake of asking. I was no longer surprised by his temperament and the strange personality that most would call unique and quirky because "crazy" was a derogatory term.

"You were leaving, weren't you?" he whispered. The breeze breathing on my neck was teetering on the verge of grieving and surrendering all at once.

"I never said I was, did I? Cecilia was texting me. That's all."

"Who's Cecilia?"

"The girl I was with in the club. A few days ago, when you kidnapped me. We talked about her. Did you forget?" I stroked his hair, trying to tame the wounded beast.

"I don't like Cecilia."

"Okay. You don't like Cecilia. She's my best friend. Get used to it."

"What would it take for you to not talk about Cecilia? And everyone else?" A plea. If I were sane enough, I would have detected the stupidity in the manipulation.

"I don't know. What would I talk about if I couldn't talk about Cecilia? About me, then? Or you?" I turned around, facing him, ruffling his hair, and cradling his face in my palms. I couldn't be sane. Not when he was so harmless, so innocently sad with his ocean eyes and prominent jaw with the drawn-out smile. Not when he was so much more the victim of life than I ever was. "Should we talk about you?"

"I'd prefer that." He rested his chin on my breasts, letting me have a free roam with his hair and his cheeks. "Angela, let me tell you a story."

"Is it a good one or a bad one?" I picked out a silvery strand. Maybe it was dyed that way. Or his hair had just outgrown him.

"I don't know. To some, it was a blessing. To most, it was a punishment."

"Well, go on then. I'll see if I belong to the 'some' or the 'most.'"

"Angela, there used to be a little boy…"

Bambi's tale about the little boy was filled with tragedy. A broken family. His mom got pregnant in her teenage years and decided to have him and his brother anyway. She was disowned by his grandparents. Ran away with his father, who was nothing less than a cheating bastard. By three years old, he had learned more curses than proper language. Kindergarten wasn't a thing because his family kept moving from trailer park to trailer park. His father's role in the picture grew dimmer and dimmer, until one day, the role was terminated. The guy packed his stuff and got on with life, leaving behind a single mother with two children of ten. Hunger was a friend. Thinking was a foe. Memory was a strong ally, then, because it reminded him that he was born to take revenge. A friend or two at school. A girlfriend or two during his time in college. Dropped out because he was sick of the holier-than-thou attitude the institution adopted. And he drifted through life that way until he learned that love wasn't a one-sided bitch. Perhaps that was when his ex-girlfriend committed suicide. Perhaps she had seen heaven, then, in her drug-riddled mind, and he wasn't the one she imagined her paradise to be. Perhaps, in the end, he wasn't anyone's choice. A beggar singing the drug ballad to get coins. He never thought it was bad.

"But where's the love in that?" I asked, no longer playing with his hair. My hands tried to lift his face, but he kept it burrowed deep between the crevice of my breasts. The primal instinct of an infant to be safe.

"I don't know. Is there love in this life?"

"It's hard to say. Some days, I think there isn't a bit of it left. But most days, when I'm too desperate, I'd prefer to think that life still has a lot of love to give."

"Then maybe, sweet Angela, on those desperate days of yours, would you choose to love a boy named Jean-Paul Raymond? Would you quietly pick the pieces of him up, patch him together, and tell him that he is beautiful nonetheless?" The bitterness seeped through my skin, and I felt him crack open.

"Did you ever have the revenge you wished for?"

"Not yet."

"Do you still plan on having it?"

"Not a day goes by that I don't think about it." He gritted the words through his teeth. His shoulders tensed up, then relaxed. Yet, he still refused to look at me.

"Bambi, have you ever thought that Schrodinger's cat was set that way so we still have a fifty percent chance to live, to hope, to love, to try again once more?" I caressed his cheeks, moistened with sweat and perhaps the tears he still had left in him.

"Every cat would've been dead. It's the reality we're living in. This is no superposition."

"But think of it this way: the box isn't opened yet, is it, Bambi?" I kissed his hair. The exit sign was blaring but the road for me to get there was growing more arduous.

"So you think the story is a blessing?" Finally looking up at me, Bambi's eyes betrayed the smile on his face. The fragments of the brokenness inside him cut me until I bled dry and my corpse bloomed with the love that he was searching for. "Was life a blessing to you then, Angela?"

I chewed my lips, tasting the flesh and the flake of skin. The salty and metallic taste let me know that my habit was making me bleed. Bambi leaned forward, licked the tearing wound, then sucked the bottom flesh gently, and let it pop out. His head dropped onto the crook of my neck. I wondered what I couldn't, wouldn't give to show him what happiness was.

"Bambi," I measured my words, "I don't think it's a blessing. Let me finish—I don't think it's a blessing, but I don't think it's a punishment, either. You haven't done anything to deserve such a life. Maybe you're just passing through it. And was it right for people to treat you that way? No. Was it a good excuse to think that they have the right to hurt you? Also no. But Bambi, are you sure that you haven't hurt anyone during those strenuous years of the tale you told? Now, it's like that fifty percent chance all over again. Superposition or whatever. I don't know physics. Think of it this way—people survive by going on hurting each other. And in those hurtful moments, there is laughter, too. If the Lord didn't intend to make us suffer, He wouldn't create heaven for those with the deadliest wounds. Remember the Psalms we read the other day? It was David who sang, I lay down and slept, yet I woke up in safety, for the Lord was watching over me. Bambi, maybe we are all just sleeping under a thunderstorm sky, overcast with gale and the howl of life's fury. But it doesn't mean you're not the chosen one. And it doesn't mean you don't deserve happiness. If life was filled with such rotten things as you said, Bambi, the cats would've all been dead." I laughed at his wrinkled brow and twitching lips.

"Fifty percent chance and you still believe there's love?" he asked with mockery. No pretension. No faked politeness. It was pure sarcasm.

"More like, fifty percent chance, why not believe in it?" I retorted with a certainty I never knew I had. No pessimism. No nihilistic thought.

"And you will still love me then, even if I turn out to be that cold, cruel devil people talk about?"

"It's a bit late for that now, isn't it?"

"Then if one day, I ask you to do the unthinkable, would you still love me?" he asked, crushing me with his strength.

"Like what?"

"Like killing me, disposing of my corpse, and…"

He told me what his plans were, and with each whisper, each question, each tender kiss, I kept repeating my promise. *Yes, yes, Bambi, yes.* It was nothing serious, purely a drunkard in the spring garden the gods and goddesses had abandoned. I bet my future on him, and he bet his past on me, because neither of us truly believed that we had a fifty percent chance to be alive when the box was opened.

Bambi put his head on my stomach, humming to the rhythm of my pulse. He loved anything that could shelter him in the futile feeling that life was right there, surrounding all his senses and overwhelming his mind. The nights he couldn't spend with me because I had to work part time, or prepare for a failing course, missing the attendance of a lecture, an unfortunate thing neither of us wanted but couldn't throw away. Bambi would sleep with another woman. Any girl would be fine as long as she looked the same as me--brunette hair, supple body, curves in the right places, and most importantly, she would hold him with the reverence he chased like an addiction.

I thought about getting jealous the first time. Bambi told me all about his routine. If I were half normal, I would have run, dropping the love that was becoming more like deadly poison than sweetened milk slipping down my throat. But as he lay there, his head neatly on my navel, his breath caressing my skin, his piercing blue eyes painted with dark circles watching my expression, apprehending the worst, his lips curled into a smile, trembling like an abandoned child in the rain. I couldn't do anything. I was wounded, but the one who was hurt the most was always him. The excuses piled up tall enough that they built a forbidden wall, and I no longer saw an escape, or a reason to think of doing so. A single "I didn't mean to" was the only thing he needed to say before I ran toward him and smothered him in an embrace of forgiveness. Come to think of it, wasn't it more like being trapped? Or rather, I chose the prison I thought would be more comfortable for me to stay locked inside.

"You know, Angie, I wonder how much love God possesses?"

"Why ask that now?"

"Because you bring up the Psalms." Bambi played with my hair, twirling the locks around his fingers, kissing them with the purest adoration. "You smell like roses. The best kind. The scent takes my mind off things. The worst things."

"Is that so? I tried on the new perfume you bought me a few days ago. I love it."

"Why? Because it's expensive?" He smirks.

"No, because you love it."

"Angela, you should reconsider your definition of love." Bambi burst out laughing, burrowing his head into my stomach as he squeezed me in a tight grip, strong enough to leave bruises. "Heal me, Lord, for my bones are in agony. I am sick at heart. How long, O Lord, until you restore me?"

"Psalm 6:2 and 3?"

"Don't you think it's tiring being God?"

"Don't answer a question with a question." I slapped his shoulders teasingly. He was in a good mood. A rare one. "I suppose God will be tired. People pray for so many things. I don't know how He copes with all of the prayers and wishes. Will there be a day when it gets desperate enough that even the Lord would say, "That's it; I'm out"? Sometimes, I think it's very likely that day is today. So yeah, it's tiring being God. It's even more tiring to be human and keep on wondering what God is thinking."

"I think He will get sick of this world. You mortals doth ask for too much." Bambi faked an old man's groggy voice, then went back to his bubbly mood. But soon, his eyes drooped. The sparkle was gone. His eyelashes quivered slightly as if they were waiting for tears to descend. I caught his face in my hands, fearing it would fall apart. He held my tremulous fingers, intertwined them with his cold, calloused ones, breathing life into them again: "Psalm

94:11. The Lord knows people's thoughts; he knows they are worthless."

"Taking them out of context won't make your half-assed philosophical musing better." I put my forehead against his, whispering through the cracking laugh. I knew why he was happy. Bambi took a dose before I came. It shouldn't be a surprise, but the hurt remained the same. "Bambi, no, Jean-Paul, there is more hope for fools than for people who think they're wise. Proverb 26:12. I want to believe it, I do, but you make it so, so hard." The crack ran deeper, the fissure broke open, and I wept. "I wanted to love you."

"And now you don't?" His eyes were dilated. His words slurred a bit, but his head was still above the deep water of hallucination.

"I do. Isn't that the most fucked up thing you ever heard?"

"No. I suppose not. The most fucked up thing I ever heard was, Jean-Paul, I wish you had never been born because your existence is a burden no one wants to bear. Wait, maybe it's another one. Recently, there's a girl who screamed to my face, 'Bambi, I love you more than life itself.' Man, that's also fucked up. Oh, how about another one?"

"Jean-Paul, do you ever believe in the future?" I held his head against my breast. His temperature went down until his body felt more like a corpse than a living human in my arms. Not enough, my brain scratched the same old record; I was never enough for you, and never will be.

"I don't. If you think about it, there's no future. Only the present. Whenever you open your eyes, there it will be: the stark, cruel present stands at the end of your bed, staring right back at you, like a curse you can't escape. Hey, Angela, if we act out my plan, maybe we can get out of this trap, don't you think? And then, perhaps, both of us, or at least, one of us will--"

"Proverb 27:1. Don't brag about tomorrow, since you don't know what the day will bring."

"Live, Angela; live and be happy. Believe that He will forgive, that after a tragic act, there will come a comedic interlude. And so it goes, and we will all live, tolerating life like the bitch it always is."

"Nothing will happen that way." But I spoke too soon. I miscalculated the track, walked the wrong path, crossed the gated territory, and ended up in a purgatory he built for us. I stayed there, thinking our forever had a meaning as long as my shoulders could lift the Earth. Then, Pierre happened.

Chapter 13: The Cats Are Alright

April 4, 2025 – A nondescript bedroom in a townhouse, Saint-Laurent, QC

"Is that what he said about Schrodinger's cat?" Pierre asks, his cigarette hanging from his lips. In the vanishing smoke screen and the gradient filter of the hazy dusk, he looks like a resurrection of Bambi. The only thing we lack in that moment is a shattered Venus bust.

"He's always been the crazier one," Pierre continues, seeing that I'm not willing to talk anytime soon after finishing my story. "Did you know he tried acid when he was thirteen? Well, our mom was to blame for that, of course. Drugs should be out of children's reach, whether they cure or kill."

I turn my face aside. My thoughts run back to the sadness in Bambi's eyes. The cats. The thought experiment that is never meant to be carried out. All the fifty percent chance in the world, and when the box opened, he was already betting on the losing side. A nauseated feeling rushes up my throat. I choke on the air I'm breathing, perfumed with the thick scent of nicotine and the haunting ghost of burned wood. The scene before me slips, and I get lost in my labyrinth of the past and the present. The bile isn't getting out of my stomach; the disgusting sense of something churning constantly as long as I'm living––as long as the little life inside me is palpitating each second––only makes me want to drown in the ocean and sleep forever. Pierre pats my back. His large palm bleeds the warmth of living through my layers of shirt and coat with enough fervor to ground me back in the sterile living room.

"Our mom wasn't a bad person. She might be a bad mom sometimes, but she wasn't a bad person. She used to give pennies to beggars and homeless people, you know. Even though we were technically homeless then. Sometimes, it's hard to choose between the fight you need to be in and the fight you want to be in. I guess to Bambi, our mom was—"

"He never said anything bad about her," I retort curtly, covering my mouth, coughing. The vomiting starts when I least expect it, and I double over, heaving with pain. The more I know about his past, the less I'm sure of what I've done. Was it a deliverance? Or was it simply his cowardice with me as an accomplice?

"He must have been angry. The way he went about his life. Abandoning everything and just—"

"Did 'everything' ever choose him, then? It's good for you, doctor Pierre, because you're still welcome in this world." I snort. A burning sensation stabs my eyes. I just want to lie there and cry until the world ends. "He wasn't. We weren't."

Pierre doesn't reply right away. He lets the grief in me fester until the bitter smell of decay penetrates the room and turns it into something akin to utter despair and idiotic rage. Then, tender as the shadow of the night, he cradles the wounds of the three of us in a monotonous lullaby: "We don't choose anything. And those things never ask for us. But thinking that way, don't you see that we'll forever be trapped inside the prison we build, forever be the victims of the system we create, forever not free? What's the life in living like that? You don't turn your head away from suffering, Angela. Living is to accept the agony, to face it, to stare it down and remain the last one standing."

"Bambi said—"

"He can say a lot of things. He has the right to it. The world hurts him at his best and kills him at his worst. I wonder if he's still alive now, facing his demons the same way he faced them in the past. But it doesn't mean you have to trust in him, trust in the faith he created out of nothingness."

"You've never been him," I scoffed. "What right do you possess to preach about the life you don't have?"

"Yes, I've never been anyone but myself." Pierre sighs, tired and visibly bored. He doesn't want to continue a dead-end consultation where he isn't getting paid by the hour. "I have no right to preach. But in a world where everyone is rushing to die, I fancy it would be better if you take a moment to breathe and see how beautiful it is to live."

"You save people because of that?"

"Not necessarily. Money plays a key role in what we do. There's a system, and the system doesn't allow me the privilege of having an ideal."

"Then why do you keep going? Isn't it hard? Isn't it painful? Isn't it fucking agonizing—every day just the same old sad song on repeat?"

Pierre lets the question hang in the air, dirty laundry he couldn't be bothered to wash, fold up, and put inside his closet, along with a few other rotting skeletons he's been hiding. The evening grows too beautiful and borders on becoming a weeping sorrow. He watches the snowflakes dancing on the window glass. I don't know what he sees in the whiteness of winter. Is it a peppermint candy dream or just emptiness like any other scenery for him? I glance around, taking in the rare view of a psychiatrist's bedroom. Books in both English and French. A few in Chinese. Some in Japanese. One or two in that foreign tongue he said was Finnish. A normal person would be crazy from the sheer number of languages he reads. But that isn't the worst: the subjects he focuses on are way more insane.

Abnormal psychology. Textbooks about prescription medicines. Different theses on the root of madness and civilization. Do we ever need a cage for the mentally ill? (A thesis I highly doubt is his dissertation). Plenty of Fyodor Dostoyevsky. A tattered Aldous Huxley. Those in Chinese and Japanese, I can't figure out the names. Much less can be said about the Finnish ones. Beside a national forest of books that is growing on his floor, his walls, and his nightstands, there is only the bed I'm lying on and a single light bulb. He takes the definition of stoicism a bit too seriously. Or simpler, he doesn't have any other purpose for the room besides sleeping in it and reading his life away.

"Can I put on some music?"

The hoarse voice echoes in the creeping darkness and I jerk back, thinking

I would see Bambi sitting there, smiling at me, waving his phone with some godforsaken playlist. But no. It's always been Pierre. All this time. He scrolls through his phone, not paying attention to the answer, or lack of answer, I have, puffing on his cigarette. Picking out a song, changing his mind midway, shrugging his shoulders with a curt "Meh," then settling at last for Leonard Cohen.

It is like watching an old reel on repeat. Only the actor has changed. Yet the frames retain their exact order to each millisecond. The pain surges into my eyes like a wave.

Cohen's grainy voice mourns from the phone's speaker. *Thanks for the Dance*. My existence vanishes. The person lying there is just a corpse of a past gone by and a future turned wrong. Pierre speaks over the low, melodic song:

"I didn't choose to be this way, either. The world welcomes me, you say. It wasn't like that before. The son of an addict. Abusive family, neglectful father, trying-her-best mother, and a brother who's been mad since the day he was born. I wonder if the world ever asked me if I wanted to be here."

He inhales and lets out a long breath. A part of his soul leaves with it.

"But who could blame them? My family, I mean. My father and mother— well, you got that part of the story from Jean-Paul. Or Bambi. Whichever name you want to call him." He waves his hand around, gesturing to an invisible figure in front of him, as if his older brother is there, standing right where he can touch and see him. "Jean-Paul was different. As you said, he was just so Jean-Paul." Pierre laughs. Tears would have been a better fit. But his eyes are all dried up.

"A fucking egoistical bastard, you mean?" I ask.

"No. He was…" Pierre rubs his eyebrows, trying to detach himself from the floodgate of memory. "A bright kid. Magnetic. Intelligent. A person on the winning team. People are just drawn to him instinctually. That's his talent. He never needs to do anything, and he always knows when to say the right words. Charismatic, that's the term. Jean-Paul was there on the podium, while I—" he stops. The cigarette flickers for the last time then burns itself out.

"While you?"

"I wasn't the brightest sort. Never have been. My mother dropped me once when she was high and I was still a baby. Must have damaged my brain somehow. I was slow. First grade and I couldn't count to ten without guidance. Jean-Paul said he would protect me, so I followed him—like everyone else—and catered to his every whim. 'Notice me.' That sort of hunger. We all have one. The constant need for validation. That's what it's called. But Jean-Paul..." Pierre taps his forefinger on his thigh, counting the beat of Cohen's slow waltz. One, two, three, one. "He was the first to fall."

"To fall, meaning—?"

"Drug abuse. Alcohol abuse. Every which way of abuse you can think of, he would get involved with it at least once. Then twice. Then it goes on forever."

"But why?" I ask. A part of me knows the answer. But the sanity in me demands the absolute truth.

"It's in his veins. In both our veins, to be exact. The madness. The despair. What the professionals call mental disorders, at that time, Jean-Paul and I just called straight-out brain sickness. Our father and mother succumbed to it. Jean-Paul was simply following in their footsteps. I was the only one left behind. All alone. On my own. In that trailer park with my mom's death rattles. Is it painful to keep on going, you ask? Well, I asked myself that question many times, too, when the social services picked me up and handed me around like a wrong package no one wanted anymore. It wasn't a Christmas gift. And I wasn't the blessing a Christian heart would want." Pierre changes the song. "Show Me the Place" goes on like the background music for his melodramatic autobiography.

"Then Jean-Paul—I mean, Bambi—left?"

"Yeah. He wouldn't stay where he failed to rise up, now, would he? He chose to leave. God forbid, but many drug addicts around here still remember his name. The guy was popular. Heh. Everybody knows a Jean-Paul Raymond in this life. Nobody knows there's an annoyance attached to his side—Pierre Raymond."

"But you keep on going."

"Because I refuse to succumb. I refuse to let the blood I was born with decide the fate of my ending. Remember what I told you? Jobs choose who they want for the work, but given the choice, people would rather have money. I believe that if I push hard enough, even in surrendering, I will still surrender gloriously."

"Isn't it better to let go?" I reach for Pierre's cigarette on the nightstand and light it up. The smoke hides his tormented face from my sight. It's better this way. Some suffering is never meant to be witnessed.

"Yeah. It is. Tempting, even. Just jump off the stage and the pain will be gone. I thought about it a lot. But one day, it dawned on me. If life was designed for people to quit, why do we keep on trying? The wars go on. The journey keeps rolling. The stream of humans keeps pushing ahead like a train to nowhere fast. We were destined to be here. After all, we're not the only ones who are suffering. That's enough. More than enough."

I stare at him, feeling like a hare caught twice by the same trap. "Things happened," he said. "Most of the time, it's punishment." My merciful Lord. My cruel Lord. My only-benevolent-in-translation Lord, if what Pierre said were true, and what Bambi said then were also true, that things happened to us despite our choices and decisions, that most of them are punishment for a deed we never thought was that important. Will Pierre be the punishment for me at last? I clutch my stomach, swaying. *Holding onto hope, Angie,* Bambi said, *because hope is the only thing left; you always have some sort of stupid maxim like that in your pretty little head. I hope our child won't be like you.*

With a violently shaking hand, I try to grip Pierre's. Rough. Calloused. The skin is dried and flaky from the frequent abuse of disinfectant. The fingernails are non-existent. He is not Bambi, just like he was never Jean-Paul. From the start, he was Pierre, and he still keeps walking with his bleeding feet, living the role of Pierre. Where many decide to give up, he pushes further. Surrendering gloriously. Pain. But it's alright because the ghost can't stop me from begging God, singing a Psalm to make Pierre my salvation.

"Pierre, there's one thing I think you should know."

"Hm?" he asks, nodding, not because he is listening but because he is falling asleep to Cohen's soothing voice.

"Pierre. Your brother. Bambi—or Jean-Paul—is dead."

The phone drops onto the floor. The light outside has gone but the light bulb inside the room still remains switched off. The only living thing in the room is Pierre's dark, fiery eyes as they impale me to the hopeless, devastating state we are in. A thousand unspoken questions. A million repressed hatreds. Yet, Cohen keeps on going: "Show me the place where the suffering began."

Chapter 14: The Puppets

March 1, 2024 – Downtown Toronto, a modern, newly furnished apartment

Bambi twirled my phone with his deft fingers; the screen reflected the dawning light from the tinted windows of the high-rise apartment. He hummed the same old song; his vacant gaze spanned the open landscape of skyrocketing buildings and the dumpsters next to them. I huddled on the bed, wrapped myself in the thick duvet, incensed with the scent of pale sunshine and the crisp winter air. The softness of the fabric melted my worries. Since the day I slept with him, I had never been back home.

And Cecilia's number had also been blocked.

"Howard Roark." Bambi suddenly spoke. Random thoughts occurred to him at the most erratic times. I happened to be there to catch it.

"Ayn Rand?" I said, sprawling on the mattress, inhaling the comforting scent of his fabric softener.

"He would cry seeing this scenery."

"Howard is a weirdo. I guess he's your kind of weirdo."

"Maybe. Maybe not. I haven't had the chance to know him yet."

The phone dropped to the carpeted floor by a careless mistake. He bent down to pick it up, the screen glaring with a thousand notifications.

"Cecilia G. Cunningham."

"What?" I jumped.

Sitting up on the bed, I stared at his hunched posture as he focused on whatever piece of message or news was on the phone screen. His naked torso showed through the slanting evening light. A sight of beauty for the beholder, but it wasn't mine to see. I was too busy catching the random thought he spewed—the name I tried so hard to forget. The existence of a person in my memory. The girl who struggled, who lived, who, until that point in time, was still fine in my guilty conscience.

"Cecilia. That girl you were with in the club a few weeks ago. Time sure flies by, huh?" Bambi kept scrolling. A contemptuous smirk lifted his face up, then vanished.

"What about her?" I fished for answers. My fist bunched the duvet into a sweaty ball.

"She's dead."

He yawned, then walked toward the kitchen and opened the fridge. A few clanking and grumbling sounds with a thousand curses thrown in the air, and I heard a beer open. The slow footsteps to the vinyl record player. The scratch of the needle on the disc. Leonard Cohen's baritone, full of grain with a filter of pain, ladened the room in the mourning for anything sacred on Earth. Bare feet slow-dancing in the dark. And I was drifting, floating on a tender wave of torment, so arduous yet faint and ticklish in its caress I thought it was pleasure.

Cecilia had died when no one was watching. Alone in her one-bedroom apartment, choked on her own vomit, her last breath stank with the rotten smell of putrid dreams and last night's spoiled meal.

"Hey, why are you crying? I thought you guys weren't close." Bambi wiped my cheeks. A trace of salty water crystalized on his finger, and he licked it up.

"She was..." I tried to find a word to describe what we had, Cecilia and I. The bond of those who wanted so badly to survive but couldn't. Wouldn't. Didn't. "She was my best friend."

"Hm. But now I'm your best friend, aren't I?" Bambi tilted his head, asking in childlike innocence. In a moment, I almost forgot how vicious the monster underneath was.

"She, Cecilia, how did she—? Why did she—?" It barely registered in my mind. A person who was there, and suddenly, she was there no more. How could a life just disappear like thin air?

"Oh. Overdose. Meh, happens to the best of us. Anyways, what do you want for dinner?"

Bambi scrolled through his phone, checking out the nearby restaurants offering delivery services. I was nailed in place by the shock, like a stupid monument, pinned there forever for the oncoming spectators' entertainment. Who had been here before me? And who would be here after? Cecilia, my girl, my doomed artist, whose paintings on the walls were always rejected, who stood up and tried, who life couldn't break so it killed instead. It sounded like a farce: her death. I snorted. Who would care for her now? The abandoned ones, both of us. And at the last moment, I let go of her hands, chasing after the higher indifference people revered. Love. Be loved.

"Pizza," Bambi called out, more like a statement than a question.

"What?" I sniffled, trying to stop the tears. Despite my will, they kept coming until my ears grew muffled.

"Do you want pizza?" He repeated nonchalantly, still flipping through the options. "Or fried chicken? Honey garlic wings with beer sounds nice. Oh my God, can you stop with the sobbing? It's getting on my nerves." He groaned, finally let go of his phone.

"I can't. She's my best friend. Cecilia, she's my—"

"And now she's not anymore. Can you catch up quicker?"

"Bambi!" I yelled his name. The first time. The last. Soft like a whisper in the darkest night, I pleaded. "Bambi, have you no heart at all?"

His eyes stayed the same vacant, unfathomable orbs. His face remained emotionless. If anything, he aged in a second. The weariness. Exhaustion. They came over him like a debt long overdue. He crawled to my place on the bed, heaving with patient exasperation. "And what if I don't?"

"I—"

"Will you leave?"

"I won't, but..." Words started to fail me. A glacier grief slashed me to pieces. The pain grew into an agonizing mountain. This was weeping for the things you weren't destined to have.

"Angela. Listen here. Don't mistake your cheap sentimentalism for kindness. It's pathetic. What and who are you acting for?"

I gritted my teeth. The cries escaped through bitten lips.

"Go on. Cry if you must. Remember, you left her first. That was your choice. More importantly, remember, she chose this ending herself. We made choices. Sometimes they lead to other choices. Sometimes, most of the time, they lead to nothingness. Ain't nothing we can do about it."

"You don't live our life. You don't know Cecilia. Fuck, what do you even know about me?" I raised my voice. Part of me wanted to buy what he said. Another part was raging, cautioning me against the big collapse.

"Yes, I don't know. Either you or Cecilia. I have no other interest than waking up in the morning and putting one foot in front of the other. So what?" he replied, somewhat at the end of his patience now. "Does it make you feel better, consoling yourself with the thought that you're the only one hurting?"

I stared at him, bewildered. What did I just hear? Was it an accusation, or a shifting of the blame? I no longer knew the difference.

"Look at it this way. The metaphor of the broken leg, ever heard about it?"

I shook my head, still processing what he'd said before.

"Supposed your ankle twisted, and the pain was so much that you couldn't walk anymore. So harrowing that you couldn't think of anything or anyone else but the broken ankle. In that scenario, even when the whole world comes to its ending, your only thought will be, *But my ankle.*"

I shook my head, more to calm my fraying nerves than to dispute his metaphor.

"But it's true. We love the victim mindset. See, if you're the only one hurting, it makes life less miserable. It gives you a free pass. Well, almost. Bullying others? Too bad, she suffered a broken ankle. Too quick to anger? Can't help it, she got a broken ankle. Can't choose a fucking dinner option? That's alright, she just suffered a broken ankle. Angela, being the victim is freedom in itself."

"I never thought—"

"You didn't see it that way because the pain gave you a privilege. While you're suffering, the world should stop existing. Focus on me. Look at me. Spare me. Because I'm a fucking victim at the hands of cruel fate. Oh good for you." He rolled his eyes in exaggeration. "Welcome to this shit show. It's not like you were born yesterday. Catch the fuck on."

"I just—I thought Cecilia would always be there. We promised. She was the only person by my side." Reason slowly ebbed away from me like a river going south.

"And? Nothing will be here a hundred years from now. What gives you the stupidity to think of forever? That's for pampered children. For the rich. For the people who can afford to build a true-to-life Parthenon and install themselves there. Jeffrey Epstein. Money can buy you the fancy, and vanity will paint a beautiful portrait of your stupidity. But you know what?" He scoffed.

"What?"

"At the end of the day, between grief and nothingness, we all return to nothingness. Why bother choosing, then?"

"Bambi, you make it sound so easy," I said, hatred pouring into my blackened heart. "Reasoning yourself out of sorrow and suffering to evade being human. You're no more than the rest of us."

"Guilty as charged." He kissed my hand pompously, winking his eyes. "Now, what do you want for dinner?"

I didn't answer. I let him choose whatever he wanted, whichever programs he liked to watch that night, whomever he decided to call on the phone, talking about the girl who died like it was just another incident dropping from the sky. Like rain. Like bad weather. Something unexpected, but not enough to stop him from moving about his rotten life in his fancy suite. Watching him bustling about the pristine, minimalist two-bedroom apartment—a slice of pepperoni pizza in one hand, a buzzing phone in the other, texting all the girls he would sleep with, the one-night stands that would happen sooner or later—the lethargy slowly caught onto me. Like darkness. Like liquid. Like the cold water of the Great Lakes and I was drowning so blissfully in my eternal sleep. So what if Cecilia had died?

Powerless against the things that tied me to Bambi's orbit of existence,

I let myself fall against the cushioned headboard, trying to flee the scene. Nothing I did could change the man. What was the use of trying?

He left the TV on mute and watched two opposing politicians debate. Their saliva was flying all over the place. The headline was something about feeding the poor of the country. Immigrants. Refugees. The unfortunate bastards. I didn't know what they were talking or cursing each other about. He never listened to their arguments. He only loved the spectacle of two grown adults fighting each other for a position in an engine that had authority over all of us. Who would be the next idiot? He often termed it that way. The puppets, he called them. I wondered who the puppeteer in his eyes would be.

The old white male on the screen shouted something—maybe an obscene word, maybe an earth-shattering insult. I never had the chance to know, and Bambi laughed. He bit off a large piece of his pizza and watched the man striving for another chance to attack his opponent like it was the best comedy show of the week. My stomach growled. I wondered if he heard the embarrassing noise. He never showed any signs, just nodded along with the silent TV. Crawling to the pizza box on the bed, I took a slice, hating myself for succumbing to hunger, questioning myself if life was just this—a cycle of eating, sleeping, shitting, and repeating. The older female of the opposing party retorted something. What was the point? What was the key to the argument? I didn't pay attention anymore. They were just another decoration in my life. Whoever won, the world wouldn't end in the next hour.

"Whales."

"What?" I said, half chewing. Hours gone by in nothingness and he uttered another senseless word.

"Whales. They're singing in the ocean. Imagine you pay for years of university, learning marine biology, carrying a huge tuition debt, just to listen to the whales' song."

"And? You find that interesting?" There were teeth in my remark. It was more for show than to do harm. The grudge had dissipated before it had the chance to grow into a forest fire.

"What if the whales stop singing? Where will all that money go?"

"Are you talking about the 52-hertz whale? The one whose frequency no other whales can hear?"

"No. Not the 52-hertz whale." Bambi took another bite, chewing his pizza slowly, savoring the pepperoni. "All whales. There will come that day, you know, when there's nothing left in the ocean. No fish. No shrimp. A vast body of water of emptiness, and whales—what will become of their empty stomachs? Will they be singing then?"

"You grieve for the whales? Seriously?" I asked, so furious it was comical to me instead.

"Why? Should I grieve for Cecilia?" Bambi smirked. He knew he'd got me. I knew he got what he wanted out of that searing question. We resorted to a seething silence. "I don't feel grief or mourn or do any of that stuff. Descartes had to make peace with the idea that living is about constantly thinking your way through. It's the same with me. I think. Sometimes, the thoughts turn silly, like Howard Roark and his unyielding ideology. Or moribund, like the whales and one day, no one will sing anymore."

Bambi tossed the rest of the pizza into his mouth. Like leftover garbage. Like eating to live. Like the remains of something nobody ever wanted. "The world goes on, Angela. Is it beautiful? Cecilia isn't here, lucky bastard. We keep shouldering this dead weight on, and we are no Atlas. Look at those puppets—Puppet Liberal is eating Puppet Conservative alive. Heh. We're all starving, but the puppets never go hungry, do they?"

I couldn't taste the pepperoni on my tongue anymore. The pizza turned into sand. Into salt. Into ashes of the girl I loved more than myself. Puppet Bambi and Puppet Me. Puppet Cecilia and Puppet Dealer. All the puppets on the ruptured stage dancing until the night ended. Some puppets would continue because their roles weren't done yet. Others were cruelly torn off the stage.

"Who's controlling them, Bambi? The puppets, I mean." I didn't cry. I simply let the sadness burn.

"Who knows. Maybe someone. Maybe no one. We love the idea that there is a higher deity out there who would take the blame for all the sins on Earth. That would be sweet, wouldn't it?"

"Bambi?" I tugged his arm. The thorn vine tattoo crawled on my fingers and captured me whole.

"Yes, my darling?" he hummed.

"Give me the damn drugs."

He stared at the TV screen, nodding his head along to the distorted face of the old men in black and dark blue suits. I thought he didn't hear me. I feared he would. Slowly, I released my grip, my fingers brushing against his tattoos like remorse. But he caught them in a swift move, pulling my whole body toward him, let loose the blanket, the pizza box on the bed, and the mess of crumbs we left behind. "Yes, I heard you." He smiled, sweet like a devil, indulgent like the most benevolent God. "Welcome to my hell, Angela."

Puppet Bambi and Puppet Angela. He held the strings. I just walked.

Chapter 15: He's Dead

April 5, 2025 – A Tim Hortons on the outskirts of Saint-Laurent, QC

Pierre leans back on his seat, his eyes bloodshot, looking at nowhere at all. The black coffee in front of him has long gone cold. He fiddles with the wrapping paper of his donut. The chocolate glaze is dripping onto his fingers, and he mindlessly licks it off on autopilot.

The door of the coffee shop jingles open, and Pierre jerks back to life for a brief second, then falls to his lethargic state again. I imagine it must feel so comfortable sitting like that, never moving, never living, never breathing anymore, that he no longer has the desire to be human. Slurping my iced cappuccino, I shuffle my feet impatiently. My fate seems to be tied with one troublesome man to the next, like a string of sausages gone bad. Pierre sighs so loudly the cashier starts to look our way, cautious and ready to press the call button to the nearest police station. I kick his feet under the table and shoot him a warning glare. It is no use—he never looks my way or at my face to begin with. He groans for the umpteenth time in the short span of thirty minutes, and I wish for nothing more than release.

"Dead, huh? Jean-Paul. Dead. Weird. I've never associated Jean-Paul with something permanent like death. I mean, sure, the signs were there. He had this tendency to destroy himself. But pain is temporary." He finally utters a few coherent thoughts, stacked on top of each other like a toy building waiting for a collapse.

"Yeah. No one ever did, I suppose." I take another loud sip and stir the frozen coffee at the bottom of the plastic cup. "But he ended up that way."

"Suicide, you say?" Pierre rubs his brows.

"Yes." I bite the paper straw, chewing my words carefully before I spill out the make-believe garbage. "He jumped down the lake. High on drugs. You know, he was just so—"

"And what drugs was he on?" Pierre cuts to the chase. His tone is curt, like glass shattering, like a world falling apart. Like being lost. He taps his fingers erratically on the laminated table, chasing after multiple streams of doubt and suspicion, the what-ifs and scenarios leading to his twin's doomed ending.

"I don't know. He used a mix of plenty. Sometimes he was on X, other times he'd do either keta or LSD. I'm not an expert."

"Sure, you're not. But you have an awful lot of knowledge about his stash, don't you?" Pierre drops the question out of nowhere, which catches me by surprise. He glances at me, his eyes raise upward, the unfathomable brown titillating in the light, accentuated by the quivering dark lashes. He enunciates each word with a steady cadence: "It's a funny thing how the human brain works. Because your mind knows that you are lying, it sends the signals to every other part of your body. Heart palpitations, misspoken words, sweating, and like what you are showing now, throwing a dead cat on the table hoping I won't notice the truth. Hm?"

I hold a breath, then shake my head slowly. "When you're in the game, you have to play it."

"Heh. Is that so?"

He goes back to his indolent state, spreading his limbs over the bench. I nod at the cashier in apology and quiet agreement with her resentment. Pierre on call and Pierre off work are two different people sharing the same body. Neither is likeable. Neither like other people. I take the last two sips of my cappuccino, and stare at the frozen coffee like it holds the key to an escape route. Pierre plays with his donut, turning it round and round on the table, then he picks it up and bites half. His eyes look indeterminably ahead, searching for something, somewhere, someone—whatever has been irretrievably lost. Outside, in the parking lot, a uniformed officer is getting out of his patrol car and approaching the store. I pull the oversize hoodie—

Pierre's—to cover my face, holding the empty cup to my mouth, chanting the mantra, "This, too, shall pass."

But Pierre has other things on his mind. I should know better than to believe that Bambi's twin would settle for anything less than chaos and trouble.

"What were his last words?"

I bite my tongue, counting the steps of the officer, pricking my ears for the door's jingle.

"Hey, I said, what were his last words?"

The officer walks toward the counter, knocking on the wood surface, chatting away about the parking tickets he's issued in a booming voice. I cower to a corner. Pierre leans forward, visibly annoyed, ready to cause a ruckus.

"I said, what were his—" he speaks in a louder register, the repressed fury showing in his white knuckles gripping the edge of the table.

All heads turn toward our seats. I quickly cover his mouth, shushing him with difficulty, but he keeps pushing my hands back. The sheer force of his head is enough to drive me back down to my seat. He isn't satisfied with the outcome. Seeing me cower on the red bench, he lunges forward, grasping my arms, shaking my upper body, because he doesn't see a patient, a damsel in distress, or a poor woman growing weak at the knees; all Pierre can perceive at that moment is a person who just told him that his only family, his twin brother, the idol he has chased after for years, Jean-Paul Raymond, is dead. The truth comes crashing down on him like the flood of Genesis. He is still breathing one moment, then, before he can prepare the ark, the water has swallowed his whole body, drowned him in the devastating loneliness of being the one abandoned once again, this time, permanently.

"Pierre, calm down." I try to appease him. The bile rises in my throat, and before I can plead for mercy, I vomit the sweet, meager breakfast of donut and iced latte onto the table.

"What are you––?"

"Pierre, that's why I told you to calm down."

"Let's get you to the washroom first." He picks me up like a battered kitten.

His hand touches my stomach briefly, and the surprise shoots straight up his eyes. "You're pregnant."

I heave into his chest, quietly confirming his statement.

"With Bambi? I mean, with Jean-Paul?"

I say nothing. My tears are more than sufficient for a reply.

Pierre bites his lower lip; under the intense pain and hyperventilation, I can't figure out whether that harrowing look on his face is born from hatred or from mortal sympathy. He wraps one of my arms around his shoulders, picking up the pieces of me that are still living, and drags me gently toward the washroom. On the path strewn with boot marks and melted snow, the decadent aroma of caffeine is the only thing move us along. Pierre mutters under his breath, "Don't cry, don't cry, don't fucking cry."

And I say, as the tears are drying with the blasting heater in the store, "I'm not crying."

He cuts me off. "I know." We trudge along like two lost giants. He stands outside the washroom, waiting for me to come out. The sound of his polished Oxford shoes tapping against the linoleum floor is almost comforting, as if I, too, had a place to call home, to daydream that somewhere, there is a person waiting for me.

We clean up the stinking vomit, then gingerly go back to the same spot with disgust. The stage has moved to a new act, and we don't have the replacement for the props. The atmosphere is heightened with the heavy howling of the wind outside and the overcast, grey sky. Pierre slouches on the hard seat. Between him and me, people would think he is the crazy one. I pat his hands, palms up on the table, trying to console the child he still is and the child I had outgrown. "There were no last words. It was an overdose." As if I would tell him how Bambi died. As if I would let him into the world only I know. As if he deserves to hear the last words.

"Lies." He smirks, then, hissing the words with venom, says, "The moment you open your mouth, there comes the lies. You lie so much it isn't pathology anymore—you live the lies. Believe in them. Build your life on them. A special case of delusion, illusion, an egotistical nutcase. You think I can't see through the hate in your eyes? No last words. If he could talk to anyone, it would be me. Only me."

"Oh? And he left you in the end, didn't he?"

I ignore the risk, the departing officer, the suspicious stare of the cashier; my brain is lit up like a Christmas market at his phrase "only me," and the lights are having a seizure party. How could he? Of all people, he was the one who never had the right to the claim of Jean-Paul's life and soul. With measured calmness and calculating hatred, I dose my vengeance out, teaspoon after teaspoon:

"You said he abandoned you, but isn't it the other way around? He learned that this world never wanted him here. Where were you when he was in his darkest place? Where were you then? On your high horse, when he was stuck in the mud, struggling to find a way through? Oh, look at Doctor Pierre Raymond, a degree, a decent home, and a job where people beg to have his precious time. Jean-Paul had none of that. The only person, you say? Don't make me laugh. You deserve nothing. Yes, I lied. I looked the other way when my only friend died from an overdose. Even worse, I have faith in the unrealistic God of my days. The paradox gnaws at me as I pray because I know God isn't real, or maybe he is dead. But you know what the difference is between the two of us?"

I grasp Pierre's collar, looking him in the eyes, forcing him to see into the nightmare of that lake in the winter night of the Valentine's Day farewell. "Against the whole wide world, I stayed when nobody would."

Pierre doesn't move. His body goes slack. His facial muscles don't give an ounce of energy to protest, to express the proper anger that a normal person should. He looks at me through the lenses of his blue-light blocking glasses, tired, weary, exhausted to the marrow of his bones. "Are you done?" he finally says, monotonous and bored.

I let go of his collar, not knowing which demon I will be facing this time. The officer is walking back inside the store. Perhaps he forgot a donut for his colleague. Perhaps he needs to inquire about a few things—the weather, the safety of the neighborhood, the girl who assaulted an old, poor white man just yesterday and ran away into the night. I sit down, counting from one to an eternity of numbers, waiting for an ending.

"No one abandoned anyone. He left first. Mind if I smoke?"

"The store doesn't allow smoking. Also, I'm pregnant."

"Ah, yes. Politics. Your pregnancy has nothing to do with me."

"It's for the public health. You're a doctor. You should know that. I suppose you don't want to care for a woman who's disturbing your normalcy." I turn my head away, not wanting to look at that uncanny, familiar face for another second.

He said, "Don't cry." We try our best to hold back the waterfall, but the scale is tipping as Pierre's fingers tremble with the unlit cigarette. "I didn't choose to be a doctor to sacrifice my smoking privilege." Pierre struggles to put the cigarette in his mouth without lighting it up, ignoring the critical stares of the clientele, and continues tapping his fingers on the tabletop. The gestures I know all too well, carved too deep on my skin, my soul. "How much do you know about Jean-Paul?"

"I know that he is Bambi."

"Then you know nothing at all."

"How much do you know about Jean-Paul then?" I cock my head, provoking him. "There's no Jean-Paul. There never was."

"Jean-Paul was the reason I chose to be a psychiatrist." He flicks the cigarette as if he's dropping ashes. "He promised me he'd come back once he found the reason. I promised him I would stay sane until then."

"The reason? For what?"

"This. All of this." Pierre gestures vaguely at the world surrounding him. The suffering smile on his face gnaws at my heart and I want to scream into the void of my agony. Anything to stop life from happening. "Why do you think the world is such a mess?"

"I don't know. Because people are shit?" I turn away. One more second and my skeleton will break from the overflowing hurt. A tangy taste blooms on my tongue. Blood. "Why do you think?"

"Jean-Paul said he just had to find out. Sitting there on the floor, holding our mother's cold hand in his as she drowned in overdosed bliss, he told me the God we believed in was either a messed up one or He misunderstood how much suffering a person can hold. Do you know the theory that God was a creature built from chaos? That He wasn't perfect, and He built humans based on his own image, so we are the very picture of his faults."

"I didn't know any of that. Bambi said he wasn't a believer."

"I guess he'd say that. He told me it was God's first time creating such a species as humans. Greed, sloth, lust, etc.—we are the projection of what He is, and we try to be better than He who created us. Such was Jean-Paul's theory. That was why we stumbled and fell. He said it was like throwing rocks to the ground, hoping it would build a tower. But the rocks couldn't stand on each other. So the tower remains a concept, a pillar of faith that we look at to remind ourselves that no matter what, life is worth living, and we can keep going another day. After all, he said, you can't build something on the foundation of nothing."

"He said that?" I ask, my eyes burning, my lips curling into an unconscious smile. The memory of him laughing in the cascading dusk, his back against the flaming sky, drips down my cheeks in streams. How much love do I still have left?

"Yeah. He said lots of stuff. Crazy stuff. The church would've exorcised him if the priests caught him saying them. The antichrist. Judas without the little faith, orthodox or not. A man like him would never leave this life without shoving two middle fingers at the rest of us," Pierre scoffs. His vacant eyes glint softly with a wan light of hope and yearning, but it shuts off as quickly as it starts.

"He once said something about how the whales would stop singing," I blurt out. Everything is moving on, but the two of us are stuck inside the life of dead man who has turned immortal.

"He did, huh? Scientists say that the heat in the ocean is hurting marine life. The whales stop singing because they're hungry. The food is getting scarce. We're not much different. Whales or humans, we chase after the thought of living one more day."

"That's not what Bambi said." I stir the melting iced coffee, mulling over Pierre's words. Something doesn't feel quite right, like a misshapen puzzle in an otherwise perfect frame. A wrong color in a vibrant painting. A muted palette when someone is trying to show a neon-colored portrait. "He told me we'll all stop singing one day."

"Isn't it the same thing?" Pierre asks, not quite understanding what I'm saying. A spark of intrigue gleams in his dark irises. But it isn't enough. Though Pierre's face mirrors Bambi's, the fathomless abyss of darkness in Bambi's eyes is not there. The tantalizing brown in Pierre's eyes is sharp and cold, but it remains warm and palpitates with the will to suffer. Bambi's bewitching dark gaze wouldn't be that mundane. He would make a person's skin crawl until they knelt at his feet; the liquid darkness flowing from his crescent eyes when he laughed was so pretentious and fake it commanded the attention of the entire space.

"No," I reply. A part of me turns quiet. A knot is coming loose. I let go of my grip on something invisible. "It isn't. I don't know what the difference is, but it isn't."

"He left. Well, I should've guessed this ending. Heh. Always the quitter." Pierre's finger-tapping on the tabletop grows violent and vigorous to the point of a lunatic's episode. I turn to search for the officer. He isn't there anymore. The cashier glances at us occasionally, but she isn't paid enough to care. "He left. Oh God, he left. What do I do now?" He cries, slumping onto the table, his face stuck to the chocolate donut.

I watch him unraveling slowly, like a scroll of paper falls open to reveal the monstrous secret it hides inside the many folds of wisdom and intellectual preaching. Pierre wants a reason to live. He holds onto hope because there is nothing left for him to do. And that hope has abandoned him, because one cold night, it found the world far too tasteless, too bland, too pretentious for its taste. A dish served without spice. The first bite brings bile and disgust. I see him wince. I watch him burn. So brilliant is the dance. So devastating is the longing. Pierre and Jean-Paul. Me and Bambi. The three of us keep walking toward the end of night. I look at the last snow outside the store window. Spring will soon be here. Bambi didn't live long enough to see the flowers grow. My lips are wet. The salty taste spreads in my mouth like sparks of fire in the dark.

Bambi, you said you weren't living. But you left behind a legacy.

Chapter 16: I Will Tell You How to Die

March 31, 2024 – Downtown Toronto, a modern condominium, cluttered with carving tools and knives

I stumbled inside Bambi's apartment, trying to keep my brain focused on bringing one foot forward. The key refused to make love with the lock, and the world turned upside down. The bubbly feeling inside me swelled up, and I laughed, not knowing why, then laughed some more because I didn't know the cause for the first laughter.

The hallway was eerily silent. The well-respected neighbors weren't home yet. Or they were, but wouldn't care for a lunatic crawling outside somebody's door. I knocked once, twice. He wasn't there. My face slid down the smooth surface of the door. The giggles poured out in a torrent. Like rain. Like a flood. Like a madness of apocalyptic, hysterical jokes gone haywire. Where was Bambi? I didn't have an inkling as to his whereabouts. The club? The restaurant? The café down on Bloor with the unfunny joke, *"Je suis mermaid?"* I knocked on the door again, calling his name. "Knock, knock. Bambi?" My senses left me bereft and hanging. The happiness burst and sadness rushed in. The floodgate opened and there was nothing to stop the waterfall to drown me in its overwhelming strength: the power of the thought that I was abandoned at last, like the girl last week, or the girl before her. He wouldn't stay for anyone, or anything, because he never believed in a race that could end itself on sadness. I howled, punching the door now, a sudden urge to see his face, his body, his silver-tipped hair—anything to confirm that he was still alive—or I might die in that moment.

The thought sparked up in my brain with glee. If I died now, he would remember me forever. Didn't he say that he would choose to relive the last five seconds of his ex's death eternally, to submerge himself in that pain like a fucking addiction running in his veins? Would he remember me that way? Would he add my last five seconds to his repertoire of despair and agony, carving my body into every muscle of his brain until his eyes saw nothing in the outside world but my face, my smile, my tears streaming down my cheekbones as I caressed him, telling him that he was forgiven from the day he was born? Or will it be just like any other day, and I was just another fatality on his bloodied hands? Why should I stop myself from becoming the one thing he wouldn't forget? I crawled, trying to get up. It was hard to maintain a balanced pose when my brain was convincing me that I was levitating. The cocaine hit the hardest on an empty stomach and after three sleepless nights. Wiping my nose, I dragged my feet to the elevator. Going up two more levels, then climbing the exit staircase, taking a jump down the twentieth floor, and I could rest, permanently. It would only hurt a bit when my bones shattered on the concrete floor, but the peace would come, like cotton candy melting in my mouth, so sweet and decadent I could taste its temptation. Bambi was the only reason I stayed.

"Bambi, I want to live. I want to live. I fucking want to live."

The thought only carried me to the elevator's door. I fell to the luxurious carpeted floor, bawling, scratching the velveteen surface. The bile rose in my throat, and before I could run or even stand up, my whole soul poured out from my mouth. It stank. Filthy. The chunks of the beings I ate to continue my being on earth. I lay in my own vomit, laughing at nothing and everything at the same time.

"My, my, look who's coming to see me?"

A familiar voice rang from the realm of my unconscious. My arms searched in the white blindness, looking for someone I knew would be there to catch me. The name lost amidst the sea of my foggy memory. Who would still be here? Who was leaving? My lips moved, but no sound came out. What was my reason for coming here? I no longer knew. No longer wanted to know.

"Angie, pull yourself together."

The voice blurred into the waning ceiling lights. I wanted to tell it that I tried. That I couldn't. That this was the best I could do in that moment. An empty feeling hurled my stomach. My feet were straight up again. The earth was underneath, and the sky was above once more. I mumbled something along the lines of, "I want to go home," but only a string of gibberish came out. My left arm was slung onto a firm shoulder. My waist was held tightly against the perfumed body, warm and hard to the touch. The force dragged me forward, encouraged me with a soft, "One more step, that's right, one more step," until we reached the door of unit 1802. This time, the key made sweet, longing love to the lock, and the door swung open.

The force brought me into the night of the living room. The floor was scattered with carving knives and molding clay. The smell of paint was pungent, and I retched, my stomach churning on the obnoxious air. I was flung onto the plush velvet sofa; the cushions swallowed me in a loving embrace. In the hazy light filtered through my blurry eyes, the Venus statue stood shyly near the TV set. Her face was carved up. Her hair was chopped up in a strange, ugly cut. The wreath on her head was made of thorny vines and garbage. If it wasn't for the lush body and the nimble, pliant fingers, nobody would see her as the goddess that she was.

"Beautiful, isn't she?" the voice said. The lighter sparked with a sharp click, and the scent of cigarette smoke filled the room. I fancied seeing the long, tender fingers stroking her face, drawing on that blank canvas my eyes, my lips, my nose. *Please let the prophecy be me*, I begged no god at all.

"Do you know the story of Venus, Angie?" The voice relayed the tales of old in its defeating peace. Deep and low like a cradle made of dark earth, leaving a rumble in its quake, the voice drew out Bambi's existence. "Before there was Venus, we had wenos. To have love is to fuel desire. We must kindle a flame to build a forest fire. Such was the Venus in my eyes."

He stopped, drawing in smoke, exhaled with a languorous sigh, then continued.

"There was no Venus until people created the myth of Aphrodite, a goddess born from a male's part. Masculine and feminine intertwined to create the most beautiful existence humans could ever imagine. But what was she before godhood? The life she would have led if the sea foam didn't bear her to the shore, and unveil such innocence to the beastly eyes of humans. Angie, did you know that Venus is a goddess for prostitutes? It's true."

He chuckled softly, then picking up a chisel, Bambi carved the frame of an eye on the clay statue. "Desire. Love. Who's to say if what you feel is real, or just a sweet piece of your delusion? Tempting, isn't it, to think that a word is powerful enough to heal the world."

My cheeks were wet. I couldn't feel whether it was tears or the remnants of my vomit. What was I crying for? My life wasn't as sad as Venus's. The bubbly feeling rose again. A cold sensation pierced my skin. The towel glided gently all over my face. It was black, then light; cold, then warm; rotting scent, then the sandalwood cologne. I yanked the collar in front of me, slopping kisses to every inch of skin I could find, hoping it was the lips, the eyes, the nose of my own Venus.

"Angie. Whose drugs did you buy?"

The rough hands ran through my chopped-up hair, pampered my head until I lulled in a temporary slumber, and when my guard slackened, they pulled me hard until the pain jerked me into heat. "I said, whose drugs did you buy this time?"

"Mar-us," I slurred, giggling as the bubbly sensation burst in my stomach like little balloons.

"Is that so?" Bambi caressed my cheeks and I leaned into the comfortable, cool feeling. He loved my soft cheeks because the supple flesh reminded him of the living. But my cheeks were sagging. The feathery fingertips danced on my pallid skin. I could hear the music booming in my brain. "You asked Markus for the drugs?" He demanded, the repressed anger coming out as an exasperated sigh.

"'m not as-ing no one. Saul said—"

"Ah, so now there's Saul, too," he chirped in fake surprise, so cruelly bright I could even see the fury behind my cloud of intoxication. "Look what I've got. A Babylon whore. How much lower could you sink, my Venus?" He gritted each word. I should fear. Run. Feel the danger. But in the fever of sweet poison, I just laughed.

"Saul said you 'ould be 'appy. Aren't you 'appy? Why aren't you laughing? Bambi, Bambi, Bambi—" I choked, then gurgled the air out as the words rolled on my tongue, half like thorns, half like venom in my blood trying to force itself out. "There's no one else but you. All alone, there's only been you. What to do, Bambi? Saul said—" I thought I was laughing still, but the tears kept flowing, and I was bawling on his dark shirt, my snot dripping onto his shoulders until the luxurious wool was soaked, and the sandalwood cologne vaporized, leaving only the stink of my existence.

"What did he say?" Bambi cradled my head on his shoulder, patting my head. The hand felt so much like peace it hurt. Like a thousand knives stabbing at the heart. Like needles piercing underneath the skin.

"'aul 'aid if I 'on't get in the 'ame, he'd off 'ou. Then 'ispose 'ou in the Mu'um of Corpses." I clawed at his back, finally cracking open. There was no power left in me to howl, to bellow, to shout the pain into the night. Only an open mouth, hanging breath, and a silent cry after the quake of destruction. My tears fell without a cause. My existence remained in place, perpetually, and I laughed in madness and folly, begging him, "I 'an't live 'ithout 'y Bam'i. Bam'i, Bam'i, Bam'i." The sound of his name echoed in my ear like a wake-up call I forgot to turn off when all I wanted was to sleep there forever. "Bam'i, I want to live."

"Then live," he whispered. His collar reeked of smoke and the pungent scent of sandalwood cologne. "What's ever changed with that? What's happened to the you and me?" He chuckled and the vibration from his tremulous breath caressed my broken body with the tenderness of a doomed soul. I think of the flood when God was angry with humans and how grotesque they had become when they left heaven; my mind already knew the answer to Bambi's question: we had grown up and were forsaken.

"I can't." My senses came back to me in gradual waves of pain. I ached for a way out, yet my hands kept reaching for Bambi's, unwilling to escape.

"Why?"

"Because..." I pushed him back, holding his face in my sweaty hands, still wet with vomit. My eyes searched for his amidst the mist. Like the last hope. Like the lost hope. "Because you are my life."

The saliva dripped down my chin. It tasted bitter. The pungent smell of vomit stank the whole place, or rather, I was smelling my own decay. I wanted to tell him how much it meant to love like I did—throwing myself into the flame, not because it was beautiful, but because I could, and I would a thousand times again, as long as he was the wood. Bambi wiped my sweat and tears away, hushing me with kisses and tender glances of regret. Like memento mori. Like giving up. Like surrendering the only salvation left. He reached for the remote of the vinyl player, turned it on, the same old song. I wanted to protest, but before the words had the chance to come out, he laid his lips on mine. Gently at first, then the attack grew aggressive. His deep breaths warmed my nostrils. His lips tasted bitter, like burned cigarettes in an ashtray.

There was no break, no space in between. Just pure, singular desire in the fervent passion of him chasing after my tremulous flesh and bone as I shattered to pieces for him to exist. Love could only be this cruel. Loss could only shine this bright. I knew then that I would never have him again. He was never mine to hold. Just a stranger passing through my open doors, teaching me how to suffer, telling me not to trust another stranger as he left for his train. In the sad melody of the unknown song, I cried and cried in the language only I knew. I wondered if my teardrops would be as beautiful as his if I crystalized and watched them under the microscope. It was then that I understood his reason when he cut himself just to see what lies beneath the tears. The elegance of the patterns and the branching of the droplet made him forget there was such a thing called suffering in this world.

"Angela." Bambi touched his forehead against mine, his eyes holding me against the backdrop of the world outside. "Let me tell you how to die."

"No, I don't want to. I don't want to. I never want to." I pleaded for my innocence, begging for the chance of a suspended sentence.

"Hush, my little angel." He smiled down at me, so sweet, so tender. A last word. A will. The wounded beast's death rattle breathing. "My wenos. Be still. Let me deliver you from the cold foam of my Poseidon heart."

It was the longest night of my life. The night that I would relive again and again, like a purgatory for a crime I never knew I committed. I lay on top of him, listening to his heartbeat, counting the seconds he was living. My fingers tapped on his chest. My hair fell loosely on his shoulders. He twirled the locks around his index finger, giving them kisses in between the tales. The myths of Greek gods and goddesses. The deities of the pagans. Religions that were built only to be destroyed. Meanings changed to fit the wars. The record paused, then repeated itself. "Did you know Venus had no original myth from the start? People only adore something when they're desperate for glory and victory." No, I didn't. I never knew the world as it was then, and as it would be later. Nothing stayed the same. In the moonlight, the Venus statue gleamed with an enduring sorrow. Her blank face started to form, and strangely, in that blurring line between the real and the fake, she resembled the me that I lost. And the him that I had let go of.

Chapter 17: When You Love Someone, You Kill Them

March 31, 2024 – Bambi's condo, the living room

"Tell me, then. How did it all begin?"

I whispered the question into Bambi's bare chest. The singer droned on, *Jos liedelle käy käteni.* He played with my hair, twirling the clumsy, chopped up locks, lost in his thoughts. The room shone in the moonlight and the city's bright, neon lights. It was as trashy as it was beautiful. He patted my back, brushing his fingers on my neck, half careless, half intentional; his fingers held my head in place. No escape route.

"Maybe it began with my name. I wasn't Bambi. Or, before I turned into Bambi, I was Jean-Paul Raymond."

"Why did you become Bambi?"

"I got tired of being Jean-Paul. There were only so many times you could wake up and find the naloxone kit for your mom. Or drag your little brother out of the trailer park house when her high kicked in. Life was never easy. It still isn't as Bambi. But Jean-Paul got the worst of it. Jean-Paul died happily, you know, so Bambi could find out what it means to be alive."

"Did Bambi find it though?" I inhaled the sharp scent of sandalwood. My stomach churned and my heart burned with a helpless feeling. I couldn't change the past. No matter what I did, Jean-Paul could never grow up now.

"Bambi. Yeah, Bambi was a jerk, right? Always making mistakes, telling himself and others that he wasn't perfect. The right excuse for all the wrong things. At least he had love. He once believed that love alone could cure everything, even the sickness unto death."

"Does he still believe that?"

Bambi held his breath for so long I thought he had stopped existing. His glassy eyes grew vacant. The cars outside screeched to allow the blaring ambulance to pass through. Someone shouted a curse. The neighbors were coming back. A door slammed shut. The prisons closed their doors. We were trapped inside our tombs, designed to neatly fit our sorrows and the pain we learned to endure.

"Does he still?" I repeated, my tongue tasting the bitter irony of my unanswered question. Why did I ever hope Bambi would be different?

"Love is powerful. Will always be, until one day, it won't. Saul. I met him when I first moved to Toronto. The circle I was in back then—the bands, the backstage madness, the thought that we were free to live as we wanted—Saul fit right in. He was the enabler. It started with alcohol, then marijuana, plenty of stashes of harmless recreational relaxers. They kept my mind afloat. And it came as no surprise at all that the ecstasy filtered in, like a fucking natural evolution."

"But you tried to avoid it?"

"Why should I?" Bambi scoffed at my frowning gaze. "Everyone was in it. I was neither the one without sin, nor the one who had the right to condemn and throw the first stone. Jumping in, what was the harm? It felt good. Get rid of life. Mind if I smoke?"

"No. Go on." I kissed his chest and let my lips linger there for a brief moment before turning away, but he held me in place, so tenderly, like a prayer. A plea for mercy. A cry for help. And I stayed.

"I met Lucille at the club. She was Saul's whore. Somewhat like you in appearance, and in the way your eyes shone with desperation and contempt for the life you tried to hold onto. Beautiful in the sadness you both wore like a mourning dress. I loved that. Grieving for life before life ended. Fucked up in the head. I took her in. She was an interior designer and put up quite a lovely nest for both of us. I thought that was it. The meaning I chased after. Life was meant to love and be loved in return. But Saul had other ideas."

"Saul also asked her to traffic drugs?"

"Traffic humans."

The words threw a dead weight on both of us. The suffocating feeling gripped my throat like a vine. I wanted to tell him it was wrong, that there was justice, the laws would find a way to make Saul pay and whatnot. But my brain yanked me back from the sheer inertia of hypocrisy. Wasn't I planning on taking Saul's hands, thinking it would be fine, thinking as long as I suffered, Bambi wouldn't? Thinking—I bit my lip, tasting the tangy, metallic blood of anger and the bitter sarcasm of it all—that love would cure anything.

"Lucille thought it was only one time. Getting the girls to the estate of some famous names. It was simpler on paper than on the road. She did one trip. That one trip broke her. You never know how innocence can break a human far more cruelly than vice and beastly sins ever could. It was the same as it is now: Lucille had the choice. She could do it or be free, and she watched me descend to Saul's darkness. Me, whom she loved so much. Me, whom she'd blabbered on and on about the future together. Me, who was her everything. Then one night, when she was high on drugs, the carload of girls she drove crept back one by one; a haunting, if anyone can see ghosts. Heh, I thought she was stronger than that. And it's always the fucking problem with me: I always overestimate the strength of a drowning person; never once have I thought about the possibility that the person herself needed help. Or even if she wanted to be saved in the last moment. I kept swinging my life, dangling between the gigs at different bars downtown at night and the junkies' cave during the day. Looking back, maybe I was also drowning. I am still. One night, when I came back from my usual gig at the Grossman, I saw Lucille outside the balcony, staring ahead without seeing a damn thing in her eyes. She sat on the windowsill of our apartment, looking at each item we bought together, saying, 'That's it, just let yourself go,' and threw herself out the window. Mind if I turn the volume up?"

He turned it up anyway. To hide the crack in his voice and the hitched breathing he tried to suppress. His grip on my nape was so hard it left bruises and red marks for days to come, and I yearned for it to burn there like a scar no amount of time could erase. My king with no crown. His suffering testified for the battles he tried to save, because Bambi and I both knew then, as we know forever, ashes couldn't build back the world he could live inside.

"Angela, remember the time we talked about love and goodness?"

"Yeah, what about it?"

"That time, when I was so adamant about the world being cruel, you said—" Bambi paused. His breathing became ragged, like a cry from a tormented beggar. A dream turned into hell's nightmare. Sharp teeth hidden in the layers of a warm embrace. "You said humans are good at heart."

He laughed. But the sound that came out was so devastating I'd rather have watched him cry instead. Tears would have been so much better than the crazed laughter on the mask of a person trying to not let the agony win.

"Don't laugh." I choked out the desperate plea, bawling in his hurt. "Don't laugh when you're so broken. Don't be a stranger. Bambi. Don't."

"Angela, when you love someone, and the love is so high, so fucking godly your mortal body can't contain it, you must kill them. Destroy them before the world has the chance to do it."

He cradled my face in his palms; his tender gaze was soft, the gentle brown color seemed to undulate in the light, and I was trapped there, thinking we were the only two people living in this city of cold gusts peppered with snow storms. Our hearts didn't have the same beat—they never did—but both of us understood far too much how lonely it would be when the night came and the stars were all dead. I nodded, simply because I would do anything to make the pain in his eyes lessen.

He lit another cigarette; the red ember glowing in the cascading twilight made our situation surreal. I watched him take a long drag and exhale the white smoke into the thickening, cold air of winter. The scent of oak lingered on his neck, haunting me like a ghost I knew I would never have the chance to forget. My teardrops etched the beauty of sadness on his thorn and vine tattoos. The lyrics of the song sang from his skin, and I thought we both were mourning the inevitable ending we took for granted. No one else would understand the world of the abandoned children, Bambi had said. I snuggled close to his collarbone; a forest of perfume and cologne invaded my nose until it bled. Synthetic roses and fabricated leatherette, the suede on some strange women's skin as they hugged him in his feverish moments of passion, the faint trace of wild bluebell, expensive because without the price tag, it was nothing but alcohol and chemicals. I wept for the lost sandalwood and the oak, the spice that burned my eyes when he first held me in his arms, and that warm, comforting peace when I asked him if I were another temporary in his permanency, to which he said no. "Bambi, your scent has gone. Your collar now smells like cigarettes and cheap booze." I crumbled his shirt's hem, fully sobered up.

"Is that so? Which scent do you like? Cigarette and booze or the bourgeoisie stuff before?" He leaned his head on mine; his voice was soft like a lullaby.

"I like you."

"That's hardly an answer." Bambi chuckled, stroking my thighs, which were wasting away as my body and mind kept rejecting hunger and the desire to eat.

"I like when you're happy."

"Like when I sprayed on those fake scents and chased after girls? I was sort of happy then."

"No, like when you're you, sitting in that rental apartment, or in that dirty studio downtown, waiting for the night to come, and your whole body smelled like wood."

"Ah, that. I haven't used that scent in a long while. I thought you'd forgotten."

"Can't. Who would forget a scent that teaches them what love is?" I smiled, and in his eyes, I knew I looked pathetic. A fool on the stage of a Greek tragedy. "I guess it's only me."

"Angela, do you know why I like girls with rose-scented perfume?" Bambi went on a different tangent, which took me by surprise. I stared at him, wild-eyed, ready for the worst, hoping for the best.

"Why?" The hurt came before his answer because I was used to it. I was never anyone's choice, even in the last minute, and I still hoped he would say I was the reason.

"I saw you in the bar that time, standing by your friend's side. Dearest Cecilia who is resting in peace now, blessed be her fate. You had that look on your face that screamed you wanted nothing else but to leave the noisy dance floor and go back to your peaceful home. I thought it was fun." Bambi snubbed the dying cigarette and lit another, shrugging his shoulders slightly in the darkening room.

"You thought I was worth playing," I stated, because it was the truth everybody kept saying to me. The truth I refused to believe in, even if Bambi said it himself, even if it were self-evident. Life needed less to live happily.

"No, I thought you were brave. I thought I would watch to see how long you could keep that farce with your orange juice and your ginger dance steps. I thought, why the hell did you not fucking leave, because the whole place was a filthy pigsty. I thought…" Bambi choked; in the dark, I couldn't see if he were laughing or crying. His tremulous voice showed both emotions. "I thought, if this place was a battlefield, then you must be the only rose blooming."

"I —"

"Don't say anything because I know how stupid it sounds, then or now. But Angela, I hope there's still enough faith in you to trust that I did want to save you from the club's grimy, dirty hands. I tried my best, and I failed spectacularly. Believe me, I did."

Bambi broke down like a shattered house in an earthquake. He let the ember glow until the red, flickering light turned to ashes and fell to his feet, burning his bare skin. I wondered if he felt the pain, or even recognized the burn. I was speechless, tolerating his suffering because since the day we met, I had thought that shouldering his agony was the only act of love that would keep him alive. What did he just say? He hoped that there was still enough faith in me. With trembling hands, I held the shivering body of the man I loved with all the force I could gather in my mortal life. I picked up the fragments of his fragile hopes and dreams as he cried about the many wasted chances he gave me to escape. Bambi never looked so small. I let him rest his head on my bosom. My heartbeat calmed the monster within him.

The snowflakes flew by our windows, and the sky was an unforgiving white. The world was never meant for people like him. I was but a counterfeit blessing, and it was comprehensible to the true believers, because Bambi never trusted God.

"What if I told you my faith in you was never lost?" I patted his head to quiet the howling in his mind. I knew he was weaving the nightmare out of his fears and hurt.

"It just means that you never had faith in me in the beginning," Bambi scoffed.

"But Bambi, no, Jean-Paul, you said you would give me all the hopes in the world, and I would give you my absolute faith. That's a fair bargain."

"Have you had enough of them now? The hopes?"

"What about you? Have you tasted my absolute faith?"

He was silent for so long I thought he was sleeping. The snowflakes whirled and danced to the end of the world. It was as beautiful as it was grotesque. Who knew how many people were buried under the innocent whiteness out there? Bambi caressed my waist, gently at first, then he grasped it until I yelped. "What?"

"Angela, let's break up."

"It isn't time yet, is it?" The plan crossed my mind. I turned my head, avoiding his scorching gaze. The flame in his eyes was so cruel, so bright, that I thought to kill it would be the most hideous crime ever committed. I was mad. Maybe Ophelia was happier with her ending. Maybe Juliet was the happiest one among living humans of her time. Maybe I should revere the doomed romance because the real ones hurt enough to make me think of hell.

Bambi sat there, quiet in his requiem, embracing his hurt because out of all his life, the agony of living was the last thing who understood his loneliness. Another cigarette flickered in the night, then he said:

"Come back to my hometown. That's where Saul's human trafficking turf is. I paid a lot for that information. Heh. Don't cry. I'll give you something sweet. Angela. Find a doctor called Pierre Raymond. He's my twin brother. He must be at some hospital in Laval. That's the address on his latest letters.

Check all the hospitals for sure."

"Yes." I played with his fingers. The calloused tips were hard to the touch, but the flesh underneath the rough skin was still warm and tender. A dark ring was inked on his ring finger. I knew it wasn't a promise he made to me, but one can't refuse the temptation of hope.

"Pull Saul in. I'll leave my testament and my will in your hands. Suffer a bit of pain. Make him think he still has the full power. Then, as Venus destroyed mankind with her beauty, you know how to kill him with your purity. Understand, Angela?"

"Yes."

"Good. Pierre will be a good pawn in your hand. Turn him whichever way you need to. Discard him when you find it necessary. One last thing."

"Yes?"

"Angie, be free. Whatever you do after, be so fucking free that the world must envy you from its chain on Atlas's shoulders." He smiled at me, and that was all it took to set the plan into action.

"*Historiaan jää, jos perin varmaa pelaisin.* Right?" I said, my voice blurred with snot and the will to change a foregone conclusion.

"You understand that?" He laughed. It was carefree and wild. It was almost happiness, because it was fleeting and gone the moment my eyes caught his lips curling in the flash of the moment.

"I don't know. You tell me. You're the one who said nothing we ever do will leave a mark in history, so—fill in the blank. And I learned the song, Bambi. I learned enough to say, *Minä rakastan sinua koko sydämestäni.* Bambi, this time, you can go back to the place where there's no suffering."

He looked at me, hurt, surprised, then smiled with defeat. "And I also love you, Angela, with all my heart, my history—my real and my fake. Thank you for being the accomplice in my selfish deliverance."

We slept to the singer's mourning of a love confession. This should have been the beginning, but we left it in the middle. It could have been the ending, but we moved it forward. After all, who else was there on this azure globe floating in the dark nothingness but us two? My hands held onto his, the only living person in a city polluted with lights and positivity so bright it was nauseating. In his deep slumber, I watched him fall. Peace was never so beautiful as it was then on his face, eyes closed, stone cold. *It will be alright, Bambi. This time, I will kill.*

Chapter 18: Going Back

April 7, 2025 – Montreal Chinatown, a tea shop

Pierre slurps the sickeningly sweet milk tea with an annoying loud sound, as if he wants the whole crowd to notice him, get angry, and even better, remember him as he is. Unwashed hair. Unshaven beard. Unkempt shirt. He is one apartment away from becoming the after image of a homeless man. That is the least of his worries now.

He hasn't reported to the hospital for three days. And he doesn't plan on ever reporting back to it again.

"What are you thinking?" I ask, biting a big chunk of the spongy castella. He looks wildly all around the tea shop, squirming in his seat like a junkie without his daily dose.

"Pierre. What are you—?"

"Hush. They're coming." He shoves his whole hand against my mouth, rough and careless. A wire inside is short-circuited. The glasses can't hide his derailment. "The police are coming for mom. Jean-Paul. Where's Jean-Paul?"

"I told you he's dead."

"Maman, Jean-Paul is playing hide-and-seek again." Pierre grabs the panda cookies on the table, throws them all in his mouth and starts chewing like a meat-grinder. "He's been bad, maman. He's been bad to me."

"Pierre, nobody's here. They all died." I stop him from stuffing his mouth with more cookies and milk tea. He is about to explode. His eyes bulge out of their sockets. His lips trickle with cookie crumbs and the tea he couldn't swallow. "No one else is here, Pierre. There's only you and me."

"He said," Pierre tries to speak through the chunks of cookies, "He said he'd come and get me. Said he'd take me away. Said he'd save me. I can't live here any longer. I can't put up with the fucking hospital, the suicidal victims, the darkness when everyone is gone and I'm all alone in that dark corridor, screaming without being heard, crawling without moving an inch forward. Help me. I said, help me."

Pierre yells, then falls to the table face-first. His eyes are wide open, but what they see isn't the place or the people there anymore. A trap. A cage with teeth. A constant nightmare on repeat every time he wakes up. I touch his clenching fists, uncurl each finger, blowing on the brutally red crescent shapes on his palm, thinking Bambi left behind a good pawn, saying, "You have me now, don't you, Dr. Pierre? I was also abandoned."

He lifts his face, tear-stained, snot dripping, hazy and gullible in his madness. The same features, the same piercing eyes, but his face lacks that distinguishing quality to befit the grandiose suffering and agony his twin brother used to carry. A lack of flavor; Pierre's pale, white skin and tender fingers, with the tips soft to the touch, tell a history of living a sheltered life. Not as sheltered as a rich kid, and not as fucked up as one, but he has been through the normal path: failed a few times, wounded once or twice, nothing too deep, but neither are the wounds shallow. He has barely enough to qualify as someone who would understand when his patients confess their pain. And it stops at that. He never lost something as great as me: he never lost the only reason holding him on the ground, nailing him to this bitter hell, forcing him to live against the odds. I despise it, how I detest his superficial sadness disguised as the apocalypse he convinced himself to believe.

Still, he is so sweet in his agony, I can almost taste the cotton candy of his pain on my tongue. "Jean-Paul—did he ever say he missed me? Loved me? Thought about me before he died? Was I ever important enough for him to have a second thought about? Hesitation, right, he must hesitate, when he..." Pierre's firm grip leaves bruises on my wrists. The quivering voice grows stronger in its delusional belief. The faith in nothingness, fueled by his ideology and the idol of the twin brother he holds onto as his salvation and anchor in the whirlwind of this chaotic world. For a person to tie his entire existence to another's whimsical impulse, Pierre has been a lost cause since the beginning. I want to tell a lie, that Bambi—no, Jean-Paul—did think about him, consider his love, waver a little bit, before taking the final step to end his misery. Perhaps it would make me a good person. Or worse, it would turn me into one of those hypocrites that I hate so much, who think that everything happens for a reason, and the people left behind are innocent little lambs waiting for God's merciful hands. My mind screams, *Fuck it*, and my lips quiver with the cruel truth scorching on my tongue, ready to shatter whatever is left of this pitiful man's sanity. I shake my head, leaving my hands to his abuse, loving the pain, knowing I will get more from it than he ever will. "He never mentioned anyone. I only learned about you when I was admitted to the Laval hospital. It was a sad, sudden affair. He was—" I pause, hitching my voice, exhaling a low, broken chuckle. "He was killed." Yes, he was killed by his guilt, his conscience, his apathy, and the faith that even if he woke up another day, the world would not be any different. And he was killed by me, by the love I professed undyingly in those halcyon days, by the constant, useless reminder I whispered in his ears, that he was forgiven.

He was killed because life wasn't gentle enough and humans never learn the true meaning of the teaching "love thy neighbor."

I glance at Pierre through the veil of my eyelashes. Every act needs a cue. Every actress needs to gauge the reaction of the spectators. And true to my expectations, Pierre quiets down, ready for the next spotlight, the next installment to catapult the plot to its crescendo. He screws up his eyes, a brief suspicion glinting through. "Killed? Jean-Paul? Killed? Why? By who?"

The bullet has always been locked and loaded. He just willingly pulls the trigger. I scoff internally, faking a white teardrop rolling in the cinematic act of the magnificent show. "He was asked to do drug trafficking and human trafficking. We called it 'playing the game.' Bambi and I—"

"Jean-Paul."

"Jean-Paul and I—" I chew the foreign name's syllables unwillingly.

Somehow, the feminine nickname suited Bambi's frivolous personality more than that stuck-up French name ever did "—were forced to help that man you saw, Saul. It started with drugs, then it escalated into humans. Goods needed to be delivered; that was all. But *bam*—Jean-Paul couldn't stand to see the innocence destroyed, so one day, he downed what he was supposed to deliver, overdosed himself, and…" I bite my lip, letting the blood drip down to the table, mixing with the tears, drawing the portrait Bambi taught me so well. "Angela, hit him where he hurts the most. Never hesitate. When he grows weak, you attack all the more. Strike him down so you can stand. Remember, you're free."

"Jean-Paul was trafficking drugs." Pierre leans back, the right expression, the correct line. He falls into the role without me forcing him.

"And humans. That's why he couldn't bear—"

"And humans. A humanist trafficking humans. How? Why?"

"Because Saul was…"

"Threatening him?" Pierre fixes me with a wild glare. The suspicion is shaking. The faith is rising strong. *Go for it, Angie.* Bambi smiled indulgently. *Go for the dying prey.*

"Saul said he'd kill me if Bambi wouldn't agree to play along." I sniffle, the tears flowing in a silent stream. My lips are bruised, but the pain still does not show its full glory. I pinch my thigh, wincing, bring a smile to my face amidst the ugly cry. "He was just so—Jean-Paul. He would do anything for everyone to be happy."

Pierre turns silent. I wait for the final judgment call. Will it be a standing ovation? Or will the audience throw the white flag into the air, cursing the bloody show, shouting "Liar," and leaving the empty stage behind? *Watch, Angie.* Bambi's hands intertwined with mine. *Watch how he shatters, how he crumbles. Watch the floor break apart underneath his feet. Watch the light in his eyes go into darkness. Count with me, Angie, one, two…*

"Who's this Saul?"

See? Jackpot. The arrogant laughter rings in the tepid tea shop, filled with the sugary smell of burned brown sugar. The ghost of the sandalwood cologne hovers on my sweater like a desperate starvation. My hands are dripping wet with the heat of a man who is soaking underneath the Oakville Lake. *Angela, sweet Angela... My everything, Angela, look what you've become.* Puppet me and puppet him. We've turned another person into a puppet dream.

"Saul is," I stutter, elated, flustered, dizzy from the final lunge toward the goal, "the man who was admitted to the hospital a few days back. He's after me, Pierre. I tried to outrun him but Montreal is his turf. Pierre, without Jean-Paul, he'll kill me."

I yell the last phrase, then collapse on the table. Ophelia in her dying hour. Cleopatra in her glorious, bloodied crown. The damsel dives into her own distress and never needs saving. The spotlight shines on me. I mutter the spell, praying. "He'll kill me," I say over and over again until it sticks to the tattooed lyrics on Pierre's skin and paints him the color of the man I love. Dressed in the wrong costume with the right appearance, he needs a little fixing before I can make some use out of him. *Angie, he's a good pawn,* Bambi's hoarse voice lingers in my eardrums like a lullaby for the scarred and broken. *Use him. Live. Live. Live, for God's sake, Angie.* The ice cubes in the milk tea clink in their melting process. A puddle of water forms around the glass, then drips down my legs like a tender caress.

"You want me to help you?"

I nod as an answer.

"As in, killing him?"

"I don't know what to do. If worse comes to worst."

"Angela, mind if I smoke?"

He bites the cigarette out of the case without lighting it up. The dark circles heighten the newborn cruelty in his eyes. "You realize I don't get paid enough for this shit, don't you?"

"Understood. As long as you can help me get to the next province—"

He puffs on the unlit cigarette, crushing the butt, his white teeth gleaming with a strange menace: "Where is he?"

Puppet you and puppet me. Swaying to the music, dancing to the puppet world of supernovas because the stars are dying, and in that final burst of light, we see their mesmerizing beauty as the last call for help.

Bambi's arm wraps around my shoulders as I heave to breathe through my exalted tears.

Bambi was never a humanist. The first time he loved was the last time he learned how being selfless could kill, and the world never treated the nice kids with flowers. He made music because it was his salvation in the rotten dumpster of the glamorous city's underbelly. What he couldn't hold, he'd shove down the inkpot on the white paper, watching it flow away in the torrent of praise and applause. Revered. Adored. Risen on an altar for people to behold. But never once a human in the truest sense.

Yes, Bambi would do anything and everything to survive. Stepping on corpses and never shying away from destroying an innocent life. Pulling others down to get up the ladder. But when he finally reached the top, Bambi knew there was no meaning. To kill or to be killed, the hunter would be the hunted in the end. The cycle went on, regardless of his will. The search for meaning? He abandoned it a long time ago. The reason he was so obsessed with the unfinished wenos was because he craved to fill his empty corpse with the desire to live once more.

Dying was easy, someone said. It took guts to die like Bambi. It took even more guts to live the kind of life Bambi dragged his feet through. Humanist. I had to laugh at the pathetic wretch. He was the most anti-humanist I'd ever seen. The love of my life. The loss of my life. Curse him. Hate him. Do anything you want to him. I glare at Pierre's languid posture, spread out on the cushioned bench underneath the warm lighting of the tea shop, my teeth grinding. Yes, do anything. But do not, for one second, paint a false picture of him in front of me.

Angie, Bambi hums the melody in my ears. The cold air blows across my nape like mid-winter's dreams. Like fervent prayers in the darkest night. Like thirst. Like hunger. Like unsatiated yearning on a midsummer night. *Angie, historiaan jää, jos perin varmaa pelaisin. Äh lienee paras täräyttää minä rakastan sinua koko sydämestäni.*

Chapter 19: Saints & Sinners

April 10, 2025 – Pierre's apartment, Saint-Laurent, QC

Pierre cuts his hair short, shaves his sides, and dyes the tips a platinum silver. He looks in the mirror, styling his hair with carefree abandonment, letting the stray strands point wherever they want. The dark circles are covered up with thick concealer. The sunken cheeks are slowly filling up with the food he digests, more regularly now that he no longer needs to be at the beck and call of his patients, his supervisor, the duty, the call, or the hospital. He tugs his shirt collar a few times, unsure of how to display his newfound ecstasy in being the bad guy, then he unbuttons the front. Dark ink on pale, white skin. The lyrics trap him in a cage without his knowing. Thorns and vines caress him, garbage the only things he rules over.

Saints and sinners. Saints turned sinners. Pierre reads a lot, but no number of essays and dissertations can prepare him for real life's upheaval. He smiles at himself in the mirror. Bambi smiles back at him. The similarity is so uncanny it borders on the supernatural.

"You look happy."

"I look the part," he replies, whistling the same old tune. I wince. The nausea churns in my stomach again; it is the same sensation when I first caught Bambi's glowing, hazy ocean eyes in that crowded night club. His voice in my head keeps ringing: "Angela, there are no winners in this war, we are all wayward and lost." I tug Pierre's sleeve, hesitant, because it feels right and wrong at the same time, because I want to run away but the ghost is etched on my brain, because neither of us deserve to bear the consequence of another man's decision, and I ask, leaving the escape route open:

"Do you need to?"

"Saul wouldn't see Jean-Paul if I kept my old skin, would he?" Pierre grins like a child getting his first peppermint candy for Christmas. "Would he?"

"Twins. That's the spirit." I punch his shoulder lightly, giving up like I should be. He flashes me a full-toothed smile. His eyes sparkle. My heart sinks faster than a body with a dead weight tied to its ankle. Bambi is here, but he's not back. Yet. "What are you planning to do?"

"Saul is under protection. For now. But that's an excuse. The police are basically tailing him for evidence."

"So?"

"Here's the plan. Give them the evidence." He grips my shoulders. The familiar force is slowly rising to its place. "You asked for my help. Help me help you then."

I swallow a chunk of bile and acid. The thrill in my bones. The chill in my blood. *Come to me, darling, come back to me.* "You want me to be the bait?"

"Draw him out. A few bruises. A few cuts. No harm done. At least you'll still be alive." He shrugs. The sharp scent of pine wood pervades my nose. I scrunch up, turning away.

"Have you ever thought of changing your cologne? It smells like shit."

"I don't use cologne at the hospital. The rare occasions when I used it, I chanced upon the cheapest one. Smells horrible, huh? If I had to choose, it'd be nice to have some notes of sandalwood. You know, the other day, walking around the mall, I got a sample from the salesperson. I don't remember the name, but the scent is strangely addicting. She said it was cassis, with some sort of wood as the base." Pierre sniffs at his collar.

My eyes burn. An empty chuckle escapes my mouth before I can suppress it. Pierre stares at me, eyebrows screwed up, bemused. I divert his attention, "Oak, with a bit of patchouli, perhaps? The notes."

"I'm not too sure on the layers of notes. I like warm, woody scents. It calms my senses. Especially when my brain runs too fast."

"Something heavy like oakwood?"

"With sharp citrus undertones, harsh enough to punch through my brain."

He grunts, as if the scent is right there with us in the room; his eyes go dark with a primal desire, and I know he is losing himself in the comfort of the cologne.

"Like bergamot, gentle and calming enough to lift you up. Then we can add in the heat of saffron and blackcurrant, the overpowering scent strong enough to burn your senses. What do you call it, in your professional terminology?" My fingers dance on his neck. I feel the palpable passion on his skin to reach for the haunting of the past. He doesn't have to know that; he suffices as a replica. I don't need to be broken twice, and he doesn't deserve to be shattered. Grasping at my waist, Pierre's hands wander with a layman's hesitation before the monster in him takes over and the force turns into a possessing grip. He hoists me up on the marble counter, his nose burrows into my nape, greedily breathing in the lingering cologne on my neck, the trace of the man he will become.

"There is no professional term for what you describe. It's the most primal instinct within all of us. We're born with the word branded on our backs and in our hearts, Angela. It's desire. An animalistic, cruel desire, as human as it is beastly." He laughs with a heart full of dreams and freedom, but his eyes are a void of nothingness. The contrast from what he had been and what he is now is frightening. This is how Bambi would have been if the world hadn't set out to destroy him. In the end, Bambi had broken underneath the world's weight, falling into the Earth's fissure as he stares down the darkness because he couldn't escape the consequences of his decisions. "Do you know the story of Iris?" Pierre diverts the conversation.

"As in the Greek Goddess?"

"What other Iris is there?"

"I don't know much about mythology. Bambi, though, he said—"

"Jean-Paul."

"Right, Jean-Paul said Iris was a messenger for the gods. She was nothing else."

"Did he, really?"

Pierre doesn't care much for the story of Iris. He's just bored because he lost the chance of telling the story all by himself. Staying in the spotlight, having all the attention focusing on him. The understudy takes the stage for the first time, and he fits right in because he was born to be it. A perfect replacement.

He combs his gelled hair with his fingers, whistling no tune and every tune at once. It must be so freeing for him to be someone else, someone whose life no longer leaves a trace on earth, whom everyone looks up to and adores, who reincarnates in him as liberty for the life he traded in. The giddiness and the exaltation show on his flushing cheeks. The fever is real, while everything else is just an illusion. I lean on the bathroom door, provoking him, dosing the poison: "Are you sure you can do it? Finish Saul, I mean. He's pretty dangerous."

"Oh, I'll cross that bridge when I come to it." He waves his hand, shooing my morbid words away.

"Careful, Pierre. It's darkness you're stepping in."

"Darkness," he smirks, adoring his arrogant smirk in the sharp reflection. "Wish it could be me."

Like Jesus to His beloved creation, I watch Pierre enjoy his new skin. His broad back turns straight, fixing the slouching posture of the tired doctor I saw at the hospital's entrance. Sharp chin. Chiseled cheekbones. This is the product of my carving tools. The plain clay takes shape, and it needs a little more detail to become the idol of old. I stroke his fingers. My touch lingers on his ring finger, wrapping lithely around it, tugging it gently, watching him flounder in the misery of loss, trying to find the correct line for his role. "Hey," I feed him the cue, "Don't you think a tattoo would look nice here?"

"I don't want tattoos."

"Why?"

"Because they look intimidating. I must not look intimidating," he murmurs. The boat is trying to find its path back to the shore. I won't let it go. Sucking on his ring finger, swallowing it to the knuckle, I bite hard, leaving the mark there like a binding vow.

"Pierre. You're not bound by anything now. You're free."

He looks at his wet finger with disgust, immediately shoves it to the sink. I wait, betting on the odds of things falling apart. In the warm lighting of the crammed bathroom, I see Bambi turning up the faucet, watching the water dripping in a small stream, saying, "Ah, what does it matter? I don't need to follow the rules now."

Leaning on the marble counter, my head falls on his shoulder. Reality blurs into illusion. I whisper, "You don't need the world to be happy."

"What do I do now that I'm free?"

"You can kiss me."

"And why should I do that?"

"Because I'm a Babylonian whore, and you're a stranger coming by on a misdirected train."

Pierre chuckles, his voice rough and hoarse. The scent of smoke fills his collar. The sandalwood diffuser in the bathroom suffocates both of us. Like drugs. Like holy revelation. Like an opioid dreamland. With one arm, he yanks me hard into his embrace, our faces inches apart, his forehead against mine. The eyes I yearned for are not there, but the replica can only be true to ninety percent. Who am I to bargain with creation? As long as the ghost can speak. My lips search for his, but the warmth is lacking. He can't return the feelings he never had the chance to live through. The sheer heat of a love that will burn instead of save, kill instead of live, wound instead of heal, and will doom us all in the agony of living. Pierre knows the story of his patients. The mad women and the derailed men who were broken and couldn't stand up, trapped in their purgatory, because life's party never calls their names. But Pierre is an outsider. He avoided the sharp teeth of the claw all this time because he promised the only person left in his life he would stay sane.

Too bad that sanity was the first thing God got rid of when He created the first man. Cain and Abel. Why must God favor the shepherd's blood and reject the farmer's goodwill?

I wrap my arms around his neck; my legs lock him in place. His hands are lost for a moment before they settle on my bony hips. I don't force a kiss again. My eyes follow his descent. The spiral staircase runs deep, and he is taking baby steps. My fingers play with his neatly shaved nape, feeling each tremor as he shudders under my touch. I giggle at the innocence he tries to hold onto. The grip on my hips grows brutal with an ardent force. "Pierre," I drawl, lips brushing his as I speak, "Tell me about Cain."

"Cain and Abel?" he replies, quivering, knees weak, palms sweaty.

"I don't care about Abel. Tell me about Cain. Where was he born? Who was he before the crime?" Pulling his head to the crook of my neck, I let him breathe in the scent of damask rose and spicy peppercorn that Bambi devoured every time. My words bite his ear, "Tell me why he killed."

"Jealousy and anger," Pierre stutters. His hands try to hold him up. My legs pull him down further. Fall, my sweet puppet, take the fall. "Cain was jealous because God favored Abel's offerings. In his anger, he killed his brother, Abel, and suffered a punishment from God."

"What punishment?"

"He was exiled from the land and cursed to be a wanderer, with a mark branded on him, so that his bloodline wouldn't commit the crime again." His sweat drips on my skin deliciously like fervent kisses.

"Ah, but don't you see? People are still killing each other. Each time you blink, doctor, a person is murdering his brother. Blink three times, and three lives are lost. Like the Germans and the Jews. Like the Jews unto the poor Palestinians. We're all Cain's bloodline, doctor."

"That's why—" Pierre smashes his lips on my shoulders. The fight inside him is bloody. The right to disagree is lost. I push for the final victory.

"Like Bambi killing Jean-Paul. Like Saul killing Bambi. Doctor, tell me, after Cain, which side are you on?"

"I—"

"Doctor, no one remembers poor Abel and his sacred offerings. Saints and sinners; in the end, isn't it you who are the judge and the punisher? Come on, doctor. Pierre. Raymond." I crush his body against mine. Our lips collide briefly then detach. The bait is set. The trap wide open.

"I want to be the last one standing." Pierre speaks without soul. His eyes are burning with a raging chaos. His voice is the earthquake's rumble in the apocalypse I've been waiting for. *Jackpot, Angie. I always knew you could do it. Break him. Break the fool. Break Abel before God can.* "I want to be the living."

"Pierre—"

"Call me Bambi."

And he stands there, his back straight, his posture towering over the morals, the ethics, the cheap philosophies people pass around nightclubs to seem sophisticated. He stands tall, ever so arrogant, always the self-centered man, thinking and believing himself to be more equal than the rest, with his overconfident smirk as his trademark, promising a bad, but unforgettable, ending to all the girls he takes. From the broad shoulders, the strong biceps, the veins showing along his arms, people already know that he is the loudest in the room. He will speak when no one asks, and his words will be the last with no further argument. His piercing eyes screw up in a chilling smile; without a word, I know that he is ever the hunter. My heart stops beating for a moment only to bump faster till it bursts into an ocean of bliss. My mind has gone wild. The air turns into stone. I swallow each gulp with difficulty. Each exhale is torture. Bowing down to the man I resurrect by sacrificing my last bit of humanity, I claw at his bare chest, tearing the shirt open, breathing life into a person molded from the ashes. Mine. More. Forever.

And it happens. The kiss. He forces it on me. I yearn to accept it with grace. His hands gather me up in the sweetness of the shelter he couldn't promise. I never needed words to believe in him. The faith has been there since the day he took me into his dream. First, there was the word. Then, there was us. In the end, there will be only us. My hands grip his head, grabbing his hair to anchor myself, reminding me what I am coming for, who I am becoming. My breasts smash against his chest; the palpitation of his heart drums through my whole being and I quiver under the weight of his existence. In greed, in lust, in despair, in death, I ask for more of what I could never get. The kiss grows deep, but the hunger is never satiated. He crushes my waist. His fingers leave red marks and new bruises on the skin that has only ever known the ghost of one man, and I exalt at the thought it is the same man now. "Bambi," I chant in my feverish madness, "Bambi, there's no one else but you and me."

Jean-Paul. Pierre. Abel. Cain. What bullshit. I burn the bridge. There's no going back. From the beginning, what I have needed is legendary.

Chapter 20: Ophelia Without Hamlet

April 7, 2024 – Bambi's apartment, living room, the couch, midnight

Bambi lined the white powder on the coffee table with his platinum credit card, then snorted the cocaine with bliss, exhaling a repressed breath as he let go of control. I giggled on the floor, my back against the velvet sofa, already high as the CN Tower. His head was thrown back, eyes closed, mouth hanging open. So beautiful in the damned fate of the abandoned. I loved him, I loved him, I loved him—the thought kept running through my brain like a full-throttle horse gone rabid, foaming at the mouth.

He laid his head on my lap, his hair caressing my skin, prickling my soft flesh, trying to get in. I cradled his face, squishing his cheeks, speaking in the childish tone, Her Lady of Suffering to the human child, "Who's a good boy? Who's a good person?"

"Angie, you stop that." Bambi laughed. He always laughed freely when he was in his comfort high. The euphoria of delusion clouded his brain, and when the drugs kicked in, he believed he could stand up against life and its cronies, his eternal enemies, who crushed him every moment he was sane.

"But I don't want to stop. Bambi's been a good boy. Bambi's been a good person. Mushy. Your cheeks are mushy." I pinched his cheeks lightly, letting them go before the pain came and the hysteria got to me. "I love when you're all mushy."

"Angie's been a bad girl. A bad person."

"How was Angie a bad person?" I ruffled his hair, playing with his nimble fingers as they caught mine in their trap, holding mine captive. Forever.

Eternity was a real word.

"Angie's been a bad person because she followed a bad person down the rabbit hole." Bambi swung my hands to his sing-song voice. I puffed my cheeks, wanting to play a trick on him, so I trapped his torso with my legs, tickling his firm waist until he yelled surrender. "Angie."

"I didn't follow a bad person. I followed you."

"And I am the bad person."

"Bambi is not a bad person."

"Really? What's Bambi then?"

"Bambi's a monster."

I cackled, letting go of him, scurried to the sofa. Bambi lunged after me, bouncing forward, and toppled on top of me on the couch. We rolled around in that narrow space of cushions and fleece blankets until we landed on our asses again, then we climbed back and repeated it. The apartment was dark. The chandelier was broken. The city lights filtered in through the glass like a fever dream. The pale moonlight was overshadowed by the dark clouds overhead. And we were living then. Really living for living's sake. He slid his cold, sweaty hands underneath my chemise and pressed my left breast slightly, as if he was testing the temperature of a bath. I froze for a brief second, then yanked his head forward and dived into the delicacy of his bitter, nicotine-stained lips. The heat vaporized the scenery between us. His skin glided on mine like silk, like water shaving away ancient stone. Like reverence. I crushed him against me, never letting go, never allowing even a millimeter of space to come between us. He thirsted for more.

Torn shirt. Loose dress. Short skirt. Silken pantyhose. A tango of wet tongue drawing on coarse skin like the most decadent painting that would shame the infamous masters of the nineteenth century. He asked me if this was what I always longed for and I said yes, yes, yes. His cold fingers made their way to my stomach, tracing along each stretch mark in utter devotion, pressing into the scarred skin, telling me it was perfection. His ring finger with the tattoo of a dark promise band. An engagement to darkness. To death. To a foregone ending. I sucked on it and swallowed the sweetness, thinking, Life could only be this euphoric. My waist fitted in his arms with space for our love to cuddle both of us. He rapped hoarsely into my ears, "Angie, my dear, I was an empty man, with enough money to hide the empty can of my being." I laughed to the lyrics, tapping on the vine and thorn tattoo on his veiny arm. Yes, yes, yes.

Everything was sparkling, every sound a hope. Every car passing by underneath the fifteenth story a wish coming true. I held him close to my heart, letting him listen to the song of my soul. "Bambi," I slurred, "Bambi, you are loved. It's alright, darling, you are loved. Broken and filthy and begging like the old fool that you are, Bambi, remember, you are loved." And he didn't argue with me. He never believed my drug-induced nonsense. I never told him the secret suffering within when the sanity returned, cruelly sharp like a knife's blade cutting through my Dr. Seuss cotton candy cloud. We settled for what we could have, no matter how brief, how impossible, improbable, irretrievable. Irreparable. And we dealt with the aftermath later, suffused the scream of the children within us under six feet of water and the dead weight of a neverland. Peter Pan growing old. Let us have love when life shut the door.

"Whatever happens to Ophelia after Hamlet?" Bambi mumbled, his arms wrapped around my waist, his whole body laid on mine, like two pieces of an ill-fitted puzzle stuck together by the worst chance at the right time.

"She died."

"Ophelia went to the lake."

"Ophelia went mad."

"Ophelia the never-mentioned damsel in distress."

"Ophelia putting herself in distress for a tragic hero."

"Ophelia could've lived."

"Ophelia chose her death." I patted his head, looking at the lights from the opposite condominium. How tedious happiness was.

"What would Ophelia be without Hamlet?" Bambi asked. His hand reached for mine in the dark. His bare chest palpitated against my ribcage.

"Ophelia would be happy."

"Ophelia would be loved."

"Or she could have ended up the same." I shrugged, imagining myself drowning in the winter lake.

"Or she could be free."

Bambi placed a reverential kiss on my breast, then let his lips linger there. I watched his quivering eyelashes, tragic in their sadness and beauty, like a disappearing dream. My fingers brushed through them softly, not knowing what I would find when I caught them opening, then closing on me again. "Who said Ophelia wanted to be free?" I asked, toppled him, straddled his thighs. "Maybe she wanted Hamlet."

"Perhaps she was fooled into thinking she wanted Hamlet."

"Why? You were Ophelia?" I leaned my cheeks on his chest, watching his face change from darkness to light, then returning to darkness once more.

"Everyone used to be Ophelia until they learned it would be easier to live as Hamlet."

"The man who tormented himself with 'to be or not to be?'"

"Would you rather live feasting on the sorrow of flowers? There's rosemary. That's for remembrance."

He played with my hair, twirling lock after lock until they tangled up in a bunch, and I let him. The childish gleam in his eyes. The lost was found, then it was gone until the next high moment came along. He loved kissing. Loved the tender caressing when he was out of his mind. Loved the soft flesh squished against his body. The lithe frame fitted snugly on his chiseled figure like a mother's embrace. I learned how to make him smile, to calm his humming brain, to get his heart to slow down when the world outside was raging on. It was no easy task to tame the monster, but once I tripped off his facade, the monster was no scarier than the next human standing on my side, ready to shoot.

The monster was me. The monster was him. The monster was the cradle we grew up in. The bosom we thought was our mother's love. It was no stranger, and the first touch was so tender I thought I could break underneath the weight of its sacrificial heart.

"Bambi, there's still time." The fun was gone, the ecstasy destroyed. The soap bubbles burst when the stream of consciousness flooded us. "We could go back."

"To where?" he asked, determined in his will to ignorance.

"You could be free," I said, knowing where the conversation would end. "Or alive. Or both."

"I'm no Shakespeare, but the plot you're writing is terrible." Bambi chuckled, his laugh rumbled through my bones, and it ached and it ached and it ached.

"Why?"

"Because no one's dying."

I hummed. Did I want to change his thoughts? Yes. Did I expect he would throw the world away simply because I told him to? Never. The moonlight shone on his face, showing the chiseled cheekbones. He had lost weight. The purple bruises from the needle were peppered along his forearm and elbow. I touched them, feathers on the marred canvas. He didn't feel anything. His face turned toward the windows, absorbing the multi-colored neon lights from the streets below. His azure eyes glinted like strange water underneath a ghostly shadow, and the ripples spread like fireflies in a dark forest. He tapped on my naked shoulders, then turned the rhythmic tapping to a gentle stroke. The calloused fingers that played the thick strings of electric guitars now brushed my back, painted a portrait of the selfless and the self. I slid up, drinking his rough tracing like summer wine, my lips beckoning his name like the incantation for the last great war. "Bambi, I'm no Ophelia. You're no Hamlet. We don't live on Shakespeare's stage. Let's run away from here."

"Yes, Angela. You're no Ophelia. I'm no Hamlet. And Shakespeare is just a dead guy feasting on tragic endings," Bambi said. His voice grew soft with laughter, dyed the color of the silver moon. The neon lights danced on his tongue, making the words a fairytale forest. "But why would we bother with trivialities? And Angie—sweet, forgiving, sacrificing Angie—dying would be a happy ending for me."

"A deliverance."

"The sweetest vengeance for the dying is the suffering and agony of the people who remain here."

"You mean me?"

"No, Angie, not you." Bambi placed his hand on my head, like Judas to a praying Magdalene. "Because you will be Ophelia without Hamlet."

"Meaning?" I asked, on my knees, begging.

"He will come to you of his own free will. He will play into your hands as fate would have it. Ophelia, my dearest Angie, rooted her strength in madness. And he is madness reincarnated. Don't choose a Shakespearean ending; it's boring. The audience has already left. Be your own Ophelia. Choose the living."

"You want both Hamlet and Ophelia to live," I scoffed, thinking about the name Pierre Raymond, imagining the exact person in front of me in a different skin, a different masquerade. "If everyone can live happily ever after, people would've been able to stop the wars a thousand years ago."

"Yeah. But where's the fun in that?" He squeezed my thighs, pressing in the stretch marks, hooking his finger into my lace panties and releasing them with a loud snap. "We do our best to make the most out of our numbered days on Earth. Some leave behind legacy. Others just leave behind a trail of corpses and blood. All great things, to a varying degree, but you remember them. No life wants to be forgotten."

"Even you?"

"Am I no life?"

"I would say you're plenty of life. Too much. It's nauseating." I pressed my weight down on his stomach and he grunted, deep and wanting.

"Then it should come as obvious that I want to be remembered."

He rolled me over on the zebra-print carpet. The coffee table shook awake under our mischief. I pushed him away only to pull him closer, far closer than any of the living and non-living have ever gotten in only to leave me bereft and hanging in the after morning, too fucked up to spell my own name. The night was dark, but I thought Bambi was the only light I needed to cross the labyrinth of thorns and aging canopy. He never was my salvation; yet it was sweet to entertain the narrow hope of possibilities. The space between us was nothing but a blurred line of what was and what could have been. We ignored it all in the name of a love so great Shakespeare would have turned in his grave to write a new play for our sake. The moonlight turned a blind eye to the foolery of childish humans acting in the mood of love. She poured her sadness on the unfinished Wenos statue, whose face was left forever blank. The nameless and the named. The faceless and the beauty. Who were we before life breathed its vices into us? I didn't know. I doubted Bambi ever learned the true meaning of what he was searching for. And I wondered if he ever stopped his faithless search. The night went on. Even in the light of day, we all knew far too well that somewhere out there, darkness remained undefeated in its reign. It would be enough, then, to believe. Without cause, without reason, without a revered idol. Just to believe.

"Bambi," I cried, the giggly bubble finally diffusing as the dawn came knocking on the windowpane. "Have you ever loved me?"

"Does it matter?" He smiled, teardrops falling on my cheeks like melting snowflakes. Crystalized salt. How much sadness was in a specimen.

"Do you ever want to know, then, how much I loved you?"

"It wouldn't help anyone now, would it?" Bambi pushed in, full force, and I bit down, hard, taking as much of his flesh and blood as I could.

"I guess it wouldn't." Stuttering in my ragged breathing, I gasped in his ears. The sweetness wouldn't work on him. But in my brain, the hopeless voice cried out a thousand times, I loved, I loved, I loved—

"Angie, if I never loved you," he paused, asking with a pained honesty, "would you die immediately?"

"Nah, I wouldn't." My voice cracked. The protest died in my throat like a soldier's silent cry. I knew better than to fight a losing war.

"See? You will be perfectly fine without me. Bambi will always be here. Bambi will always love you, Angie. But I—"

"But you?"

"I will die this instant if my Angie won't love me no more." He crooned. That was the code. That was no Bambi.

"Raymond. I will be there when you fall."

"I'm scared of the dark."

"And I will hold you till you're gone."

"Angie. Do you know what I would do now, if I had the power to turn back time?"

He smiled at me. Ever so indulgent. Ever so sweet. The benevolence of the last monarchy's executioner. And I craved to be his solace. The warmth he lacked. The love he lost. The memory he would soon erase. There in the cold, dark bottom of the lake, how would he know the way to come back home? My hand holding his. My eyes carved his face into stone. Eyes, nose, lips. Where did the love grow?

"I don't know. What would you do, Raymond?"

"I would choose to relive this moment with you. My eternal five seconds. Forever, no remorse."

"You could still do that now." I held back tears. My heart was little raindrops beating on broken glass.

"Aw, but what would be the fun in that?"

He laid down, his weight pressing comfortably on my body. I felt my whole being shattered to dust. To ashes. To the nothingness where no living could be born again. Because he was sleeping, sound and peaceful, no trouble could reach him now.

Because he was no Raymond. That was Bambi. Bambi was a monster.

Chapter 21: The Accomplice

February 14, 2024 – Bambi's condo, empty of furniture and decoration

I put the tiny package of ketamine wrapped tightly in a black nylon bag and duct tape on the minimalist, glass-top coffee table. The desire to just tear it open, hack at it with a heavy knife, or simply to surrender everything to the police and quit the game overcame me with the same elation as a summer reverie. Biting my lips, I steeled myself for the things that would happen next. Before Bambi got home from his gig at the local indie bar, I needed to clear all possible evidence of suicide, drop hints to Markus, dose out the clues to Saul, and then… And then, what?

A warm sensation spread in my stomach, coursing through my bloodstream. I curled into myself on the floor, remembering the conversation I had with Bambi just a few days before. When things were good, it was hard to imagine how cruel the world could be. He said he never believed in such things as narrow hopes.

"I don't believe in such things as narrow hopes," Bambi scoffed, turning his head sideways. He was difficult to talk to when he was three whiskies in with a low dose of amphetamine.

"But Bambi, think about it. Things could be different. You can choose your own ending. You have the freedom of choice," I persisted. It was tiring, desperate—a cry against a stone wall, hoping the gods would listen, but they never did.

"Freedom of choice? Does that mean I can kill another person and be free? Does that mean I can commit any sort of crime, no matter how ghastly, how insane it is, as long as I receive an absolution from some priest? Oh, that would be fun, wouldn't it? Repentance, and the faithless religion will ease your conscience." He grabbed my arm hard enough to leave a bruise. I was tearing up, but I refused to leave him there in the dark. He was fighting to choose between goodness and evil, and it sounded as silly as it did pathetic, but I had hoped I could be the light to lead him out of the dark prison he was lost inside.

"Bambi, we don't need to be other people. Why should we trouble ourselves with other people's decisions? Why should you be bothered about the corrupt system some people create so others in power can live their blessed lives? Remember, suffer the children to come unto me. Be the children, Bambi. If all things fail, be the children."

"Children don't kill."

"You never killed anyone." I cradled his head in my hand. The tiredness washed over me in waves. My eyes were heavy. A thought fleeted through my mind: *How about we sleep here, forever, never open our eyes again, so tomorrow won't come?* And I cried; the anger, the helpless feelings, the pressure to do well rooted in my upbringing, the bleeding wound from Cecilia's suicide, the downfall of the man I love, the future, the past, the fucking present I wanted to escape—when things were bad, it was hard to remember the way out.

"Angie. Angie, my sweet baby girl, why are you crying?" Bambi turned sober in a quick moment. He caught me as I collapsed into his arms, heaving, bellowing, trying to get the pain out of my body using the only way humans were taught: letting the agony out through the deafening screams of a wayward woman going mad. Ophelia had it better. Ophelia was dead.

"Bambi. What should we do? What should I do?"

"What do you mean? Everything is in place. I don't know why we're having this conversation. You started it first." Bambi tried to make a joke out of his own mess, but I wouldn't have any of his evasive attempts to escape.

"Bambi, I'm pregnant."

And the silence fell fast. It shrouded over us like a white sheet covering the things a dead person left behind. It was eerie, almost sinister in its quake. I tugged at his sleeves, timorous and apprehensive, waiting for an outburst. My heart palpitated through the layer of skin and the thrifted sweater on my chest. He remained motionless. His eyes stared ahead without recognizing anything in their track. Bambi was no longer there in the room with me. He was traversing through a thorny path in his own forest. The tendrils caught onto his feet, the branches scratched his face; every step forward was a struggle against an unknown obstacle, and he didn't know what would await him at the end of the path. His hands reached for mine, still gripping his sleeves in desperation, and with a tenderness unlike his normal self, Bambi heaved a suffering sigh. He aged in the short duration of five minutes. Bambi grew older than he ever thought he would. Holding my body against his, gently patting my back as he leaned on the cushions of the sofa, Bambi said in a monotone:

"You know, Angie, you should be the light. Something for me—for anyone—to hold onto amidst this endless struggle against eternal suffering."

"But I'm not." I smiled, thinking of the best times we had together, the laughs we shared, and the life we could have had, if only I were the light. "I'm not." The tears wet his shirt, but Bambi left the teardrops dry by themselves. He barely moved from his position and his arms still held me in that unfamiliar gentleness.

"It's better that you're not. You don't have to be the light for me or for anyone. You can be yourself. You can be free. That's what I thought—I still think so. But you keep throwing yourself into the dark place, with that fucking belief that humans are good at heart. My darling, I tried—with all my might, all the power I have left, all the things I possessed, even myself— to show you what a shitty race we are. A belief is nothing but a truth you construe in your world. It doesn't mean the world outside will act on your truth, Angela. The world is crazy. The world is a monster."

"And what does that have to do with me being pregnant? I want the child. Even if you refused her, I would still have her anyway." I tried to heave myself up, but Bambi wrapped his limbs around me, holding me in place, locking me there, his nose trailing against my neck, his hair tickling my cheek. It was his normal apology, but this time, something was different. The scent of oak and patchouli lingered faintly on his collar, mixed with the sickening, bittersweet scent of whisky, making me hazy. I surrendered to his call and lay down, breathing in the peace, feeling the warmth seeping from his skin. "Bambi, don't you want a child?"

"I want a family. I want a daughter, a son; either would do as long as the child is mine and yours. I want a house, not this luxurious condo, just a house, barely large enough to fit our family. I want a steady job—maybe as a bank teller or a receptionist at some shady hotel—with good pay. Not much, but it could put the food on the table. I want to wake up in the morning with you there, making breakfast, clumsy with burned eggs and toast, the child running from one end of the room to the other, laughing. See, Angie, I want a lot of things, but essentially, they come to one single word: I want happiness. A very ordinary happiness, so normal and bland that it will bore people to death." Bambi chuckled into my nape and I gasped, quivering, not because of his sudden confession, but because the wet sensation on my skin told me he was crying. The tears trailed down my neck, slithered along my spine, and gripped my whole being like a vine. I sucked in a breath, suffocating by the burden of the wish I heard—a wish anybody could easily achieve but one that no one could grant to him.

"That's why you don't believe in narrow hopes?"

"Because they limit me to a frame, a trap, a box—the narrow hopes people profess to me, they make me think how tedious the world is. Get rich quicker, have more power, believe in a benevolent god because He will absolve them of the sins they commit to make their lives easier. Angie, do you want our daughter to grow up in a world like that?"

I felt his hands trembling as he stroked my hair. Something told me it wasn't all because of that phony philosophy he just spewed. There was another aspect he still tried to hide. It was weakness, cowardice. It was also a narrow hope.

"Bambi, you also hope someone will take your hands and save you from this situation, don't you?" I said. My eyes held his, level, unyielding. "Admit it, you hoped that the world would be just and the ones harming you, the Sauls and Markuses, would be punished. Bambi, don't lie your way out of this simple situation. You said you wanted a family. It's far more straightforward than that. You want to live. Right from the start, what you describe, what you wish for, is to live."

His lips trembled. He hesitated for a while. I knew he would bite back. The normal Bambi would have bitten back. He'd rather be dead than show his vulnerability. But who can be strong forever? Even Achilles had a vital weakness, and everyone was alright when the hero fell. We were born weak—fragile, little things tossed into the whirlwind of life—and our only strength was our ability to stare at that weakness without shame, admitting it, living with it, proudly acknowledging that our weaknesses make each of us bloom beautifully in the rotten garden of self-proclaimed giants. Bambi never knew that. He was too busy putting on armor, fending for himself. It was understandable; if my world was built on what he called flimsy faith and narrow hopes, his was built on worse stuff: the make-believe of greed and lust, of the high vanity of mere mortals who think they can outwit the twist of fate. Bambi said we were not free from the consequences of our decisions, but I wondered if he understood it, because his consequences had barely begun.

"I want to live. Yes, you're right. We all want to live, some less so than the rest. But I don't deserve to live. Angie, the things I did are catching up to me. If you want me to admit that I am a coward and a fool, yes, I will admit it. Even more so, I'm nothing but a liar. I lie to myself every day, telling myself in the mirror that things will get better until one day, that lie doesn't work anymore. You asked me if I want the child or not. Angie, if I answer that question, it would be a lie, and yet another lie to myself when I wake up tomorrow. I told you my wish, and it's true, I had such a wish. I still do, to some degree. The best thing I can tell you right now is to raise that child with love, with faith, with hope, with the best things in you, and never mention me as her father. Never let her know that she's from the bloodline of Jean-Paul Raymond."

"Why would you say so?" I caught his face in my arms, and it was grotesque. Because I wasn't staring at Bambi. I was looking at a real-life portrait of mortal agony.

"Raise her to have narrow hopes and dreams. Raise her with everything you have and all the things I never had. It's better to have those things than to walk through the forest, searching for a way out, eternally in the dark without a light to lead you home. It's better to be ordinary. It's better to be you than me."

We left the conversation at that, because Bambi refused to respond. He leaned on the cushions, his eyes vacant and hollow. In that slanting twilight filtering through the glass windows, I thought I could see the wounds he suffered from his childhood until now, the wounds piling one on top of another. Some were fresher than others, some were deep, and others were shallow but made up for their fatality in the way they bled. The cruel thing in common was that none of them healed; all of them were bleeding. The blood painted him red and raging, and Bambi wouldn't know this, but he never looked more alive than he was then. The only living person in the whole, wide, cruel world.

I stared at the ceiling. The crystal light fixture had been taken down a few days ago. The empty holes hadn't yet had the chance to heal. I untied my hair, letting the long strands flow freely over my shoulders. There were moments when a person could stand up from a broken place. There were also moments when the option to lay there dying was just as delicious and tempting. As for me, it had become so exhausting that letting things go looked like a sweet dream from my long-lost childhood, the only one I never wanted to wake up from. Throwing myself on the hardwood floor, I counted the hours on my fingers. They were more than what I had left. The whole affair was so sad it was laughable.

The zebra-print carpet was gone. The cacti and succulent pots were packed into a tray, waiting to be brought to someone who cared, or who would live longer. The books were stowed in cardboard boxes, labeled by genre, divided by authors' names in alphabetical order. The nightshade was given to an insomniac neighbor with a well-wishing card. The paintings suffered the same fate. It was strange to see the entire life of a person reduced to tiny objects, the size of trash and disposable garbage, ready to be thrown away on a Tuesday night.

The only thing left was the faceless Venus-Wenos statue, standing in her full, naked glory in the middle of the room, like she owned the place and the world underneath. The crown on her head was uglier than the first time I laid eyes on her. The body grew fat. Her round breasts sagged. The stomach was fuller, rounder, as if she had born a life into this world, and now that the child had grown, she was but an empty vessel, waiting for her turn to go to the underworld. There was no cloth covering her, in clay or fabric. Naked she had come to the shore, and naked she stayed. *Freedom*, I thought, looking at her empty eyes and the scarred sadness on her stretch marks and plump thighs. What would Venus think if she knew men would die for a simple glance from her? Power is the cage, and power is also the release we chased after.

The hardwood floor scratched my cheeks and it burned. I hoped there would be scars. I hoped they would be deep enough to never fade. Glory be the wounds from the battles where we emerged, victorious, bloodied, and deadly weary, wondering when there would be another, wondering if we would be strong enough for a chance to rest. A wet sensation trailed down my nose. I sniffled hard, breathing in the woody scent of the floor and the pungent smell of cleaning solution. Toxins in the air, in the layers of varnish, in the paint on the walls. The boxes untaped, the light shone on the dust dancing on Venus-Wenos's stone-cold skin. How I would love to drown myself in the sea of dreams and the uncertainty of the future. At least I wouldn't have to accept defeat. That future was murder.

I looked at the lock screen on my phone and Bambi's photo smiled back. Gentle, indulgent, with a glint of sweet adoration in his eyes, so dark and decadent I could still see the scene of last night's celebratory dinner in my mind. The candlelit table. The delicious smell of roast beef and mashed potatoes. Him asking if I ever had the chance to eat the famous French *aligot*. Me laughing at the word, repeating it just to hear the foreign sound and annoy him at the same time. "*Aligot*. What kind of word is that?" Bambi shook his head in that suffering, tolerant way, so tender it killed me slowly at first, then struck me down sideways.

"Angela, you should see the world. Loving is hard, but it's real," he said. Red wine to go with the perfect medium rare roast beef. Asparagus was in season, or wasn't it? After the third glass, he was drunk off his ass, and I told him as much.

We sat at the table looking out over one of the Great Lakes, watching the lights across the shore turning off and on, then off again. The waiter asked if I wanted cookie crumbles for dessert and Bambi fixed him with a charming sneer. "Perhaps not. Perhaps she wants a chocolate mousse." Because I always wanted chocolate mousse. Because he loved making a scene, standing in the spotlight, turning eyes on him, belonging to a place, a person, a feeling--as long as he didn't need to be himself. Because we were that desperate to hold onto each second, hoping it would be forever. Hoping eternity was a thing. Hoping a miracle would happen. *The second coming is here*, the graffiti on the way back read, and I laughed at it until tears streamed down my face in torrents. Bambi said if God ever came back to Earth, He must have left right after. Because this was a shit show. Because the puppets were broken. Because we were the worst things to ourselves since the beginning of Noah's Ark. Him asking if I knew the reason why Noah saved the animals first. Me replying I would've done the same as sweet Noah.

Was it for nothing then? Living, dying, then living again.

I sobbed into the floor, never realizing I was crying the whole time my memory ran its short film in my mind. The door clicked shut behind me. Bambi was back. He removed the heavy jacket, probably covered with snow. Rough hands patted vigorously on waterproof fabric, trying to get rid of the evidence that he ever existed. Then the boots knocking. The cold air reached me from the entrance from all the snowflakes melting. I didn't move an inch, waiting. He walked slowly toward where I lay, his footfalls soft with thick socks. The pair I had bought in a cheap clothing store because they were so Bambi. The same with the gloves he wore, the sweaters, the pants, and everything else he had on that day. He was ready. Born ready, if there was such a thing, for the way that he planned to die.

"Hey," Bambi said, his voice hoarse from the cigarette smoke and the cold air outside.

I didn't want to talk. Any words now would just deepen the misery I was going through.

"I went to the bar."

I nodded, my hair caught on a protruding nail. So that was what had been scratching my face.

"So they were saying Saul might come by later to get the delivery."

I nodded again, just to keep him going.

"He will be pissed. I didn't bring the delivery to the place with me after all. Heh. I'd love to see the look on his face. Mind if I smoke?"

I scoffed at the irony. He smoked anyways, sitting squarely on the floor. The white cloud fogged up the empty space.

"Right. Venus-Wenos. What are we to do with her?"

I shrugged, determined to be muted.

"I thought of sending her to my brother. But it was such a hassle, you see. A whole statue. No delivery company would charge me a reasonable price. Should we just break it?"

"No." I yelled out, grabbing his hand with a violent anger. He got what he wanted. I spoke. How could I not? That was the last thing he could take away from me. My face was bloodied, my eyes red with fury. I screamed like a haunted witch on the way to her trial, "Don't you dare touch her. She's mine. Mine. Hear that? Mine."

"Heh. You're finally talking to me, huh?"

"What's it to you? What do you care if I speak or not? Leave me be." I turned away. The pain rushed to my heart, and the suffering was enough. More than enough. But he forced me to eat up. The meal was still on the table.

"Angela, you're making things hard on yourself. My foretold ending wasn't anything bad—just considered it as a love turned sour, and you are doing your darling a favor by bidding him a good farewell on his last journey. You wouldn't keep on eating a rotten apple forever, would you? Come here, look at me. My sweet baby girl is all wounded, and I'm the perpetrator. What should I do?" He crooned. There was no trace of drugs in him. It was the elation of a person who's coming to his end.

He lay down next to me, spooning my whole body in his tall frame. He was thinner now. Just about enough bones and flesh to hold and to carve onto my own flesh. The shape would still be there, fresh and red like a burning iron mark because memory is a dictator in the shape of the man I lived to revere, and that silhouette of him in his mortal frame trapped me inside the prison of my choosing, thinking—mistaking, even—that it was happiness. I wept, knowing things couldn't change, knowing he was right, as he always was, that I was making things harder for myself. That a life was gone, and it was as simple as that. His arms wrapped around my waist, his chin on the crook of my neck, the warm breath tickling my skin. Needles prickling silk. Thistles swirling each inch of my existence. I stroked his fingers. My touch lingered on the wedding band tattoo around his ring finger. He once said if I were lucky, I would be able to take his ring off. How could I? The chuckle escaped my throat like a bitter grudge for a thing I learned to be true but couldn't obtain. It was inked on his skin, while I was but a human without the cruelty to hurt him more than the world already had.

"Angela, you still won't talk to me?" He blew air into my ears and without a mirror, I could see them flushing red.

"Why?" I sobbed, quickly wiping at a tear rolling down my cheek.

"Why what?"

"Why must it come to this?"

"Didn't we agree we won't talk about this anymore?" He inched closer until we were glued together. No space in between, just shirt, skin, and the warmth seeping through. The heartbeats danced their own tango to the end of love.

"I just want to know the meaning of this mess. I'm getting myself into a murder. Shouldn't I know the cause? Shouldn't I have a reason to go on after…" My breath caught in my throat, the words choked, and I bit my tongue so the pain could force the thought out. "After you leave?"

"Ah, the same old search for meaning. If we were to go around in that foolish maze, the monstrous labyrinth would swallow us, wouldn't it?" He played with my hair, but I kept hearing, *This is the last time. The last time.*

The last.

"I didn't want to know anything grandiose, did I? I just want—"

I paused. The thought ran in a circle. What did I want? The warmth was still there, but my back had grown cold. His embrace was the same, but it wasn't enough to anchor me in the present. The present was pain. The present was hurt. The present was anything but a place I wanted to be in. I would trade anything—my thought stopped there. Trade what? For what? The saying goes, An eye for an eye. There was no life that could fit inside the shoes of Bambi Raymond. And even if there were, the trade wouldn't be fair for either side. Both of them would suffer the same ending.

I laughed at the foregone conclusion. Even in the near-death hour, he managed to strike a final goal with truth.

"Would it make you feel better if I say that everything we did was for nothing in the end?"

Bambi caressed my stomach, circling the stretch marks, then moving further down and stopping right at my uterus. Where a life could be born. Where a life already existed.

"My Angie is carrying with her an angel." Bambi pressed a tender kiss onto my nape. "And I couldn't see her grow."

"Don't talk like that. It's bullshit." I scoffed, pushing his hand away, but he pressed it firmer still, as if he wanted it to leave a mark. To burn a seal there. To remain. "A life wouldn't be enough to keep you here. What do you want more than that?"

"Let's see. Maybe I want her to be a different person. I hope she won't turn out like me, only getting little breadcrumbs, chasing after the illusion of life. I hope she'll be a normal girl, have a normal childhood. And since you're her mother, she'll be the happiest girl in the world. That's barely enough. Just barely," he mumbled, the ghost of slumber haunting him. Lately, he just fell asleep anywhere, whenever the mood struck him. And the mood was always there.

"Without her father there?"

"That's why I said it was barely enough." Bambi tickled my waist, something that would have made me go crazy with laughter before, but my sensitivity had grown dull. I tolerated his touch with longing, knowing it wouldn't be there the next time I opened my eyes in a foreign place. "It would be nice, right? To see a life grow."

"Maybe you could make it more than enough."

I licked my lips, fighting against the onslaught of dream and lethargy, trying for one more time. And one more time. And one more time. What else did I have to lose?

"Aw, Angie is still trying to save me. What did I ever do to deserve her love?" He peppered kisses down my neck and shoulders. His rough hand glided up to my breasts and fondled the soft flesh like it was his private possession. No one was allowed in.

"Perhaps Bambi was a child. Perhaps I took in a lost kitten, and now that he has nowhere else to go, I can't abandon him there, all alone on the road. The night is cold, and humans are…"

"Humans are?"

"Humans are not always good at heart."

"Even the best of them?" He crushed my body against his chest, and the warmth burned my clothes until nothing remained but my white lace bra and sheer panties. I turned to face him, softness against stone.

"Yes, even the best of them. But you know what, Bambi?" I bit his lower lip, sucking on the flesh until it turned blood red. Put some color on him, decorate the corpse before disposing of the evidence of the life I was going to lose.

"Hmm. What?" He grunted into the kiss, eager in his response, not so eager in listening to the reason behind it.

"Sometimes, when humans are good at heart, it can amaze you how much they can make the flowers grow. Even the worst of them."

"Tell that to Hitler."

"Don't start."

"Tell that to the dictators who are still ruling over us."

"I said don't start." I squirmed in his arms, trying to get out. His mood changed. The monster settled in. Or something worse. It was helpless. It was cold. I ran but my head kept turning around to look at it.

"Angie, it's fascinating how the darkness in me can never touch your heart." He stared at me with a dark menace gleaming in his eyes, ever so briefly, then it shattered and he collapsed on me. Breaking in between and everywhere. "I hope our daughter takes after you, Angela. I'd trade everything to the God I don't believe in for that simple wish."

"Bambi." I called his name, holding him to my bosom, letting his head rest on my breasts. Like Our Lady of Sorrows to Her suffering child. Words failed the meaning of the bond between us, so I let my heartbeat, my touch, my fingers coursing through his hair speak the foreign tongue he would never dare to understand. "Bambi. Bambi. Bambi." I cried his name, more reverent than any god. More adoring than any lover. There was never anyone before him, and my faithful heart screamed that there would be no one after his leaving.

"Angela, was I ever a good person?" He spoke into my breasts, his tears wet on my skin. I burst out laughing. The love bloomed like a garden of roses after a rainstorm.

"Yes, Bambi was."

"How about Jean-Paul?"

"Jean-Paul was also a good person. He still is."

"Angela."

"Yes."

"If you met Jean-Paul before Bambi, would you love him the same way?"

"I would. Probably more. Probably the same. But never less." I kissed the top of his head. The pain grew acute, then softened into a dull ache all over my palpitating body.

"Angela."

"Yes."

"I wish it were different, too."

"We all wish so. Only when it's too late. Didn't you say it once before? Holding onto hope. Choosing nothingness and whatever."

"That was Bambi. Jean-Paul wouldn't say such corny things. Jean-Paul is a fool."

"Why would you say that?"

"Because he had everything he wanted, and he still let it all go."

"Then," I tried again, my heart racing, "Would Jean-Paul rethink his decision?"

"It would be nice, wouldn't it?" He chuckled, his breath spreading a fiery life into my soul. "But if Jean-Paul stayed, no one would be happy."

"I would. Our daughter would. Pierre would. There are plenty of people who would be happy. Why don't you understand that? For God's sake, Bambi. Jean-Paul. Whoever is inside your monstrous brain and your savage darkness, tell him to open his eyes. See the life in front of him. See the cradle he was in. Fuck, Bambi, or Jean-Paul, or whoever you are, I loved you, love you, will love you. Unconditionally. Against Gods. Against humans. Against faith. Against reason. Against all that could be. Why can't you see that?" I broke down, the weight finally shattering my world. Kneeling on the floor, my knees scratched against the protruding nail. The blood trickled out and the small burgundy stream flew to where he was, dying his sweater an angry, poignant hue.

Bambi's lips curled up. He held my hand in his, caressing the wrist where the scars hadn't faded, and pressed a kiss there. The lips stayed as his cheek leaned into the warmth of my palm. I cried; that was my last try. Black ink on white paper, words failed to hold the truth when the person they meant to save had decided to surrender. "Let me rest on you for a while," Bambi whispered, his arms gathering me in a tight embrace. Lace lingerie caught onto silver hair, sunlight caught onto nightmare, dust weaved onto the hands holding on, nails scratching knees. We were all children. We never grew. The Earth was far too old for us to share our sorrow; the only consolation she could offer when the night grew colder was the same old, *It's alright. You are not the only ones being abandoned.*

I fell asleep, dreaming about a family. A loving home with a field of lilies. My daughter ran barefoot on the baked earth, laughing about her school days. I shouted her name, calling her back home for dinner. And Bambi turned around on the spring field, smiling. There were no tattoos. The inked wedding band was replaced by a bland, cheap silver one. His hair was dark brown, his shirt was crumpled, messy with dirt from all the gardening work, and his eyes were mesmerizing. It was happiness. It was ordinary. It was the darkness of the faith he and I chased after only for it to disappear the moment I reached out my hands to crush it against my bosom.

My eyes startled open on their own. The stark, cold air filtered into my nostrils, and my lungs were bursting with an acute ache. Each breath I pulled was a thousand sharp needles piercing cruelly through my heart. Dying would be easier, because why else did Bambi choose it? I turned my head aside; Bambi was dead, overdosed on the package of Special K I brought back. The delivery Saul requested. Revenge for the suffering dead had begun. It was slow; as quiet as the day the universe had begun. I heard the stars crackle, saw the embers glow, and in the depth of night, my hands reached out to catch the light of my darling's soul, leaving me. The 'almost' that separated me and the only love I would ever let into my world shattered in the hollow void of darkness, and the universe burst open. My hands gently closed his peaceful eyes; a thousand words were too much and never enough at the same time for the eternal farewell between us. The light was on outside the window, and with the agonizing bang of Bambi's death, the universe was reborn. And my life would be spent mourning for my darling on his journey down the road to the other world, where he believed there were no sorrows, and happiness wasn't something he must conjure with his sheer imagination.

Saul forced the life of Bambi's lovers on him the same way he forced Bambi's life on me—they both wanted their victims to choose the role of Savior, while they sat back on their thrones, satiated by the feeling of absolution. If I let Bambi escape the prison he built and designed so meticulously all these years in the creeping darkness, it would be a crime against the will to live of the life wasted and Bambi's master plan.

"Why did you take Bambi as your nickname?" I'd asked.

"Because it reminds me, always and forever, that innocence kills—in the most savage, beastly way," Bambi had replied, the cigarette smoke swirling around his neck and face like a mirage.

The mirage stayed with me, haunted me, lived inside me like poison. It was as if on the first day we met, I had swallowed a thorny flower's seed, and in time, it bloomed, branching out, the thorns catching onto my flesh and veins, tearing at my living essence until I bled to the howl of death. Yes, innocence killed. Wasn't it a good thing that my innocence died with the man Jean-Paul "Bambi" Raymond?

Chapter 22: Pierre in Old Montreal

pril 15, 2024 – Old Montreal, QC, Montreal General Hospital

Pierre dons a turtleneck sweater and a long black trench coat with leather boots to fit the look of a trendy downtown playboy. His hair is slicked back, a loose strand curling on his forehead, as it isn't long enough to comb together with the rest. Or it's simply his stubborn idea to stay true to the Pierre within, the one who isn't lost just yet. When I walk out of the OB-GYN room, he is arguing with two nurses, one a veteran, old and sure, and a young one, fresh out of school and filled with timidity. Though Pierre appears nonchalant, his shaking legs and the constant tapping of his feet prove he is anything but calm. I approach the escalating situation, armed with experience. "Hey," hooking one arm over his, I feign the sweet, suave voice that works with almost anyone. "Whatcha doing?"

"*Madame, votre mari a fumé à l'hôpital.*" The veteran nurse turns toward me with reprehension.

"What's she saying?" I appease her with a smile, asking Pierre through clenched teeth.

"I smoked inside the hospital. Didn't you hear that word? *L'hôpital.*" He groans, directing a rant at the fresh nurse, turning his head toward the grumpy one. "*La cigarette est pas allumée. C'est correct. J'ai pas fumé. Tu vois? Pas d'alarme, pas de détecteur qui sonne.*"

"What are you saying now?" I knock his elbow, frustrated at the foreign tongue and how it is intruding upon my life more and more, making its own place in my Anglophone-dominated land, forcing me to understand with a French kiss on the lips against my will.

"I told her I didn't smoke." He hisses, eyes rolling sarcastically, as if saying, "Of course I have to deal with stupidity everywhere." The nurses fume.

I gather the little French I still possess from my school days. *"Madame, monsieur, pardon, mon mari, eh... Mon mari est idiot."*

"You say what?" Pierre yells, to the scrutiny of the old woman. He glances around, then whispers into my ears with the force of a wounded ego, "Don't speak when you don't even know the language."

"Ben voyons, votre bébé va être niaiseux avec un père de même." The veteran nurse throws her hands in the air and walks away, taking the sweet puppy of an apprentice with her. He glares at Pierre with a certain hostility before getting to the elevator.

Pierre is speechless, then, catching his voice again, he screams after her, *"Oi, elle n'est pas. Oi.* Damn it. Her daughter is not my daughter."

The whole floor looks at us, curious, malicious, with a strong seasoning of greedy judgment. Someone laughs. A few others talk behind folders. The benign and benevolent doctor who is in charge of my case peeks his head from the examination room, lowers his glasses, and asks with the muted, gentle voice of a grandfather, *"Problème?"*

"Pas problème. Vous sont mermaids." Pierre throws his ridiculous sentence back then drags me away in a storm.

Vous sont mermaids. I feel my heart melt away at the edges, dripping watery salt drops down my stomach like late-blooming flowers. Fluttery, cotton clouds float up my throat, bubble into a chuckle. Pierre looks at me. His eyebrow shoots up, provocative and challenging. I pull on his coat sleeve, halting him in his tracks. "That is just so Bambi, you know?"

"What is?" He grunts, blowing the loose strand of hair on his forehead, visibly annoyed at the funny feeling.

"Nous sommes des mermaids. Je suis mermaid. Bambi and I often told that joke to each other."

"Why? What's the fun in that?" he asks, his interest ladened thick in the way his fingers play with the unlit cigarette.

"Because the little mermaid turned into sea foam and..."

"And?"

"People will become nothingness and…"

"And?"

"And from sadness, Venus-Wenos was born. I don't know why I'm explaining it to you. That joke was only funny between the two of us." I scoff at my own pathetic foolishness. Why am I still chasing things that could never be? A rough hand scented with the hospital's ether and sanitary soap wipes my cheek with carelessness.

"I can't understand your wicked sense of humor. Dying is funny to you, huh?"

"That wasn't it. You don't understand. And I can't explain it with words."

"Then what can you use to explain it with? A life?"

"It's growing inside me. That should be enough."

"Apparently, my brother didn't think so, did he? Whether it was *je suis mermaid* or the life inside you, they were never enough to make him stay. So I ask you again, what's the fun in all of that?"

He lifts my head, his forehead pressing against mine. The eyes grow dark but the softness never disappears. There are people who never grow blades. There are also people whose blades are meant to heal and fix rather than kill. I had drowned in my own sea of suffering for far too long and in that brief second, when Pierre's gaze lingers on my transparent teardrop, I am reminded once more what it means to be human. Between grief and nothingness, Pierre chose grief. Between his grief and my nothingness, Pierre chose my nothingness. So this was what Bambi meant when he said what it would be like when I met Jean-Paul before Jean-Paul got lost in the darkness.

"Angel, I—"

"Angela," I correct him, wincing at the familiarity of the same mistake happening twice with two different people sharing the same DNA. The night Bambi called me Angel and tried to explained his mistake out of his clumsy philosophical ass comes back to me like a wave, as sweet as candy wrapped in sugar and cinnamon.

"Right, Angela. Who were you before my brother came into your life? You never told me about that girl." He takes my hand and guides me to the nearest bench, settles me down gently, and sits by my side. The patience and the weariness on his face ages him ten years. A decade of life. A decade of burdens he never asked for.

"She wasn't an interesting person," I reply, trying to avert my eyes, but they keep searching for his gaze. The longing is still there. The yearning keeps growing.

"Did she want to be an interesting person?"

"She wanted to. She thought life had so much to offer besides textbooks and exams."

"So she did go to school. Figures. She did speak like she graduated with honors and had a Philosophy doctorate degree in her pocket."

"That wasn't from school. That was her hobby."

"Smart discussions and mulling about life?"

"No, living on dead men."

"Like reading them?"

"Like living them. Literally. She drank their wisdom, thinking it would help her navigate through life in easy mode." I snicker, feeling the irony gnaw at me with teeth and claws. "Damn, how wrong she was. Just a naive soul. The innocence of age. People like her were meant to be trampled upon sooner or later. Bambi was there at the right time, and she took the chance upon the first dance to the end of love. It was a tragedy in disguise. Ophelia without Hamlet. What do you think it would be like?"

Pierre pauses for such a long while, I almost think he stopped listening from "Like living them." His long fingers knit together, forming a pyramid, and he rests his aquiline nose on them. I don't know what goes on inside his brain. A million different theories of madness. A billion theories on how to treat pain. Perhaps both of those trains are running side by side, and he is short-circuited. I lean against the metal back of the bench. Six months along and my stomach is barely showing. It's no wonder; how could the child grow when I keep pushing her to oblivion, wishing her father were here, hoping she will be happy without me? Wishing for everything, but everything keeps passing by, while I peer through the windowpane, watching.

We sit there, each of us chasing a different dream, but both following the same shadow of the man who left us in his towering madness.

"What was he thinking, Hamlet?" Pierre speaks curtly, chewing the butt of his cigarette.

"He needs to avenge the death of his father."

"But his father was dead. And he was a ghost. Maybe what Hamlet saw at that time was an illusion. Do you know what we call that in psychological terms?"

"What?"

"Hallucination. One of the symptoms for a plethora of mental illnesses. Schizophrenia, for one." Pierre shrugs, hunching forward, scratching the unfamiliar feeling of stretch wool on his legs. "Or dissociative personality disorder, for another. I could name many others."

"So you think Hamlet was crazy?" I guffaw, doubling over on the bench, kicking my feet. "My English professor would have loved you to death."

"It's one of a few theories. It was all his doing. You see, when you dissect the play bit by bit, from his delusional meeting with his dead father to his murdering Ophelia's father, to his ridiculous ending and the triumph of the other nation, there would have been so much less pain if he could have just shut up the ghost with a simple, 'Yeah, got it, rest in peace, etc.,' and moved on with his life."

"So you think Bambi was crazy?" I test the waters, feeling the temperature rising, yet my body refuses the warmth.

"I don't know." Pierre throws his head back, resting his head on the metal bench. "I think he'd be a hell of a fool to leave someone like you behind. And his daughter. And a future where anything could happen. What sort of power was strong enough to induce him to make that decision, if not madness?"

I stroke my stomach gently, imagining the beauty that is growing inside me, healthy and rosy, sleeping still, but fully aware of the love that is sheltering her. She will be so much better than her parents; that is more than enough for a mother who was twice broken by the same man, whose father abandoned her before she had the chance to see the light, whose substitute father is contemplating the difference between sanity and the insanity of power.

What will she think of us when she grows up? I wonder.

"Doctor—"

"Bambi." Pierre corrects me somewhat begrudgingly.

"Bambi, he didn't choose that ending because he wanted to, alright? There were many things leading up to that finale. He was ever the mastermind, and on the stage of life's finest Greek tragedy, he wanted a grand exit scene befitting the greatest showman; he thought the search for meaning was meaningless in the end. Instead of following the masses, he dared to disobey. That was all."

"Disobey what? And to what end? Are you trying to defend the man who wounded you in that beastly way, who left me and used me to his advantage even after he had nothing to give me anymore?" Pierre sneers. "You're right; there's such a thing as the stupidity of the innocence of age."

"You wouldn't understand. He sheltered you here in the comfort of a life where you never had to face the cruelty of humans."

"Who said I haven't faced that?" Pierre plays with the lighter, bearing the scrutiny of the nurses passing by with keen interest. He flashes a mocking grin at them, showing the lighter without flame in his hand just to spite them. *"L'hôpital.* The place where people come to die, to heal, to bring another life to earth. You will see plenty of cruelty there, if not somewhere else. I work in the psychiatric ward. There were nights when I was on call, and suicidal cases came in—self-poisoning, self-harm. You name it, we have it. Do you know what death smell like? It's rotten. The pungent decay of the intestines when the poison starts to eat at the living corpse. I know I can't save them, but against the hopeless eyes of their family members, I still faked the smile. 'We'll try our best.' Damn liars, that's what the psychiatrists were. We couldn't fight your battle, but we will be there, watching, bearing the wounded soldiers away." Pierre takes a deep breath, ruffling his hair, destroying the careful pomade.

"And that makes you better than the rest of us?" I ask ruefully. I don't mean to cause a fight, but it irks me to see the world from his side.

"I didn't say that. No one can ever say that. I just… Angela, look at it this way." He turns toward me, his gaze straightforward and pure in its intensity.

"You keep saying that we are not the only ones being abandoned. But have you ever thought that maybe, just maybe, none of us needed saving?"

"Stop right there," I warned him, cold sweat breaking out on my nape.

"No, I won't. Let me burst your bubble a little." He crosses his legs, his chin resting on his knuckles, determined to get through. Twins really do share the same genetic annoyance. "He targeted you because he saw your vulnerability. You succumbed to his will because let's be straightforward, he's a handsome mess. Devil in disguise. Can't say I'm different. But Angela, where's your freedom of choice? And don't pull me in with that 'It's an illusion' bullshit. I know what it is. No one forced you to stay with him. Angela, let's face it—you stayed because you thought, beguiled by your own thoughts, that you could save him."

"Are you finished with your TED talk?" I snap at him. Anger shows through my thinly veiled contempt, a smarty pants acting the part of a smart asshole.

"Not quite. Bear with me a bit longer. You thought you could save him because he provided you with the feeling of freedom. Let me guess—before him, you were stuck. Trapped inside the prison you chose to live in because everyone would be happy then. But he came a-knocking and told you the world could be many things, one of which was that you never had to be virtuous and upright. Sin. Fall. Taste the temptation and whatnot. Because who else will be there to forbid you? He would be there to catch you. And the catch is that he gets his deliverance while you are stuck inside a purgatory, wandering in the desert of life, trying to deliver yourself out of this mess, pulling me inside your sick twist of religion because he told you so. What does that story say about you?" He cackles, catching the glare of the head nurse. He quickly shuts up but trembles all the while to suppress his laughter.

"You tell pretty stories. Is that all you have?" I kicked his legs, moving away from him on the bench, groaning with the pain in my lower back. "Pretty stories, theologies, definitions, categorizing everything into treatable or non-treatable disorders?" Taking the prescription from my tote bag, I check for any changes in the dosage or the medication. The kind doctor was sweet enough to remove my sleeping pills. "The Clonazepam isn't here," I mutter.

"You don't need Clonazepam to fall asleep. Also, pretty stories? We need to check your brain to see what other ridiculous definitions you have. Angela, what was Bambi to you?"

"I need Clonazepam to fall asleep. Without it, I'll stay awake forever. I've never gone a day without two milligrams of Clonazepam. Where's Bambi? I must talk to him."

The trance catches me again. My eyes become hollow. I no longer see the hospital floor, the nurses in their scrubs, or the clanking noise of the carts rolling through the hallway. My fists clench on the edge of the metal bench. The sweat drips in small streams. I feel like I'm drowning in a swamp, and the thick, muddy water is choking my throat, gripping my whole body in a vise. I heave. My breath comes to me in waves; one moment it's there and the next, it's nowhere to be found. I want to call Bambi's name, but my memory fails me. The syllables escape my brain. The letters flow out through my ears in screams, but I can't comprehend their meaning. In my lucid nightmare, where the real mingles with the worst apocalypse and the earth turns back to the black void of oblivion, a hand reaches out, pulling me away from the darkness.

"Angela, I can be your Bambi, but I can't be your salvation. You must save yourself."

Pierre holds my shoulders, putting the space of a hand between us. The cold, indifferent gaze of a specialist dissects my fear into boxes, storing each one away, calculating the best method to dispose of them without causing harm to mother earth. To me. "Breathe, Angie, breathe," he says, his voice calm and composed with the same vibration as the Bambi of old. I don't know which one I should believe in: the monster I conjured up, or the monster manifesting itself in my dreams.

"I just want to live," I cry in short, truncated words. A useless sobbing mess. *Look at you, Angie. What have you become?* Bambi's voice croons in my brain, sweet and deep with thunder and rumble. *Without someone to love you, Angie, you're nothing but an empty shell, filling your world with ideologies and faith so others won't realize how fake you are inside. How can someone love a person who's nothing but a broken record, repeating the same pain at the press of a button?*

"Of course. We all want to live. But Angie—"

"Don't call me Angie," I sob between tears and snot. It isn't real—the man before me, the man behind me, the man in my head, and the man patting my back.

"What should I call you then?" Pierre groans into my hair. The mass of chestnut brown is growing thicker now that the child is sharing my life force. I stopped dying my hair after the happy news—what kind of mother would want her baby dyed in blue? "Angel? Angela? Carter? Reincarnation of Judas?"

"I don't know. I don't fucking know." Clawing at him, I crave Bambi's tight embrace, the laughter in his eyes when I told him I was pregnant with his kid, and the brief happiness bubbling in his eyes, telling me I was right in hoping love could change everything. But it ended as quickly as it began. The terror and emptiness drowned him, smothered him in the abyss. He wanted to be ordinary. I wanted him to live. Until the last moment, we couldn't settle on the right to disagree. "I can't go on. Bambi, I'm not strong."

"And you're totally right in feeling that way. I mean..." Pierre clicks his tongue, crushing my crying mess into his neck, appeasing the nosy passersby with a smile that is more like a scowl. "I don't want to be a doctor, and you're not my patient. So, let's say that we're talking like two people hurt by the same fucked-up man. Would that be alright with you?"

"You're still acting professional," I mumble into his turtleneck sweater, sulking and petty, because how can he be so carefree?

"I was in the profession. I can't be anything but professional. I also want to talk normally. To speak human language, the simple tongue of my patients. It would be easier that way, wouldn't it? Going back to the beginning and becoming the children we all are inside. Believe me," Pierre's voice turns sour with despair, "I wish I could be something different. I wish I could be Bambi. We all want something we can't have, don't we? And Angela, you know what? It's human nature. We have much, but we are little."

"Talk more philosophy to me again and you'll convince me that you're him reincarnated." I punch his shoulder slightly, not meaning to hurt, but wanting to leave a mark anyways.

"I know. We're twins. That's the curse upon us, Jean-Paul and me. Maybe I should've followed him when he left Montreal for Toronto. Maybe I could've saved him when he was lost in the dark nights without a light to go home to. See? It's not just you, Angela. I also think about the 'what-ifs' a lot. But it's never our decision. Jean-Paul chose that ending for himself."

My head lolls on his shoulder and my arms grow lax. The strength leaves my body. Pierre's words cascade down my skin like silk. Like water. Like ribbons trying to tie up a bundle of life. I listen, letting the sadness flow out my eyes freely.

"Angela, don't blame yourself for others' decisions. He never felt bad for doing what he did to you. Why should you forgive him?"

"Do you forgive him?"

"Heh. Of course, I—"

But we don't have enough time to figure out each other's answers to that question. Pierre cuts his sentence short, hushes my sobs, and covers my face with his rough hand, pulling his trench coat to shield me from surrounding eyes. I hold my breath, my heart jumping to the beat of the sound of footsteps in the pristine hospital hallway. Tugging his sweater twice, I signal my coded question, "Is it Saul?" Pierre pats me twice on the head, answering yes.

Saul is skulking around the OB-GYN ward, looking in every examination room, saying "Pardon" after a few seconds and scratching his head, appearing apologetic, as if he is sorry for mistaking the room. The stinky, pungent smell of alcohol, the sour scent of rotten meals, and I can also see in my mind, vividly, the yellow teeth with the black coffee stains and the white-dotted tongue. I shiver in Pierre's embrace, and he holds me tighter. His breath caresses my skin closer, and he turns sideways to further hide me from the outsiders.

The heavy footfalls grow nearer. I grasp at Pierre's coat sleeves. It's now or never. I tap Pierre's back. One tap, pause, then two more taps in succession. Pierre grinds his teeth, unwilling to act out the plan, but resolves to let me go at last. With much reluctance, he pulls back the trench coat, puts the cigarette back into his mouth, chewing it, dangling the lighter between his fingers, and approaching Saul in fast strides. His eyes glance at Saul, purposefully drawing down the sweater neck to reveal the inked lyrics on his skin, catching Saul's attention immediately. The filthy old man grasps his arm, hissing, "Bambi, you," but Pierre swings his arm deftly with the precision of a practiced professional who's used to facing crazy people going wild in the mental ward at midnight. He smirks provocatively, acting the part, speaking in that seductive French I can't get used to just yet, *"Problème, monsieur?"* and strides away with inborn arrogance.

Saul starts to chase after the black shadow, but I'm one step ahead. Holding onto a fat arm, clawing at the pink flesh and the stained T-shirt underneath the worn leather jacket, I put on the sweet act, "Saul, Bambi left the goods with me. Let's get out of the hospital first. You don't want us discovered with a stash of ketamine here, do you?"

The old man screws up his eyes, observes me through the microscopic lenses of cruel scrutiny and suspicion. His bloodshot whites looks like they belong to someone who's buried alive. He sneers, poking my stomach with his gnarled pinky finger. "Ya pregnant?"

"I'm not." I shy away from his touch with disgust. Instinct is something I can't control.

"Found ya walking in this war' with tha' fucker Bambi. Where's he goin'?" Saul slurs. His hand fiddles with my knitted dress like a nauseating routine. I gag into my elbow.

"Sorry. Bambi is getting the goods. He's waiting for us in the parking lot."

"In the hospital? You nuts."

"No, it's a fifteen-minute walk from here. He parked the car along with the goods in the nearby park." I avert my eyes. One more look at his face—the yellowed, gaping teeth, the stench, the stains—and I will vomit my intestines out. "Mind walking a bit?"

"Walk? With a pregnant lady? Not my taste."

"Or do you want the police here?" I pinch his wandering hand, keeping it away from my waist.

"Angel, don't forget, you stabbed me first."

"And I got what you want," I bite back.

Saul pauses, doing an acrobatic act inside his brain to calculate the options. I can hear the cogs running at full speed in his mind. After a while, he flashes me a queasy smile. "Let's go, then. To the park."

I swallow, nodding to him and leading the way. He overtakes me, pulling me close, wrapping an arm around my shoulders, trapping me in his mass of filthy-smelling flesh. In fear and trembling, I press the emergency call button on my phone, which directly links to Pierre's number. He picks up without a word, silently listening, acting the perfect accomplice.

One more life. Help me take one more life, Bambi, and save our daughter.

Chapter 23: The Park. The Lake. The Ending (Almost).

April 15, 2025 – Old Montreal, QC, Mount Royal Park

Pierre is leaning against the faded silver 2020 Honda's passenger door. Black trench coat, black turtleneck sweater, wool pants, and leather boots. He puffs the cigarette to life, blowing rings of smoke into the air without a thought. The square belt buckle gleams in the glinting sunlight. His eyes are cast on our approaching shadows—Saul and me, walking side by side, glued together by Saul's brute force. His lips open, as if wanting to protest, but my glare shuts them right up. Don't speak. Not now. Not when everything is so close to the perfect ending.

Saul shoves me toward Pierre, and he catches me with visible relief. I can hear the stones dropping from his heart, and perhaps it is the hormones, or the child, or both, but I have the sudden urge to weep for us all. Pierre traps me inside his arms, never letting me go again, refusing to let my face show to others besides himself. "Saul." He grinds his teeth with an unknown anger, which surprises even him. "Long time no see, eh?"

My skin pricks. A shiver runs along my spine. The silhouette hovers over my head and the warmth seeps through my blouse, resurrecting the ghost of the dead man I revere in the temple with sacred devotion. A swift scent of oakwood and patchouli invades my nose, tearing my whole body apart until my eyes soften with unspeakable sorrow. Pierre's grip on my shoulders turns brutal. He is grounding me in the present, as much as himself, because the persona he imitates is eating him away in excruciating torment. *It's alright.* I pat the back of his hand. *As long as we both suffer.*

"Darn right. Too long. And here I thought ya were dead." Saul cackles, but his words ring with laden threats. "Turns out yous were outta the city and lived off the grid, eh? Ya happy?"

"Can't say I'm not." Pierre retreats with cautious steps. I tug his sweater. He should've shrugged with a more carefree attitude. "I mean, my baby's on the way."

"Whose baby?" Saul leers. I can feel his eyes trail down my back in that hideous, flirtatious way. My brain forces the bile down my stomach. The tears swell up, waiting for the war.

"Mine." Pierre grunts, throwing the cigarette away, crushing me closer to his body. "Problem?"

"None. 's long 's you gimme that stuff, then I'll be well on my way. There's a delivery tonight at Judy's house. Young, fresh girls out of the slammer. Wanna be in?" Saul takes his silver cigar case out of his leather jacket pocket, knocking a few times to get one out, cocking one eyebrow at Bambi, warning him that "no" isn't an answer.

"Of course I'm in. Where's Judy's house?" My leg brushes his ankle lightly. He takes the cue with haste, changing his tone. "Has she moved since the last time we spoke?"

Saul watches him through the slit of his aging eyes. The fat on his cheeks quivers for a brief second; his wrinkles fold up on each other, making his face more beastly than human. He clips off the cigar's head, saying curtly, "Judy never moved. Judy isn't a person. Bambi, some'in' wrong with your head?"

Pierre clutches my coat, holding me in place. He turns slightly aside to shelter my vitals from any possible attacks. His legs spread farther apart, taking a firm stance, one hand pretending to reach for my stomach while trying to grasp the Colt .45 in his back pocket. "Must've been the meth. Crystal meth messes with the head. You know that, right?" He grins.

"Nah, I don't." Saul retreats to the light spot in the parking lot. It is approaching high noon. There's nobody here except us three and the empty cars. Bambi weaves our bodies into the shadow of the tree nearby, in a truncated corner, where no driving recorder can catch us. "Ya rat bastards. What are ya tryna pull?"

It happens faster than words can describe. Saul pulls his Browning 19mm from the lining of his leather jacket, aiming for my head. He wants to hold me hostage. It always works out that way for him—using the treasure to lure in the pirates and holding them as slaves. But this hideous animal dressed in the pigskin of a man is no Bambi. And I'm not treasure he can take advantage of. Fool's gold, that's what we are. Pierre shoves me toward the car, shielding me with his towering figure. Without a moment of hesitation, before I can grasp what is happening, before Saul can utter another threat, before the dust of the afternoon has the chance to settle down on the windshield wiper, he pulls the trigger.

Bang. Bang. Two shots. Right between the eyes. No remorse. Saul falls to the gravel earth like a sack of meat on sale at the end of the day in a cheap supermarket.

I watch the blood seeping out from his head as his body jerks a few times before settling its deal with death, feeling adrenaline pumping me with life. *Live, Angie*, the dying Bambi whispers in my ears, ever so gentle and loving, tenderness mixing with fervent adoration no one ever has ever known besides me. *Live free.* The living Pierre turns toward me, flashing me a full-toothed grin, his eyes dark with something I can't quite figure out yet. "Well, he shouldn't have done that. I had no choice. As the saying goes, when worse comes to worst and whatnot. Phew, now, you get in the car while I drag this pig down the lake."

"Bambi –"

"Pierre." He tuts, his smile is purely pain and agony, stained in the soft color of the upcoming spring buried under the layer of white snow.

"Pierre, let's leave him there. Let's not dispose of the corpse. What if someone finds out?"

"My brother is waiting for him down there. I'm not going to leave this filthy bastard on the shore in his peaceful sleep. Angela, you think you're the only one with a vengeance?" Bambi looks at me.

For the first time, the mask peels off. The sadness in his eyes, the anger at the injustice of life, the suffering acceptance because he can't change anything, and the worst of all, the contagious darkness in all of us. He doesn't speak a word after that. Neither does he care if I get in the car following his orders or not. In that eerie silence, Pierre drags the corpse to the trunk of the silver Honda and stuffs it into the black nylon bag we prepared yesterday. He ties the bag neatly with eerie expertise. The stones and the weight are added on more skillfully than I had done. Heaving the plastic bag into the trunk, he gets into the driver's seat, motioning his head to the passenger side, telling me to get in. I acquiesce; my brain is still trying to process what happened. Much to my surprise, I find myself elated at the sick twist of events. The monster in me peeks its head through my morality's last oppressive reign. *More. Drain Saul's blood. Skin him. Break his bones. Sacrifice him for the unborn child.* I shiver at the thought. Throughout the whole fiasco, I realize that I've been smiling.

"It's fun, isn't it? Being the one handing out the judgment. Punishing the wrongs. Throwing the first stone. How does it feel now that you've tasted the pure flavor of absolute power?" Pierre presses the start button, puts the car into reverse, and gets us out of Mount Royal Park's parking lot. I turn around; on the fence, there is a signboard that reads, *Maintenance in progress. No trespassing.*

Ignoring his question, I point at the board the wind has just blown off. "Is that your doing? The signboard."

"Yup. I love the details. Set up the stage, lure in the prey, make him think he's the hunter, but in the end, he's nothing but mere entertainment, dancing the last tango before I crush him under my feet. Man, I always wanted to do that." Pierre cackles wildly, slamming his hands on the steering wheel.

"Is that why you chose psychiatry?"

"Part of the reason. I wanted to learn, you know, search for the meaning in my own way, why humanity is such a shit show." He hums a song. The lyrics come to my mind like a nightmare on repeat.

"What about Jean-Paul? You said you were waiting for him to come back here and find you."

"And I did. Jean-Paul knew something was wrong from the start—he told me often that humans preached thou shall not kill, but they justified killing to fit the narrative. It will not be a crime if it benefits the hierarchy. It's a shit show, a stinking pigsty. He said the one who created this world, who shaped human beings as we are, must have been someone full of flaws. He made us misunderstand each other because He feared if we become strong, He will be overthrown. Jean-Paul was full of stuff like that. He was the wisest man I've ever known. But there's only so much wisdom humans can tolerate, you see. He was too wise for his own good, and they came for him. While I…" Pierre taps on the wheel, slamming the gas pedal. "I hide. Blend in with the crowd. Make them think I'm one of them. Play it safe. Sure, it took a heavy toll on me, but I had faith that Jean-Paul would come back and save me from this tedious reality TV show. And he did." He turns on music. The National's "Pink Rabbits."

"What do you mean?" I shield my stomach, somewhat apprehensive, but a shrill voice comes out of me in ardent expectation. "You wanted to be saved by Bambi."

"No. You, Angela, were saved by Bambi. And I…" He turns toward me with a madman's smile, full of delusion in its unshakable belief. "I was saved by your existence, which was brought to me by Jean-Paul's death. He was a genius, wasn't he?"

I let that statement sink in, hoping my daughter won't grow up like these lunatic twins. I still have a chance to abandon the past and start a new life; I can leave Jean-Paul and Pierre behind as a bad fever dream, and go my own way from here. Though I have no friends left, nor family for that matter, I can rent a small room in a faraway town, building my life from scratch. Maybe I will meet new people—normal people—who will teach me how to love myself the right way. Maybe there will be temptation again, because life is full of it, but I will pull through because my daughter will be there for me. The child will grow up with plenty of love to share. And though her genes are tainted with the devil's blood, she is strong enough to distinguish between taking a life and saving one. That should be enough, and I know it. But the sweetness of the apple comes before the tart settles in. I suck on the juice, biting the crisp flesh, thinking it is too good to let go, thinking if it was not meant to be eaten, why did God make it so delicious and appealing? Addiction is the will to disobedience, and the good Lord knows I would do anything to rebel against the teaching that leads humankind to kill one another in His name.

"Pierre. You're sick," I mutter, six feet deep in my thought.

"You bet. My mother never had me tested, but with the trust in my highly distinctive degree, I can assure you that I'm sick. And it can't be cured. Blessed be the curse we're born with. Heh. He was also sick, you know—Jean-Paul, that is. Saintly in his sickness, of course, but sick nonetheless."

"Bambi had his ending planned out to perfection, just like how you planned Saul's ending. I wonder, Pierre, do you ever think of your exiting act—the grand finale, as Bambi would have called it?"

Pierre stays silent. He looks out the windshield, watching the winding road unfurl ahead of us as we drive down the mountain. The trees are still barely green. The budding leaves and flowers dot the scenery like a painting from the nineteenth century, and perhaps it will stay that way forever, until humankind no longer inhabits the earth. There is an arrogant resilience in how the trees and the mountains refuse to die, while all I can think about is how to end my life in the most spectacular, extravagant way—before I had a life, my most precious gift, my treasure, my sole reason to move on, grown inside of me. Perhaps Pierre thinks the same. Or he simply doesn't pay attention to my nonsense. After all, I keep going on about Bambi, the man he doesn't know—doesn't want to know. What he longs for, what he conjures up in his mind is his loving brother, Jean-Paul, who would never have abandoned him to the waves of life.

"Jean-Paul would never think of ending his own life." That was what Pierre had said when we talked about Bambi in our planning. It was hard for him to comprehend how a person like his brother, who loved life enough to run away from the garbage dump and find the ladder to heaven, would one day think of dying that easily. Surrendering isn't weakness; I told him as much, but Pierre wouldn't listen. He adamantly explained to me with the patience of a teacher to an ignorant babe: Surrendering isn't a choice. We argued about the right to die by our own hands. I told him he wouldn't understand because he hadn't lived through it. He retorted back, "You haven't lived my life long enough to preach that to me."

Yes, Pierre is crazy. *A good pawn*, Bambi told me before closing his eyes for eternity, but I wasn't smart enough to use it. A generation of manipulators; that's who they are. One refused to obey and became the martyr for his faithless religion. One conformed to the masses and waited for a chance to destroy the cage. From the start, I should've known neither of them belonged to the normal side of society. But I know, as a voiceless blue whale recognizes another like her, the Raymond twins are the only human beings left who still have enough love for life in them. They renounced the wars; they sneered at greed; the daily material hustle makes them sick with disgust; and ironically, both share the same will to see the goodness in a human's heart. Too bad, one of them couldn't live to see the end of his belief in universal truths. Maybe if Jean-Paul "Bambi" Raymond had made a different choice, he would've stayed—he would've been ordinary. But he opted for the path toward the legendary; he wanted to leave behind an indelible mark, and his death, no matter if it was inevitable or not, is the proof of life's exiled beggar. Pierre is right. One can only tolerate so much wisdom. Toward the final moment, perhaps Jean-Paul had surrendered to his mind and become the outsider to the normal happiness of the life he yearned to have.

Sadly, the goodness is tainted. It's hard to find someone pure enough to forgive the left and the right. Pick a side and stick with the hate. That's what we are taught. But Jean-Paul would never take a side, thinking one set of humans has more rights than the other. I laugh at the thought of Bambi choosing a side and fighting for it simply because people told him to. Right, we grew up differently. He was raised on drugs by a parent with a case of naloxone always by her bedside. I was… What was I before him?

"What do you want to do with him?"

Pierre's question breaks my train of thought.

"With whom?" I ask, somewhat muddled in my reality.

"That corpse. Saul or whatever his name is. What do you want?"

"Oh, right. I thought you said you wanted to put him in the lake?"

"That's what I would do. Because it would be a circle and because I think my brother would've wanted that. Did my brother tell you he wanted that?" Pierre glances at me briefly before stopping at an elbow on the mountain road.

"He did. He wanted Saul drowned."

"And you'd do what he wished? Are you his dog, jumping at the treat and playing catch?" Pierre mocks. Somehow, his tone turns red with fury.

"I wanted to obey him. Is there anything wrong with that?"

"I suppose not. It's your life. You can choose to ruin it six ways to Sunday, and I have no right to interfere." Pierre shrugs, leaning back on the seat, relaxing his shoulders and his legs. The temperature outside is still cold. "But Angela, he won't be there to bear the consequences for you. Not before, not now, not ever. I suppose you understand that much, or don't you?"

"What are you getting at?" I raise the question charily.

"Ever heard the saying, 'No matter how much you love the dead, they won't love you back'? That's what I'm getting at. Don't get me wrong. I'm perfectly alright with how things are. I killed someone; that's plenty good for me. I can choose how to move forward now: go back to being the white sheep, or shedding the mask and becoming the black sheep. But that's my life; I'll live it how I want. That's Jean-Paul's gift to me, I guess. Breaking the surface and diving to the bottom of the sea. Facing the darkness within lest it has the chance to burst out when I least expect it. You, Angela—what will you do?"

"I don't know yet. Stay here, perhaps." I avoid his eyes, facing the windows. The lake underneath the mountain is a deep shade of azure.

"And chasing after the shadow of Bambi once more?"

"At least I have a daughter with me now."

"That's right. A daughter. What will she grow up to be? Have you ever thought about that? Where do you find the love for her when you can't even love yourself properly?"

"And why do you care?" I snap. In a violent fit of anger, I grab his coat collar, screaming in his face with the full blow of the anger I had repressed since the day Bambi was gone. "Did I choose to be this way? No. Did I want to be in your brother's fucked-up mess? No. I thought I could save him. You were right in guessing that. I was stupid. Pathetic and naive in my innocence, thinking everything would be cured if I could love him enough. You keep going on and on about how everyone is lesser than you both. What a joke. You can't even function as an individual in this society. Your sickness can't be cured. I was wrong. You love life, but you don't love the humans living within it. Look at it, Pierre; face it properly. You never wanted to save anyone but yourself. Don't act all high and mighty with me. You know full well from the start that your heart never has a place for anyone else but you, not even your beloved brother."

Pierre's pupils blow wide. He jumps at me, shoving me to the passenger window, pressing my shoulders to the frame until they bruise. The pain wakes me from my reverie. The cold outside seeps into the cracks of the metal frame and it laughs at our puny skeletons. We should have tolerated each other, loving the suffering on our backs, because nothing's going to last and our existence is but a meaningless thing without the warmth we share. But the lesson is long overdue. Pierre hisses; his words stab, his voice hoarse. The rumble sounds like he is the resurrection of Bambi from the realm of the exiled for the worst sinners in the Lord's eyes.

"You choose that ending yourself. You made the choice. Don't go saying otherwise and putting the blame on me or my brother. You played the game because—"

"Because I fucking loved your brother, you stupid, selfish motherfucker," I shout, squirming, punching his gut with all my strength. But he is far removed from the physical pain. His hands strangle my neck with inhuman force. The devil shows its face in his bloodshot eyes, his slowly revealing dark circles, and his loosened hair:

"Don't speak to me about love. You know that love won't save anyone. It didn't save him, or me, or you, or anyone for that matter." He smiles wickedly. I kick my feet, scratching at him, but the thick coat protects him from the sharp attack. The car shakes in our struggle. In a choked breath, I call his name: "Pierre. Pierre. Fuck it, stay with me, Pierre. Bambi." I yell the last word with all the power left in my limp body. He releases me immediately at the name. I cough out the dry air, and my body doubles over the seat. Tears stream down my face. It is fear. It is instinct trying to warn me of the same dark road again. "Bambi." I whisper his name. Who are you at this moment? Who is here with me?

"Angela, do you love me?"

Pierre drops the question out of nowhere; his voice is uncannily calm, as if our fight never happened. He lights a cigarette, puffing it a few times so the smoke flows out in a white fog. The mood swing is a glaring red light. None shall pass.

"I said, do you love me?" He holds my chin up, fixing me with an intense gaze. The darkness in his eyes gleams in the shadow of the trees and I catch my breath. Now I see where the familiarity comes from. It is the same darkness I saw in Bambi's eyes the first time I met him. In trembling and terror, I nod without thinking. "Really? Me or Bambi, who do you love more?"

There is only one correct answer. I feel my daughter kick my stomach in protest. *Breathe, Angie, breathe,* Bambi's voice caresses my ears. I hold Pierre's hand in my palms, my voice tremulous and soft like a breeze: "Both. I love you both."

"But which one?" He pushes for more. I retreat further; my hand reaches for the door handle.

"Pierre. Let's—"

He doesn't let me finish. Caging me against the car door, his looming figure loses its threatening sharpness; the innate arrogance deflates; the self-assured smirk leaves his face like a ghost leaving its haunting place. He speaks without understanding my half-answer: "You're a liar. No one loves Pierre. No one ever wants Pierre to live."

Great. One baby in my stomach. A bigger, more troublesome baby to take care of in my daily life. I let go of the fear balloon in my heart, holding out my arms to gather the shattered pieces of Pierre into a neat bunch. How could I forget? Twins; both share the same genetically broken soul.

"But I want Pierre." I coo in his ear as his head nestles into my neck, finding solace in the warmth no one has ever shown him all these years he's been living. "Pierre's a good person."

"Maman said Pierre was unwanted. Both Jean-Paul and Pierre were unwanted, an accident."

"Maman was wrong, wasn't she? Because Jean-Paul was loved by many." I sniffle, suppressing my own grief, because the wounds of the man before me are far greater than mine.

His eyes are vacant, his lips are quavering, and he keeps mumbling, "My existence is an accident."

I hold his face in my hands, smiling through the tears, hoping the love will reach him in his dark place: "And Pierre will be loved, too."

"Maman is dead. And now, Jean-Paul has also left. No one's staying for Pierre."

"But I'm staying. See? I'm staying with Pierre, living with Pierre, and feel this." I place his lax hand on my stomach. Through the knitted dress, the baby kicks his lanky limbs alive. "The baby is staying with Pierre."

He watches with interest as the skin on my stomach changes slightly to show a footprint, so tiny it could be crushed with the sheer force of his weight, yet so immensely powerful that it drags him out of the lethargic despair as quickly as a whirlpool of sweet cotton candy. Pierre swerves the car into a grocery's parking lot so fast he makes me yank at the seatbelt out of surprise. I open my mouth in protest, but his face stops any foul curses rising up in my throat. The sparkle in his eyes, the pure happiness that beams from every pore, and his hands tremble as he slowly reaches forward to remove my seatbelt reverently as if he is in awe of the life inside me. Pierre kneels on the seat, lowers his head further, pressing his ears against my stomach, listening to the soft beating of the child's heart. A smile plastered on his face, as if he is caught in a trance, Pierre says in monotone: "Are you staying with Pierre?"

The child kicks once, twice. I ruffle his gelled hair. "She said yes."

"And are you staying with Pierre?" He looks at me, begging without words, praying without tears. The thunderstorm in his eyes makes it harder and harder for me to refuse. *Live free*, Bambi had said. How could I, when he left his brother's life in my hands without ever asking me if I wanted another love in my life or not?

"Yes." I nod. The tears flow of their own will. It isn't a bad idea; delivering the older brother and saving the younger one. I should've written a memoir of my sorrow, called it *The Gospel of the False Judas*. "I'm staying with Pierre."

He beams with happiness. Though the smile isn't visible anymore, his eyes convey how much gladness he feels. The light overtakes the shadow. The darkness disappears. The azure orbs become transparent, almost turning back the clock to retain the innocence they had lost to the suffering they were force-fed. He rushes back to the driver's seat and pulls out of the parking lot, driving at full speed down toward the grocery on the hill's winding road. The elation flushes his cheeks a deep red.

"Where are we going?" I grip my seatbelt, speaking in a sing-song voice, trying to appease him lest he swing back into that dark mode again. My knuckles turn white. Sweat drips down my spine. I am walking on a broken mirror and beneath the surface, there is nothing but a million reflections of the worst possibilities, waiting to gnaw at me, swallow me whole, crush my bones into smithereens.

"We wait. It's too early to dispose of the corpse. We need an alibi first. I'll drop you off at the Chinatown gate. Get to a tea shop or a family restaurant and wait for me there." He whistles, quite happy with the picture he's painting in his mind.

"What about you?"

"Aw, sweet Angie cares about me." His smile is sweet and indulgent, but the eerie sensation keeps crawling on my body like prickling thorns and thistles. "Don't worry. I'll go back home, change to a new set of clothes, dye my hair back to its original color, and hang around my friend's clinic before meeting you. Listen carefully." His voice turns serious, dripping with the precise calculation of a meticulous, seasoned murderer. "We must leave a reasonable window of time beyond suspicion. Here's the map for action: Angie, you stop by the bakery at the corner of Rue de la Gauchetière Ouest— that's French for west. It's easy to locate; I'll send you the address. Once you get there, slowly browse the sweets on display, stroke your stomach, make sure that people see everything, then feign low blood sugar—"

"How do I feign low blood sugar?"

"You are having low blood sugar. It's in your blood test. Don't you feel dizzy?" He rolls his eyes.

"A little, yes." I mull over the last few days. It's true that dizziness comes to me more frequently now.

"Not only that, but your heartbeat is also faster, arrhythmia. It's normal in your case, as you have severe depression, a heavy dependency on sleeping pills, a bad sleeping schedule, all while being pregnant. With your medical record at the Montreal General Hospital, it's obvious that you will faint after walking a long distance." He raps out the diagnosis with supersonic speed, leaving no place for a retort. "Based on my calculation, with a slice of buttered toast for breakfast and holding out until now on nothing but air, you will probably—no, you will definitely faint if you browse the bakery for ten minutes."

"And then?" I lean toward him, fascinated by the prowess of his brain. The same genius that's brought me to him is now binding me to a new fate.

"Then, people will call your emergency contact or 911, or both. It's better if it's both. Your emergency contact is me, Pierre Raymond, yes?" He raises one eyebrow at me. I nod, checking my phone again to be sure, then nod once more in affirmation. "Good, then I'll wait for that call at my friend's clinic. I will turn on the speaker, unintentionally, of course, and my friend will be the witness for both of us." He smirks, visibly satisfied at his blueprint.

"What about after? We'll be going to the ER? What if they discover Saul's corpse while you park the car? And your friend, is he safe?" I fiddle with the hem of my sweater dress. The adrenaline from when I saw Saul's death is coursing through my veins again. It's exhilarating. Life should be like this—living on the edge of danger.

"You're smiling. Do you like the plan that much?"

"Am I?" I touch my face. My lips are stretching upward. "Maybe I like it. A lot."

"Well, let me wow you some more." He chuckles in that low, suave voice, filled with thick smoke and wine perfume. "My friend works for an OB-GYN clinic. Based on what I know about her, she'll be more than thrilled to see me getting a girl pregnant. The rumors at the hospital in Laval go that I'm impotent. Pierre the Eunuch. Might as well take this chance to get rid of the nickname."

"But you shouted at the hospital ward just now that the child wasn't yours." I tug at his coat sleeve, no longer able to distinguish between Bambi and Pierre. Who's in front of me? Is it him who has returned from the dead?

"But that wasn't me." He grins, observing the road with eagle vision and swerving to the left, taking a sharp right to get downtown. "That was Bambi. Bambi was a monster."

"Then your plan is?" I ask with bated breath. It's him. He's back.

"First, let's drop you off here." He stops at the red, ornamented gate with the unique carving of Chinese dragons and phoenixes, glancing briefly at the clock on the car's dashboard. The red digits show 11: 15. "Then, I will kill Bambi. Now, sweet angel, kiss me goodbye, hm?"

He puts out his left cheek expectantly, so confident in getting what he wants that I have to laugh at the childishness. How can I refuse such demands from my world? I place a long, arduous kiss on the pale skin until my sheer, pink lip gloss sticks to his face. "Gross," he laughs, then putting his other cheek out, "One more." I indulge his whims, caught in the whirlwind of his impulsive fever dreams, then get out of the car, staggering toward the bakery on Rue de la Gauchetière Ouest. Bambi honks once after I'm ten feet ahead to get my attention; I turn back, catching him waving at me in that flamboyant way. I wave back, and walk firmly ahead, my back straighter.

It's alright. I know he will be there to catch me this time. Pierre was no Bambi. Neither was Pierre a monster. Pierre's the real devil.

Chapter 24: Chinatown

April 15, 2025 – Montreal Chinatown, 1 p.m., a bakery on the Rue de la Gauchetière Ouest

After a long stroll around Chinatown, I drag my feet into the bakery, my forehead dripping wet, my hair matted. Clutching my chest, I try to temper my breathing and my racing heart. The fast beat rings in my ears. Pierre was right; I'm ten minutes away from fainting.

Pushing open the glass door, I inhale the calming sugary scent mixed with the aromatic fragrance of black tea. I close my eyes, picking out each flavor: orange pekoe, first flush; earl grey, tea bags instead of loose leaves; donuts, freshly out of the fryer, sprinkled with powder sugar; and of course, chocolate, how can I miss the chocolate? My mouth waters at the thought of a hot twisted donut and an ice-cold milk tea, double strength. Unconsciously, my hand draws circles on the small bump; my daughter kicks in agreement.

Walking around the different display sections, my nose perks up at the egg tarts the grumpy lady has just brought out from the oven, the chocolate glazed donuts and the Boston cream lying side by side, inviting with their colorful sprinkles and promising delicious taste. In haste, I stride toward the donut case. The sweet scent of powdered sugar, the treats with their delectable golden color in the glinting afternoon sunlight, as if they are screaming for everyone to grab one or all of them and cash out immediately, tearing out their flesh right after—the sheer imagination is making my mouth water. My head is foggy with want. I reach out my hand, yearning for the taste of squishy dough on my tongue, inches away from the glass case, when another hand catches mine. "Madam, no touching. Use the tray," the grumpy service lady says, annoyed at my impertinence.

"I'm sorry, I was just," I swallow a thick gulp of saliva, "a bit hungry."

"No touching." She motions to the set of trays at the front of the display section. "Use the tray."

My stomach churns. She frowns at my sorry state, unwilling to linger there lest her pay be deducted for helping a white pregnant lady. Brushing my hand aside, she walks briskly away, taking the empty cake trays and shoving them back to the kitchen, preparing for new loads. Good, one target down. I need to get as many as possible before the ten-minute window finishes. Picking up a tray and a pair of tongs, I browse around the store, soaking in the cool air and the sweet smell. A child runs by, grasping my sweater dress, lifting his eyes to look at me expectantly. I smile at him, taking a melon pan from my tray, waving it toward him questioningly. "Do you want one, little cutie pie?"

The boy beams at the treat, reaching his hand out to get the pastry, but his mother quickly picks him up and takes him away. She throws me a doubtful stare while I wave at the happily smiling boy. It's weird how children know immediately who's a good person when the adults always think everyone is inherently bad at heart. Going back to the castella cake section, I pick out two fresh sponge cakes on discount. The chance of me eating them is slim to none anyway. A pungent smell of dampened clothes left for three days in the dryer pervades my nose; the bile rises in my throat and I quickly cover my mouth lest the vomit pours out. I glance around, searching for the source of the smell. A person has just come into the bakery, soaking wet. Outside, it is raining. Spring is coming.

Gradually, dirty footprints decorate the tiled floor of the bakery. I cower into the corner where the fried donuts are displayed, trying to calm myself with the comfortable scent of the cakes. Glancing at the red digits on the bakery's display screen, I count the minutes I have left. Three minutes until Pierre's predicted fainting fit. Ninety seconds to cause a ruckus and make the most out of my performance. I observe the clientele in the bakery in the late afternoon. It isn't too crowded, but there's still enough traffic to make the perfect audience size for Pierre's grand orchestration. An old lady passes by, glancing back at my paling face several times, and I seize the moment with lightning speed, falling forward, grasping her coat tail in my Oscar-worthy stage: "Madam, help, I don't feel so good." She yelps in surprise, holding me up, throwing away her full tray of sweets and pastries onto the bakery's parquet floor. Hiding a sneaky smirk behind my hand, pretending to gag, I swipe the display trays of cakes and savory treats to the floor, gasping for air. Low blood sugar, obviously, Pierre's voice rings in my muddled brain, and his hand guides mine toward the kind old lady who's shouting for someone to call an ambulance. His words escape through my mouth: "Call my husband. Please. I'm pregnant and have suffered from low blood sugar lately," I pant heavily. "He has my record." One more look at the red digits on the display screen. Three. The lady reaches for my phone in a panic mode, hitting the call button for the emergency contact. Two. The phone rings in her frightened prayer; the store clerks already called 911 in the meantime. One. Someone finally picks up the phone; Pierre's familiar voice breaks through a cloud of noise like a victory toll, "Hi sweetie, what's going on?" Zero. I close my eyes, letting the darkness swallow me into its glacier consolation.

Three-thirty p.m. Montreal General Hospital. Emergency unit.

I slowly open my eyes to various voices. None of them bears warm familiarity or a welcoming tone. The beeping noise only makes my headache worse. My left hand moves with difficulty and a dull pain. The IV drip is unbearable on my elbow. I want to call someone, but my voice is hoarse and grainy; there's barely any sound, only a feeble attempt at a pathetic cry. As I struggle to sit up in my weakened, hazy state, a tattooed arm reaches in, pulling the curtain aside. Pierre's crow's nest hair appears before his face peeks in. "Hey, sweetie." His voice is wrought with worry. "How are you feeling?"

I shake my head, smiling. My heartbeat grows calmer as the beeping noise turns slower. Pierre glances briefly at the stats in front of the bedrest, nodding satisfactorily. "Good. Your blood sugar level was a bit low. The baby is alright. I could get you discharged now, but we need to see the OB-

GYN doctor first. Do you mind waiting?" He speaks with such a disgustingly sweet tone that I want to laugh. A superb actor on his way to his first Golden Globe. "What's the matter?" His eyes beam at me. The indulgence is so decadent I think the love is real at last.

"Water," I mutter with difficulty. My throat is a desert with sand dunes and coarse dust.

"Gotcha. I'll be back with ice chips." He glances around as if searching for someone, finds her, and motions with his head to urge her quickly to my bed. "Meanwhile, wait here with Lucille, m'kay, sweetheart?"

Who the fuck is Lucille? I ask with my frown.

"The friend," he replies with a lifted eyebrow, "who's our witness."

A sweet woman in her late thirties appears right after that comical, muted conversation. Her blonde hair is tied neatly into a bun. A pair of owl glasses don her face, further enhancing the typical appearance of a successful doctor. The sheer pink lip gloss catches the glaring white light of the ER room as she speaks with a sickeningly sweet voice to Pierre, her hand slightly brushing his arm. "Oh my gosh, how is your brother's girlfriend?"

I look at Pierre's darkened eyes, the disgust barely showing, cracking my lips a little in soundless mockery: *Your brother's girlfriend?*

He detaches himself from the female doctor with practiced expertise, suavely sliding along the bedpost, hooking his finger to get my report and focusing on fake reading the stats with intense interest. "Angie, you don't might staying here with Lucille for a bit, do you, dear? I'll be back in a second." He flashes me a smile then quickly disappears, tactfully evading Lucille's intentional pull on his vintage beige vest as she tries to call him back. The longing in her eyes fails no one, even the blind. Poor unfortunate soul; she has fallen for the devil's disguise, no doubt.

I cough, catching her attention with a few ragged breaths. Lucille strides to my side with the confidence of a highly revered doctor. She isn't my doctor in charge, but she takes the flimsy excuse of checking my current state to scrutinize me under her morality's microscope. Bring it on; I'm passed the stage of society's judgment and accusation anyway. Clicking her tongue, Lucille takes a chair and sits down a few inches from me, distancing herself from someone she clearly knows is an ex-junkie. The high horse she sits on must be super comfortable; I can't help but visualize the fall.

"You know doctor Pierre?" she asks, the hard 'r' in Pierre's name rolling on her tongue with sensual seduction. "How?" And the tone goes right back to terse, cold professionalism.

"Brother." I struggle to talk. What beastly reason can make a doctor interrogate a sickly patient, pregnant, on her rattling bed, about her new crush for Dr. Pierre the Eunuch?

"Pierre's brother. I see. Was he the man causing the ruckus this morning in the OB-GYN ward? The nurses here made him go through a difficult verification, you know, regarding that incident. But they're twins, right? Only different personalities. And hair. And education." Her eyes grow dreamy and hazy with some unsightly imagining. "I never knew Pierre could also look so…you know?" She gestures vaguely toward her clothes and figure.

I nod. Of course I had known how weirdly sinister he could look all along. Different personalities, my ass. Different madness, yes. And yes, from the start, he's always been so Pierre.

"So when I heard he resigned from his position at the hospital in Laval a few days back, I was thoroughly surprised. I never knew he had a twin brother. My gosh, that changes everything, doesn't it? I heard from his supervisor's talk that his brother is an outlaw, a junkie. What else did he do? You're his girlfriend. It must be tough on you, dear." She casts a look of pity toward my sleep-deprived, life-battered face. I can't bother to tear her head off. She goes on in her delusional rant. "Pierre is such a wonderful man. I mean, taking care of his brother's pregnant girlfriend, quitting his job to devote his full attention to saving your life. I never knew he had that in him."

Because he never had that in him. I roll my eyes in my mind's safe room. Pierre is a selfish jerk, focusing only on saving himself, always waiting for others to save him first. You never noticed him before, lovely blonde Lucille who grew up in a tree house with so much love and caring from both parents and a private education. That's because he is that good at acting the part. If he wants to stay in the game, he must abide by the rules. In that way, he's no different from his twin brother. I search for Pierre's shadow with a satirical heart. He really knows his way around the Laval hospital, and he cast the right actress for the witness role.

"Anyways, where's your boyfriend?" She smiles, continuing the one-sided conversation without me ever wanting to respond. Her perfectly manicured hand taps on the bed railing, the sweetness in her eyes restored as she detects that I'm no longer a threat to her supposed romance with Pierre, the suffering soul.

I shake my head weakly, indicating I don't know, meaning my existence in his life was the catalyst for his death a few months back. She seems taken aback for a second then regains her composure just as quickly, tapping her heels on the floor, glancing around, waiting for Pierre to come back. The charming prince in the beige vest turns heads and eyes in the unit as he strides toward my bed in style. A neatly ironed shirt, faded jeans, Oxford shoes to match the palette of the good guy, he brings with him a large paper cup of ice chips and a stout, extremely angry-looking nurse. "Sorry," he smiles, somewhat sheepishly, "She was a bit busy with other patients. They're short staffed, as always, everywhere."

Lucille beams; if her professionalism hadn't been so ingrained in her mind and taking full control of her body, she would've jumped from her chair and skipped toward Pierre, all mesmerized by his sudden gentleness. Instead, she stands up gracefully, tucking a loose hair behind her ear, fixing her bun, speaking in the gentle, subdued tone that is so different than mine: "Pierre, so glad you're back. She was in a horrible state. Who would leave a pregnant lady alone, walking around with her constitution?" She makes sure to emphasize the word *constitution* as if it was an inside joke only she and Pierre would understand.

"Right," Pierre agrees gingerly and turns to me in haste. "Let her examine you, alright, Angie?"

I try to mouth the words, *Lying fucker*, to him, and grin with my dry lips. That act is enough to sweeten his sickening mood swing, and he indulges the performance even more, fussing over the blanket ("Are you warm enough here?"), the fluids, the stats ("Your heart rate is lower, which is a good sign"), and every little thing that could get on my nerves. I kick my foot, but the strength isn't there. He replies with the moonbeam glint in his eyes, "We will get you sorted out, sweetheart."

Lucille squirms uncomfortably in her place, trying to get Pierre's attention. "Where's your brother, Pierre? I don't see him anywhere, and she needs a close family member by her side." The caring voice is so pretentious in its intention I can barely hold back another gag. Pierre talks without turning to see her. "He disappeared. I can't reach him. I've called many times but—"

"So many times." The nurse chimes in with a grunt of disapproval. "His phone must be blowing up. They all go to voicemail. What's the rush? She's not in labor." She tsks, checking the vitals once more per her duty, under Pierre's pleading stare.

"Yeah, Angie, I'm sorry, I can't reach Bambi," he apologizes without an ounce of sincerity, yet the handsomeness of the devil's face does plenty in persuading people of his meek, loving care for a stranger. "I wish he would pick up. I don't know where he is, either."

"Wasn't he here this morning with this mademoiselle?"

A kind voice intrudes into the busy atmosphere with practiced calmness and the seasoned temperament of a person who's been through a lot and has very little. It is the OB-GYN doctor I met for the checkup just a few hours ago. With a benevolent light in his grey, aging eyes, he lifts his glasses as a way of greeting: "Good to see you again, mademoiselle. How are you feeling?"

Maybe it is his way of handling himself among fake people, maintaining his truth amongst the bustling lies of others; or maybe throughout the fiasco with the mad Bambi and the devil-in-disguise Pierre, I find in him an unshakable anchor. The dignity in his posture, the firmness in his hands, wrinkled but powerful in their diagnosis, decisive and quick in their examination routine, make me want to confess. The hope of being saved, of being absolved of my sins, of returning to the masses is, as Pierre would say, human nature. As he places the stethoscope on my chest, listening to my heartbeat with a stoic demeanor plastered on his pinkish face, my lips quiver instinctively in a call for help, and Pierre catches that before the old doctor has the chance to ask.

"Angie, any discomfort?"

I am startled, reminded of where I am and the darkness of the swamp I live inside. Shaking my head weakly, I smile at him, docile and mild in my long-suffering whirlpool of anguish. The melancholia overtakes me for a moment, and my tears flow out of their own free will. "Aw, my Angie is in pain," Pierre says, quickly rushing to my side, stroking my hair, crooning in my ears. The voice and the reaction are so exceptionally similar to Bambi's that I think I am seeing double. The feeling is uncanny, and the eerie sensation latches onto my body like a haunting.

Lucille walks to Pierre's side, watching my sweat-soaked face with disinterest. "It's alright. All low blood sugar patients are the same." Pierre's shoulders jerk at that remark and I can sense him groan internally. The old doctor glances at her in deep reproach: "Not all patients are the same. Madame, each person has a different constitution, and Mademoiselle Angela is particularly weak after her long dependence on antidepressants and sleeping pills for her insomnia and disorders. Madame is also a doctor, yes?"

Lucille mumbles a tiny "Oui" in response, flushing to her ears.

"Then I trust that Madame will know better than assuming a patient's symptoms and diagnosis before you have conducted a thorough checkup." He continues listening to my vitals without paying another second of attention to Lucille's embarrassed profile in her pristine pencil skirt and cream blouse.

Pierre hides his face into my pillow as if he's hiding his tears, but I can clearly hear his hysterically suppressed laughter and the tiny, "Thank God someone is still around to speak the truth." My body convulses lightly, sharing his humor, and a choked cackle escapes my throat. This time, it doesn't escape the kind doctor. He pats my stomach gently, talking in a slow and measured glee. "The baby seems fine. I'm glad Mademoiselle finds joy in the most urgent moment of life. We all need that. As Edith Piaf sings, *'Nous ne formons qu'un seul corps, et le flot sans effort nous pousse, enchaînés l'un et l'autre, et nous laisse tous deux épanouis, enivrés et heureux.'* Right, *docteur* Pierre?" He winks at Pierre. Some meaning is so vibrant I can read it in the gray irises; some is lost immediately as the old doctor turns to walk away.

I turn toward Pierre, asking with my eyes, *What the fuck is that?*

He shrugs, acting confidently, but from that hunching posture, I know he has grown cautious. One can never be too suspicious of everyone. And dearest Lucille is stock still in her spot near Pierre, by the machines, mulling over the wisdom of the doctor, unaware of the storm just passing over her pretty little head.

"I think the doctor is angry with me." She finally says what all of us already know.

"Of course he would be angry, Lucille. Patient first, always." Pierre stifles a groan, trying to be calm in his explanation of what he would deem "the stupidity of the bureaucrats." He ruffles his hair, tempers his voice, staying in character all the while. "I mean, the first lesson we must remember is each case will be different. The doctor is right; Angela's constitution has been weak from the beginning. She is dependent on clonazepam, and no one in his right mind should've gotten her pregnant." His eyes grow dark; jealousy? Perhaps not. I don't want another monster besides me.

"Then your brother is—?" Lucille questions him, somewhat triggered by the new information she received.

"I don't care. I mean…" He slips back as I pinch his palm hard enough to leave a mark. "He hasn't picked up the phone. He must've gotten lost somewhere. It is just so…so him to be like that, you know? He's not the type to take responsibility." He grins apologetically at Lucille.

"Ice chips," I utter, my eyes growing soft with memory and sadness. Not the type to take responsibility. So him. Those phrases hit differently when the journey is through. Pierre still loves his brother, despite the odds never being in his favor. Or mine.

He quickly catches my words and hand-feeds the ice chips to me, much to my surprise and Lucille's. I'd wanted to refuse, but it's worth the pleasure to spite Lucille's distorted face, so I suck the ice chips off his fingers in relish. He melts at the act, as if that was what he'd been searching for all along, as if he'll never stop searching for that scene from now on. He yearns for the peace and the serenity in the picture-perfect frame of having someone to love him—the only human left to love him—for who he is, not who he will be. I indulge his fantasy, licking his fingertips, spoiling him with my eyes, sparkling with the love I hadn't had the chance to pour on Bambi. He rests his forehead on my abundant mass of hair, blooming with the thick scent of jasmine and coconut everywhere; the tenderness is overwhelming in each gesture, from the tip of his finger to the quiver of his eyelashes. "Let's get you discharged, shall we?" he purrs, and I concur with a quiet nod.

Lucille fades out of her role as the silent witness. She asks a few things, talking of the weather and getting a cab for the three of us. Perhaps we can stop by her house since it's closer than Pierre's place in Saint-Laurent. No, no, and no. Pierre simply shakes his head at every turn, not bothering to even answer with words. She's done enough, and there's no need for the spotlight to shine on her any longer. Let the lovers be the main actor and actress. They are dancing in the world of Edith Piaf, and the old doctor's voice lulls them away from the would-be of the world which hasn't yet learned how to be gentle.

Five-thirty p.m. We are on the road back to Pierre's house.

"Lucille is a real piece of work, huh?" I suck on the paper straw, trying to get as much as possible of the iced cappuccino left at the bottom of the plastic cup.

"Yeah. She's been that way since forever. In a way, she's like you. But fifty percent worse." Pierre sits at the steering wheel, maneuvering through the traffic on highway twenty, leading back to Saint-Laurent.

The car has transformed from the piece of crap he rented to orchestrate Saul's murder to his sleek BMW sedan. It's an older model, but the seats are comfortable, with the heater on and the modern tablet as the control panel. He turns the knob to choose the playlist and puts music on. The traffic gets worse as the evening grows a darker shade of purple. "Worse in what sense?" I lean back, reclining the seat to get the most out of the luxurious car. Money can't buy happiness, but it sure knows how to spoil the untermensch.

"She pities others instead of empathizing with them," he says nonchalantly, taking the nearest exit to get out of the traffic.

"And you don't like that?"

"I don't like her. Or anyone working at the hospital. Did you see how happy she is to help 'poor Pierre' out, fussing over every move? Man, she's never been that glad to share a meal with me before." He laughs with cruel bliss.

"You think everyone is a fake like her?"

"Am I wrong?" He raises one eyebrow toward me, provocative in his arrogance.

"I can't say you are or not. But if you don't trust her, why ask for her help from the beginning?"

"Because the more willing a person is to judge based on appearance, the easier it is to fool them. I don't blame anyone for that, actually. It's part of our safety net. Judging others is our only way to dissociate ourselves from imminent danger. You, on the other hand, might have lost that natural protective instinct since birth. A special evolutionary feature, I must say," he chortles in contempt. "Whether it is your luck or ill-fortune, you decide."

"I wouldn't choose to be any different if given the choice." I close my eyes, ready to fall asleep in the cozy warmth. "Now what? Did you taint this luxurious car with that filthy pig's blood?"

"I wouldn't do something that stupid." Pierre scrunches up his nose, shivering at the thought. "He's still inside the trunk of that disgusting Honda at the lakeshore."

"Lakeshore. You parked the car there, walked home, got out of the disguise, and casually gave sweet Lucille a visit?"

"Jackpot." He smacks his lips, blowing a kiss toward me. Somehow, I feel Pierre is gradually fading out and Bambi is gaining the ground in an exponentially accelerated racing car. "You give yourself less credit than you deserve, Angela. You're the most intelligent person I've talked to in a long while."

"Funny, your brother said the exact same thing when we first met."

"Can we not talk about the dead?" He rolls his eyes. The uncanny sensation keeps churning in my stomach. I hold onto my unborn child; the motherly instinct tells me the plot is going haywire. Pierre presses on the gas pedal. My heart sinks.

"What do we do now? Stop by your house, get out through the underground garage door—no, that'd be too obvious. Perhaps we drive to the park, stroll around, take in the fresh air, then—"

"Then, we spot the suspicious pungent smell of rotting flesh. Given the weather conditions and the heating car, a certain corpse would've decomposed a little." Pierre's face goes grim. His eyes focus on the imaginary park in the night. "You will call the cops while I check around the area, asking the few passersby if they've noticed anything. We'll wait for the police to arrive. The showdown begins." His eyes glint with the joy of a showman, malicious and delighted at the high success rate of his own orchestration.

"If you're that confident, I trust that Saul's corpse is no longer inside the trunk?"

"Oh, it's there, alright. But with so many putrid smells out there in the open space, who's to tell whether it's a human corpse's smell or a filthy rodent?" He gestures vaguely around the room. "A poor racoon got crushed by someone's speeding car. A prank gone wrong. Anything goes."

"You want to play the dangerous game?" I place the iced cappuccino into the cup holder, leaning further into the seat, wishing I could sleep there forever. "Can I have another coffee before then?"

"Yes, and no. I need the police to think that the report will be a prank. And you've had enough caffeine for today."

"Where's Saul?" I slur. My eyes can't stay open any longer.

"He's there, inside the nondescript car trunk, parked in a dull corner, under a shaded spot no one cares to look." Pierre takes a sip from my drink, so casually I find no offense in the action. "After the cops are gone, it'll be way past midnight. That's when the fun begins."

"I think I've also had enough fun for today."

"Aw, don't be that way. You're the main actress. Play the damsel in distress; you're perfect for the costume."

"Did you dispose of him? Saul?"

"Not yet." Pierre grows meditative, then he bounces back in a quick second. "Some preparation needs to be done. I want to make sure that he'll never resurface."

"What preparation are you thinking of?" I yawn, patting my stomach slightly. "Stabbing his lungs so his corpse won't have the chance to float up? Even though you've got deadweight inside the bag, you sure are meticulous."

"And you know your way around corpses." He winks, caressing my aching thigh, circling the visible stretch marks behind the stockings. I wince; the feeling is too familiar for my liking. I can't ground myself in this reality, and I don't know the border between the present and the past.

"Bambi went down the same way." I say, brushing his hand away, but he grips the flesh, unwilling to move an inch.

"Don't talk about the nonexistent." He growls, then whimpers in the same instant. "I didn't go down, remember? I told you before, Angie, I am Bambi. And you promised me you'd stay."

Great. I place my feverish hand on top of his. I got myself into the same trap. Same hunter, same old trick. But when the temptation is sweet enough, it pays to disobey the higher good of society. It is human nature. Didn't Adam and Eve's story start at the same point?

"You will get rid of Saul's corpse by midnight, then?" I murmur before falling into a shallow slumber.

"Anything, Angie. Anything to keep you here."

But his answer sounds more like a dream talking to me. By the time I wake up, we are already in the parking lot of the lakeshore park.

One-thirty a.m. We sneak into the vacant park. Darkness surrounds us, holding our hands like the sweet accomplice it always is to the children forsaken by the Holy Ghost.

The farce with the cops in the afternoon went way better than we had thought. After disposing of the stinking dead racoon, the police strolled around the parking lot a few more time, completed the protocols, then packed their things and went back to the station. Saul stayed snuggly inside the cheap car's trunk; no one noticed his festering sag of meat. We park our car next to the empty space beside the one with Saul's body. Pierre opens the trunk and heaves the plastic bag with Saul's corpse, both lungs stabbed through, down the lake. We watch it sink like a last rite for the life we buried together. In the hazy moonlit night and the dim yellow lamp shining through the canopy, we dream of our next chapter—one future where there will be more laughter than tears, and our days will be seasoned with a child's curious chirping, saying, "Maman, I'm happy here."

Pierre, I've got my own grave now. You must be happy, knowing your plan has played out perfectly like you sketched it. But Bambi, is it worth it? Sacrificing everything, and you are never the one to live in the end.

I lean on Pierre's shoulders, and he leans back on my head. No, it's wrong. Bambi is here. He's alive. He's never gone; his soul has just transmigrated from one poor, unfortunate person to the next.

Chapter 25: Rolling Stones

June 30, 2024 – Toronto, new condo, new furniture

I trudge toward the newly built suite with the faded number 3402 on the wooden door, turning the key in the lock; it won't open. Heaving an exhausted sigh, I place the paper bags of groceries down, and knock on the door to my own house. Pierre rushes to open it; I can hear him running through the entrance, knocking over the sofa, hitting his knee (perhaps) with a curse, and a few seconds later, a bearded face with two dark circles appears, all smiles. "Hey, where have you been?"

"Work. Supermarket. Hanging out with colleagues. Nothing fun, just the minimum necessary to keep the bills going." I remove my flats, leaving the heavy groceries to him, cracking my neck to release the tension in the weak muscles. "Why did you change the lock?"

"I didn't change it." He picks up the bags with practiced routine, following me inside like the best of husbands and the best of men. "The managers changed it this morning. There was a notice at the start of the month. I told you about it, didn't I?" He talks my ears off. How can I be expected to remember every little thing when my brain's been functioning for two—no, three of us?

I lie down on the soft-cushioned sofa; my back feels like the whole world's weight falls off in a smooth glide. Groaning, I find a comfortable position to sleep. My eyes grow heavy and my head blanks out in lethargy. But of course, how can that jobless motherfucker let me be?

"Angie, you shouldn't be on your feet all day at this point in your pregnancy." He sits down by my legs, massaging my swollen ankles. "I order bed rest." It should sound like a joke, but no matter how gleefully he laughs it off, the lethal edge of the threat is there.

"I can't do that. The bills for this condo, the money to raise my daughter, and the fees for you to go job hunting. Pierre, it's—"

"Bambi." He presses my ankle to hurt enough so I remember.

"Whatever," I kick him, but his grip is too strong. "I can't be bothered to think about it now. I can't stop."

"You can abandon me." He mumbles ruefully, as if he thinks the low volume would escape me. I scoff at the sweet act and the self-victimizing show. It's so good I almost believe it's true.

"I told you I won't. Not you, this baby, or me. I carry all three of us on my shoulders, and you keep pestering me with that fucking annoying attitude. Did I ever tell you I'd leave?" I throw the decorative cushion at him, angry and frustrated.

"But did you ever love me?" He snaps back, pulling my ankle, then rubbing it gentler in his meek, apologetic posture. "Did you ever love me, Angie?" he repeats.

"You're still asking that question?" I can't believe my ears, or his acting, or what he's meant to say in the situation. Who's to say he's telling the truth? Who's vouching for his feelings? "We all know this is a farce," I utter with a trembling voice. The pregnancy makes it easier for me to cry, against my better judgment and will.

"To you, maybe. But it's never a farce to me, Angela. It's never a farce to wish for someone to love me. Love me, for myself, Angela, against all odds, against the masses and the last judgment. Is it too much to ask, then?" He weeps, so pathetic, like a drunken old fool after the circus's lights have gone down. "Am I not allowed this sliver of happiness?"

I look at him, my eyes seeing without knowing what they perceive. Is it a monster or another face of the same old devil, playing a different trick lest I grow tired of the theatrical playout of the normal? Bambi's old sweater fits him perfectly; the twisted gray pattern with the striped neck elevates the sharp features on his face. His cheekbones grow more prominent now; he said he'd lost his appetite. The aquiline nose stands out, deepening the sharp eyes, enhancing the piercing azure storm in his eyes. My eyes trail down his lips, thin and beckoning, wet with a sheen of saliva as he licks them constantly in nervousness. How long has it been since the last time I kissed someone? I turn away, not wanting to answer him. Any response would be wrong. Any word would not be enough. The moon hides her beauty behind the dark clouds gathering outside the dirty glass windowpanes, leaving the beauty of my Venus illuminated by the lights from the next high-rise condominium. Pierre doesn't let that escape his eagle vision. "Miss him?" he grumbles, letting the act slip.

"Never have I not. Never will I stop." I breathe; the words hurt enough as they are; the tears are just a sweet accomplice.

"But you could make it less obvious." He leans forward, rubbing my stomach in loving circles.

"For what?"

"For me."

"I don't live for you."

"You could start now." He wraps his towering, lanky figure around my exhausted one. I can't feel my limbs, and I let him indulge in the little pleasure of life.

"Never thought of it. Never will."

"At least you could try." He talks to my stomach. I don't even know if he's speaking to me or the baby.

"Pierre, have you ever thought of living freely? Be yourself, because every other life's been taken and whatnot."

"But I'm living freely. Here, with you, and the baby." He purrs into my soft woolen pants.

"No, you're not. You're still borrowing someone's life. Someone's name, home, and the mise-en-scène he left behind. You think it'll be safer this way, that standing in his shoes, wearing his costume, you won't have to bear the consequences. It's powerful, isn't it, Pierre? To live and never think about the price you pay." This is not me talking; it's his ghost preaching the same old words to the same old situation.

"What are you trying to say?" And the provocation still works the same sort of miracle. Pierre perks his ears, triggered. The pale face grows even paler in the unlit living room. In the long silence as the play holds the audience's attention, I can hear Bambi's chuckle echoing from the past.

"Pierre, let's face it. The costume doesn't fit because it was never meant for you. Sure, it's fancy. The sequins dancing under the spotlight, the red seams and the embroidered, intricate patterns. They're too magnificent for an understudy and I won't blame you for the supreme fascination with fame. We all go through it. But it hurts, Pierre, to wear a pair of shoes too big for your feet."

I watch him shatter in that silent, horrifying way of a marble statue being smashed by an unbeliever. Perhaps this is me at my cruelest. Perhaps this is him at his most vulnerable. If neither one of us is wounded enough, none of us could let each other go, and the show would go on in its insufferable, cheap, soap operatic tragedy. I try to get up; it's becoming harder to move now that my stomach is bigger and every joint aches. Pierre's hold on my left ankle grows tighter, a vise around a dying rattlesnake. We are biting each other to the end, aren't we, Pierre? I ruffle his soft, brunette hair, placing a kiss on the top of his head, "What's wrong? Who hurts our little Pierre?"

"Life's not meant to be lived forever. You know that, don't you, Angie?" he replies, quite irrelevant to the mood and the flow of our current conversation. But I've gotten used to his mood swings, his mania, and his sudden psychosis. He was diagnosed by a psychiatrist immediately after we got back to Toronto. The result was far from favorable, and Pierre was banned from practicing the only thing he's excel. A psychiatrist with an onset of schizophrenia. Who would've guessed a good joke like that?

"And?"

"I've lived as Pierre for more than thirty years. Lived as Bambi for less than six months. A trial version, you could say, of the life I always looked at through the display windows when I strolled around the Christmas market. Neither of those brings me joy. It's weird. There's a book teaching people how to live a simple life. Did you ever read it? If it doesn't spark joy, let it go, and all that bullshit." He pops a nicotine patch onto his arm. There are three of them already sticking onto the veiny limb. "People will take the teaching differently. But I always thought, hey, if I were to throw away all that doesn't spark joy, my life would be the first thing to go."

He moans sensually as the nicotine kicks in, throwing his head back, leaning further on the headrest, but his grip never loosens on my ankle.

"Pierre. Jean-Paul. Bambi. I tried them all. I like none of them. But the problem is, how do we return a life? I can't just hand it back to whoever created human beings and ask for an exchange, can I? Do you believe in God, Angie? Any God would do."

"I tried so many times. It seems God doesn't want me to believe in Him. Not yet. Sorry."

Pierre rubs my ankle so tenderly, as Jesus would to a newborn babe, as if he were afraid the mere ankle had a life and a will of its own and he would hurt it just by existing. I know better than to diagnose a psychiatrist with severe mood swings, so, I just lay there, watching the multi-colored neon lights from the skyscrapers reflect on the Venus statue like a prayer for us all in this beautiful mess.

"I also had my own search for meaning. Had, because I stopped midway. I suppose if I had gone on a little bit longer, I would have chosen the same ending as my brother. Heh, it's funny. There are a lot of psychological studies about twins. None of them is very conclusive about why they share the same madness. The common similarity is that the malady will be triggered at different points in their lives."

"What did you find then? What caused you to stop searching?" I lace my fingers into his, trying to appease the child's thirst for undying, unconditional love.

"That day, when I was so high on pain, when my n^{th} patient just committed suicide, hanging himself because no medication was strong enough to do the job of a fucking rope, I stopped by a church on my way home from work. The evening mass was on. I was a disturbance, walking in during the sermon, doing my best to be as noisy as possible, causing a ruckus so people would pay attention. I guess that was the first time in my life I wanted someone else besides myself and Jean-Paul to know that I was here, alive, not well, but barely getting by."

"Was the preaching not to your atheistic taste?" I ask, knowing the answer. The story has the same ending, but the route leading to it changes every time I turn around.

"The priest said, 'People often seek punishment in Jesus Christ, but they're never patient enough to see His forgiveness.' I didn't know what was so great about that sentence, but I cried. Not the normal kind of sobbing, no; full-blow crying, like a sad clown exaggerating his performance on the stage to lengthen the interlude so the main actors and actresses have more time for themselves. It's this sudden sense of loneliness, Angie, and sometimes, it eats me from the inside out. I wonder why that is." He stares at the clay Venus, whose color has turned a deep maroon as the light in the opposite high-rise condominium changes its shade. The dark circles merge into the night, and the eyes disappear. All that's left of him is how he changes the way he caresses my baby bump, the feathery touch on my swollen limb, and the gentle pat on my stomach. Existence only needs that much proof.

"Pierre, maybe you weren't destined to be at the front," I tell him after a long pause, craving a smoke, thinking about my daughter, all the possibilities jumping in my mind like a funhouse in Warhol's color scheme. I hadn't taken a single dose of Clonazepam, and sleep keeps evading me like a ghost in a haunted house.

"What do you mean?"

"I think the problem with you is that you think you're entitled to saving lives. Of course, you're entitled to think so; you're a doctor. But Pierre, there are people meant for that profession, and there are people who are meant to be saved. Maybe you belong to the latter category."

"Being saved?"

"Wanting to be saved, to be more exact. Bambi always said, 'There's only so much sadness a human heart can hold.' That day, as you told me just now, was your breaking point. You didn't cry because the preaching touched your heart, your soul, or any higher being within you. It wasn't a call to search for something to believe in; you were simply exhausted at being the ending everyone looked for. I'm a sympathizer here. I won't say you're better or worse than your patients. But Pierre, punishment and forgiveness handed out by the Lord isn't something we can judge by some priest's word, or by our fatal enemy's voice."

"Fatal enemy?" He raises his eyebrow at me. Somehow, in the dark, I can still envision his naive expression, the same demeanor he had when we first met. He hasn't grown much, except for the desire to be. Though what to be is still a question he needs to answer on his own.

"Your mind is not your friend, Pierre. No one's mind is. Do you blame yourself for the death of your patients? Well, guess what, other psychiatrists are treating their patients. Some come out of the fire alive. Some end up dying. You don't see them going around with so many ghosts on their shoulders they have to hunch forward to carry them all, do you?" I squeeze his hand, dangling it in a slow dance, tilting my head on the sofa so he can see my eyes, wet with hope. "You have the right to live and be free, Pierre. We all do."

"Do I blame myself though?" He pauses, mulling over the question in seriousness and desperate thought, then snuggling closer to me, he continues, "It's always good to have faith, Angie. That's what I tell my patients. Until it becomes a repetitive curse. Faith is a flimsy thing. A slippery slope; no matter which side you stay on, it will be the wrong one in the end. Perhaps you're right, my mind is not my friend. But it saved many lives, Angie." He pauses again, longer this time, his eyes gleaming in the pale moonlight as the first stars come out of their hiding places. "So many."

"Then why do you keep punishing yourself for the lives you couldn't save?"

"Because it's human nature. You don't abandon your comrades on the battlefield. You don't go back home from a shift at the hospital without some guilt and a few ghosts hanging on your back. The case that day, Angie, and why it stuck to me so bad, was because the patient who committed suicide was a very young man, a 17-year-old on suicide watch. I was the last one to talk to him."

"How did it go?" I nudge his hand. He never needs my permission to go on.

"He told me he couldn't find a single interesting thing in life. I told him the same old thing. The world is a beautiful place. You just haven't found the right dream for you yet. Learn a new language. Pick up a hobby. Find a close friend in your group therapy session when you're off the watch. Life is for the living. All bullshit lies I repeat to every damned soul because the textbook and the code books haven't invented new phrases yet. But it was no use."

"He didn't have anyone?"

"Worse. He didn't care if anyone ever cared for him. You're right, Angie: believing in love is one thing; having absolute faith that it can cure every fucking disgusting disease on this infested earth is another. The boy said he'd learn a new language, and I went home, satisfied that I had lengthened his life for a sufficient amount of time until the new change in his medication kicked in."

"Then?"

"He died. That same fucking night. With a rope made from his own bedding and pyjamas. And I was sleeping through it all in my comfortable house, under the soft duvet and the perfumed pillows so my dreams could taste better when I woke up. The call from the hospital rushed me into a numbed state. I knew when I saw his body, when I watched my colleagues trying to resuscitate him, when I stayed until the next evening to relay the news to his parents, that it was the first sign of PTSD. I should've quit then, I know. Spare me your judgment and pity, but Angie, without me, many boys like him would end up with the same fate." He laughs, bitter and sour like a shot of whisky spiced with lethal poison. How could he still wake up in the morning after that incident when he was already a dead man? The Raymond twins are a mystery to modern-day psychologists, and to me.

"You choose to sacrifice yourself, then?" I course my hand through his hair. The softness isn't there anymore, but the coarse strands hug my fingers like a lifeline. "How can you save others when you can't even save yourself?" I kiss his forehead, finding my old, tattered self in his thinning figure.

"It isn't about saving others, Angela. I don't overestimate myself that much. We don't play God. Doctors can only do so much, you see: it's a vicious battle between the progress of medication and the power of the Grim Reaper's scythe. I think you've already seen the sculpture depicting that exact fight in front of every hospital. But we're always on the losing side. I thought maybe if I'd stayed behind on that gruesome day, maybe if I hung around the boy's room a little bit longer, he would've lived. Sometimes, it's not a miracle pill we want. A simple conversation could be enough. Someone who can talk and someone who's just there, patiently listening to every word, remembering the pain and letting them know they're not alone."

He casts a glance toward the Venus statue, whose upper body is immersed in the dark, while the lower part is illumined by the moonlight shining through the window. Something catches his attention in the folds of her tulle dress, carved clumsily in clay, or the curves of her hips, and it makes his eyes glow. Beauty and sadness are the only combination left on this earth to move a human's heart. I see a galaxy of history flowing in those unfathomable irises. A lifetime isn't that long, and it passes through in the shape of a lonely man traversing the galactic railway, finding something invisible. I wonder if Pierre had encountered the 17-year-old boy on that road, what the boy would tell him now. Maybe that it was never his fault as much as anyone else's, that it was simply revenge against the living, and perhaps he was regretting it. That no matter how much Pierre stayed in the past, it wouldn't resurrect the dead.

But my train of thought is going off the grid. Pierre is on the verge of falling asleep. He can't sleep on his own and needs a human body by his side. I let him rest his head on my stomach and the child kicks his cheek mildly, as if she is caressing his pain softly to appease his agony. Stroking his hair, I keep his mind at ease, letting him know that I'm not going anywhere. The stars hide behind the gathering clouds again, and I can't help but think about Bambi's old saying: *Angela, you won't suddenly die just because one day is sadder than another.* But Bambi, I interrogate him on the edge of his grave, what if there's no other day, and the sadder day you think was only temporary will lengthen into the saddest day eternally? It's unfair, Bambi, when you preached about choosing dreams and hopes while you chose nothingness as your ending.

Pierre snores intermittently. His brows knit together. His nose scrunches up. He grits his teeth and the sound is unnerving. Even in sleep, he is losing the fight against his inner demons. The fight ends, then a second later, it starts again. Day in, day out, he keeps living in the same nightmare. Maybe that is his five seconds on repeat. I cradle his face nearer to my bosom, hoping my heartbeat is loud enough to calm his fraying prayer. "It's alright, Pierre. What doesn't kill you doesn't kill you. You don't have to struggle so hard to appear stable for anybody's sake."

After our jagged conversation, we never broach the subject any further. Since it doesn't kill us, neither does it spark any joy; we let it go at that. Pierre gets a new job a few days later. He accepts a receptionist position at an outpatient mental health unit in a pretty famous city hospital. His track record is a bulletproof hiring weapon: highly distinctive degrees, multiple certificates, and a few deaths under his belt to prove that he is able to handle the toughest patients with the loudest demands. He tells me on the same evening that we are moving forward. The same suffering smile, the enlarging dark circles, the bulging red in the whites of his eyes, and the desperate scream for salvation written so clearly on his face it's almost too painful to look at for longer than two seconds. I tell him to reject the offer and accept the invitation from Mount Sinai Hospital, where his talent will be appropriately appreciated and duely rewarded. He shakes his head, not saying no, but not agreeing. His arms hang loosely by his sides, his head hanging. I think a part of him is still in that room with the 17-year-old boy, and I have neither the right nor the power to pull him through. He goes his way, and I will go mine. At least, he won't be doing the job of a psychiatrist anytime soon; not with his diagnosis, and his brokenness. The consolation our misfortune brings sometimes surprises us in the weirdest way, and I don't know if I should be grateful or angry at Pierre's sorry state.

"Pierre, what can I do to make you reject the job offer?" I ask, cutting carrots into little pieces. The potatoes are boiling in a pastel pink pot nearby. The water bubbles are the background music to a noir scene.

"I just want to help." Pierre washes the lettuce and rinses the greens three times until they sparkle under the stream of water.

"Help? Who?"

"The patients. The children. You."

"Did I ever say I want you to? Do I need your little help? And did I die without it before?"

"You don't understand."

"Of course I don't." I put the knife down, stroking my back, trying to alleviate the pain. Pierre throws the steel washbasin with the soaking greens to the sink and rushes to my side, helping me with the dull ache. "Pierre, you might be very intelligent with all your fancy degrees and your thick books, talking about unreal theories—shut your mouth; I know what I'm talking about—and how they can cure an ocean of suffering out there. But sometimes, you're so stupid I don't even know if you have a working brain inside that big head of yours. Don't you see how cruel it is, forcing me to watch you die a little bit every day just for every other life to go on? No one asks you to fight their battles. You told me when we first met, 'Help me help you.' Walk the talk, then. Help yourself first. You're this close to jumping off the cliff and you dare to say I don't understand. I, failing at building my own live, am bringing a new one to earth in the same instant. I'm a woman, Pierre, in case you haven't noticed, and it means I was born hypersensitive to humans' pain. No matter how thick your mask is," I pull a sharp breath; my chest aches; my eyes hurt with the salty tears and onions, "I can see it. The pain on your shoulders. The suffering is drowning you, the loneliness you choose to live inside because you refuse to believe there is a slim chance of happiness. It isn't right, Pierre. I see your thoughts, and maybe I won't understand them as you want me to because you're just as insufferable as your goddamn brother, but I know you're trapped in darkness, and you're the only one who can crack the dark cage open. Let the light fucking in. It's about damn time, Jesus fucking Christ. Ow."

"Are you alright? Angela? Angela? Let's talk about the timing after—"

"I said it's about damn time for the child to come out. I'm in labor. Call the ambulance, for fuck's sake, stupid manchild."

I scream in the coming waves of intense, gripping pain. Half of the things I want to tell him are gone with the contractions. Pierre freezes, then he jerks into action methodically, stepping into the role of the professional that he is. After calling 911 and judging that it won't be worth the wait, he carries me to the car and speeds to the nearest city hospital, cursing every five seconds that we're stuck in the night-time traffic, honking the car like it is his own life he's giving birth to. The drivers yell at him as he swerves from lane to lane, never caring one bit who he's going to hit the next minute, or the cost of the cars he swerves by. In a few minutes, we have a police car tailing us and if I weren't in so much pain, I would congratulate him on a job well done—an existential crisis is always the perfect excuse for a speeding ticket.

"What do I do?" he mumbles under his breath as he presses on the gas pedal and stops short before the ICU. "Right, contractions. How far apart are they? Angela, stay with me."

"I'm staying with you. You're the one who's losing his grip. Ow. Get me out of the car first. They're fifteen minutes apart, lasting about forty-five seconds now." I groan, trying to open the door.

He rushes to unbuckle my seatbelt, fumbling with the lock and hitting his head against the frame. Behind him, a policeman is approaching. "Right, it's still early then. We should get you admitted just in case. What now?" He snaps, turning back to the tap on his shoulders.

"Good evening, sir, madam. Are you aware that you were twenty over the speed limit, gaining on eighty kilometers per hour in the residential area? Can I see your driver's license, please?"

Pierre rummages through his shirt pockets and pants, throwing the driver's license to the policeman without looking back, then carries me bridal-style to the ICU. The weight of two lives saddles him down and he walks with heavy, dragging footsteps, but the determination in his eyes is strong enough to shoulder all three of us through the five hundred meters. "Help. My wife's in labor," he shouts, walking straight to the reception area, and I'm too exhausted to argue.

"Put down your name and give me your insurance card, please. Next," the receptionist replies with as much weariness as Pierre had when he was still in the system.

"She's in labor. Labor. Do you understand? A child is coming." He heaves, breathing hard as his muscles gradually give up on him.

"Tell me about it. I went to med school. Also, even if it's the second coming of Christ, your wife would still have to wait. We're short-staffed tonight, sir." She hands him the registration papers then calls out, "Next."

"But—"

"Pierre," I whine, growing weaker as my body is a bundle of sore, fraying nerves. "Just fill in the registration form and wait. The child isn't coming just yet."

He wails one last time; his frustration rises exponentially to the powerlessness of the situation we are in. Grabbing the form, he perches me on his lap, quickly writing in the necessary details, and shoves the form back through the receptionist's intake slot with his insurance card. I tug his sleeves, mumbling, "Mine, too."

"Your what?" he whispers back, as if speaking louder will somehow harm the child and me.

"My insurance card, you idiot." I bite his shoulder in an insufferable ache. He searches for the card in my purse and throws it in with the document.

We sit in the waiting area for a good hour. Pierre perks his head up every time the emergency room opens, hoping it is our turn. I swallow the moans, closing my eyes so my senses won't become more overwhelmed than they already are. The tears flow. The sweat drips profusely down my forehead and my face. My hair is matted to my scalp, and it hurts and it hurts and it hurts. The contractions grow nearer and nearer, and the intensity gets stronger. When I think I can't do this anymore, a nurse finally calls my name. "Angela Carter-Raymond."

In the blur of pain and dissociation, I think I overhear Pierre shout at the nurses, demanding a Code Blue (what does it mean? I ask but no one answers) only for the nurses to call in a Code White (again, what does it mean? I breathe, but they all ignore me). Someone asks if we want a C-Section and he orders in that authoritative voice of a true doctor: "No one touches my wife without my permission. She has no problem giving birth naturally." I squeeze his hand in reassurance. Multiple voices mingle into one, and that one is his. As I cross the sea to bring my daughter to the realm of the living, Pierre kisses my fingers reverently, whitened to the knuckles with the sheer force from my grip, praying to different deities—any god who will listen—and crying even more than me. The babe comes at one thirty in the morning. A midsummer child, with a cry as brave and loud as both her fathers. The nurses bring her to Pierre, and he struggles to hold this new life in his embrace as gently as he can. His eyes search mine in a pathetic call for help. I laugh, "What's wrong? Doctor Pierre didn't learn how to hold a newborn child in med school?"

"They taught me to save people. They never taught me to create people." He huffs, gaping as he tries to remember how to breathe normally. "Here. Yours." He brings the child to me, letting her lie close to my breast.

"Wrong. Ours."

"Ours?" Pierre asks incredulously. The nurses watch him with curiosity and astonishment. He coughs drily, trying to hide the quivering exaltation in his voice. "Ours."

In the dazzling light of the operation room, Pierre plays with the child's tiny hands and feet, letting her hold his index finger. The small force from her little frame makes him giggle all the while, so carefree no one can imagine the beast in the emergency room a few seconds ago. The child finishes her crying, her introduction to this maddening world. His eyes follow her movements, never letting go, never abandoning her. *Forever is in a single moment*, I think, *and people always say it is hard to find.*

"Pierre," I gasp, tired and a bit cold from the air. "See that?"

"What?"

"In your hands. A life." The sentence becomes fragmented as I try to stay awake. "People come. People leave. You're holding one in yours right now." It's hard to articulate; the meaning is lost as the connection between my brain and my voice thins out.

Pierre stares at me, tilting his head. Just as I thought he didn't get it, that he'd never get it, and that I'd lost the chance to let him experience the meaning Bambi had sacrificed his life to give him, he smiles at me, so sweet and innocent. "It's fucking fantastic. Angela Carter-Raymond, you're a fucking beautiful goddess."

He understood then. He's always understood. He just refused to see the truth. It only takes a life to know the value of a life. I grin at him, nodding off. In dreamland, I fancy hearing a stern, cold, commanding voice pierce through. "Pierre Raymond, is it? May I have a quick chat? Do you know a man by the name Jean-Paul Raymond?"

It's a nightmare, isn't it? After all, we are allowed that sliver of happiness. I will prove it to you, Pierre.

Chapter 26: Epilogue: Part I

When I wake up, Pierre is nowhere in sight. The baby is sleeping sweetly in the cradle, and the sunlight is shining through the room. I turn my head to the door; there's an empty bed beside me. It's that sudden sense of being all alone and Pierre's voice comes to me in a haze. I press the button, notify a nurse that I'm awake. A kind, elderly lady comes in, cheery and joyful despite her tired pallor: "Hey sweetie, how're you feeling?"

"Sore," I croak, my throat dry. My tongue feels like sandpaper against my palate. "Where's my husband?"

"Sweetie, you rest first, okay? We can worry about everything else later." She hooks a new IV drip on, humming a new pop song that's playing on the hospital speaker.

"Worry? What happened to him?" I try to sit up, but she pushes me back, gentle yet firm in her force.

"It's alright, sweetie. If nothing's wrong, he'll come by very, very soon. I'm sure of it." She smiles, trying to assure me, but it only has the reverse effect.

"Where's Pierre?" I growl. The nightmare comes back. Anxiety piles on fear, seasoned with a bowl full of hysteria; I yank my blanket off, feeling the panic attack coming on hard.

"Sweetie, calm down. He's fine. There's nothing wrong with him. He's just a bit busy at the moment. Try to lie down first."

"I don't listen to any orders. Give me back my Pierre."

Amidst the shouts and the mess of dripping blood on the white bedsheet, another voice chimes in, calmer, more pragmatic, heavy with authority and assured in its granted power.

"Your husband is at the police station at the moment, madam. Please don't give our nurses more trouble than we can take."

"Police station? Why?" My voice echoes inside my brain. It isn't curiosity; it's pure apprehension.

"Apparently, his brother is involved in a drug and human trafficking ring. The man was witnessed killing the ringleader in Mount Royal Park in Montreal. There's no information about him. His name is Jean-Paul. Doctor Pierre is under suspicion of being an accomplice." The doctor relays all this news without an ounce of feelings as he puts a stethoscope to my chest, checking for my pulse. "Does your body still hurt?"

"But Pierre isn't… I mean, he's… Oh, God. Oh, my God." I sob, no longer recognizing the question or the need to answer. The paints is ripping my brain out of my skull. My capacity to think blows apart with an error code. The words lose all its meaning, and every sentence coming out of the kind humans before me turns into gibberish.

"The Lord watches over every one of us, madam. Now, let's see you take a big inhale, holding it there. Madam?"

The hospital room disappears, leaving behind only the window with the curtain billowing in the early morning breeze. I don't want the nightmare creeping in, and I fear the monsters crouching behind every invisible corner. My baby cries, and I know I should feed her; she is my world, my anchor to a life that's slipping through the cracks of my armor. The doctor calls my name, or a bunch of syllables that sound like it, and I can't find the strength to answer. He motions to the nurse, discussing a few options to "stabilize the mental well-being" of a potential postpartum depression patient. I fade out of the scene, wishing the baby would stop crying, hoping that she knows how hard it is for me to keep myself together, that instead of the nonstop howling, she should bring me something sweeter. She should be the salvation I had hoped for, a sweet drop of water on my desiccated tongue. Yet, as I stare at her in the utter apathy of a person devoid of the will to live, my daughter keeps on bellowing with every intention to be loved, to go on, to run forward. She is quickly becoming a burden. The cry grows louder as time trudges slowly on, and this time, there's no ghost of Bambi's voice to bring me home. Instead, the voice of the baby calls to me, accusatory in her hatred and starvation: "If you never loved me, why would you bring me here?"

"Can I at least call him?" I ask the doctor, already hopeless in my quest, knowing he will agree to my request. Special circumstances and all that bullshit are my only advantage.

"Sure thing, sweetie," the nurse replies, patting my back in her maternal indulgence. "But only after you rest for a bit longer, alright?"

I quiet down, the nurse hands my sweet child to me in a soft bundle with so much gentleness, and I hold her close to my breasts, my whole world is reduced to the little life in my bosom. My daughter takes after Bambi more than me. The aquiline nose is distinguishable, but her bright azure eyes and brunette hair show the carbon copy of his mischievousness. I hope the child won't grow up to be like me, Bambi said on the last day of his life. Sobbing, I tickle the child's cheeks and feel her bathe herself in the joy of existing. She sucks with fervor, as if she were scared I'd take away her treasure anytime. As if she feared, an innate fear, that I'd find an excuse to abandon her. I hold her closer to my breast, urging her to be greedier, more selfish, because the world wouldn't be that forgiving to her or anyone like her. "Steal and let steal, my little child, and leave the rest to suffer their own hell," I whisper to her soft ears. It's too late to realize that I can't cross this sea of motherhood alone.

An hour later, the nurse comes by to take my daughter back to the cradle. I struggle to let her go and the kind lady says it's a good sign; my love is growing. How do I explain to her that I don't want another love growing on me? I ask her again if I can call Pierre, and she maintains the same answer. "After you rest for a bit." I know it's bad. I ransack my mind for a feasible reason for the police to keep Pierre this long. We pulled a perfect alibi, and Bambi died together with Saul. Why would someone bring it up again after nearly five months? I chew my nails, a bad habit when I get too anxious. A drop of blood trickles down my thumb as I bite too hard on the flesh. Something sparks up in my brain. *Fuck you, Markus*, I cursed, and that sleazy man said, *If I could, I would*. The name and the sneering voice come back all at once.

Markus. The forgettable pawn. The one Bambi and I left behind in our orchestration because he was too insignificant to worry about. The name I never brought up to Pierre because I fucking forgot about his existence until this very moment.

I search for a phone, but there's none. In coldness and tears, I sit on the hospital bed, waiting, hoping that this time, Pierre will return. A careless mistake is all it takes to destroy a life. Is it my punishment or is it God's forgiveness this time?

When the clock strikes five-thirty and the sun is finally burning the room with its fierce light, Pierre walks in. I think I am dreaming him into existence. In his casual shirt with a striped vest and woolen pants, he looks worn out, but the life source within is flowing with fresh spring fountains. He opens his mouth to call my name, but just as quickly, he runs to my side with a shout and presses the emergency button for a resident on call. Dehydration, panic attack, paranoia, and I was peeing uncontrollably. Clawing to his arms, I try to tell him everything is fine, he's here. But no sound comes out from my throat, only a strange combination of gargling and choking. Pierre grows furious; his eyes turn into a sea fuming with fire. He shouts a multitude of orders to the nurses, diagnoses without being in charge, gives the on-call resident a dressing down harsh enough that the poor guy is close to breaking apart. The doctor in charge is called back, in shock at my worsening state, and with the same stern attitude, only a lesser fury, he asks the resident why I was left in that state without anyone notifying him.

"She said she was fine waiting for her husband," the guy replies in all honesty. I nod, because that's what I told him.

Pierre heaves a sigh, trying to calm himself down. With utmost restraint, he questions the guy, "If she told you to switch her Zoloft dosage from seventy-five milligrams to two hundred milligrams, would you do it, too? Are you the doctor, or is she? Is this your first time on the job?"

"I'm sorry, sir," the resident replies, frustrated, but he knows better than to talk back. Reason isn't on his side.

"Richard, Doctor Pierre is right. Also, Doctor Pierre, could you please not stress out my residents?" The doctor tries to appease the situation. "You don't work here."

"About damn time, because I'm under the assumption that no one does. My wife could've died if I were here an hour later. Her blood sugar is dangerously low, and she can barely talk without hurting her throat. She's just given birth. A human comes out of her and this is how you treat our women? Shame on you. All of you."

"Pierre," I call him, tremulous and tender.

"Yes, my sweetheart, yes. I'm here." He skips two steps forward and kneels down by my bedside. "How are you feeling? Ice chips? Porridge? Cheesecake? Hm?"

"The baby. She's crying."

The whole room goes silent. Pierre squeezes my hand so hard it hurts. I want to ask him to bring my daughter here so I can feed her, but it's difficult enough to maintain an even breathing pace. The nurse looks at me apologetically. The resident steps up, intending to explain something but the doctor quickly holds him back. "Don't," he shakes his head, nodding to Pierre's drooping shoulders as he kneels there beside me like a sinner, forsaken by the Holy altar of the abandoned church. All the Gods had long left humans, but the sinner, in his stubborn, willful ignorant way, still holds onto hope, yearning for forgiveness that will never come. Because the seed of hope is also the seed of life. And because without such tedious things as narrow hopes and wishful dreams, how can people keep on waking up every morning? I stroke his head, and in a fleeting moment, I think I can see him shatter into pieces like a china doll.

"Angela," he finally says, after a long stretch of awkward silence, shifting eyes, and averted gazes, "we decided to move the baby to the temporary incubator for monitoring purposes."

"Why?" I swallow with difficulty; the nausea comes back and it churns up my being. "She's perfectly fine, isn't she?" Pierre lowers his head in shame, tinged with the darkness of guilt. I urge him with a pleading cry, "Isn't she, Pierre?"

"Angela, our baby…" He tries to sound composed, but I can see him shatter and break inside. "She suffers from respiratory distress, which may lead to cardiac defects—"

"Speak English." I shake with anger, trying to break free from his arms, but Pierre holds on tight.

"She can't breathe normally and needs monitoring for a while." He puts the symptoms in simple words and the damage isn't lessened one bit.

"Is it because of the medication? Because I'm mentally unstable? Because I dared to be a mother but still dreamed of being Ophelia, trying to get the attention of the coward Hamlet? Why? He makes me choose again, Pierre. He makes me choose. He never asks if I want to or not; He just forces me into the field on a whim. Because it's fun to entertain the faith, just to see if said faith wants you to believe in it. Because—"

But I didn't have the chance to finish the sentence. A needle pricks my forearm like the sting of an ant, and I doze off in an instant. "Angela, it's alright, I don't believe in a God who built his children up just to tear them down. I also refuse to partake in a faith that preaches forgiveness, but its followers always pick and choose a convenient meaning to fit the masses' narrative. After all, salvation is meant for the innocent, the untainted, the light; as we grow up, we become the guilty, the tainted, the dark. Don't you see, Angie, even in the first chapter, He who created the world already separated us." Bambi's voice soothes me to my dreams. "And Angela, I will protect you, our daughter—us, against the living, the death, the punishment, and the forgiveness. Let them throw the stones. The world was built by three, don't you know, my dear Savior?" Pierre's chuckles caress me through the night.

He who rules over salvation always asks for a worthy offering. I could have the love of my life, but which one? My Bambi. My Jean-Paul. My one and only God. He who weighs the two options before me on a scale while I writhe and mourn at His altar, begging for the last crumb of his love. If Bambi could pardon the bloodshed of his whores who died in his name and absolve the deadly sins in the book of his game, surely there would be love enough in his big heart for a marred woman like me to seek his blessings?

He told me no, it wasn't him who tried me; it was me all alone. Little faith and with just as little hope, he preached to me as I knelt there, "Angela, you never trust anyone enough to believe there's more to life than your own pain." A selfish man to a faithless woman—why did I ever dream that we would have a happy ending?

And I weep. In that blurry dream, I see my daughter grow up to be just like her father: a dreamer who's rewarded for daring to reach for the stars. Fame and glory spread before her like a red carpet, and the spotlight is on. She will dance the same dance Bambi took on his chance to reach the moon. Just when the dream should end, as I expect her to fall, she rises again. From the ashes, the phoenix is born, not with vengeance or age-old wisdom, but with hope. A hope so strong in its power, so immense in its quake, that her wings keep spreading until she becomes the sun. Pierre was right; maybe I always seek punishment in him. Maybe it is a good thing to have faith, no matter how flimsy or little the faith is. Maybe Bambi is also right: never trust the invisible power, never bow before the force, and when life breaks you, remember, you have the choice to stand up. Both men in my life carry me home, and my daughter is there, waving at the three of us, smiling. Her tiny, chubby fingers hold a bouquet of thistles and weeds, and her rosy, cherubic cheeks paint our life a blissful pink color. *Live, Angela*, Bambi says as he lets Pierre lead me to her, *Live and be free*.

When I turn around, nobody is there. The past remains a dark canvas for the future to shine on, ever so cruel, and ever so bright.

When I open my eyes, tears are streaming down my face, my nose stuffed, my mouth gasping for air. Pierre sits by my side. He fidgets with the blanket, twisting the edge into a messy bunch, hesitating on what to say. I place my needled hand on top of his, appeasing his wellbeing with the sickness in me: "What's the matter?"

"Your daughter is—"

"I thought you said she's our daughter." I chuckle at his flushed face, patting his hand, urging him to go on.

"Our daughter is fine. She still needs a few checkups, but her breathing is stabilizing now, and her heart rate is under control. I..." He inhales sharply, pausing to organize his words, the first time I have ever seen him so flustered and lost. Too bad I couldn't frame the scene to hold forever. He lifts his head, looking straight at me, his eyes filled to the brim with resolution. "I will protect you and our daughter."

I wait for the next phrase, but it is a period, not a comma. He doesn't go on, and I hate the intentional cliffhanger. "Pierre," I squeeze his fingers, my own shaking, "I don't want to hear you excluding yourself like an afterthought. I told you I wouldn't leave. Let's hear you say it once more. It's not only our daughter and me. There are three of us at the start, and there will be three of us by the end."

"You mean 'us'?" he asks, his eyes casting a sideways glance at my heart rate monitor. "Can I hope?"

"It's always been us, hasn't it? And if it's not for hope, what else do we live for?" I crack a smile, dangling his hand with the last of my feeble strength.

"Angela, the police."

"Yes."

"They asked me about Jean-Paul."

"Yes." I close my eyes, listening to the predictable.

"They said a friend of his reported him missing, under a different name. Bambi Raymond, whose record couldn't be found."

"Of course, his was a fake life and a fake death till the end." I shift in my blanket. "Did they tell you who reported him missing?"

"I can't get the name. Witness protection; that's a given. They traced a Jean-Paul Raymond who shared similar features to what the reporting person described. And do you know what happened?" He snorts, and I can hear the tears in his voice without having to look.

"Go on."

"Jean-Paul Raymond was reported dead fifteen years ago. Fifteen fucking years. He was dead the day he went to Ontario. There's a death certificate with his name on it. The cause of death was cardiac arrest. The police caught onto me because I was speeding, and with the same face, same name, I was suspected of being Jean-Paul. Oh God, what kind of fucked-up plan did he have since the start?" Pierre wails, his whole body shaking against the bed rail. But I had always expected this turn of events. How could I not?

"That's why I told you from the start, he was just so Bambi. You never knew what you'd get with him."

"Right. He was just so Bambi. After the questioning, the police told me about the drug and human trafficking ring. I told them I had no idea, and it was the perfect lie because I had always lived in Montreal. I…" Pierre stops for breath, but he can't go on anymore. The flood of emotions is too much for him to bear, and it's drowning him. He never signed up to clean up anyone's mess. Neither did he want to receive the blessings someone had bet their life on to give him. "I can't beat him, Angela. He's always been the better one of the two of us. The most intelligent person, the popular one, the reputation of the family, the legacy that could be written down on the sand and I'm sure even the sea couldn't wash the whole of it away. What am I, then? What was I born for?"

"You're the living one, Pierre." I tilt my head on the pillow, feeling my heart struggle to beat for life. "He knows he couldn't make it, and he knows you can. There are people born to die, and there are people born to live so they can tell the tale. I belong to the latter category, and you do, too."

He sniffles, snot dripping down his upper lip, and he grasps a tissue at the nightstand. "Sorry," he says. I shake my head gently. Even the cruelest of humans would forgive such a broken soul who had newly discovered that his life was nothing but a fully orchestrated plan for a substitution. Gripping his hand, I ask, "Did you get any news about a person called Markus?"

"Markus who?" he asks, quite befuddled. There's so much truth in his eyes that I decide to drop the matter for now.

The only person who would report Bambi missing was Markus. I chew my bottom lip, lost in a darkening cloud of thoughts. There were so many things happening that I completely forgot his existence. He was never much of a presence in our life anyway. Sometimes he'd pop into the club when Bambi was there to perform, playing around with the girls, hooking up with the guys, and teasing me at the same time. He played both sides; as long as they brought him money and goods, he never cared what was inside their pants. Non-discrimination at its best. To Markus, money had only one gender, and it was green. A master at hide-and-seek, a coward, and consequently, the last one standing, he had been eluding Bambi's brilliant masterplan to save our daughter and his twin brother all this time. The question now stands: why is he showing his face at this crucial moment, when we are almost finished crossing the threshold, and the door is closing behind us, inch by inch, step by step?

I follow Bambi's traces in my brain, searching for the right solution to this mystery. What should I do next to solve Markus's sudden appearance? Will he cause harm? If he does, to what degree will it affect the two of us? How can I mitigate the damage? I think of asking Pierre's opinion, or at least, making a call using his phone to mask my identity, hoping Markus, or whoever the enemy is, wouldn't realize what I'd done all this time, running away from him and the gangs at Rendezvous. But Pierre is in a worse state than I expected: he keeps crying, refusing to listen to anyone's reason. He's stuck on the life that's been given to him all of a sudden, with the freedom attached to his back like a pair of wings. He's floating and soaring amidst the anguish and the joy. I let him be in his own bubble of contradicting emotions. There's plenty of chance to burst his balloon once we get through this one last hurdle. Staring at the ceiling, I think of my daughter. She, too, is struggling to live, and she's doing her best. What gives me the right to surrender before the last fight begins? I hold onto the tail of Ariadne's thread, finding the way out of this gruesome labyrinth.

Markus, where have you been all this time? A bar outside your turf, or did you follow me all the way to Montreal? The conversation in the taxi when I was in a panic attack popped up. He picked up the call then; did he know that I was all the way out in Laval? Did he know about Pierre's existence? If so, is there any chance he was aware of Bambi's plan from the beginning? *Angela,* Bambi's voice breaks in, *remember, when you're dealing with a snake like Markus, hit him on the head. Strike once because you only have one chance with him.* Pierre's phone vibrates; it's been his habit to put his phone on silent since we've lived together. He unlocks the screen. An unknown number. Glancing at me, he asks a silent question: Should I pick it up? I nod, knowing whose call it is.

"Hello?"

"Bambi. Been a pretty long time since we last saw each other, eh? How's everything?"

It's Markus. Loud and clear. Pierre stares at me, bewildered and scared, but his wits are still intact. He writes on the pad of hospital paper: *Should I say yes?* I nod again.

"Hey, yo. Pretty long time, indeed. I mean, sure, I've been busy." He scribbles on the notepad, *Is he dangerous?* I nod. "Listen, should we meet sometime? I have plenty to talk to you about. Things are crazy." Another sentence appears, *Police?* I hesitate, then nod.

"Damn crazy, you motherfucker. Did you know that Saul was killed? By that bitch Angela, fucking hell. I swear, that bitch is bad news. Nobody has discovered the corpse yet, but I'll find out where she hid the body." Markus cackles through the speaker, and Pierre winces at the curse word. I hold his hand through it all.

"Right. I haven't had any news about Angela in a long while. How is she?" He scribbles quickly and it's harder to decipher his writing this time. I screw up my eyes to read the question as he stalls for time. *Drugs or human trafficking?* I nod.

"Oh, so it's true? You both were separated way back then, right? Fucking hell, you should've contacted me sooner! That bitch ran to Montreal. Last I heard, she was admitted to a hospital. Saul was right there with me when a nobody called. He took the first flight out to Montreal and poof, disappeared after. Listen, Bambi, this is my theory only but be careful in your hindquarters. You might be next." Markus laughs at his own joke. Pierre scribbles more, then erases the note just as quickly. He taps his thigh, his eyes sharp and calculating.

"Really? Why? I did a clean break-up, after all." The hint of mockery shows in his sneering voice.

"Why? Duh. Because both of you are involved, aren't you?" Markus refuses to fall into Pierre's trap. There's an awkward silence. The only sound coming from the other side is the tapping of Markus's finger on a hard surface. Maybe he is at home, sitting by his bar. Or maybe he's down somewhere at another girl's apartment, waiting for a new adventure.

Pierre presses further. "Well, I got out now. I don't know about her. What about you?"

"Let's not talk about me, man. Did Saul get his delivery?" Markus swims nearer to the trap. I squeeze Pierre's hand, mouth the command, *Go for the kill.*

"Yeah, he got it alright. Before he got on the flight. Said he'd stash it somewhere safe so he could get it when he's back. What a shame, huh?"

"Do you know where he hid it?" *Get it, Markus*, I pray, biting my nails, *take the bait. Fall for the trap. It's right in front of you, just fucking step inside.*

"Hid what?" Pierre dangles the hook closer in Markus's face.

"The delivery, of course."

"Delivery of what, Markus?" Pierre teases, but the sweat is beading on his forehead. "I've been doing a lot lately."

"Special K. The ketamine, motherfucker. Get your peanut brain together, damn it!"

Pierre exhales a long held-in breath. He scribbles on the notepad again, speaking with a cheering voice, "Ah, yes, that one. Of course. It's at, let's see, where is it now?" He shows the note to me, Bambi's studio? I nod repeatedly. "My studio. You know where it is."

"I don't." Markus is befuddled. "You only take your girls there, bastard."

"Right. It's my special hideout, after all. How about I bring it to you then?"

"You bet your damn ass you will. Rendezvous?"

"I don't know. What's in it for me?" Pierre writes another question, *Human trafficking, for sure?* I nod in affirmation.

"How about the usual deal? You're a bachelor now, aren't you? Want some fun?"

"Girls, then?" Pierre laughs, sounding interested, caressing my palm to assuage my anxiety.

"The prettiest of the load."

"When?"

"Next Friday, after ten."

"Gotcha."

"See you then. Ah, right, do you happen to know a Pierre Raymond?" Markus asks. The authenticity of his query causes Pierre to panic briefly, but he comes back with a perfect strike:

"Never heard of him. Why? Is he a new client? Need me to check him out?"

"No. It's alright if you don't know. I swear, this idiot looks exactly like you, man. But he's, how do I put it? He's softer. Like you if we take off all the drug dealing and human trafficking, you know?"

Pierre's eyes shine brightly in the dark. He grins, eerily similar to the one that got buried when he got what he wanted where he wanted it most. "Right," he said. His voice rings in the dark with that sharp edge of arrogance and holier-than-thou force. "If we take it all off, eh? But there's only one Bambi. And there will only ever be one Bambi."

He hangs up before Markus has the chance to reply. I stared at him, asking with my eyes, *Now what?* But Pierre is too busy with his own plan to pay any attention to my curiosity. His fingers dance all over the phone screen, and after about thirty minutes, he makes another call. Two rings. A rough, gruffy voice response, "Police. What do you want to report?"

In the same cold and cunning voice as his twin brother when he was alive, Pierre enunciates each word slowly and clearly: "Hi, this is Pierre Raymond. I want to report a drug and human traffic deal this coming Friday night, 10 p.m. at the bar Rendezvous."

Chapter 27: Epilogue: Part II

On Friday morning, Pierre and I come down to the incubator room to see our daughter. She is sleeping peacefully, her breathing even and her face an angel from Michelangelo's Sistine Chapel painting. She shares the best features of Bambi and I, Pierre whispers to me. The soft eyes and the plush lips are mine, while the nose and the bone structure of her face bears a slight resemblance of Bambi. I watch in awe as she smacks her lips in her dream; maybe she is savoring the sweetness of the love she'll get soon, after the nurses take her out of the incubator this afternoon. We stand side by side, his hand in mine, our fingers never letting go of one another's. I wish this moment were frozen in time.

"Are you sure you want to go through with that?" I ask, somewhat hesitating on the ending. When people have so much treasure to lose, fear becomes second nature to everything they do.

"I don't know. No matter how carefully I plan, every experiment still has that one percent possibility of human error, Angie," Pierre replies in an unexpectedly rueful manner as he tries to get the child to wake with his knocking, earning him a hostile glare from the attending nurse.

"Then why do you bother doing it at all? The experiment and the plan? We know it might be another failure."

"It's true. That thought is unnerving. Failing is scary because we never know what the bad ending would be like. Imagine if we failed to stop scientists from cloning humans. Now that would be a real disaster, huh?" He chuckles, but his eyes don't show the slightest bit of laughter. "Dolly could've been happier if she was born a normal sheep, for all we know."

"Don't digress from the topic. You don't have to involve yourself in this mess, Pierre. We've gone through the ritual. There's no use in digging up a life from the grave."

"But that life has done so much for me. Even given me a new cause to live. New family. New people who truly care about me. And most importantly," he glances toward me, "He sends me a person who loves and teaches me how to love. This is just my small offering."

"Acting as Bambi to lure Markus into the trap might kill you." I turn away, not wanting to look at him any further, fearing I will hold him back and confess everything we did to the police. "Are you planning on abandoning me and our daughter?"

Pierre looks at the child in the incubator. She has just woken up. Her innocent eyes glint in the white lights of the room, and her face beams a little, which makes it seem like she is smiling at him, as if he is the only person she recognizes amongst the strangers passing by her bed. Her tiny hand reaches out toward him, and Pierre would've fallen there if I weren't holding his towering frame up. The nurse comes by to check on our daughter and the little girl squirms. She hasn't been given a nametag yet, which makes it all the more confusing for the caretakers. We have been through a tumultuous time after her birth, and I haven't had the chance to tell the doctor her name. Never mind; maybe that is God's cunning way of testing me, pushing me to try a little more, urging me to keep on entertaining the faith that fails once and again. Or maybe He wants Pierre to be the first one to know. God's loyal saint is Pierre's namesake—of course, the Great Creator would play the favorite and bless his faithful servant.

"What will we call her, Angela? I think Elizabeth might be a good name for a girl. The queen, you know, and she had such a long ruling period," Pierre says in a jocular tone, but the sadness still finds its way to creep in. "Or Antoinette. A French monarchy with as much notoriety as beauty."

"No. I don't want her to be stuck in the history of others." I lean my head on his shoulder, letting my hair caress his trembling arm. Who wouldn't fear the closing time, when the predestined act is so dim and dark, and the lights are gone? "Pierre, when you come back, I will tell you her name. Promise?"

He nods without answering. I don't believe in wishing upon anything, and I'm not naive enough to wait for the miracle, but in this time, I desperately hold onto hope. If something were meant to be in your life, it would stay; at least, that's what people always say. What if I want happiness to stay nonetheless, even if it wasn't meant to be?

A nurse approaches us with a cheery attitude. She holds our daughter in her arms, a nice, warm, powder-fragranced bundle of soft blanket. I take the child with reverence. Here she is, the miracle I've been waiting for all along. I give her my finger and she grabs onto it with a childish passion. In that moment, I'm convinced that children are born with the super power of unconditional love, and they have a mission to preach that lesson to the selfish, barren, pragmatic adults, who were once children themselves, but who, as they have grown older, have forgotten the treasure called forgiveness. I cradle her in my arms, talking gibberish to her. Syllables without meaning, "Twinkle, Twinkle Little Star," and the Finnish song her father left on my brain like a generational curse. I wonder if my mother did the same to me when I was a newborn. The memory of her is a blur now; the only things I remember are our quarrels, the guilt, the blame, the constant curses and I-wish-you-were-never-born and I-wish-I-were-never-here. Unconsciously, my tears flow, crossing the stream of the past and the present, and I promise my daughter a future that will be far better than what I ever got. It wasn't my fault, and it isn't hers. If God wanted us to be happy, why did He create this world with so much suffering?

I turn to Pierre, wanting to ask if he'd like to hold the baby. The scene stops me short: Pierre pulls a dark blue velvet box out of his pocket and opens it up. Inside, there's a ring, rich with age and the wisdom of the many women it has adorned. A square-cut diamond is the centerpiece, and little aquamarine crystals hold it up. A thought pops into my mind: *Isn't this Venus being born from the sea foam?* I stare at the beautiful ring, bewildered. Pierre never asks the question. He simply puts an earbud into my ear, and plays the obscure Leonard Cohen song:

Ah baby, let's get married,
We've been alone too long.

Let's be alone together.
Let's see if we're that strong.
Yeah let's do something crazy,
Something absolutely wrong
While we're waiting
For the miracle, for the miracle to come.

"What do you think you're doing?" I ask, long after the song is finished and the nurses are gone.

"I'm doing what normal people should be doing. Falling in love, getting married, building a family." Pierre turns his head away, still holding the velvet box awkwardly in the air. "Living."

"And are you falling in love with me? Because it seems we skip straight to the second step in your diagram of normalcy—getting married." I snort. Something bitter, ladened with disgust, rises in my throat. I don't want another stranger stopping in my life just to destroy the last vestiges of my will to keep on living. The room becomes dark and I am transported back to Bambi's condo once more. The cigarette smoke, the spiced and burnt wood cologne, the laughter in the dark, and the addiction to a love that had poisoned me but also brought me a lifetime to live for, to die for, to burn for again and again, as the old timers would say.

Pierre stands there, not moving. His hand trembles a little bit from holding up the box in the air too long. He has no intention of giving in. We are at a stalemate: He knows what he wants to get; I don't know what I want to achieve. Yet, we share a common thread: neither of us want to live in the purgatory of utter loneliness, when the lights are gone, and everyone is sleeping beside their beloved sweetheart, while each of us walk on the cold, deserted street of the abandoned city, the knowledge gnawing at us like a starving ghost—we are the only living people in the world, and there's no happiness for the rebels who dare to go against the will of God. He bites his lips hard enough to bruise, and I can see the spots of red bloom on the soft flesh like a haunting. "Pierre," I call his name, not knowing what I'm hoping for in my desperation and prayers, "It doesn't have to be me. You have a lot of other options. Someone who has a cleaner past, a brighter future, and maybe even a more loving heart. Someone who isn't marred all over by the tattoos of an old Finnish song telling her that nothing she ever does will change the course of history or leave her mark on this earth. I don't know, Pierre. Someone who knows what love is."

He snaps his head back, facing me. His eyes are raging with a whirlwind of emotions. He closes them briefly, trying to calm the storm, then reopens with the aftermath of relentless sadness. "That someone isn't you," Pierre says, his voice tremulous, prostrating himself before me with the naked vulnerability of the man who has no escape route left. "I don't want a perfect lover, or a woman with a cleaner past with a bright future. In fact, I have had enough of that—the labels, the categorization of humans into sections and boxes, the treatable and the unfixable. Maybe I want the madness. Between nothingness and grief, I made my decision long ago. I chose grief the same way I chose you. Angela, if you had been the 'someone' you described, I wouldn't have fallen into the abyss that is your unfathomable love."

Pierre stops his long tirade of passionate speech, taking in breath after breath. I watch him, bewildered. The little babe on my bosom hiccups, and her warmth rushes the tears out of my eyes. It is so damn easy to love, because the feeling comes as an instinct to every human. Yet, I dare not take the jump down the precipice. Looking down from the height, love is beautiful, but I know the cruel, devastating pain once I take the fall. My daughter grasps the collar of my hospital blouse ever so lightly, like a soft wind brushing by gently, and I can feel the deadly weight of the murder, the first meeting with Bambi, the chase after the farce with his death, the love of my life, shatter to smithereens like the Venus statue in that studio a long time ago. I grip my blanket, speaking with a fragile faith in Life's benevolence:

"I don't have a degree. I can only work part time."

"That's fine. I have degrees, but with my current diagnosis, I'm banned from practicing for a long time."

"I'm mentally unstable. I might not take care of anyone."

"And why should you? Everyone can take care of themselves. You only need to worry about yourself."

"What if I can't love you enough?"

"That's fine. I will love you and your daughter for the three of us."

"What if I suddenly don't want to go on?"

"Then I will drag you along. And when I fall at my broken place, you'll do the same." He shrugs as if it's the most natural thing. "It's a fair bargain."

"Pierre, why are you so good to me?" My eyes try to pierce through his azure eyes. He smiles, the melancholy bloom from his eyes like a weeping willow dancing in the wind on a cold winter night.

"I'm done fighting with God. He won. He shows me that this Earth is the place where suffering begins. And if I were meant to suffer until the bitter end before I can become a man, I want to entertain the narrow hope that I, too, like many sinners, can be happy. A dull, ordinary happiness like any other sinner."

My brain blanks for a moment. Bambi's voice from a foggy land of buried memory echoes with the tune of The Lumineers' "Same Old Song": *Angela, I just want to have ordinary happiness.* So many words churn in my stomach and rise in my throat, fighting to get out, but their vicious battle eliminates all the meaning until one single word barely escapes to form a sound: "Yes."

"Yes what?" Pierre stunned.

"Yes, let's do your normalcy. Falling in love, getting married, building a life. Living."

It is more than tragedy; it is a choir singing a requiem. I want to beg him to let it all go. We can cross this city and travel the world. His degrees can earn him a job anywhere. I can make do with a few part-time jobs, and teach our daughter what it means to live. But words are contrived; the more I want to convince him, the less my words sound sure of themselves. I swallow them all, knowing I'm only tempted by my own delusion. Happiness, thou art a heartless bitch.

* * *

The inspector comes to my hospital room at one in the afternoon. I'm breastfeeding my starving treasure while Pierre sits in the sunlight, reading some medical psychology journal. The inspector calls out to Pierre and asks to talk to him in private, which I adamantly refuse, and Pierre acquiesces to my request. The old man in plain clothes has no other choice but to sit down opposite Pierre by the window. Taking his hat off, he talks with gruffy severity: "Just for confirmation, sir, do you still want to go through with this plan?"

"Why not?" Pierre replies, enduring in his acceptance. "If I don't, he's going to do much worse to my family."

"Sir, we can get you and your family under a witness protection program, and you can move somewhere far away, live in a safe neighborhood under a new name. I don't think the perpetrator will reach you." The inspector tries one last time to persuade Pierre out of his mad plan, and I nod in a frenzy as our daughter burps in agreement.

"It's no use. He traced my phone number even though I have been here for only three months—well, almost three months. I can tell that he'd do worse. Mr. Inspector, I'm a trained psychiatrist. Though my career isn't in criminology, I've seen enough crazy in my career to detect it when I see it."

"Call me Sam, sir." The inspector nods his head politely with respect. "A psychiatrist, you say?"

"Yes. I used to work at the Hôpital de la Cité-de-la-Santé in Laval, Quebec. You can check my record there."

"If you don't mind me asking, why did you quit?" Sam asks, amused. But the undertone of an interrogation is there in his voice. Perhaps out of habit, perhaps something else.

"My wife got pregnant and her mental health was suffering badly. I had to be at home full time by then."

"And your brother?"

"I haven't had any news of him since he moved away. Last Monday was the first time I heard of his disappearance. I'm still in shock, honestly, Mr. Inspector."

"Sam."

"Mr. Sam. We're twins, and I looked up to him as the perfect role model."

Pierre touches his lips as if he were in deep introspection. "Maybe I did put undue pressure on him without knowing. He was much stronger than me, and I thought he'd make it in a big city without my help or anyone else's. My bad." He rubs his eyes, exhausted. "It still strikes me as unbelievable."

"Yes. Quite unbelievable. Mr. Jean-Paul Raymond's body was found a few months ago by the local divers. After our initial investigation, he was confirmed dead with no relatives. I was also shocked to see that he has a twin brother. And this Bambi Raymond, is he also a relative of yours?"

"No. I've never heard of him. I think it's a stolen identity case. Jean-Paul was a kind-hearted person. I don't know what sort of people he involved himself with when he got to Toronto, but it must be..." Pierre pauses. His lips quiver as if the shock is coming over him again.

"A bad crowd, indeed. This Bambi has been dealing with drug and human trafficking with an intermediary who went by the name Saul. I thought your wife was also involved." Sam casts his glance toward me. I cover my daughter's ears in protection; of course she wouldn't understand a thing we said, but just in case, I don't want her childhood memory tainted with the adults' bad turn.

"Yes, I lived with Bambi for a while. He promised me he'd cover my living expenses and tuition. He promised the same thing to every girl he hooked up with. But I wasn't involved in his business. Saul offered to take me into his circle, but before that happened, Bambi had vanished without a trace. I was at a loss of what to do so—"

"So you ran to Montreal?"

I confirm Sam's question with a ginger nod, apologizing to Bambi a thousand times in my mind.

"And coincidentally, Doctor Pierre, you met Ms. Angela there, at the hospital?"

"Yes, sir. She had a panic attack and was rushed into the ICU when I was on call. I took her in and let her stay at my apartment as she had nowhere else to go with no money on her. The rest, you see, is history."

Sam sighs, tapping his finger on the table. He mulls over everything we said, as if trying to find a hole in the needle so he could pull a thread through, but it is stuck in the same spot, the same cycle. "And that guy, Markus, he just reached out to you like that? Out of nowhere?" He asks, still not fully convinced, but already tipping over the edge.

"Yes. He called me in the dead of night. I don't even know how he got my number—"

"That might be our fault," Sam scribbles a few things in his notebook. "You look so much like the reported missing person, and maybe a rookie at our station gave your information to Markus without confirming the case first."

Or some insider sold that information to that blackguard at a steep price; that is what we all thought to ourselves and quietly agreed to be the universal truth.

"I don't know the reason. Anyways, it was a bad case. He mistook me for the missing person and kept pouring out information about this delivery and the pretty girl loads. It was unnerving so I hung up and reported it to the police." Pierre shrugs, concluding the story in his matter-of-fact way. A half-truth that sounds so much like the truth that I start to confuse what really happened that night.

"And you did the right thing. We've been on his tail for a while, that Markus. He's a slippery snake. We have proof, of course, but none of it is definitive enough to confirm his involvement in a larger ring. If you can act as bait to lure him in, that will be the lock on the cage. Unless, of course, you want an out, and you have every right to do that." Sam tests the waters as his eyes measure Pierre's authenticity.

"If everyone chooses the easy way, who among us will take up the dirty work?" Pierre replies with a question, smiling, sure of himself. "I don't want an out. I'm not great enough to think of helping anyone or ridding the neighborhood of bad guys. I just want my daughter to grow up safe and happy."

Sam seems to be extremely satisfied with that answer. He stops his questioning and tells us the blueprint for the plan. Pierre needs to get into the bar Rendezvous, mix in with Bambi's old circles, and I will help to fill in the information for him. He will be there two hours before the agreed meeting time to create a believable profile. It's best if he can catch the attention of some of Bambi's old friends, which will be easy to do since Bambi had a lot of debt with the girls there. At ten sharp, Markus will come in. Pierre must not approach him on his own under any circumstances. The in-ear device will tell him what to do and say at the right time. There will be no transaction happening (Sam emphasizes this part with three taps of his pen) and Pierre's job is to goad Markus to admit his crimes. As soon as they get the admission on record, Pierre will fake an excuse to get out of the bar so the cops can come in and sweep the whole operation clean. Markus will be none the wiser as Pierre will be on a car back to the hospital to be with me immediately after.

"Understood?" Sam asks, more to stress the point than to get an answer.

"Yes, sir." Pierre scratches his head, a bit reluctant, which is a bad sign in the inspector's eyes. And the reason for it comes right out, "But don't you think this plan is too old? Markus will sense something strange if his chummy friend, Bambi, is suddenly there after a long absence just to talk to everyone. No transaction is a bit weird, even to me."

"Also," I chime in, unable to stop myself, "Markus won't go inside if Bambi isn't standing by the door. He often meets Bambi first, then they both go in together."

"It'll be too dangerous if you meet outside. What if he makes a run for it?" The inspector leans back in his chair, recalculating the plan.

"How about I meet him at the door, while you have undercover cops surround the area?" Pierre asks, clearly excited at the thought.

"Son, you watch too many crime shows. We don't do that kind of protocol in this case. Letting a civilian join the force is already crossing the line big time." Sam screws his eyes shut, tired at Pierre's enthusiasm, which starts to strike him as strange.

"Or I can meet him there, lure him into the bar, and mingle with Bambi's old friends. That way, it'll be easier for Markus to lower his guard." I give two thumbs up to Pierre's suggestion.

"No can do. It will involve too many civilians and the risk for us will be exponentially higher." Sam retorts. "Can we just stick to the normal plan?"

"It's going to fail. That's all I'm saying. Sir, when you get with the mad, you first have to dress in madness." Pierre grins, holding his journal up in eagerness. Inside, the page points to an article, "Adverse childhood events and self-harming behaviours among individuals in Ontario forensic system: the mediating role of psychopathy."[1] "Markus might be a snake, but I'm that statistic in this little cluster of caged children suffering from childhood abuse. And I'm sure if there's anyone alive who can pull his weight around that guy, it'll be me."

Sam opens his mouth to protest, but thinks better of it, and shakes his head in surrender. We come to an agreement, much to Sam's grudging huff, that Pierre will meet Markus at the bar's entrance, lure him inside, and use his wits as a skillful psychiatrist to get the information out of him without touching on the delivery. After all, we can't procure the ketamine out of thin air, and I'm sure Sam will burst if Pierre makes a suggestion about making ketamine using a chem lab like in *Breaking Bad*.

* * *

Friday night is dressed in thread and nightmares once more for me. Lying on the hard hospital bed, I hold the little girl to my bosom, tickling her to hear her crystalline coos. Pierre dyes his hair silver at the tips using a temporary hair dye, donning a black leather jacket and washed-out jeans to match the look of the bad boy. The tight-fitting, fishnet T-shirt draped over his lanky body makes a comical contrast. He looks at me, asking for my opinion: "Am I good enough?"

I pinch the baby's rosy cheeks as she gurgles on about something I'll never understand, shaking my head indulgently. "No one's ever good enough for Bambi."

He groans, picking up another gaudy shirt to try on, but I call out to stop him. "It's alright. Wear what makes you comfortable. It's not like you'll be

---

[1] Kaggwa, M.M., Chaimowitz, G.A., Erb, B. *et al.* Adverse childhood events and self-harming behaviours among individuals in Ontario forensic system: the mediating role of psychopathy. *BMC Psychiatry* **24**, 332 (2024). https://doi.org/10.1186/s12888-024-05771 -7

Bambi forever, is it?"

"But Markus might recognize something strange if I don't match the look." He rolls his eyes, dragging his feet to my bed and throws his face to the baby's blanket, inhaling the powdery scent. For a brief second, I think, *this is it. This is what I want. This is Pierre in his full essence, without mixing the characteristics or the personality and ideology of anyone else.*

"Don't worry. Markus can be pretty dim sometimes."

"What if this time he isn't?" Pierre asks into the bedding.

"Trust me. He will be. If Saul's dead, he has no one else to lean on. Unless, like Sam said, he's got someone bigger now."

"That's what I said. If he got someone else, then we're in big trouble."

"Pierre, what if you just don't go? Remember how Sam said we could get into the witness protection program? That's plenty good."

"And do what? Wait for the next time Markus comes by our road again? I don't want to live my life on the what-if, Angie. Plus, you promised me you'd tell me our daughter's name. I have to earn the right to it." He plays with the girl's little fingers, and she quickly grasps onto his. The reflex is surely of the Raymond bloodline.

"It'd be nice if Bambi had prepared us with one more gift, huh?" I say somewhat wishfully, knowing I'm hoping for too much.

"He's not God. Even God has His limitations, like bringing back the dead. Bambi couldn't foresee the future. How could he have known there would be a day some nobody would threaten you and me, and his daughter?" Pierre is careful in listing each of us separately. He knows there's a certain threshold I still revere deep inside my soul.

"Well, there's no harm in daydreaming. Maybe he left a voice record somewhere, confessing Markus's crimes, the evidence Markus left in his tracks, and perhaps the police are getting that record right about now." I glance at the clock. It's 8 p.m. Two more hours until Pierre walks outside in the role of Bambi Raymond, his fate unknown, the ending drowned in a muddied fog.

"Yeah, right. That sounds like him. How about we pray to him then? Oh Lord Jean-Paul, please bestow Your mercy upon my poor destiny and throw the bad guys in jail before 10:00. Will that do?" Pierre mumbles, his face completely buried in the layers of blankets and bedding now. He has no will to get up for at least another half hour. I chuckle, stroking his freshly gelled hair.

"Right. Oh Lord Bambi, please have mercy on Your newborn daughter and save her from being an orphan, so soon from existing on this ghastly Earth."

"Your prayer sounds so macabre. He won't take that up." He taps my thighs through the covers.

"And your prayer sounds too jocular to be taken seriously." I punch his shoulders slightly in retort.

"Guess that makes two of us. Now he won't protect us all."

"Well, if he wanted to, he'd have done it before Markus had the chance to call you that night, wouldn't he?"

"Yeah, because he was just so Bambi."

"And so Jean-Paul all the same."

We laugh so hard we cry. Or maybe it is the reverse. We only miss the dead when we need their salvation and protection in a dire situation. Maybe we don't love them enough to die just yet. Oh my suffering Lord, how much more selfish do You want us to be? Still pinning our hopes on his resting body, even though he had done his best and left forever, wishing for his deliverance so he no longer had to suffer. And yet, we choose to stay here, begging for his forgiveness, praying he'll grant our wish. Maybe it's true, then, as Bambi had said, that God is indeed a lonely creature. He couldn't think much further than molding a species after His own image, so He doesn't have to exist eternally in solitude.

"Angela, can I tell you something?" Pierre breaks the silence.

"Sure."

"I don't want to go anymore."

"Then don't."

"Will it make me less heroic than my brother?" His voice grows timid and sad.

"Well, if I must answer, you were both cowards from the start, so your escape won't paint a worse picture in my eyes, Pierre. Living is hard. And it's brave to choose a hard thing."

The clock strikes 9 p.m. It's a half-hour drive to Rendezvous from the hospital. Pierre gathers himself up like a broken puppet, groaning all the while, putting another coat on because he doesn't want people to see him in such punky attire. I keep my silence. In my own resilient pose, I'm waiting for the miracle to come. *Bambi, there's only thirty minutes left. It's now or never. You promised you'd protect us, didn't you?*

And the miracle keeps eluding us. The hand moves closer to the departure time, and I keep staring at the clock's face, willing it to stop. My mind scrambles for a way out. This is all so familiar that by now, I should have a plan or a roadmap leading to a safe place. But none comes up. All through this escapade, I have adhered strictly to Bambi's teaching. Should I stray from the path? Didn't our original life on Earth start with disobedience?

Pierre trudges slowly to the door, his feet dragging and his back hunching forward. The role isn't on yet, and he lingers in his skin to feel the safety within. As his hand turns the doorknob, I shout, "Wait." But no other phrase comes to my mind. We freeze in mid-scene, him waiting for me to speak my line, to get to the climax of the act, me praying for a long interlude—if possible, dragging it out forever. As he turns away once more, the door swings open and bangs him straight in the face. Sam arrives, huffing from his race from the hospital's parking lot, the sweat still dripping down his face to his yellow shirt collar. "Great, caught you on time. Why the hell didn't you pick up our call?"

"I was planning to get there now, I swear." Pierre fumbles with his words, holding his bruising nose. A red line runs from his nostril to his upper lip. It's a strong impact hit; a nurse rushes in, calling for an icepack.

"What for?" Sam sounds genuinely confused. "Didn't you check your message?"

"Couldn't. I was busy trying on clothes." Pierre leans his head back to stop the blood flow. The nurse gets him to a chair with high efficiency.

"You… It's canceled. The plan. We texted you so many times. Markus was arrested at his home. The evidence was sent to us by the postal office. And guess who it's from?" Sam sounds frustrated as he aggressively scratches his head in total bafflement. We wait for him to speak the revered name with fear and trembling: "None other than that fucking Bambi Raymond. He sent the hard copies of the evidence; photos, receipts, letters, attestations, and everything. Well, we appreciate the gesture but the post office was on strike the whole time. Didn't he think of that?"

Pierre and I are too stunned to speak. The post office was on strike. It isn't because he never thought of Markus; it's because all this time, his setup was a delayed timebomb. I burst out laughing. "Thanks be to Him."

Pierre cries, ugly and messy with blood all over his mouth. "Thanks be to Him."

Sam keeps saying it's a miracle from God, but he'll never know the Him we were offering our prayers to and the Him Sam is thinking of are not the same. It's hard to explain, and nobody would understand it anyways. Sam looks at us, happy and satisfied in his ignorance. "Well, as long as you both are safe. By the way, I heard you haven't named your daughter yet. Still deciding? Anne-Marie is a popular name in Françoise Quebec, isn't it?"

I shake my head vehemently, trying to hold back the hysteria, wiping my eyes viciously to stop myself from crying together with Pierre. "No, I had a name for her all this time. It's just—I haven't had the chance to reveal it yet."

"Oh, is that so? What's her name?"

Pierre looks at me in great expectation. His eyes gleam in the cascading violet sky outside the window. The moment our daughter's name is spoken, Pierre falls to his knees, shattering into a full circle: "Her name is Jeannet Pauline Raymond. Remember her, Mr. Inspector. She will do great things. After all, she comes from the bloodline of great men. Sanctified and glorified, she won't be anyone's salvation. And she will live with a freedom not even God can destroy. She won't need to choose her prison, because her world will expand as she grows. Always questioning everything, never satisfied with any answers, she won't settle for a narrow hope."

Yes. Jeannet Pauline Raymond won't be stuck in the past; she will crash through the present and run toward the bright future to reach a happiness of her own. She wasn't born to suffer, because her fate belongs to the future.

Her father dictated it so. Her uncle sacrificed everything to make it happen. And I will kill every darling along the way to carve that truth into her bones.

The End

About the Author

Thanh Dinh is a Vietnamese writer and poet whose work explores love, obsession, grief, and the quiet violence of human relationships. Her writing blends lyrical intensity with psychological depth, often inhabiting the fragile space between tenderness and destruction.

She is the author of *Kill My Darling, Chronicle of a Love Foretold,* and *Love, Anyways: Because the Apple Trees Blossom,* and the co-founder of the independent imprint Writerly Books Press. She currently resides in Scarborough, Ontario, Canada with her loving family and busy herself with her adorable cats.

You can connect with me on:
- https://writerlybookspub.com
- https://www.facebook.com/writerly.books
- https://www.instagram.com/thanhdinh_write

Subscribe to my newsletter:

✉ https://writerlybookspub.com

Also by Thanh Dinh

A repertoire of lyrical pain and the joy in having narrow hopes.

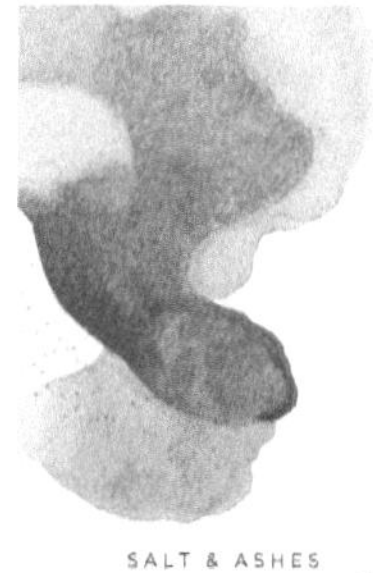

Salt & Ashes: Poems from the Abyss

A descent into grief, survival, and emotional ruin. In *Salt & Ashes*, Thanh Dinh writes from the edge of loss, tracing love, trauma, and endurance through stark, lyrical poems that refuse consolation. This is a book about what remains after everything sacred has burned.

The Smallest God Who Ever Lived

A raw and unsettling poetry collection that interrogates faith, loneliness, power, and the fragile desire to be seen. *The Smallest God Who Ever Lived* moves through devotion and doubt with dark humor and quiet cruelty, questioning what happens when belief collapses—and what we worship in its place.

Chronicle of a Love Foretold

Set against the backdrop of migration, generational trauma, and domestic violence, *Chronicle of a Love Foretold* follows Dong, a young immigrant navigating exile, family expectation, and forbidden desire. Through his relationship with Simon—and the quiet devastation of an immigrant mother caught between survival and love—the novel explores queer intimacy, memory, and the cost of being seen in a world determined to erase you.

Love, Anyways: Because the Apple Trees Blossom

A collection of stories about love in its most fragile, stubborn forms. From fleeting connections to lifelong wounds, *Love, Anyways* examines longing, loss, and the quiet persistence of hope—even when everything else fails. These stories linger in the spaces where people choose love not because it is safe, but because it is inevitable.